Trained as an actress, Barbara Nadel is now a public relations officer for rethink severe mental illness's Good Companions Project. Her previous job was a mental health advocate in a psychiatric hospital. She has also worked with sexually abused teenagers and taught psychology in both schools and colleges. Born in the East End of London, she has been a regular visitor to Turkey for over twenty years.

Barbara Nadel's previous books, BELSHAZZAR'S DAUGHTER, A CHEMICAL PRISON, ARABESK and DEEP WATERS have all been highly acclaimed:

BELSHAZZAR'S DAUGHTER

'Best crime fiction of the year by a new writer was Barbara Nadel's *Belshazzar's Daughter* . . . great blooming baroque plot (ditto talent)' *Independent*

'This is an extraordinarily interesting first novel' *Evening Standard*

'Really refreshing to encounter something as idiosyncratic and evocative among debut novels' *The Times*

'Unusual and very well-written' *Sunday Telegraph*

'Intriguing, exotic . . . original' *Literary Review*

'Will have you looking over your shoulder' *Scotsman*

A CHEMICAL PRISON

'*Belshazzar's Daughter*, with its brilliantly realised Istanbul setting and innovative protagonist was a hard act to follow. But she pulls off the trick triumphantly' *The Times*

'Even better than Nadel's extraordinary first book . . . A depth and detail unusual in a crime novel' *Evening Standard*

'A thriller that presents a Middle Eastern city populated by human beings rather than specimens of oriental exotica, and a British writer who can get inside a foreign skin' *Independent*

'A first-rate author' *Good Housekeeping*

ARABESK

'The delight of the Nadel book is the sense of being taken beneath the surface of an ancient city which most visitors see for a few days at most. We look into the alleyways and curious dark quartiers of Istanbul, full of complex characters and louche atmosphere' *Independent*

'The Istanbul atmosphere is as thick as Turkish coffee and the novel is crammed with fascinating information' *Evening Standard*

'Particularly interesting for its discussion of Turkish customs and beliefs' *Sunday Telegraph*

'A bewitching style . . . a story that carries the reader forward willingly along until the well-sprung denouement' *Scotsman*

'Barbara Nadel continues to go from strength to strength with her atmospheric and idiosyncratic Istanbul-set thrillers . . . one of the most original crime series currently in progress' *Crime Time*

'As before Nadel presents a gallery of richly created characters along with the superb scene-setting we have come to expect from her' *Good Book Guide*

DEEP WATERS

'Intelligent and captivating mystery recalls Michael Dibdin's Aurelio Zen stories' *Sunday Times*

'As always, it's the characters which make this series so fascinating' *Sunday Telegraph*

'My reader rates this author higher than Donna Leon' *Bookseller*

'One of the most exciting of new crime writers' *Good Book Guide*

Harem

Barbara Nadel

headline

First published in hardback in 2003
by HEADLINE BOOK PUBLISHING

First published in paperback in 2003
by HEADLINE BOOK PUBLISHING

10 9 8 7 6 5 4 3 2

ISBN 0 7472 6720 0

Typeset by Palimpsest Book Production Limited,
Polmont, Stirlingshire
Printed and bound in Great Britain by
Clays Ltd, St Ives plc

HEADLINE BOOK PUBLISHING
A division of Hodder Headline
338 Euston Road
London NW1 3BH

www.headline.co.uk
www.hodderheadline.com

I've had a difficult year and have had a lot of help from many people. This book is dedicated to them, particularly my mother, my husband and son, my friends Peter, Kathy and Alison and all my colleagues at Good Companions. In addition, I'd also like to say a big 'thank you' to my agent Juliet Burton; Anne Williams, Sarah Keen and Zoë Carroll at Headline and Senay and Sırma at my Turkish publishers, Oğlak in İstanbul.

Prologue

Blood had never been part of the equation before. But now, suddenly, there it was. Of course things had been . . . deteriorating for some time. But he'd closed his eyes to that.

He looked down into the depths of his huge crescent-shaped pool and thought, I'll have to sort it out. Not leave it to Vedat any more. He then added out loud, 'I will have to go home immediately.'

After all, it wasn't just him, was it? Others were involved too – people far above him in the scheme of things. People who were counting on him to sort it out. People who, even now, still didn't know the whole truth . . .

G had said, 'Well, they're your people, you know them. Do something or we will have to.'

That had made his blood run cold, that and the whispers of fear he had picked up around the pool earlier in the day – whispers from men who had been his friends. Men who now said they would 'hang him out to dry' if the shit hit the fan.

With a determination born only of fear, he opened the door to the pool house and went inside. A young blonde woman lay on a huge leather couch watching an old episode of *The Cosby Show*.

He called across to her, 'We must pack tonight. I have to go home.'

The woman, startled by this sudden pronouncement, turned and looked up at him.

'But we are home,' she said. 'This—'

'I mean my home,' the man responded bluntly. 'Türkiye.'

Chapter 1

Çetin İkmen finished what was left of his coffee and placed his cup down on the breakfast table. The hot İstanbul morning was already making him tetchy and so the last thing he needed was a disgruntled child. He looked up at his pretty teenage daughter sitting opposite.

'Well, Hulya,' he said, 'if you don't want to continue working in the pastane then what do you want to do?'

'I want to work in entertainment,' she replied.

İkmen rubbed the sides of his face wearily. 'In what capacity?' he asked.

Before she replied, Hulya looked briefly across at the young boy sitting next to her. Only when she was certain that he was totally engrossed in the book he was reading did she say, 'I want to be an actress.'

But Hulya miscalculated badly. The boy, Bülent, flung his book to the floor and burst out laughing.

Hulya rounded on him angrily. 'I wasn't talking to you!' she said. 'I was having a conversation with Dad!'

'Children . . .'

'You need talent to be an actress, you know!' Bülent, unmindful of his father's warning, teased. 'And you have to sleep with everybody—'

'Bülent!'

'Well, I'm only saying what I think.' Bülent shrugged off

3

the mounting anger on his father's face. 'And anyway, Dad, since when were you prudish about such things?'

'I'm not!' And then turning to his daughter, İkmen added, 'But your mother is.'

'Oh, so I can't even think about it because Mum wouldn't approve!'

'No!'

'It's what you're saying, Dad.'

'Yes, it is,' her brother agreed. 'It's definitely what you're implying.'

'You keep out of this!' İkmen now roused to fury pointed a warning cigarette at his son, 'Allah, but it's been like a war zone in this place since your mother left! Surrounded by teenagers! Is it any wonder a man can't take his rest in comfort!' He lit up what his son knew from experience was at least his fifth cigarette of the morning.

Bülent rose from his seat. 'Well, I'm going to work anyway.' He smiled at his sister and added, 'Not all of us can spend our time dreaming about stardom.'

'I'm not.'

'The name of this family is İkmen, Hulya.' He patted her shoulder in a deeply patronising fashion. 'Our dad's a policeman which means there's neither glamour nor money in our lives. Learn acceptance.' And then with a smirk he left.

His furious sister made as if to go after him, but was restrained by her equally furious, if more weary, father.

'Oh, leave him be!' İkmen said. He let go of his daughter's hand and slumped back into his chair. 'You and your brother, you're like a pair of cats fighting over meat. Every day I get this. Argue, argue, argue! How your mother controls you I don't know. I can't. All my adult life I've worked as a police officer in the toughest city in Turkey and I can't control my own children!'

'Dad—'

'When, İnşallah, your mother returns from visiting Uncle Talaat, I may well break with a lifetime of atheism and give thanks to the Almighty and Merciful.' Noting the shocked look on his daughter's face, he continued, 'Yes, it is that serious, Hulya! Two weeks now and all I get from you and your brother is complaints, rudeness and bad attitude. Uncle Talaat is very sick and so your mother needs to know that we are all managing when she calls. She's looking after your uncle and all your little brothers and sisters too, it's as hot as a hearth out there in Antalya and yet every time she calls I have to speak to her against a background of your bickering!'

Hulya lowered her large, dark eyes. 'Dad—'

'If your older brothers weren't so busy I'd send you both to stay with them. Split you two up.' He puffed furiously on his cigarette before putting it out and lighting another.

'I'd happily stay with Çiçek,' Hulya said, naming her elder sister who now shared an apartment out by Atatürk Airport.

'Oh?' her father replied acidly. 'Would you?'

'Yes.'

İkmen crossed his thin arms and looked down his considerable nose at the cowed girl before him. 'You who cannot get to your place of work on time when you live only fifty metres from it, you want to live at least forty-five minutes away?'

'I've told you, I don't want to work at the pastane any more, I—'

'Oh, yes, of course, you want to be an actress, don't you?'

5

He leaned forward and smiled unpleasantly into her face.
'I'm so sorry I forgot.'

'Dad!'

İkmen rose smartly from his seat and headed out towards
the hall.

'I'm going to work now,' he said, 'I have no choice.'

Hulya, who was not unaware of the realities of life despite
her wants and her protestations, slumped forward onto her
elbows and put her head in her hands.

Out in the hall, a grey-faced İkmen was just taking his
jacket down from one of the hooks on the wall when the
doorbell rang. With a sigh of resignation, knowing that if he
didn't answer it no one would, he opened the door. A small
woman dressed in the navy blue uniform of the Zabita, or
market police, stood before him.

İkmen smiled in recognition. Hürrem İpek had lived in the
apartment opposite the İkmens' place for nearly ten years. A
widow, Hürrem was a hard-working mother of two young
girls, her careworn face belying her thirty-eight years.

'Oh, Inspector İkmen,' she said, 'I am so sorry to disturb
you. But I wondered if you or in particular Hulya have seen
my Hatice this morning?'

The eldest of the İpek girls, Hatice, was one year older
than Hulya and also worked at the Sultanahmet pastane. The
girls had been firm friends since high school.

'No, I haven't.' He ushered her into the apartment. 'But I
expect my daughter saw her at work last night. Maybe she's
gone out to buy something.'

'Her bed hasn't been slept in, Inspector,' the woman bit
her bottom lip nervously. 'I went to bed early last night, I
was tired. Hatice usually gets in at about ten thirty, but I
was asleep by nine.'

'What about your other daughter?' İkmen asked. 'Didn't she hear her sister come home last night?'

'Canan is staying with my sister at the moment,' Hürrem replied. 'It's better for her in the summer. There are cousins there for her to play with . . .' She looked down at the floor.

Hulya entered from the kitchen.

'Did you walk home with Hatice last night?' İkmen asked his daughter. The girls usually walked home together when they worked in the evening, as they had been instructed to do. Sultanahmet in the height of summer could be somewhat rowdy.

'Yes,' Hulya replied. 'Why?'

'Did you see her go into her apartment?' İkmen asked.

Hulya lowered her eyes. 'Yes. Or at least I saw her at the door.'

'You didn't actually see her go in?'

'I don't know,' she shrugged, 'maybe.'

İkmen sighed and then turned with a thin smile to Hürrem. 'I'm sorry about this, Mrs İpek,' he said, 'but as you can see this particular teenage mind is not very attentive.'

Hürrem managed a small smile of understanding in response.

'Oh, well,' she said, 'I'm sure there must be a reasonable explanation. But if you do hear of anything . . .'

'We will let you know, of course,' İkmen replied. Then as his neighbour left the apartment he added, 'Maybe she just sat up watching TV and then went out. Children do such things these days – I know mine do.' He smiled. 'Hatice is a good girl, I'm sure she's fine.'

'Thank you.'

When he had closed the door behind Hürrem, İkmen

turned his attention back to his daughter. She was, he noticed, still intent on the floor in front of her.

'Why,' he said, 'do I get the feeling that you know more about Hatice's movements last night than you are prepared to admit?'

There were, so it was said in some quarters, shops far better than the one on the corner of Kütlügün Sokak and Dalbastı Sokak. There were some that, in addition to traditional groceries, sold children's toys, covers for mobile telephones and even cheap clothing. But no other, or rather none that Neşe Fahrı had ever come across since her migration to İstanbul in the 1970s, boasted a shopkeeper who actually came from her village. Selim Bey, though many years older than Neşe, had not only lived in the same street as her but had known her late husband, Adnan. It was a background that to Neşe was more valuable than gold. For whatever else he might have been – unemployed, faithless – Adnan Fahrı had been, as well as the father of her son Turgut and daughter Fatima, the love of Neşe's life.

As she entered the shop, Selim Bey reared up from behind a large box of Winston cigarettes.

'Good morning, Neşe Hanım,' he said. 'I trust you are well.'

'Allah still bestows good health upon this old woman,' Neşe replied with a sad smile. If only the Great and Merciful had extended such an honour to her Adnan.

'I'm very glad to hear it,' Selim Bey replied. 'And how is Turgut?'

'The boy is well.' Neşe sighed and then leaned over to open up the glass bread cabinet and remove one of the corn husk-shaped loaves. 'Still waiting at table, but he is well. Do you have any green olives?'

Selim Bey reached down into the chilled cabinet in front of him and then frowned. 'No. But I do have some excellent black ones.'

'Mmm.' Neşe looked doubtful. 'Well, if you recommend them, Selim Bey.'

'I do.'

'Then write half a kilo in the book.'

The shopkeeper set about weighing the olives, nodding just briefly as he did so to a young man who came in and took a packet of cigarettes, placed some notes down upon the counter and left.

Neşe glanced behind her, scanning both the shop and the street for other people. When she was certain that no one else was coming she tilted her heavily bound head towards the shopkeeper.

'A good, strong shovel can also go into the book too, if you have one,' she said.

'Oh, I always have one for you, Neşe Hanım,' the shop-keeper said with a twinkle in his eye. 'I still have faith.'

'İnşallah, once we have found that which we seek, I can pay off everything in the book and much more besides.'

Selim Bey poured the olives from the scales into a plastic bag and then twisted the top of it into a knot. 'If Adnan believed that treasure existed, even though he never told me where it might be, then that is good enough.' The shopkeeper continued, 'You are a good woman, Neşe Hanım, to keep your husband's ambitions alive.'

Neşe Hanım reached across the counter and took the bag of olives from Selim Bey's hands.

'What choice do I have? My boy deserves an education.

How else am I, a poor widow, to give him that in this city of thieves?'

Selim Bey came out from behind his counter and then reached behind a large sack of rice. Neşe Hanım's eyes lit up as she looked at the shiny new shovel in his hands.

'Well, it looks strong,' she said.

'It is.' Selim Bey replied as he banged it down onto the floor and then passed it across to her. Grave-faced, she nodded her approval and then turned her long, wiry frame towards the shop door.

'May it come easy,' Selim Bey said as he watched Neşe step out into the sun-baked street beyond. From the near by Sea of Marmara the sound of a ship's hooter echoed plaintively through the narrow streets of the battered Kumkapı district.

The pastane was only a short way from where İkmen usually parked his car. And having received little beyond sulky denials from Hulya with regard to the movements of Hatice İpek, it made sense just to see whether the girls' employer, whom he knew, could shed any light on the situation. Besides, averse though he normally was to food, İkmen possessed something of a passion for all things chocolate.

As he entered via the elegant art nouveau doorway, İkmen cast his eyes across the creamy and sugary delights that filled the glass confectionery cabinet to his left. Numerous rich gateaux, profiteroles and croissants oozing with liquid chocolate vied for supremacy with local sweets. Syrup-drenched baklava, thick rice puddings and aşure, a sticky fruit and nut dessert packed with fat and calories. But İkmen's thin frame could do with some extra bulk. And so in lieu of breakfast and because his wife was hundreds of kilometres away,

İkmen ordered a cappuccino and a plate of profiteroles. Then he sat down, lit a cigarette and waited for his food and drink to arrive. Out in the street, curly-headed Ali, one of the local waiters, also known as 'Maradona' because of the facial resemblance, nodded a cheerful greeting.

The coffee and profiteroles were eventually brought over to İkmen by Hassan, the proprietor of the pastane. A tall, slim man in his early thirties, Hassan had taken over the shop from his father, the formidable confectioner Kemal Bey, early the previous year. Hassan placed the pastries down with a small bow and then offered his hand to İkmen, inquiring after his health as he did so. İkmen gestured for Hassan to join him.

'We don't often have the pleasure of your company, Inspector,' the younger man said as he called across to the woman at the counter to bring him a cup of Nescafé.

'No,' İkmen shrugged, 'but my wife is away visiting her brother in Antalya. And seeing as a man must eat . . .'

'Ah.' Hassan smiled.

'Not of course that being here isn't a pleasure,' İkmen added as he forked a large lump of profiterole into his mouth. 'You and your father have always been the Picassos of chocolate and pastry, Hassan. It is an art that is as important as painting and sculpture, in my opinion.'

'You're very kind, Inspector.'

'It's nothing.'

The policeman continued to eat in silence, his eyes at times half closed in appreciation. Shortly after Hassan's Nescafé arrived, İkmen came to the point of his visit.

'So is my daughter behaving herself?' he asked. 'And her friend Hatice?'

'But of course.' Hassan cleared his throat with a strange,

almost feminine giggle. 'The girls are very nice. The customers like them.'

'Any particular customers?' İkmen inquired.

The confectioner's face assumed a sudden grave expression. 'You mean young men, Inspector?'

'Amongst others.'

Hassan leaned back in his chair, bathing his face in the strengthening morning sun. 'Well, the girls are young and pretty,' he said, 'and so naturally the men do try to engage them in conversation from time to time. But nothing serious takes place, I can assure you, Inspector. I take care of my staff, particularly the women.'

'But of course.'

'And besides, as far as I am aware the only male those two ever show any interest in is old Ahmet Sılay.'

İkmen raised his eyebrows. 'Wasn't there an actor of that name? Long ago?'

'Yes, the very same.' Hassan sipped his coffee before continuing. 'He's a regular but he has to be sixty at the very least. He's a contemporary of Hikmet Sivas who, to be candid, he talks about at some length. As regards Hulya and Hatice, I don't think there's anything you need to be concerned about beyond a bit of filmstar worship.' He smiled. 'Not for Ahmet, you understand, but for Sivas.'

'Our Turkish brother in Hollywood,' İkmen observed.

'Our *only* Turkish brother in Hollywood,' Hassan corrected. 'Although he is rather past his prime now, don't you think?'

İkmen shrugged. Films didn't really interest him. He was aware that Hikmet Sivas had appeared in a lot of Hollywood films in the 1960s but beyond that he knew very little about the man.

'So was Sılay in here last night?' İkmen asked.

'Yes.' Hassan frowned. 'Why?'

At this stage, with the possibility of Hatice İpek turning up at any moment, İkmen didn't want to sound any alarm bells.

'Oh, it's just that Hulya keeps going on about wanting to be an actress,' he said. It was, after all, the truth.

Hassan smiled. 'Oh well, yes, she would have probably got that idea from Ahmet,' he said. 'His stories about theatrical tours of Turkey and other countries he went to in the fifties are quite exotic, plus of course his association with Sivas.'

'So Sılay is still friendly with Sivas?'

'He has apparently visited him in Los Angeles in the past,' Hassan replied. 'I've no reason to disbelieve him.'

'No.'

'But if you want me to speak to him about putting ideas in the girls' heads, I will,' Hassan offered as he stood up and made ready to go back to his work. 'I don't want to lose Hulya and Hatice to the dubious business of entertainment, do I?'

İkmen smiled. 'No, but I'm sure that Sılay is, from what you say, quite harmless. And if the girls are just amusing themselves, there's no harm in that.'

'Well, it's up to you, Inspector,' the younger man said and then with a small bow he departed.

İkmen finished his profiteroles and then looked out of the window again. Of course nothing ever sprang from nothing and it was interesting to know the source of Hulya's theatrical ambitions. And if, as Hassan seemed to think, both girls were currently bent upon careers in the entertainment industry then maybe Hatice had gone off to try and see some of the film and theatrical agents up in Beyoğlu. Perhaps that was why Hulya had seemed so reluctant to talk about her friend. But surely Hatice wouldn't have gone to see agents in the middle of the night?

Chapter 2

Inspector Mehmet Suleyman was just leaving for work when he heard the scream rip through the upper storey of his house. Zelfa! He dropped the sheaf of papers he had been carrying and raced upstairs to his bedroom. As he entered, Patrick, his wife's fifteen-year-old cat, bounded nimbly past him heading, presumably, for somewhere where Zelfa wasn't.

His wife, whom he had left apparently sleeping only half an hour before, was sitting up in their bed, her face red and contorted with pain.

'What is it? Has it started?' he said as he ran over to her side and placed an arm round her trembling shoulders.

By way of reply, Zelfa pushed the duvet down towards her feet and then stared, panting at what she had revealed. The underside of the duvet as well as the sheet were drenched with pink, blood-stained water.

'Seems like it's time to get to hospital,' her husband said. He turned away from her and walked over to her wardrobe. He took a suitcase and a winter coat from inside it.

Zelfa, panting still as she watched what her husband was doing, frowned. 'I can't wear that,' she said in her gruff, Irish-accented English. 'I'll die of heatstroke.'

Mehmet draped the coat loosely round her shoulders.

15

'You can't go out in just a nightdress,' he said. 'I'll put the air conditioning on in the car. It'll be fine.'

'Jesus Christ!'

Mehmet helped Zelfa swing her swollen legs down onto the floor and then pulled her slowly to her feet.

For a woman like Zelfa – a professional woman, a psychiatrist, who had grown up in Ireland – to be quite so large seemed wrong and even puzzling. But then Zelfa had both craved and eaten an enormous amount of chocolate during her pregnancy, which had seemed preferable to her usual cigarettes.

'I'm like one of those toys,' she said as she lumbered, with her husband's help, towards the bedroom door. 'One of those fat clowns that won't fall over, keeps on bouncing back.'

'When our son is born you will feel better,' Mehmet said. Inside his heart beat fast and his flesh trembled inside his skin. His son! At last he would be born, bringing an intense feeling of joy but also of great apprehension. Even now, at the beginning of the twenty-first century, a proportion of babies still died at birth. And Zelfa was, after all, nearly forty-eight and this little boy was her first and probably her last child.

As they descended the stairs Mehment hugged both his wife and his child tightly to his body.

'The doctor says that they belonged to a girl who was not yet fully developed,' Orhan Tepe said as he placed the photograph of pelvic and femur bones in front of his superior, Çetin İkmen.

'OK, so you'll need to check out the lists of missing earthquake victims in that sector,' İkmen replied. It wasn't the first time they'd had to try to marry up discrete body parts with names of those whose bodies had never been recovered in the wake of the 1999 catastrophe. Nearly two years on, traumatised survivors were still being shocked by the bones and flesh of the dead that their gardens and car parks kept on revealing to them. There was also the possibility that these fragments held more sinister secrets. After all, where better to hide a murder victim than in those parts of the city that were effectively graveyards? This was why İkmen and his colleagues became involved in these matters. Unlawful death was his speciality and the fight to bring those who had committed such acts to justice had been his professional mission for almost all of his working life.

At fifty-four years old, Çetin İkmen was undernourished (due to pain from his numerous stomach ulcers), underpaid and smoke-dried. In spite of these drawbacks he was passionate about his work, possessed a loving and supportive wife and nine healthy, if at times problematic, children. Over the years his formidable detective skills and keen intellect had afforded him considerable success within the İstanbul police department. This combined with the incorruptible honesty he demanded of both himself and his officers had provided him with the kind of legendary status that occasionally allowed certain breaches of procedure to be performed without comment from those above. In short, İkmen was a phenomenon and as such he was admired and even courted by others. This was not always easy for those around İkmen. His current junior, Sergeant Orhan Tepe, frequently felt that rather more was expected of him than was reasonable. It was not an attitude that had afflicted İkmen's previous sergeant, Mehmet Suleyman, now promoted to inspector. But then as Tepe frequently observed to himself, İkmen and Suleyman were two of a kind. He was different. It was not something that made him happy. Nothing much did nowadays.

As the list of missing persons for the Ataköy area flashed up on Tepe's computer screen, he put such personal thoughts aside and concentrated on his work. On the other side of the small, cluttered office, İkmen frowned at a pile of papers until he was interrupted by the ringing of his telephone.

He picked up the receiver. 'İkmen.'

'Dad?'

It was Hulya, and from the tremor in her voice, she was nervous about something.

İkmen lit a cigarette. 'Hello, Hulya, what can I do for you?'

'Dad, I've just seen Mrs İpek and she says that Hatice still isn't home.'

'Oh?' Could it be that his daughter was finally going to tell him exactly what had happened when she and her friend had parted the previous evening? İkmen suspected that she was. Although whether this would be a major confession as opposed to just some juvenile nonsense he couldn't yet tell.

'So,' he prompted, 'do you have anything more to tell me about how you parted from Hatice last night, or are you just calling to keep me up to date?'

In the short silence that followed İkmen watched Tepe look up briefly from his computer screen to eye the shapely figure of Sergeant Ayşe Farsakoğlu who was passing by the window of their office. So evident was the younger, and married, man's lust for their colleague that İkmen turned his chair round to face the wall.

'Well, Hulya, I'm waiting.'

'Dad . . .'

'Yes?'

'I didn't actually see Hatice go back to her apartment last night.'

This was hardly a surprise, though Hulya obviously felt that it should be.

'Where did she go then, Hulya?' he said. 'After work when you left her . . .'

'I don't know.'

'Oh?'

He heard her swallow. 'No, honestly, Dad, I don't.'

'So if you don't know where she went, do you know what she might have been doing?'

'But Dad, I promised I wouldn't tell.'

İkmen swung himself back round to face the front of his office again, his features stern. Mercifully Tepe was back at his work. Not that İkmen took much notice, he was far too irritated by his daughter to be bothered by his sergeant's peccadilloes. As İkmen knew from bitter experience, promises between teenagers could be very dangerous things.

'Hulya, you're going to tell me otherwise you wouldn't have telephoned and so I would just get on and do it,' he said.

'Oh, Dad, but you're going to be so angry.'

'Seeing as I'm already furious, you have nothing to lose, do you!'

'Dad . . .'

'So if it has anything to do with Mr Ahmet Sılay or any other theatrical type you girls have talked to about your ambitions . . .'

'How did you know?' She sounded outraged and truly shocked. 'Have you spoken to Mr Sılay?'

'No,' İkmen replied sharply, 'but I think I'm about to.'

'But this has got nothing to do with him, Dad!'

İkmen puffed heavily on his cigarette. 'What does it have to do with then, Hulya?' he said.

He heard his daughter sigh and then with an almost visible shrug in her voice she gave in, as was her wont with her father.

'Hatice had another job after work last night. It was a great entertainment opportunity. Lots of money.'

İkmen, who had heard such stories many, many times before from girls even younger and more innocent than Hulya, put his head in his hands.

'Don't tell me,' he said wearily. 'Some nice men wanted her to dance for them.'

'Yes, and act too,' Hulya replied simply. 'How did you know? Have you met . . .'

'I think you ought to come down here now, Hulya,' İkmen said as he stubbed out his cigarette and lit another.

'What? To the police station?' She sounded appalled.

'Yes,' her father replied through his teeth. 'It's where I work, Hulya. I'm a policeman. You have information about someone who might be missing and in danger. Please get yourself over here. Now!'

Tepe, startled by his superior's sudden, enraged bellow, accidentally printed the list on his screen.

Although Turgut Fahrı possessed a voracious intellectual appetite, his enthusiasm for physical pursuits was rather more muted. OK, so his mother was no longer young, but why was it that he always had to carry all the tools when they went on their expeditions into the underworld? He was the brains of the family. Both his mother and his sister told everyone so and, when he was alive, his father had agreed with that analysis also. It was, after all, Turgut who had put the whole cistern idea into Adnan's head in the first place, although his mother always referred to these forays as attempts to fulfil her husband's dreams.

The cisterns which riddle the foundations of the old city were built by the Byzantine emperors. Fed with water from the Belgrade Forest by aqueducts, these enormous spaces ensured that despite drought or siege, the city of Constantine never went thirsty. It was a very successful system – for a time. During the Ottoman period, however, the cisterns fell into disrepair and were only 'rediscovered' by a sixteenth-century French traveller, who was amazed by stories of locals fishing underground. It was not until the twentieth century that any of them were extensively explored. And even then it was only one, the Yerebatan Saray, which since the 1980s had hosted daily sound-and-light entertainments for tourists. It wasn't therefore to the Yerebatan Saray that Turgut and Neşe Fahrı and their tools were headed. No. If Turgut's theory was correct and Greek treasure of unimaginable value was hidden in the cisterns, it was not going to be in the one that had already been comprehensively excavated. It was going to be in one of the others which lay undisturbed beneath bazaars and cafés, houses and apartment blocks, gently rotting into its own thick dark silt. A cistern just like, in fact, the one that Turgut was entering now.

Via a combination of amateur detective work and bribery, Turgut and Neşe had identified this particular cistern some months before. Rumours of a small cistern just north of the great Binbirdirek Cistern – which was currently under excavation – had been circulating for a while. It had only been a matter of time before the intrepid Fahrıs tracked it down. Situated in the garden of an old house on Türbedar Sokak, the entrance to the cistern was a hole in the ground which, until recently, had been covered by a rough wooden lid. Now helpfully removed by the elderly woman who owned the house, access to the entrance was currently costing the Fahrıs almost half of Turgut's weekly wages. Age had not, apparently, dimmed the owner Mrs Oncü's desire for the cheap jewellery this little enterprise allowed her to purchase.

'May it come easy,' Mrs Oncü said as she passed the shovel down into the cistern to Neşe.

Turgut switched his torch on and flashed it around what had, over the weeks, become a grimly familiar scene. Silted over until almost halfway up the columns that supported the roof; much of the filth in the cistern, Turgut reasoned, must have originated from pre-Ottoman times. So far they had not so much as glimpsed the floor.

Neşe walked over to the small pit they had dug last time and began to rake away at the dirt with a trowel. As she bent towards her work, she put one hand into the small of her back and groaned.

'I don't know how much longer I can carry on doing this,' she said as she watched her son begin his heavy, rhythmic digging. 'May Allah forgive me, but I just don't always feel strong enough. My heart is good, but I am old.'

'No, you're not,' her son panted as he shifted the muck onto the pyramid of filth they had constructed beside their excavation. 'And anyway, all this will stop when we find what we're looking for.' He paused for a moment in order to wipe his brow and catch his breath. 'It's well known that when we conquered the city, the Greeks didn't have nearly so much gold as Fatih Sultan Mehmet thought that they would. It must have gone somewhere. And just like Dad always said, it has to be somewhere that people haven't been to before. Like this.'

'Yes, yes, I know all that,' Neşe replied as she tetchily scraped away at the shifting sludge underneath her feet. 'I'm just saying that for me—'

'For you it is the same as it is for me,' Turgut responded. 'Hard work with only Dad's dream to keep you going.' And he turned away from her and started digging again.

He dug for some time, steadily, with purpose, unaware that for quite a while his mother had stopped her labours. But when he did notice, Turgut became concerned. Seemingly frozen in her painful stooping position, Neşe had one hand stretched shakily out in front of her.

Alarmed Turgut threw down his shovel and moved towards her. 'Mum!'

But she didn't answer. Her eyes glassy, Neşe just made a small gurgling sound in her throat – the sort of noise those who have just experienced a stroke might make.

'Mum!'

Turgut grabbed her around the shoulders and tried to pull her up towards him. But Neşe, frozen to the spot, would not come. Mesmerised by some place just in front of her, she kept on looking ahead until her son saw what had caught and paralysed her attention.

It was Turgut's turn to gasp as the beauty of the ancient crown hit him in the eyes. The light from his torch played across the artefact. There was gold and jewels also – emeralds, rubies, diamonds the size of babies' fists . . .

Turgut, his whole body trembling with emotion, reached past his mother and touched it gently with his fingers. The crown felt strangely warm.

Chapter 3

The two of them took their seats in silence. Dressed in shorts and brightly coloured T-shirts, their faces almost completely obscured by dark glasses, they didn't look anything out of the ordinary – for Angelinos. Had they been in New York or Seattle, they would have seemed weird, but not here in the City of Angels.

Not that the dark glasses fooled anyone. Angelinos are trained from birth to see celebrity through brick walls, if necessary. And besides, the glasses weren't meant to actually hide anything – they were part of the uniform. Vitamin pills, small scars behind the ears, Tiffany jewellery, dark glasses.

Some of their fellow travellers, the women particularly, did recognise them. But as they were, as always, travelling Club Class, none of the women actually *said* anything to them. He knew, however, that on such a long flight it was only a question of time. They would, he thought, probably use the topic of his recent marriage to Kaycee as an opener. He turned to her and smiled, watching as she attempted to make her seatbelt small enough to hold her emaciated hips.

'My God,' she said as she smiled back, her deep Southern voice drawling with intelligent contempt, 'if I get any thinner I'll be joining the spirit world!'

Her husband, the most successful Hollywood actor ever to originate from Turkey, laughed. 'When we arrive in İstanbul, you can eat exactly what you like,' Hikmet Sivas said. 'In fact if you don't, my sister Hale will be very offended.'

'So it's true what they say about you people then?' Kaycee asked.

'What's that?'

'That you like eating and big ladies.'

Hikmet Sivas laughed. 'Yes, we do,' he said. 'All the sensual pleasures . . .' And then his face darkened.

Kaycee took a hardback book out of her hand luggage and opened it halfway through.

'So maybe I can put on a little flesh for a spell,' she said, looking down at the page in front of her.

'Yes.'

'Shame I'll have to lose it again before we come back.'

'Mmm.'

And then Kaycee looked up from her treatise on the theoretical nature and function of black holes and gazed out of the airplane window. Out there was Los Angeles, their rich and privileged home. Strangely, she pulled a face.

'Fucking shitty place,' she said and looked at her husband. 'I'm for İstanbul! Can't wait!'

'Indeed.'

Still smiling, she returned to her book.

İstanbul. Hikmet Sivas inwardly shuddered. Home. It had been a while – too long. Things had changed. Time was when he couldn't wait to get home. But not now. This time it was different, this time he was under pressure.

'It is Ali Bey, isn't it?'

In response to his now rarely used stage name, Sivas

turned. The woman's sun-cooked skin resembled that of an alligator. She pulled her orange lips back in a smile.

Sivas bowed graciously. 'Yes,' he said.

'I told Miriam it just had to be you,' the woman said, indicating another, even drier woman in one of the seats to their right. 'I'd know you anywhere. I met my second husband at one of your movies, *The Man from Acapulco*. It opened six months to the day after Kennedy was shot. I shall never forget it.'

'How kind,' and then he turned his head away and closed his eyes. Ali Bey – what a long time ago that had been, and how much being him had cost Sivas.

The woman, not receiving any further response from her idol, resumed her seat.

Sivas/Ali Bey feigned sleep until the plane took off.

'It's fake.'

Neşe's eyes instantly filled up with tears. 'It can't be!'

'Well, you hold it then and tell me what you think.' Turgut passed the crown over to his mother.

Neşe straightened her back as she took the glittering article from her son and then grunted, although whether that was from the pain that moving elicited or from the sadness she now felt as she held the thing, it was impossible to tell.

'It's light, isn't it?' her son said, shaking his head in disbelief. 'Gold and jewels are heavy and cold. This isn't.'

'It's like one of those crowns young brides wear here,' Neşe said alluding to the longstanding love affair Turkish brides continued to have with crowns such as these.

'It *is* one of those, Mum.'

'Yes, but how did it get—'

'I don't know!' the young man snapped.

'Turgut!'

He raised his shovel and once again dug down into the muck around his feet. 'Just throw it onto the pile,' he said, tipping his head towards the silt they had already excavated.

'Oh, but Turgut, we could keep—'

'It's totally worthless, Mum!' Exasperated and exhausted, Turgut nevertheless dug with a fierce sense of purpose that did not easily allow for dissent.

'All right, all right.'

After some difficulty, Neşe negotiated the uneven surface of the filth until, crown in hand, she came to the pyramid of silt. With a sigh of mild regret, she looked down at the object and even though the thought that it might look nice on her daughter crossed her mind she stepped forward to throw it onto the pile. However, as she leaned across her foot caught against something and she slipped.

'Turgut!'

As she started to fall, he came running but not quickly enough to be able to catch her.

'Mum!'

Neşe hit the silt without a sound or anything beyond a little discomfort, the muck cushioning her fall. It was a pleasant surprise to find that she hadn't done herself any harm apart from being filthy from head to toe. Turgut shone his torch up and down his mother's blackened body and fought to suppress a laugh. What with all the many layers of clothes she wore on her body and head, plus the dirt, Neşe looked even more like a bundle of rags than she usually did. Poor old Mum, Turgut thought affectionately, nothing she does ever comes close to fulfilling her dreams. Poor peasant.

As he leaned towards her to help her up, he asked, 'What made you fall?'

'Something there,' Neşe replied shortly, waving a disgruntled hand down towards her feet.

Turgut shone his torch down to where she had indicated.

It looked like the branch of a tree. Long and white, it lay to one side of the muck pyramid. Turgut moved the beam of his torch along its length until he came to what should have been either a thicker part of the tree or a break where the branch had separated. But instead of either of these there was only a hand, graceful and slim, its long fingers decorated with numerous multicoloured rings.

When, after having a shower, putting on make-up and changing her clothes, Hulya İkmen finally arrived at the police station she found that her father had altered his plans and was preparing to go out.

'We'll have to talk later,' he said, ushering her out of his office almost as soon as she arrived.

Even through the haze of cigarette smoke that drifted across his nose and into his eyes, Hulya could see that her father's face was very grey. She had seen it like this before – after the earthquake and when her grandfather had died – and it alarmed her.

'Dad—'

'Just go home now, Hulya, please,' he said.

She looked beyond her father towards his deputy Orhan Tepe. But she got no answers from his blank countenance. And so with a shrug she began to make her way back towards the stairs. With any luck she might see a few young, handsome officers on the way who might glance at her carefully applied make-up and brand new jeans. If they did, her efforts would not have been wasted, even though her affections lay elsewhere. But try as she might she couldn't smile – not even at that pleasant thought. Perhaps it was because of her father's appearance, or her worry about Hatice – or rather what she knew about Hatice . . . Her heart jumped.

Hulya put as much distance between her father and herself as she could and ran all the way down to the ground floor.

As soon as he saw his daughter tearing down the stairs, İkmen put his jacket back on and checked his pockets for cigarettes.

'OK, Orhan,' he said to his deputy, 'let's get over there.'

'Yes, sir.'

When he'd got the call just minutes before, İkmen had wanted to 'get over there' immediately. In the garden, or rather underneath the garden of a house on Türbedar Sokak, a corpse had been discovered by a mother and son hunting for treasure in a little-known cistern. The body was young, fresh, and female, and İkmen had a bad feeling about it. Even before he'd learned these details, he'd had a bad feeling about it. His heart had started to race and the skin on his scalp prickled uncomfortably underneath his hair. Feelings that his late father had described darkly as either 'witch's sense' or, more commonly, 'that thing you do, like your mother'. His mother, Ayşe, had indeed possessed some very strange and unnerving abilities. Widely recognised as a witch, İkmen's long-dead Albanian mother had passed on much of her character to the younger of her two sons. Now was one of those times when that inheritance, at least to İkmen, was most apparent.

For the moment he kept his feelings to himself. He would

need a clear and open mind to deal with what was awaiting them at the scene. After all, he could be wrong. It was improbable, but not entirely without precedent. And in this particular instance he very much hoped that he was wrong.

İkmen's hopes exploded into bitterness as soon as he saw the young girl's face. Hunkered down in the organic-smelling silt, his eyes straining to accommodate both the light from the arc lamp and the dense surrounding darkness, İkmen groaned when he looked into her dead eyes. She had been, still was, so pretty.

'She's called Hatice İpek,' he said wearily to his deputy. 'She's seventeen.'

'Is she known to us?'

'No, no.' İkmen, with some reluctance, replaced Hatice's head in the silt and then slowly rose to his feet. 'No, she's a friend of one of my daughters. She lived with her mother and sister in the apartment opposite ours.'

'From the way she's dressed—'

'Since when did you see a working girl dressed like that?' İkmen said and the two of them looked down at the body again. 'Since when did you see anyone dressed like that?'

Although her clothes were covered with filth it was easy to see that the likelihood of Hatice having bought them herself was slim. The dress, if not the cheap and plentiful jewellery, was extremely elaborate. Full length, it was made of richly marbled satin which was further decorated with occasional tiny fabric roses. Cinched in at the waist by a thick metal belt, the dress was cut low to allow the full glory of Hatice's breasts to be appreciated. Around her neck, wrists and ankles, as well as on every finger, cheap jewellery glittered. Only the crown which had led

the Fahrıs to the discovery of Hatice's body lay away from
her, the only thing that was out of place.

'What do you think she can have been doing here, sir?'
Tepe asked, shuffling his feet to stop himself from sinking
into the silt.

İkmen shrugged. 'I don't know, but I suspect that she
wasn't doing anything.' He, too, moved his feet uncomfortably on the precarious dirt surface, 'I mean, I can't see
anyone having a passionate tryst down here, can you?'

'No.'

'And yet dressed as she is, she obviously wasn't just
doing her mother's shopping.' He sighed. 'I would say that
she was probably dumped down here after – something.
Forensic and Dr Sarkissian will be able to tell us more once
they've worked their morbid magic, but from the way she's
lying I don't think she was just carelessly hurled down here.'
He looked at her briefly again and then turned away. 'She
looks carefully arranged, laid out.'

Tepe, who had been looking at Hatice's body as İkmen
spoke, tilted his head upwards to indicate his agreement.

'Did you get anything useful out of the people who found
her?' İkmen asked.

'Not a lot,' Tepe said. 'They're well-known treasure
hunters. The type of people the Fire Department hate. You
know the sort, they get themselves into difficulty and have
to be rescued. The old lady who owns the property charges
them to dig here. Apparently they pay her quite well.'

'Really. And so did she, the old lady, see anything odd
going on in her garden either last night or this morning?'

'She says not,' Tepe replied. 'But then if the Fahrıs know
that this cistern is here, others may do too. Not that they've
told anybody.' He smirked. 'They're very secretive about

the locations of their dig sites, apparently. The son told me
his late father reckoned there was a lot of Greek gold to be
found underneath the streets of the city.'

'He may well be right,' İkmen said. 'Stories have been
going around for years about the gold the Greeks might have
wished to conceal from us when Mehmet Fatih conquered
the city. It's why otherwise sane people periodically get
stuck underground and have to be rescued. The lure of easy
money.'

Tepe looked about him with disgust. 'I'd rather just keep
on doing the lottery myself,' he said.

'Yes. Although in my experience,' İkmen said, 'the
possibility of discovering lost Greek gold is probably a
more realistic route to wealth.'

Tepe indicated his agreement with a rueful smile. The
lottery, like every other kind of easy money, was a long
shot. Unfortunately.

In spite of incredulous as well as disapproving looks from
several of his colleagues, İkmen – seemingly impervious to
the rancid stench from the silt – looked again at the corpse
and lit a cigarette. As Tepe watched the smoke weave and
shimmy its way towards the cistern entrance above, İkmen
said, 'She wanted to be an actress, you know.'

'Mmm.'

'She and my daughter Hulya shared a dream – apparently.' That he hadn't known anything about his daughter's
aspirations until that morning was something that now
saddened İkmen. Always too busy – even for his children.
If he'd known what the girls' interests were he could have
at least prepared them. One simply did not trust men who
wanted girls to dance for them, however great an 'entertainment opportunity' that might be. But then if he had failed,

so had Hatice's mother, Hürrem İpek – yet another parent who worked in law enforcement, İkmen observed bitterly.

'So do you think this girl's ambitions may have something to do with her death?' Tepe asked.

İkmen sighed. 'I think it's possible. My daughter said, when I finally managed to persuade her to tell me, that Hatice had gone to work elsewhere, entertaining men, after she left her job at the pastane last night. I'm just so relieved that she didn't ask Hulya to go with her.'

'So she was involved in prostitution.'

'Not consciously I don't think, no,' İkmen replied. 'The doctor will confirm whether she has been engaged in sexual activity . . .' He closed his eyes briefly against the unpleasant picture that was forming in his mind of the thick black depths of the far corners of the cistern. 'But you and I both know that the word "entertainment" is frequently used as a cover for rather more sinister activities. I think we should start at the Sultanahmet pastane which is where Hatice worked. I know Hassan Bey, the proprietor. We also need to speak to an old actor, you won't remember him, Ahmet Sılay.'

Tepe shifted his feet again; his shoes were beginning to feel damp. 'You think he might be involved?'

The two men moved out of the way to allow the police photographer access to the body.

'Sılay liked to regale the girls with stories of his past triumphs,' İkmen said as he put his cigarette out in the accommodating silt. 'My daughter doesn't think that he had anything to do with where Hatice went last night, but he could be worth talking to. He may even know those she went with. When we've finished here I'll have to go and tell Hatice's mother. If you go to the pastane and ask after

Sılay, they should know where he lives, he's been going in there for years.'

'Yes, sir.'

They lapsed into silence as the photographer took pictures of the body from every conceivable angle. Not that there was anything dramatic about it, apart from the inherent tragedy. Cause of death had not yet been established. There was no blood or even any obvious bruising. İkmen's first thoughts had been that perhaps Hatice's death had been chemically induced. All of the city's greatest mobs were known to have at least some involvement in the drug trade and if they'd given the girl a quick hit of cocaine to loosen her up and she'd reacted badly to it . . . But then what lay behind her elaborate clothing did not sit comfortably with the notion of rough, ignorant gangs involved in prostitution.

İkmen's musings were cut short by some rather chaotic sounds from the surface. Tepe walked, with some difficulty, over to the entrance and called up to find out what was happening. İkmen couldn't hear what was being said but he turned when he heard Tepe laugh.

'What is it?' he asked as he watched his deputy attempt to suppress yet another giggle. 'What's going on?'

'Dr Sarkissian has just arrived,' Tepe said. 'The men are, er, trying to work out how they might get him down here.'

Dr Arto Sarkissian, pathologist, was Çetin İkmen's oldest and most valued friend. An Armenian Christian, Sarkissian shared his friend Çetin's intense love for their native city. His enjoyment of food, however, particularly sugar, showed itself in an ever expanding girth, which was something of a problem now. The entrance to the cistern was not large and the drop to the silt below, though quite manageable for one of average height, could be a problem for a short man like the doctor. All in all, getting him down to the site was not going to be easy.

With a grunt of displeasure İkmen pushed past his deputy and made his way over to the entrance. A constable called Avcı was, without even attempting to conceal his giggles, surveying the scene below.

'I'd really rather you didn't laugh in the presence of a dead child,' İkmen snapped as he peered up into Avcı's now shocked face. 'Had you used the time you've already spent laughing you might have come to the conclusion that a ladder is the solution to your problem.'

Avcı, embarrassed, cleared his throat. 'Yes, sir.'

'The doctor is an important man,' İkmen continued, 'you can't expect him to just jump down into a hole in the ground. I'm most displeased.'

'I'm sorry, sir. I'll get a ladder right away.'

'Yes, you do that,' İkmen said. Then he fixed his eyes on a suddenly straight-faced Tepe. 'And if I catch any of you laughing again I'll exact the kind of revenge upon you that only I know how to.'

Chatter and laughter, both above and below, ceased immediately. İkmen was, as everybody that worked with him knew, fair, honourable, generous to a fault and absolutely terrifying to have as an enemy.

When the doctor did eventually descend into the cistern it was with dignity and relative comfort.

'How is she?' Mehmet Suleyman asked his father-in-law who had now joined him outside the hospital's main entrance.

'Still busy with childbirth,' the old man replied drily. Then he smiled. 'These things take time.'

Mehmet, his eyes, even beneath his sunglasses, squinting against the intense midsummer glare, lit yet another cigarette and sighed. He hated hospitals. That his wife and his father-in-law were both doctors was ironic. That he found himself in hospitals and other medical establishments during the course of his work as one of the city's foremost homicide detectives was grimly amusing.

Years ago, when he'd first started the job under the tutelage of his old boss Çetin İkmen, he'd found such close proximity to the dead disturbing. Now, however, or rather on this particular day, it was the living that were giving him pause. Patients, hundreds of them, had passed before his eyes as he sat for hour after hour in the corridor outside the maternity unit. Bleeding, attached to drips, screaming for more painkillers – they couldn't help being ill any more than the hard-pressed staff could help being too overworked to attend to everyone properly. It was just another manifestation of how pressurised all the services in the ever expanding monster of modern-day İstanbul had become.

He turned to his father-in-law and smiled. 'I had to come out here,' he said wearily. 'I was doing no good in there.'

'You know that in Zelfa's mother country, in Ireland, men go in to watch their infants being born,' Dr Babur Halman told him. 'They didn't of course when Zelfa was born. In the nineteen fifties in Dublin it was still as it is here.'

'Some men here do attend births,' Mehmet replied. 'I have heard of it. But . . .'

'But you don't really like the idea for yourself?' Babur smiled. 'Maybe not. Having experienced how my daughter can be when she is in pain, it is probably not a good idea.'

The two men shared a brief, knowing look.

'But I'm told that neither she nor the baby are distressed, in the medical sense, and so I'm not unduly worried,' Babur continued. 'You will have a son and I a grandson before the day is out. Inşallah.'

Mehmet leaned back against the wall of the hospital and turned his slim, handsome face up towards the shade that was provided by a nearby tree. At thirty-six, Mehmet was twelve years younger than the blonde 'foreign' woman who was now in labour with their son. And although it was good to hear that his wife, who was a very elderly first-time mother, was doing well, there were other things on his mind too. His son, when born, would be the first male child to have been produced by a member of his generation in his family. It was, he knew, an event of considerable significance. Not that the birth of a male child was ever insignificant, that could never be the case within a traditional Turkish family like the Suleymans.

Mehmet's family had a noble pedigree. Until the beginning of the nineteenth century his ancestors had been prominent dignitaries in the Black Sea town of Trabzon. When, however, one particular forebear, a young man named Suleyman, exhibited outstanding courage in battle against the Russians, the Sultan of the day rewarded the family with property and Suleyman himself with the hand of one of his own daughters. This ancestor of the 'ordinary' Turk now known as Mehmet Suleyman had thus bestowed royalty upon his family and he and his descendants had continued to prosper, acquiring wealth and marrying other princesses. Things began to turn sour in the wake of the Great War and with the collapse of the Ottoman Empire.

Now many kilometres as well as many years away from their old palace on the Bosphorus, the Suleyman family suffered as much as anyone from the rigours of hyperinflation. Mehmet's father, the man some people still called 'Prince' Muhammed, possessed little now beyond his blood and his love for the French language to remind him of what his family had been. A grandson was, however, some consolation and even if the child's mother was both a foreigner and of 'common' descent, the as yet unborn boy was eagerly anticipated. Mehmet's mother would want to care for the child at every opportunity and, with Mehmet himself working for the police and Zelfa busy with her psychiatric practice, there would be ample opportunity for her to do so. Or not. Just the thought of it made Mehmet scowl. Although of 'common' descent herself, Nur Suleyman had pretensions. Backed up by a vicious tongue and almost unlimited spite, this made her a dangerous adversary. Mehmet himself had displeased her – once. Now he hated the sight of her.

What, he wondered, would his mother do to stunt and twist her grandson's mind? She'd done a fine job on both Mehmet and his brother Murad. But then she would only be able to do that if he, Mehmet, let her and he had already decided that that was not going to happen. Somehow, although he didn't yet know quite by what means, he and Zelfa would earn the money they needed to provide loving and responsible care for their son. And Nur Suleyman, wife of a prince, mother of 'disappointing' sons, would have no part in it.

Chapter 4

Eventually and inevitably good fortune runs out. If it did not, then all beings would be immortal. Whether this good grace and its subsequent withdrawal originates from Allah or the fickle arms of kismet or is simply a random act is debated frequently across the globe. And although those of a religious disposition possess their own firm answers to questions about the identity and purpose of the deity in charge of events, in accordance with their beliefs, even they are not immune from the pain that proceeds from loss. All that said, however, the human instinct is not to believe what has happened. The human reaction is to gain just a few more seconds of normality by vigorously denying that what has happened is indeed the truth.

'No. No, you must be mistaken,' Hürrem İpek said as she moved backwards, attempting to disappear into the corner of her settee. 'No, it can't be my Hatice, not . . .'

'I'm afraid that it is,' İkmen said. Both he and the female officer with him stood as they told her the news. Just like the officers who had come to inform her of Celal's death, they had refused to sit. Celal! How her heart still hurt for her husband all these years on – how her body still ached for his.

Tears gathered in the corners of her eyes as Hürrem whispered a last gasp of denial. 'No.'

'Our doctor has yet to determine the cause of Hatice's death,' İkmen persisted. He was accustomed if not inured to this type of reaction.

The female officer sat down beside Hürrem and took her hands.

'But I have to warn you,' İkmen continued gravely, 'that we fear your daughter's death was unlawful. You must prepare yourself for that.'

Hürrem's only reaction was in her eyes which widened.

Officer Gün, who was a traditionally minded young woman, murmured the standard formulaic phrase for times like this. 'May your head be alive,' she said to Hürrem.

İkmen signalled his agreement by inclining his head downwards slightly.

'Oh, but I don't want to be alive!' Hürrem replied, her mouth thick with grief. 'I want to die now! I want to . . .'

And then she screamed.

'I am so very sorry,' İkmen said, his voice virtually inaudible behind the woman's shrill torrent of pain. 'Hatice was a good girl, a friend to my daughter . . .'

'No!'

She ripped her hands out of Gün's grasp. They flew up to her face and into her hair, hacking, tearing, making her grief a visible, tangible thing. Something she could later look at in the bathroom mirror and know the reality of what had happened.

İkmen and Gün for their part let her do it. For those for whom this was the way, you had to. Hürrem İpek was, like so many of the grieving relatives İkmen came across in the course of his work, a Muslim. And because all Muslims should be buried within twenty-four hours of death, not only did these relatives of the murdered have to come to terms with the demise of a loved one, they had to accept that burial within the prescribed time was impossible: cause of death had to be established, samples of tissue, fluids, etc., had to be taken and the body needed to be dissected. This, İkmen knew, was going to be very hard for the İpek family to bear.

As Hürrem İpek tore great bloody clumps of hair from her head, İkmen raised his voice through her screams and gave her the only tiny chink of light that could penetrate her darkness.

'I give you my word I will bring whoever did this to justice,' he said. 'I will not rest until it is done.'

While officer Gün remained behind with Hürrem İpek, he left to make a brief visit to his own apartment. He told Hulya, who had been instructed to wait for him, that her friend was dead. Hulya cried, burying her head in her brother Bülent's neck, until İkmen went over to her and took her in his arms. Rocking her gently back and forth he cooed into her ears in the way that he had seen Fatma his wife do when she soothed the children through their miseries.

As soon as the 747 touched down at Heathrow Airport, London, Hikmet and Kaycee Sivas made their way to the gate where they were due to pick up the connecting flight to Amsterdam and then İstanbul.

Kaycee, who was a little nervous about missing their connection, virtually ran. Hikmet, who was rather more accustomed to the way that things worked in the real world (not the USA), made his way in a more leisurely fashion.

'The flight will probably be delayed,' he said as he watched Kaycee's long blonde hair flap up and down as she hurried. 'This is Heathrow. It's the busiest airport in Europe. I've never got through without a delay.'

And, indeed, when they did eventually arrive at the gate in question the flight had been delayed by half an hour.

'Oh, shit!' Kaycee said and flung first her hand luggage and then her long, slim body down onto one of the less than comfortable chairs. 'I just hate all this waiting stuff.'

Hikmet smiled. 'Ah, well, you're in Europe now,' he said as he, too, lowered himself down onto a seat. 'The Old World. Time is viewed rather more casually here than in the US. And as we head east, you'll see, casualness becomes a virtual disregard. In my country time is almost irrelevant.'

Kaycee scowled. 'Great.' But then she, too, smiled. 'Ah, but what the hell,' she took one of his hands in hers, 'it's an adventure. And anyway, where do I get off coming on like a movie star, eh?'

He kissed her. 'I married an academic for a very good reason,' he said.

'Yeah.'

Hikmet Sivas had been married three times before. In each case it had been to minor starlets with ideas above their fame. Not one of them had ever accompanied him back to Turkey – not one of them had ever wanted to. But Kaycee Durand was of a rather different order. Although she looked like a typical Angelino starlet, she was neither as young nor as dumb as many casual observers imagined. At thirty-two she was not, in fact, less than half her husband's age and being a lecturer in astrophysics at UCLA she was far from stupid. Not that Hikmet always found her cleverness to his liking. Indeed her next inquiry was a case in point.

'So, Hi,' she said, using the shortened version of his name that seemed to sit far more easily with his American persona than Hikmet, 'you gonna tell me the real reason for this sudden summer vacation or what?'

Hikmet Sivas frowned.

'I mean, I accept that there is probably some sort of family stuff going down . . .'

'My brother and my sister are having . . . difficulties.' He took his hand from hers and looked away.

'Yeah, which you won't specify,' Kaycee replied. 'Not that it matters a whole lot. It's just that coming from the Big Easy as I do, I know all about family stuff and how weird that can be. I mean, I've had to go home before now just to take my mom over to the juju woman so she can get a husband spelled out of her life.'

'It isn't like that.' Hikmet turned back to face her, his features suddenly and unusually taut. Such an expression, Kaycee thought, made him look what she imagined 'very Turkish' to be.

'So how is it then, Hi?' she asked. 'What are these difficulties?'

'They are Turkish,' he said. 'I can say no more because you just wouldn't understand.' And then with a hardness in his voice that was totally unknown to her, he added, 'Just like I don't understand your New Orleans juju women and their doings.'

'But—'

'Read your book and wait for your airplane, Kaycee,' he said. 'You will have a good vacation in my country. You will like it. And then when all the difficulties are resolved, we will return to the States and you will have lots of stories and happy memories.'

He got up and walked over to the window. A British Airways European Airbus was slowly approaching their gate. Soon he would be home in beautiful Turkey. He was looking forward to smoking cigarettes again for a while but one would never have known this from his face which was indescribably sad.

The district of Cankurtaran lies between the glorious, monument-ridden Sultanahmet area of the city and the Sea of Marmara. Characterised by rather down-at-heel if faintly picturesque streets, it is a district of small schools, lots of children and the ruin of a melancholy Byzantine palace called the Bukoleon, now little more than a wall with three enormous marble-framed windows set into it. The palace was a ruin even when Sultan Mehmet II conquered Constantinople in 1453 and is said to have inspired the victorious monarch to quote the following lines when he first came across it:

The spider holds the curtain in the Palace of the Caesars
The owl hoots its night call in the towers of Aphrasiab.

This district, especially around the old palace and Cankurtaran railway station, is not particularly safe. Robberies and muggings happen there and women are not advised to walk alone in these parts especially at night. Alcoholics, it is said, frequently gather to drink rakı in the old palace gardens. Sometimes they can become threatening and abusive. Sometimes they just stay at home to do that. Ahmet Sılay, one-time actor, now full-time drinker and teller of tales, was a case in point. Sitting on a kilim on the floor of his small cottage on Cankurtaran Caddesi this bright afternoon,

Ahmet was entertaining a young police officer in his own unique way.

'Yes, I like to talk to the girls in the pastane,' he said in answer to Tepe's question about Hatice İpek and Hulya İkmen. 'They like to talk to me.' He took a deep gulp from his rakı glass and then wiped one hand across his mouth. 'I'm an interesting old bastard.'

Tepe, who was sitting over by the sun-flooded window, found that his eyes were drawn to a photograph of a handsome young man on the table in front of him. It was a black and white print and showed an elegant fellow wearing one of those loose suits so typical of men's fashions in the 1950s.

Sılay, who saw where he was looking, smiled.

'That's me,' he said, 'in Egypt. I was eighteen and, as you can see, I was criminally handsome. That was taken on the set of my first movie.'

'So it's your acting career that fascinates the girls?' Tepe said.

'My career?' Sılay tipped his head backwards to indicate his dissent. 'No. The fact that I've worked with the greatest director of all time didn't impress them. That I once worked with a man who went to Hollywood did.'

'And who was that?' In spite of his need to stick to the point with what was in reality a suspect, Tepe found himself drawn to ask further questions about this man's previous life. If all of the movie posters and various cinematic trinkets that adorned his home were anything to go by, he'd had a very interesting life.

'Hikmet Sivas, or Ali Bey the Sultan as he came to be known in Hollywood,' Sılay replied. 'I met him first in Egypt when we both appeared in a V O Bengü monstrosity. He took that photograph of me. We got on and even returned to this country together.' He shrugged. 'But then Hikmet went off to Hollywood and I stayed here and worked with the greatest director of all time.'

Tepe frowned. Neither Steven Spielberg nor Ridley Scott were to his knowledge Turkish.

Sılay, seeing his confusion, elaborated. 'I mean Yılmaz Güney,' he said, citing arguably Turkey's greatest and most controversial film director. 'An artist of genius as well as a true hero of the people.'

There was an element of challenge in Sılay's gaze now. But, Tepe reasoned, if he had indeed worked for Güney then he probably shared at least some of the late director's views about politics and society. The way he spoke seemed to bear this out. But then Tepe reminded himself firmly that he hadn't come to speak to Sılay about either Sivas or the frequently imprisoned Güney.

'So you didn't ask either of the girls, Hatice İpek and Hulya İkmen, to accompany you back here to see your collection of film things?' he asked.

'No. Why would I? While I'm out I'm old and interesting. Why disturb that illusion by bringing them back to this place where they can see me for what I am?'

Apart from the film ephemera, the only other notable items in the house were the hundreds of empty rakı bottles that stood in silent groups in every room. Sılay, the alcoholic, had a point.

'And last night you spoke to the girls . . .'

'As I always do.' Sılay frowned. 'Has something happened to Hatice or Hulya?'

'Just answer my questions please, Mr Sılay,' Tepe said, verbally stepping back into the officiousness of his law enforcement role.

Sılay, who had in all probability, given his past associations, come across this sort of attitude before, just took another swig from his bottle and let his shoulders slump.

'What time did you leave the pastane?' Tepe asked.

'At about ten.'

'Shortly before it closed.'

'Yes.'

'Where did you go after that?'

'I went out to Bebek.'

To Tepe, Sılay, actor or no actor, didn't exactly look like the sort of person who would go out to a smart suburb like Bebek. Ice cream, for which Bebek is famed, didn't seem to be his sort of thing even on the warmest of evenings.

Sılay knew what the policeman was thinking. He responded with a good deal of actorly arrogance.

'My father, who lives in Bebek, will substantiate my story,' he said. 'I went to visit him. He's very old now and although, as I'm sure you can see, I am a great disappointment to him, I am still his son and I keep in contact.'

'I see.'

'And in answer to your next question, officer, yes, I went to get money from him too.' Sılay smiled, but not with any warmth. 'I haven't acted since nineteen eighty-three and I can't do anything else. Someone has to keep a roof over my head and my father is very rich.'

Not the sort of person Tepe could imagine having a lot of sympathy with either the background or the politics of Yılmaz Güney. It must have been extremely galling for Sılay senior to have his no doubt beautifully educated son mixed up with communists and jailbirds. But then perhaps the old man just paid Ahmet to go away – go away and get drunk in a 'bad' part of town, well out of sight.

'I took no little girls back with me,' Sılay continued as he lit a thin cigar and then sucked appreciatively on it. 'I just collected my money, slept in my father's house for one night – you can ask his nurse if you want an independent witness – and then I came home here in the morning.'

'So as far as Hatice and Hulya are concerned . . .'

'The girls told me they wanted to become actresses and I amused them with my stories. Nothing happened. I never invited them here nor met them anywhere outside the pastane.'

Tepe felt fairly certain that he was telling the truth. Once a rebellious and socially conscious young rich boy, Sılay had never achieved the fame that he craved and so he took to drink, dining out on boasts about a man he had worked with only briefly. He was a sad, broken character whose love for and knowledge of cinema was all that he retained of the handsome youngster in the baggy suit.

Tepe lit up a cigarette of his own. 'So if you didn't have an inappropriate relationship with either of these girls, do you know of anyone who might have done? Men who might have attempted to entice the girls back with them, using their ambitions to tempt them?'

Ahmet Sılay sighed. 'Hulya's father, I know, is big in the police. Everyone knew, it annoyed her. Men, young and old, kept their distance.'

'And Hatice?'

He took a swig from his glass and again wiped his mouth with his hand. 'Well that, I think, might have been another matter.'

'What do you mean?' Tepe asked.

'I mean that if you want to know about Hatice and men you might begin by asking Hassan Bey.'

'The proprietor of the pastane?'

'Yes. Unlike his father, who is a man of both learning and principle, Hassan Bey believes I am only a harmless old drunk wedded to stories of my youth. But I have eyes in my head and I know what it looks like when a man squeezes a girl's breast and she likes it.'

Chapter 5

Although it was obvious that the girl had been sexually assaulted in both her vagina and her anus, and had lost blood from both, that was not what had killed her. She had lacerations to the pubic area and some deep bruising but the cause of Hatice İpek's death was elusive.

Not that pathologist Arto Sarkissian was giving up. There was still far more information that could be gleaned via further observation of the corpse as well as tests to be performed on tissue samples. But it was late now and he was tired. He would return to Hatice again in the morning. She wasn't, after all, going anywhere. The Armenian's large features broke into a smile as he thought about this grim little joke – the sort of dark observation that he and his friend Çetin İkmen frequently exchanged. Çetin was probably right at this moment still trying to comfort his daughter whose friend Arto's charge had once been.

Poor little girl. Whoever the man or men were who had assaulted her, they had been brutal. Surprisingly Hatice had not been a virgin before the attack, a detail upon which Arto passed no judgement even though many, he knew, would condemn the girl for that. As far as he was concerned, it was hardly relevant. Hatice had been subjected to sexual violence, the perpetrators of which were obviously both dangerous and without conscience. It was something that

Çetin needed to know so that he could act upon it – and soon. Sex crimes did not, fortunately, happen every day, but when they did the assailants had to be caught quickly. With nearly thirty years' experience behind him as well as, rather more recently, close contact with Mehmet Suleyman's wife, the psychiatrist Zelfa Halman, Arto knew that sexual brutality tended to escalate. And if what he had seen of Hatice's injuries was anything to go by, this man or men were already well down that particular road. Whether or not they had killed her, they had abused her body in almost every orifice. Next time who knew where their depraved appetites would lead them.

Arto considered ringing İkmen to give him the news but then thought better of it and decided to go and tell him in person. This was not, after all, just any body he had here, it was the body of Hulya's best friend. Çetin would have to think very carefully about how to tell his daughter what the post mortem had so far found, so it was probably best to discuss it fully with him first. He would, of course, have to take him away from the apartment in order to be able to speak freely – probably, knowing Çetin, to one of his favourite bars.

Arto scrubbed his hands and arms until they were red, put his jacket on and made his way out towards the car park. It was already gone six o'clock when he finally emerged from the confines of the mortuary. The sun was still strong, however, so he took his jacket off before he got into his car. As he fired up the engine, he flicked the switch to turn on the air conditioning – a luxury that Arto, with his palace on the northern shore of the Bosphorus and his elegant, wealthy wife, took for granted. His friend Çetin İkmen lived an entirely other kind of life and so Arto would need the air conditioning to cool him down before he toiled up the many stairs to the policeman's stuffy, chaotic Sultanahmet apartment.

As he walked from the kitchen into the hall, İkmen looked down at Hulya where she sat on the floor with the telephone in her lap, talking to her mother. Her little face, which now looked folded in on itself with grief, was still wet with tears. Earlier when Canan, Hatice's sister, had returned from staying over with one of her aunts, Hulya had rushed over to the İpek apartment to comfort her. Both girls had hugged, crying with misery and disbelief. Behind them, in the dark depths of the apartment, İkmen had just glimpsed Hürrem İpek's devastated face, now still and lifeless as if the core of her being had dried to stone. That he would have to formally interview both his neighbour and his daughter about the events surrounding Hatice's death was not something that he looked forward to. In the meantime, however, he would let Hulya talk alone to her mother.

'But, I mean, we can't really know where people go to when they die, can we?' he heard his daughter ask his wife. He watched as Hulya's face briefly resolved into a frown as she listened to Fatma's response. Just in case one or other of them should decide to draw him into the conversation, İkmen made a quick getaway into the living room and then out onto the balcony. OK, so like his late mother he might have the odd premonition, experience the occasional ghost, but the afterlife and particularly traditional Islamic concepts of it were not his province. That was Fatma's area; she, after all, almost alone in the vast İkmen household, believed.

Bülent was already out on the balcony when İkmen arrived. His sweet young face was tinged with gold as he turned his features up to the still fierce setting sun. His father sat down beside him and lit a cigarette.

'Your mother's helping your sister to come to some sort of peace with what has happened,' he said as he exhaled smoke out across Divanyolu Caddesi with its teeming pavements and packed trams. 'I'm glad it's her. I couldn't have done it.'

Bülent shrugged. 'But you see death all the time,' he said.

'Doesn't mean that I'm inured to it,' İkmen responded. 'Even when it happens to people I don't know, I'm still shocked. But when it's someone close . . .' He sighed. 'You don't get over it, you just get used to it. There are times when I think about your grandfather and the pain is so intense it feels like I've been punched in the stomach.'

Bülent sipped some water from his bottle and then leaned back and closed his eyes. At eighteen he still wasn't mature enough to be comfortable around emotions like the ones his father was expressing. And so the two of them sat in silence until İkmen's mobile phone began to ring.

Hassan Şeker, dressed in an elegantly cut suit and emanating expensive cologne, looked totally incongruous as he sat behind the old stained table in Interview Room 2. The poor light from the one inadequate bulb overhead made his immaculate appearance seem even more bizarre. Orhan Tepe knew that Şeker was in a different league from him. He is in the same category as Mehmet Suleyman, Tepe thought sourly. Back in Ottoman times, when Suleyman's family had been aristocrats, Şeker's had been the culinary artists who served such people. Patronised and flattered by their exalted customers, many confectioners, jewellers and other artisans had as a result become admired and wealthy themselves. Despite the passing of time and the declaration of the Turkish Republic in 1923, such people retained their wealth and reputations.

Tepe looked across at the confectioner again and scowled. Very like Suleyman, in fact, he thought – handsome, loved by women and rich . . . in comparison to him. His scowl deepened – which was not lost upon Hassan Şeker.

'Is something bothering you, officer?' he asked, his head held high with imperious indignation.

Tepe slid his glance across to the young constable who stood guarding the door. People were not generally so confident and up front in this type of setting and the constable looked uncomfortable.

'I was just hoping that Inspector İkmen gets here soon, sir,' Tepe replied. 'It would be good if we could get this over with.'

'I can only agree with that,' Şeker said and he looked Tepe up and down with very obvious disdain.

And then the room became silent again until there was a knock at the door. The constable opened it immediately and İkmen entered. Hassan Şeker rose to his feet.

'Ah, Inspector,' he said. 'It will be a trouble, I know, but if you could just put this stupid man right with regard to the grave error he has committed, I would be grateful.'

İkmen looked at Tepe before, smiling at Şeker, he sat down.

'If you mean that Sergeant Tepe has made a mistake in bringing you here, sir, then I must take issue with that.' İkmen lit up a cigarette. 'Had you answered his questions—'

'He and his underlings just marched into my place of business asking insulting questions!'

'Sir, we have reason to believe that you may have been having a relationship with a girl we found dead earlier today.'

'Yes, yes.' He ran one hand through his hair, his head bowed. 'He told me about Hatice and I am very sorry. It is most distressing. But as to my having a relationship with her—'

'Oh, I agree,' İkmen said, 'that I may have overstated your connection with Hatice. From the information we have received it would seem that it stopped at just sex. If indeed it got that far. But you were seen touching her breasts, and she appeared to be comfortable with that.'

Şeker raised his head a little, his eyes furious. 'And who says this?'

'Sir, you must know that I cannot—'

'Oh, but of course, I told your men the whereabouts of Ahmet Sılay, didn't I?' He laughed without mirth. 'And you believe the word of a politically dubious alcoholic. Such observations are pure fantasy, the product of a mind obsessed with celluloid.'

'Mr Sılay apart, there is a witness who can substantiate this notion who is not given to strong drink.'

'Who?' Şeker's voice as well as his eyes were challenging, imperious. 'Well?'

'Mr Şeker, I am not at liberty to—'

'But if I am to counter this accusation then I have to know who I am up against! This is a lie! I am fully aware that some of the people who work for me do not necessarily like me.'

In the face of İkmen's stoic silence, Şeker sat down. As he did so, a thought appeared to occur to him. It was perhaps prompted by the gravity that was etched on İkmen's features.

'Unless, of course, it was your daughter,' he said. 'In which case I may as well, I suppose, confess to this whether I did it or not.'

İkmen sighed. This was not a place he had wanted to go to with this interview. But when Tepe had telephoned him about Şeker, he had had to ask Hulya about her employer and Hatice.

'Sir, telling the truth might help,' İkmen said. 'Touching a girl's breast or having consenting relations with her is not a crime. We are not accusing you of harming her, we simply need to know who her contacts were. And because you must have been one of the last people to see her alive—'

'When she finished her work she left with your daughter.'

'And you didn't see her again that night?'

'No. I went home to my wife as I always do. I have never done anything with or to that girl. If some people mistake my natural friendliness for something else then that is their problem, not mine.' And then he sank back into his chair as if temporarily deflated.

İkmen put his cigarette out and lit another. 'Well, you may be right,' he said. 'It is possible some misunderstanding . . .'

'Thank you!'

'However, I stand by my officers' actions. We were, sir, bound to follow up such an accusation.'

'Well, of course.' Şeker's features had softened considerably now. Although not exactly smiling, he appeared more relaxed. It was at this point that İkmen pleasantly called a halt to the proceedings and allowed Hassan Şeker to go.

As soon as they heard the confectioner's footsteps disappear down the corridor outside, Tepe turned to his superior and said, 'Do you believe him, sir?'

'No.' İkmen frowned. 'It's his word against Ahmet Sılay's and Hulya's. I know that my daughter, at least, doesn't lie. She's seen that man with his hands all over Hatice. And besides, even if I didn't know that I would still call Hassan Şeker a liar.'

'Why?'

İkmen smiled. 'Oh, just because, Tepe. Feelings that I have about people. Call it something supernatural, for want of a more appropriate term.' He stood up and made ready to leave the room.

Confused, Tepe just reiterated, 'Supernatural?'

'Yes,' İkmen said as he opened the door to the corridor, 'as in precognition, that sort of thing. But please, don't mention it to Commissioner Ardiç, he hates that.' And then with a smile he left.

In spite of the difference in their height and the fact that Mehmet was handsomer than Murad, it was easy to see that the Suleyman brothers were closely related. The way they sat, slumped down against the wall of the hospital, their chins cupped in their long thin hands, made them resemble scolded children rather than middle-aged men.

Murad had been with Mehmet for just over an hour like this, occasionally talking but more often than not passing the hot, thick night by smoking and taking drinks from his can of cola. His sister-in-law Zelfa's labour had been going on for most of the day, so unlike Murad's experience of impending fatherhood. His late wife, Elena, a sorely missed victim of the monstrous 1999 earthquake, had given him a daughter within two hours. But she had been young; even now she would only have been twenty-eight. The thought of that, coupled with the closeness of the heat, made Murad feel slightly sick and so he distracted himself by looking at Mehmet. The younger man's face was quite white.

Murad reached over and took one of his brother's hands in his. 'It isn't exactly major surgery these days,' he said with what he could muster of a smile. 'And anyway, the doctor said he would give Zelfa another hour.'

'Yes, but if she doesn't have my son within an hour—'

'Then they'll perform a caesarean section,' Murad replied, 'as the doctor said. They do them every day, Mehmet. She will be fine. Inşallah.'

'Mmm.'

They sat in silence for a while, watching as ambulances and cars came and went, taking part in the twenty-four-hour soap opera that is hospital life. Birth, death, sickness, joy, grief and anger – Mehmet had seen it all since he had come to this place that would herald a turning point in his life. Things would never be the same. They certainly hadn't been for Murad since little Edibe's birth. Mehmet looked at his older and wiser brother and smiled.

'So what did Mother and Father say when you told them?' he asked.

Murad smiled. 'Father showed me the coin he has purchased for your son,' he said, referring to the old Turkish custom of buying a gold coin for a new baby. 'It's one of the biggest I've ever seen. He told me it's from the reign of Sultan Abdul Mecit.'

Mehmet closed his eyes and shook his head. 'But he can't afford something like that, not with you paying half of his costs on the house and—'

'Mehmet, he has to, you know that,' Murad replied simply. 'Like going to only the best restaurants and having

61

his suits tailored for him, it's what he does. It's how he was raised.'

Mehmet lifted his eyes up to heaven. 'Ah, yes,' he said sotto voce, 'by the glittering waters of the Bosphorus, with precious carpets on every floor; with servants and nurses watching him walk his family of white Angora cats around the lush, green gardens.'

'Something like that,' Murad said and then both he and Mehmet laughed. Soon, very soon, they hoped, another little Suleyman would come into the world. Hopefully, with his practical Irish mother and hard-working father, Mehmet's son would appreciate the kind, if anachronistic and unwise act his curious grandfather had performed on his behalf. Just an echo now of the princes his forebears had once been, Mehmet's son would at least start his existence in old-fashioned regal style.

The upstairs family parlour was mercifully empty. Apart from a couple of young students in the corner, it was just them. So they wouldn't be seen, which was good. Sergeant Ayşe Farsakoğlu nevertheless looked about her with large, doleful eyes. These little *pideci*, though clean and cheap, were so boring. Not that she didn't like *pide*, that thick, flat bread topped with cheese or meat or eggs or almost anything you could want. Like Italian pizza, to which it is often compared, *pide* is not easily disliked. No, it wasn't the food or even the dull, whining tunes from the radio in the corner that were bothering Farsakoğlu.

'I shall be thirty in three weeks,' she said to the man sitting opposite her.

Orhan Tepe looked up from his *pide* into a pair of eyes that shone with a heightened intensity. 'Yes,' he replied simply, 'I know. We're going out to eat in Tarabya.'

'Where no one will know us,' she said, her generous lips now tight around her words. 'On my thirtieth birthday, I go out with my lover, not my husband – at my age! – and to a place where nobody knows us.'

'Yes,' he shrugged, 'I'm married. It has to be that way for the moment.'

'I want to go to the Four Seasons, Çatı or Rejans,' she said, naming three of the city's most expensive restaurants.

The little boy who was their waiter for the evening came over and took away Tepe's empty Coca-Cola glass. He might also have been trying to listen in on their now rather fraught conversation, but if he was, neither of them noticed.

As the boy left, Tepe leaned towards his mistress and said, 'You know I can't afford to take you to places like those at this time. We have to go to places I can afford.'

'Like this place!' she said, her face now quite red with rising anger and genuine upset.

'It's just an ordinary *pideci* . . .'

'Yes, exactly!' She stared deeply into his eyes. 'And after here we will go over to your brother's empty apartment where I'll—'

'Keep your voice down!' He looked around nervously, but to his relief the students and the waiter had gone now.

'I want more from my life, Orhan,' she continued. 'I deserve it. You deserve it. A proper, comfortable place for us to relax, nice clothes, good food, some certainty that we have a future together.'

'Which I have told you we will have!' Tepe, his voice

still a whisper, snapped. 'I'm working on it. I think about it every day. Eventually—'

'Eventually, if you don't do something soon, I may leave you to the timid caresses of your frigid wife and—'

'Go and attempt to seduce Mehmet Suleyman again?' He looked at her with both desire and disgust. Somehow the lingering obsession she still retained for her ex-lover Suleyman excited him. It always had. From the start he'd envied Suleyman, but the thought that he now had what the far more cultured and aristocratic officer no longer had made him feel superior. Ayşe Farsakoğlu was both a beautiful woman and an uninhibited lover – Suleyman had to miss her. After all, what did he have now? A sharp-tongued old hag of a wife, monstrously fat in her pregnancy. Orhan smiled. Ayşe, however, did not.

'The only time I think about Mehmet Suleyman,' she said icily, 'is when I consider all the smart places he could have taken me. Places you and I must go to, unless of course you want Aysel to find out.'

With the speed of a viper, he snatched her wrist across the table. 'Don't even think about blackmailing me!'

'I'm not blackmailing you, I'm promising you I will do this!' she replied, her face set hard and determined against the pain inflicted by his hands. 'I want better than this, Orhan. I'm nearly thirty. I want us to have things. I want you! I want to be your wife. I'll do anything I have to to make that happen!'

For a moment they sat like that, their hands joined as if arm-wrestling across the table. And although afraid of what he knew she could do and say, Orhan Tepe was also excited by how Ayşe was at this moment. When she was like this, determined and manipulative, she was also very sexy. In his mind he replayed old scenes of her kneeling on the floor in front of him, taking him into her mouth as he pushed and raked at her head with his fingernails. He felt his penis stiffen.

'Come on, let's go,' he said thickly.

She pulled her wrist out of his slackening grasp and stood up.

Orhan took her to the apartment his brother used on the rare occasions he visited from Ankara. There he first re-enacted the scene he had imagined earlier and then, later, he laid her down on his brother's bed and entered her hard in the way his wife, Aysel, hated. Almost as soon as he had come inside her, he wanted her again. He couldn't get enough. Only afterwards did he give thought to how he was going to continue this. Yes, he did want to give her all the things, the good times, that she wanted. If he did that he knew she would become even more accommodating, more open to sexual experimentation. But he couldn't do that right now and it made him angry. A woman like Ayşe needed more than just vague promises to keep her interested and out of the way of his wife. If only he didn't have to spend all his money on his family. The thought of it threw a temporary cloud across his features – until, that is, she mounted him again, making all thought disappear. Orhan Tepe gladly embraced the oblivion.

They hadn't planned a stopover in Amsterdam, but when Hikmet heard that the connection to İstanbul was delayed by at least three hours, he decided that both he and Kaycee needed a break. And since money was no object, he first changed their flights and then booked them into the exclusive floating Boatel. There they made love, drank several bottles of champagne and watched the sun set over the city. It was idyllic and they were both very content until Kaycee, who was completely relaxed, fell asleep, leaving her husband alone to frown at and then turn away from his reflection in the mirror on the wall. That his wife didn't have a clue why they were really going back to the place of his birth didn't please him. With Kaycee he had hoped, old as he was, to make a new start. But in his heart Hikmet knew, had always known, that that wasn't going to be possible. He turned on his mobile telephone and called his brother Vedat.

When Vedat answered, Hikmet announced himself and then said, 'There's been a change of plan.'

'But this is urgent,' Vedat replied, his voice heavy with what sounded like anxiety.

'Yes, I know and I'm sorry,' Hikmet said. 'But the flight was delayed and I needed to rest. This has all been most . . . worrying. I'm not young any more, Vedat, I don't know whether I can—'

'So when will you be here?' his brother asked, displaying more impatience than sympathy in his voice.

'Our flight will get in at three fifteen tomorrow afternoon. Inşallah it will be on time.'

'I'll be there to meet you.'

'Thank you.' Hikmet rubbed his hands up and down his tired features. 'I'm so looking forward to seeing you, Vedat, you and our beloved Hale.'

'Yes.'

It was a strange, cold response which made Hikmet frown. He hadn't seen either his brother or his sister Hale since well before his marriage to Kaycee. Putting aside the fact that he effectively bankrolled them, the three of them were, or had been, very close and loving siblings. But then perhaps Vedat blamed him for what had happened. He was, after all, living with it, enmeshed in a way that Hikmet had chosen to ignore for some time. They'd hurt Vedat . . .

As he muttered a distant farewell to his brother, Hikmet Sivas shuddered. Today he was in Amsterdam, tomorrow he would be in İstanbul. Only Allah knew what would happen then, what was already written.

Hikmet Sivas, film star and millionaire, lay down beside his sleeping wife and closed his eyes.

Chapter 6

It was always difficult to tell when İkmen was particularly tired or strained. His usual look was, by anyone else's standards, one of crumpled disaffection. Close association with the man had, however, taught Orhan Tepe that a particularly manic light in İkmen's eyes was the key to how much rest he had managed to get. Today, given that İkmen's eyes were both very watery and a little crazy, it would seem that he had slept even less than Tepe himself. But then Tepe had been pleasuring himself with Ayşe Farsakoğlu, while İkmen had the look of a man who had been involved in much grimmer tasks.

'Hatice İpek was both raped and buggered prior to her death,' İkmen said without any preamble as soon as Tepe entered the office. 'Her pubic area was cut up, probably with a razor.'

'Indeed.' It was said coldly and, strangely to İkmen, without judgement.

'She wasn't a virgin before she was attacked,' İkmen continued, 'but I don't feel that is relevant given the nature of her injuries. She was cut and bruised. She resisted. That's rape. It's a crime; whoever did it to her will be punished.'

'So what was the cause of death then, sir?' Tepe asked as he sat down behind his desk and looked across at İkmen's long, grey face.

'I don't know,' İkmen replied. 'Dr Sarkissian has yet to discover that. In the meantime we need to find out just who was having sex with this girl. He or they could be our perpetrator. Hatice admitted nothing to my daughter, who as we know made her own observations and came to her own conclusions; but Hatice's mother is still convinced of her chastity. And then there is Mr Şeker.' He smiled unpleasantly.

'We let him go,' Tepe said, lighting what for him was his first cigarette of the day.

'Yes,' İkmen responded, 'we did. And if the stories told by my daughter and Mr Sılay did not concur so well and were not also such interesting addendums to Hatice's "ruined" state, I would probably give Şeker the benefit of the doubt. But Hatice was not a virgin and my daughter is perfectly convinced about her observations. Şeker touched her and she liked it. She was a beautiful girl and he's a good-looking man.'

'Just because he had her doesn't mean that he killed her.'

'True, but I would like to know the facts of this anyway,' İkmen said. 'I let him off last night, but that was then and this is now.' He lit a cigarette and then leaned wearily on his elbows. 'Take a couple of men and apply some pressure to Mr Şeker. Convince him that the humiliation of supplying a semen sample can be avoided provided he does the right thing. Be pleasant.'

'Yes, sir.' Tepe stood up.

'Oh, and while you're out you might also bend your mind to the issue of what Hatice was wearing when she died.'

'It was some sort of long gown, wasn't it, sir?'

'Yes.' İkmen frowned. 'Dr Sarkissian is of the opinion

that, as well as looking archaic, it is also in reality quite old. I feel it is unlikely that a modern girl like Hatice would choose such a garment herself, so the dress could point towards some sort of preference for such clothing in her assailant.'

'So you think that whoever raped her dressed her first? Like that?'

'According to my daughter, Hatice was going to dance for some nice men who had promised to introduce her to show business. Now as you and I both know, girls who "dance" for "nice" men don't generally do it wearing a great deal of clothing, much less hugely elaborate gowns. No.' İkmen leaned back in his chair and blew a long stream of smoke up at the ceiling. 'I've given it some thought and have come to believe that the people who did this are probably not the type we might be accustomed to in cases such as this.'

'Oh.'

It was a simple word, signifying little, and it irritated İkmen mightily. Tepe hadn't understood and so he just made a noise to convey the fact. So unlike Suleyman who had always questioned, commented and formed opinions. But then as İkmen knew only too well, Suleyman was not just better educated than Tepe, he was also far more adept at keeping his mind away from his private life during working hours. At times like this, İkmen missed him badly. Still, at least with Mr Şeker it was unlikely that Tepe could do much harm even if he did spend all of his time thinking about Ayşe Farsakoğlu. Hassan Şeker may very well have robbed young Hatice of her virginity, but he was not, İkmen felt, a serious contender for either the assault upon the girl or her murder. After all, both Hulya and Ahmet Sılay had said that Hatice liked it when Hassan made advances to her. The man or men who had dressed Hatice in that gown had had to fight her, hurt and damage her to get what they wanted.

İkmen sent Tepe about his business and briefly moved his thoughts away from poor dead Hatice. In the early hours of that morning, Zelfa Halman Suleyman had given birth to a son – a very large and healthy boy, according to his old partner's friend Balthazar Cohen. Crippled as a result of the 1999 earthquake, the former Constable Cohen now busied himself almost exclusively with following the lives and adventures of his friends. Always a gossip, Cohen gathered and passed on information in a far more efficient way than most media, with the exception, maybe, of the internet. He hosted frequent gatherings at his Karaköy apartment and had a variety of telephones, one of which he had used to call İkmen about the Suleyman child at five o'clock that morning.

The baby, so Cohen told İkmen, was to be called Yusuf İzzeddin. It was, apparently, the name of some noble ancestor. It had, again according to Cohen, pleased Mehmet's father who was reputed to be giving the child the largest, thickest gold coin in the entire city. İkmen smiled. How very Ottoman it all was. The child with the name of a noble, princely relatives bringing gold . . . He, too, would have to arrange for some sort of, certainly inferior, gold coinage to be bought for the child. Mehmet was his friend as well as his colleague and anyway, money or no money, Fatma would be scandalised if he didn't buy something.

That would have to come later. In the meantime it was important that he add to his knowledge about Hatice İpek, which meant talking, more formally than before, to her mother.

* * *

This was the second time that the police had visited the pastane. On both occasions they had come to see Hassan and, although Suzan Şeker tried to convince herself that she must have misheard, she could distinctly remember the name of Hatice İpek featuring in that first conversation between her husband and the sergeant. Hatice. Suzan frowned at the memory of her. She had been a nice girl, popular with the customers and good at her job – perfect, in fact, had she not been giving herself to Hassan. Suzan had only seen them once, but it was enough. Through a crack in the office door she'd watched as her husband took the girl's breasts into his hands and kissed them. Hatice's gasp of pleasure haunted her still.

But now the girl was dead and, somehow, the police had come to know about Hassan's connection with her – at least Suzan assumed that they had. To question a mere employer three times, once at the police station, was surely unusual. Now her husband was alone in his office with the sergeant. Two uniformed officers sat outside, drinking her coffee and, no doubt, listening to the occasionally raised voices from inside the office, waiting. To deploy such numbers for, on this occasion, such a long time, seemed pointless unless they were going to arrest Hassan. And yet Suzan, in spite of everything, was convinced that he was innocent. Of course the fact that he was her husband, the father of her children and the man that despite everything she loved, did inform her feelings. But there was something else as well and that was that Hassan, for all his faults, was just not a violent man. He hated violence. One of the reasons they were not nearly as rich as people thought they should be was because Hassan so hated violence. His father, Kemal, had been of a different order. When he was in charge of the business he had stood up to people like the three men who had just now entered and seated themselves by the front door. Suzan quickly finished cleaning some ashtrays and then approached the newcomers with a grave face. The men, all bright open shirts and nasty jewellery, smirked as she approached them. She was going to enjoy telling them just who was currently out of sight behind the partition in front of her husband's office.

She leaned forward to speak to the oldest of the three, a man of not more than twenty-five who wore his hair short and waxed and intimidating.

'The police are here,' she said as she nervously shuffled the cutlery on the table.

The man with the unusual hair frowned. 'What do they want?' he said in a rasping, desiccated voice.

'I don't know,' Suzan lied. 'But they are talking to Hassan now. I think you should go.'

'Why are they talking to Hassan?' asked the youngest of the three, a sad-faced, sniffling character little more than a boy. 'He's nobody. He just—'

'Shut up, Celal,' the leader snapped. He rose to his feet and said to Suzan, 'Tell your husband he is to call me as soon as he's through with them.'

Suzan pulled herself up to her full, not inconsiderable height. 'And if they take him away with them when they go?' she asked. 'What then?'

'Then you'll have to call me, won't you, Suzan,' he replied as he leered up into her face.

'We need some more coffee here.' Although arrogant and demanding, the young officer's request couldn't have come at a more opportune time. Suzan turned to look at the police-man who had just appeared from behind the partition.

'Of course,' she said with a smile. 'No problem.' And as she moved behind the counter to retrieve the coffee pot, the three men by the door left the building.

Unbeknown to them, however, they did not leave quickly enough to escape the scrutiny of Constable Hikmet Yıldız. He didn't know who all of them were but he had come across two of the men before professionally. Not 'good boys'. Yıldız hadn't liked their familiarity with Mrs Şeker. It gave him an uneasy feeling.

Kaycee didn't know what she had expected when they landed, but a huge new airport hadn't been uppermost in her mind. Vaguely she had imagined some sort of third world arrangement of shacks and in a way she was almost disappointed that it wasn't like that. The immigration and customs men were, however, comfortingly menacing, as were the police officers who seemed to favour hanging around the No Smoking signs puffing heavily on evil-smelling cheroots.

'Very *Midnight Express*,' she said as she followed Hikmet out of the customs hall and into the arrivals area.

Her husband smiled. 'I wouldn't say that too loudly around here,' he said. Then he caught sight of a small, suited man at the front of the crowd and threw his arms in the air. 'Vedat!' he cried.

The man, who was a slightly shorter, more careworn version of the Hollywood star, trotted forward into the huge, crushing embrace that awaited him.

'Brother!'

'Vedat, I am . . .' and then lost for further words, Hikmet did something Kaycee had never seen him do before and burst into tears. Amid copious amounts of water Hikmet kissed his brother loudly and repeatedly on both cheeks, stopping only occasionally to gently wipe tears away from his overflowing eyes. It was, Kaycee felt, about as far removed from the sterile 'air kissing' that took place in southern Californian society as you could get. It reminded her of those full-blooded New Orleans funerals of her youth, occasions when the bereaved would drink and kiss and beat their breasts as they gave vent to the gut-wrenching sadness of such events. As a consequence, she rather liked what she was witnessing here.

When Hikmet finally recovered himself he took hold of his wife's hand once again and, in English, introduced her to his brother. Rather charmingly, Kaycee thought, Vedat Sivas bowed just slightly as he shook her hand and then said, 'May Allah make you happy. Welcome to İstanbul.'

'Thank you,' she replied, 'that is very sweet.'

And then to Vedat's surprise, which actually bordered on shock, she kissed him hard on one of his wet cheeks. Hikmet, for some reason that was lost upon Kaycee, found this very amusing and laughed.

The three of them threaded their way through the packed arrivals area and then out into the open air. It was hot, which was pleasing, but less humid than southern California. That was a relief given that Hikmet had said air conditioning was not yet de rigueur here. What was less pleasant and indeed rather disturbing was the smell that seemed to be everywhere. Kaycee couldn't place it beyond the knowledge that it was unpleasant to her and that it was vaguely organic. But since her husband didn't seem to be bothered by it, she kept her opinion to herself. They located Vedat's vehicle in the car park and loaded the luggage into the boot. Although the car was fitted with seatbelts, they didn't appear to work and so Kaycee resigned herself to placing her trust in the vehicle's air bags. At Vedat's suggestion, she sat in the front beside him so that he could point out places of interest as they travelled. The interior of the car, which was a new Volvo, smelt of cigarette smoke and chocolate.

Within minutes they were on the broad Londra Asfaltı highway heading into a city that at first sight looked about as exotic and mysterious as New Jersey. Unless of course you really looked: for the almost totally obscured Ottoman building in the middle of a row of apartment blocks; for the minarets peeping up from behind the shops; for the most beautiful municipal fountains in the world . . . But all of this implied some sort of knowledge which Kaycee didn't have. It also required a little less speed on the part of the Volvo and its driver. But then as Hikmet observed as he took his first cigarette of the visit out of his brother's jacket pocket, Vedat, as a Turk, neither knew nor understood how to drive slowly. Allah who decided the fate of every living being would take care of the outcome, whatever the speed one was doing and with or without seatbelts or air bags.

As Hikmet lit up, Kaycee wrinkled her nose in disgust. Not only was he smoking, which was gross in itself, but whatever it was smelt very bad. Unable to contain herself she fanned the smoke away from her face and said, 'That is so nasty!'

Both men laughed. 'Ah, but when in Rome, one must do as the Romans do,' Hikmet said. 'Is that not the saying?'

'Well . . .'

'Well, the same applies to İstanbul.' He shrugged and leaned forward to give her shoulder a reassuring pat. 'Before you leave you will be eating sugar, drinking rakı and

77

dancing amongst the traffic like a true Turkish pedestrian.'
He laughed again.

Kaycee didn't. She was, as she'd said before, prepared
to make some concessions while in this country, but if Hi
expected her to change her life completely, then he could
think again. She turned to Vedat and said, 'So where's the
best place to get a yoga class?'

Hatice İpek's bedroom wasn't dissimilar to the room that
Hulya occupied. Her bed, like Hulya's, was covered with
an assortment of soft toys, jeans and jackets were casually
strewn about the floor, posters mainly featuring young male
singers covered the walls. In every way it was a teenager's
room – with one exception.

It had been Canan, Hatice's young sister, who had first
drawn İkmen's attention to the stack of exercise books on
top of the dead girl's bureau. Most dated from her high
school days: lists of English verbs, historical essays and
mathematical calculations. One, however, was much more
personal in character. Labelled on the front cover, in a
childish hand, 'My Diary', it made disturbing reading for
any father of a young woman.

Sitting on the chair beside Hatice's bed, İkmen flicked
through the book, stopping at random at what, he soon
realised, were typical entries. Frowning, he read:

4th April. Hassan Bey shut the pastane early today.
When everyone left he took me to his office. I took
off all of my clothes and he took his off too. He told
me how beautiful I was and touched my breasts. I felt
that good feeling again when he did this. Then, as soon
as he was big he went inside me. This time I sat on

top of him so that he moved me up and down. After, Hassan Bey said he was sorry it didn't last long but that it's my fault for being so beautiful.

Another entry, rather closer to the date of Hatice's death, caught İkmen's attention because it mentioned Hulya.

22nd June. Hassan Bey asked for me to suck him again, which I did but not for long. He would like to have sex into my mouth but he won't do it yet because I don't want to. He did it into my hand instead and then later on he did it into his own hand while he looked at me dancing.

When I meet these entertainment people, I'll dance just like this but with my clothes on, of course! I just hope that they like me and give me a job. I haven't told Hulya about this because they might like her better which I know is mean. But I really want to be a star and she's just copying. At the end, Hassan Bey kissed me all over my breasts and told me that he loved me.

Written, İkmen calculated, two weeks before her death, this entry revealed a side of Hatice that neither he nor Hulya knew. Selfish and sexual, Hatice hadn't just wanted to be an actress, she'd wanted to be a star. And, no doubt encouraged by Hassan Şeker's reaction to her body, she obviously thought that these people she had somehow come into contact with before her death would help her achieve her ambition. She'd only told Hulya about her opportunity on the eve of her appointment – too late, thankfully, for Hulya to arrange to accompany her. She had told her sister that she had a plan to make their poor little family richer, but she didn't go into detail. Canan, like her mother, only knew Hatice as the chaste and lovely girl she had always been.

When İkmen felt he had read as much as he could bear, he left the grieving İpek family and paid a brief visit to his own apartment.

Hulya, who hadn't been back to the pastane since the discovery of Hatice's body, was at home alone. Unusually, when her father arrived she made him a glass of tea and then threw her arms round his neck.

'You will find who killed Hatice, won't you, Dad?' she said through yet another flood of tears.

İkmen put his arms round her shoulders and drew her towards him. 'Of course I will,' he said, as ever keeping the doubts that always assailed his mind at the beginning of an investigation firmly to himself.

'Uncle Halil phoned this morning, just after you left,' Hulya said, referring to her father's elder brother. 'He'd read about Hatice in the papers because some of the articles mentioned you.'

İkmen gently let go of his daughter's shoulders and sat down at the kitchen table. 'What did Uncle Halil want?'

'Just to let you know he'd read about you.' Hulya joined her father at the table, wiping the tears from her eyes. 'I told him that you would find out who killed Hatice and he agreed. He said that if anyone could find out, it would be you.'

İkmen smiled. It was nice to know that his family placed so much confidence in him, but it was also a pressure. And with the added stress that came from the fact that his daughter's best friend was the victim in this case, life was not going to be easy for a while.

At some point İkmen knew he should discuss Hatice and

her behaviour with Hulya rather more fully than he had done so far. But not now. Now he just drank the tea she had prepared for him and, smiling, changed the subject.

'When I finish work today, I must go to the gold bazaar,' he said, 'and beggar us all to buy a coin for Mehmet Suleyman's son.'

A look that only the most keen-eyed parent could detect passed across Hulya's face; it brought a slight flush to her cheeks. 'Did you have any particular shop in mind?' she asked as she looked not at her father now but at the wall behind his head.

İkmen, ever the tease, mentioned first the place that did not employ the young man she was sweet on, but when he saw her face drop he relented and told her the truth.

'I will go and see old Mr Lazar,' he said, naming the goldsmith he knew best and also the one that employed his old colleague Balthazar Cohen's son Berekiah – the boy his daughter liked. 'You can come with me if you want,' he added. 'Lazar always gives me credit, but I could still do with someone to control my spending.'

Hulya, still not looking at her father's face, shrugged. 'If you think I can help you.'

'Yes. Yes, I do,' he said and watched the quick rush of excitement send a shiver down his daughter's slim spine. He could remember feeling like that himself. In fact he had felt just so excited the last time he and Fatma had slept together, the night before she left to go to Antalya. Grey-haired, overweight and tortured by varicose veins, Fatma İkmen was nevertheless still a beautiful, passionate woman and Çetin adored her. He was, he felt, an extremely lucky man.

'Then of course I'll help you,' his daughter answered,

as she yet again flung her arms around her father's neck. 'Shall I meet you there or will you come home first and pick me up?'

'I'll come and get you first,' İkmen said. 'So make sure that you're ready.'

'Yes.'

And then Hulya lapsed into silence, her eyes glazed. She was, İkmen thought, probably trying to decide which outfit was the best to wear for the occasion – mulling over what might most impress a young Jewish boy. And although he knew that his wife, who was religious, would disagree with him, İkmen inwardly wished his daughter and the object of her desire well. After all, Berekiah Cohen was a very nice young man who, unlike his crippled father – or maybe because of him – treated all women with great respect. So different from the men who had raped Hatice İpek – and also unlike the outwardly benign Hassan Şeker. Bad men all. Men a father would not want his daughter to even look at.

When Hikmet Sivas made his name as Ali Bey in the Hollywood of the 1960s, one of the first things he did was buy a grand house back home in İstanbul. A native of the working-class Asian district of Haydarpaşa, once furnished with dollars, Hikmet had chosen to stay on that side of the city, albeit in the more salubrious suburb of Kandıllı.

As he now explained to Kaycee, the house that he had bought at that time had mainly been purchased to fulfil the dreams and ambitions of his mother. She was the person to whom, after all, he owed everything. Widowed at twenty-five when his father, a railway worker, died in an accident, Gülnüş Sivas had even done hard physical labour, men's work, to support her three children and to enable her handsome Hikmet to get the education he needed. Now dead, she of course never knew that while the English lessons she slaved for were of great value to her son, what he did first on cheap and greasy casting couches and, more importantly, later in Las Vegas casinos was far more pertinent to what he became than his language skills. Not that he alluded to any of that now. Kaycee wanted to know what his house was like and so they talked about that.

His house, or yalı, as Bosphorus villas are called, was now lived in and retained by his brother Vedat and elder sister Hale. The yalı, which was the traditional rose-red kind, even possessed that elegant embellishment the cumba, or large bay window, which overhung the water and gave the light in the living area a sparkling, luminous quality. The business he had to conduct here in İstanbul meant he would have to leave Kaycee in the yalı for some considerable time by herself, so he trusted she would find all the features – the pools and ponds and antiques – of some interest. At the very least, out in Kandıllı she would be spared the smell of old İstanbul, that hard, subterranean tang of elderly, overworked sewers, sour cisterns and dusty Byzantine tunnels. Not that she had mentioned the smell, but Hikmet had seen by the expression on her face that she'd experienced it as soon as they arrived.

Vedat, who so far had managed to keep up a reasonable, if nervous, commentary on the subject of buildings and streets of interest, turned off the main Yeniçeriler Caddesi just after the Mosque of Sultan Beyazıt. This part of the city, which is actually called Beyazıt, is both cultured and raffish at the same time. As well as encompassing the İstanbul University complex, it boasts several imperial mosques and excellent libraries. Side by side with this, however, are teeming streets of uncertain cleanliness where businesses both openly suspect and of a more subtly 'dodgy' nature survive. Here, for all the world to see, those from Chechnya, Georgia and other now impoverished ex-Soviet republics ply their trade in just about anything, including their large-boned blonde-haired women. These females, the 'Natashas' as they are known locally, are only slightly less obvious than the businesses themselves which openly advertise their wares in Cyrillic characters.

'Soon I am going to arrive at the Galata Bridge,' Vedat explained as he dropped the Volvo down into third gear in order to deal with what was going to be slow progress up the steep, packed road. 'From there you can see all the main sights of the city.'

Kaycee smiled. 'Cool.'

Hikmet, still smoking in the back, was not so impressed. 'Since when did we become part of Russia?' he asked his brother in the Turkish he knew Vedat found more comfortable.

But Vedat didn't answer; intent upon negotiating a tricky, teeming corner graced by a huge, brightly lit leather shop, he simply grunted as the car wrestled with one of the potholes in the road.

Shaking his head at the dire state of the roads, Hikmet was just about to say something about how the local authority was neglecting its duty when the front passenger door sprang open. At first he thought that his wife had lost either her patience with Vedat's laboured driving or her nerve over the steepness of the drop behind them. When, however, dark, unknown arms plunged into the body of the car and either just before or just after he heard Kaycee scream, he realised that she was not leaving the vehicle of her own volition.

He lunged forward, attempting to grab something of her. 'Kaycee!'

But she was gone, into a thick knot of men and then, apart from the sound of her voice which called his name over and over, seemingly into thin air.

Hikmet flung the car door open and threw himself onto the pavement. As he did so, dark men and groups of blonde, cheaply dressed women gathered about him. He looked wildly around, at blank faces wet from the heat, Kaycee's voice still faintly reaching his ears. His brother had now also left the car and called across to him – a rattle of, to Hikmet in his distress, unintelligible Turkish.

And then he was pushing against the press of faces, elbows and bodies that hemmed him in. They gave way easily, but still he flung them roughly aside as he half ran, half shuffled towards the place he thought Kaycee had disappeared into. Screaming her name he elbowed his way into the leather shop where he yelled at the shocked proprietor about a beautiful blonde woman the man had patently never seen. Plunging out into the street again, Hikmet ran headlong into the back of a young policeman who turned and stared at the flushed face of the star with hard eyes.

Hikmet heard Vedat shout 'No!' just before he launched into his account of what had happened, but he ignored it. The policeman listened dispassionately as Hikmet's short account degenerated into floods of tears. He then called the incident in on his radio and asked for assistance.

Chapter 7

Though stylish, the jacket Nur Suleman had taken from her wardrobe was a rather strong yellow and so, despite the extreme heat, she swapped it for a more conventionally elegant black one. Slim and attractive if in a somewhat joyless way, Nur's expensively preserved visage defied her sixty-five years. She would, she thought, as she smiled at the carefully engineered image of herself in the mirror, provide an interesting contrast to that fat, loud-mouthed baggage her younger son had married. What had possessed her beautiful Mehmet to even consider such an elderly and common woman she couldn't imagine. But then her boys both seemed to be prone to unsuitable matches; Mehmet with this strange, foreign intellectual and Murad with a Greek grocer's daughter who, though now unfortunately dead, still exerted some influence over him in the form of his rackety Greek in-laws. It was sad really that such well-bred boys should waste themselves like this.

However, one could at least enjoy the children; Murad's daughter Edibe was a very pretty and engaging little thing and the baby Yusuf İzzeddin was going to be just perfect – in spite of his mother. She would fight her stupid, ungrateful sons for the sake of her grandchildren and make sure that the children married both money and class. Muhammed, her husband, who was far more easy-going about such matters, would naturally oppose such meddling. But then he was just a stupid aristocrat and therefore easily dealt with. After all, hadn't he just sat back and said nothing when Mehmet married his first, perfect wife, his cousin, Zuleika? Oh, he'd mumbled something about the boy being unhappy about the match, but he hadn't done anything – beyond pointing out Nur's error when that marriage failed.

No, aristocrats were almost exclusively limp, in Nur's opinion. Had Muhammed been born to the harshness of central Anatolia, as she had, he would know the value of the ambition that had carried her to the mansion of a prince, as her home had been in the early days of her marriage. It had all now disappeared but that was not her fault. Yes, she had spent money but that had not been what had caused the real damage to the family fortunes. That had come about via the numerous elderly relatives Muhammed had attempted to support. Old princes who couldn't even put their own boots on without assistance and whose idea of getting a job began and ended with occasionally selling some jewellery or antiques. Her husband was exactly the same, which was why the whole thing had failed. But her grandchildren, Nur thought with a smile, would be different. Bourgeois fathers and unsuitable mothers aside, the children still possessed rich Ottoman blood in their veins – something she was not going to let them or anyone else forget.

Nur placed a small, pill-box hat on top of her thick, richly coloured hair and then picked up the brightly wrapped parcel from the top of her dressing table. Her own little present for her grandson, from the Carousel Mall in Bakirköy – nice, tasteful, expensive clothes. Together with the largest gold coin money could possibly buy, which Muhammed had purchased via his usual dubious line of credit, these clothes represented little Yusuf İzzeddin's future which would be full of beautiful people and things. Even if his father was a policeman.

With yet another brief smile at her image in the mirror, Nur left her bedroom and walked downstairs. Her once lovely, now hollow-eyed son Mehmet stood in the hall, nervously jangling his car keys in his hands, anxious to get back to his newborn son at the hospital. As she drew level with him, Nur placed a gloved hand on his cheek. What a terrible, terrible waste!

Just before he left to go and get his daughter, İkmen received a troubling telephone call. Although his investigations into the cause and manner of Hatice İpek's death were not yet complete, Arto Sarkissian had come to some conclusions.

'Cause of death was myocardial infarction,' he said. 'Unless I can find some indication of narcotic involvement, this would seem to be natural.'

İkmen wrinkled his brow. 'What do you mean, natural?' he asked. 'The girl had been raped, buggered and cut!'

'Yes, but I believe that her actual death was unconnected with that,' the Armenian replied. 'What I think happened was that a small clot blocked blood flow within the heart. This caused tissue death in that area which resulted in a heart attack.'

'But something must have caused the clot.'

'Well, obviously, but it need not have been of a sinister nature. All the cuts the body sustained happened post mortem. True, she was held down, raped and sustained bruising during the course of her ordeal prior to death. But I can't say that the attack killed her. This type of sudden death is more common than you think. It is also unconnected with lifestyle factors, like state of health or age, or accidental damage. It just happens and if I can rule out narcotics, I will have to declare that her death was due to natural causes.'

'But she was obviously placed in that cistern, Arto,' Çetin said as he checked his pockets for cigarettes he knew were not there.

'I admit that her death could have occurred during the course of her sexual ordeal, but if so that was just a coincidence, Çetin. These things can happen at any time. It's possible that Miss İpek's attackers thought that they had killed her and so they decided to dump her body.'

İkmen, unsettled by this news as well as tetchy due to lack of nicotine, sat back down at his desk. 'Without murder and in light of the fact that the girl wasn't a virgin, it will be difficult to persuade my superiors that this was even rape. If what you say is correct, all I'm left with is physical assault and illegal disposal of the body.'

'I know. But I can't change the facts, however galling that may be,' Arto said. 'We have collected samples of seminal fluid which may be of use when matched against known offenders.'

'Yes.'

'I'm sorry, Çetin.'

İkmen sighed. 'It's not your fault,' he said and then he replaced the telephone receiver.

As he walked back towards his apartment, after stopping briefly at a kiosk to buy cigarettes, İkmen thought about what, if anything, he was going to say to the İpek family and to his own daughter. Rape of somebody with a 'reputation' was notoriously difficult to prove and if the assailant didn't kill the victim, well . . .

Arto, İkmen knew, wouldn't present his findings to Commissioner Ardiç until he was absolutely sure of the facts. And İkmen's boss was not interested enough to pursue the pathologist himself. So really, it was business as usual even if his confidence in reaching a satisfactory conclusion had been shaken.

The Hulya he took with him to the gold bazaar was quite different from the usual jean-wearing girl İkmen knew so well. Wearing a crisp white blouse and elegant pencil skirt, she looked more like someone going for a job interview than the relatively carefree teenager that she was. Not that İkmen commented upon this. The poor child would have enough trouble stopping herself from blushing when she saw Berekiah Cohen without him adding to her embarrassment.

When they entered the shop of Lazar the Jew, they were warmly welcomed by that elderly gentleman who immediately stopped what he was doing to encompass İkmen in his frail, trembling embrace.

'Oh, Çetin Bey, you have bestowed honour on our poverty-stricken house,' he said, resorting, as was his custom, to Ottoman forms of address.

İkmen, returning his embrace, smiled at the obvious mismatch between the phraseology and the expensive glittering reality around them. But then that was Lazar.

'You will of course take tea with us,' the old man continued.

'Of course.'

Lazar called for 'the boy' – his youngest apprentice and one of his grandsons – to go out and purchase tea as well as a box of Haci Bekir lokum. This latter was for Hulya who as the female relative of an honoured guest warranted only the finest brand of Turkish delight. That Hulya was, quite without reason, weight conscious, was something Lazar didn't know. As the old man led the İkmens through to his private room at the back of the shop, Çetin whispered to his daughter that she should perhaps forget her diet in favour of not causing offence. The girl scowled briefly before bowing to the inevitable.

The room they found themselves in was decorated in red – red carpets, red couches and curtains. All very comfortable, if rather hot in the current conditions. İkmen settled himself down, removing his jacket as he sat. A young man with slightly sad eyes entered from one of the workrooms, carrying a tray covered with many differently sized gold coins. Briefly his eyes met hers and Hulya blushed.

'Good evening, Berekiah,' İkmen said. 'I see that you have anticipated my needs.'

Berekiah Cohen smiled.

'The birth of the Suleyman child has been celebrated many times in this humble place today,' Lazar said as he ushered Berekiah out of the room and back to his work.

İkmen smiled. 'Good fortune then for you, Lazar,' he said. 'Babies are excellent business.'

'That the child is healthy and a male is my only concern. The family needed an heir.' The old man held the tray of coins up for İkmen to inspect. He pointed to one particularly large coin. 'This comes from the reign of Sultan Abdul Mecit. Muhammed Suleyman Effendi is one of his direct descendants. It is therefore very appropriate.'

'Yes.' İkmen raised a wry eyebrow. 'It is also extremely expensive.'

'Ah, but Çetin Bey . . .'

'I'm just a policeman, Lazar. I mean, I want to do the very best that I can for the child, but . . .'

If there was one thing that really bored Hulya, it was haggling. And because her father was so very good at it, she knew that it could take an extremely long, tea-and-lokum laced time. She could, therefore, slip away for a while. So she did.

'Hello, Berekiah,' she said as she entered the workroom.

The young man looked up from his current piece of work which involved setting diamonds into a ring. 'Hello, Hulya. How are you?'

'I'm well, thank you.' She moved towards him, noticing as the light crossed his face that he had a thin smattering of gold dust across his nose. 'What are you making?'

'I'm setting a ring for a lady who is shortly to be married,' and then tipping his head in the direction of a mannequin which stood in the shadows at the corner of the room he said, 'Everything must be in keeping with that dress she is going to wear.'

Having only just gained access to Berekiah, Hulya didn't really want to move away from him. But since he seemed very interested in his current assignment she felt bound to at least take a look at the dress. When she got close and Berekiah had switched on the light above the mannequin, she was glad she had made the effort.

The full-length dress was made of a thick, white satin. It had long, elaborately decorated sleeves, made of lace. Small white roses covered the skirt and the tiny waist was shown off to marvellous effect by a thick, metal belt.

'It's real gold,' Berekiah said in answer to Hulya's unspoken question about the belt.

'Really?'

He smiled. 'The lady's father is a very wealthy man.'

Hulya ran her fingers gently around the plunging lace-edged neckline of the dress and sighed. 'Oh, what it must be like to get married in a dress like this!'

'Well, you'll never know, will you?' Her father's voice was as harsh as it was unexpected.

'Dad!'

İkmen moved with what was for him unaccustomed rapidity. 'Get away from that thing,' he said as he roughly pulled his daughter away from the mannequin, his face grey with what looked like fury.

'Where did this come from?' İkmen asked a shocked Lazar who had entered the room behind him.

'The dress?'

'Yes. Where did you get it? Who does it belong to? What—'

'Çetin Bey!' Lazar held up his hand to silence this man who appeared for some reason to be raving. 'I don't know what all this is about but from the look on your daughter's face you have upset her considerably. The girl was doing no harm to the dress.'

'She didn't touch it, Çetin Bey,' Berekiah said. 'She was only looking.'

Hulya, who did indeed have a shocked expression on her face, smiled inside. Berekiah had, in a very minor way, deceived her father for her. What joy!

İkmen, his seeming fury now spent, slumped as he continued to look at the dress.

'I'm sorry, Lazar,' he said as he shook his head slowly from side to side, 'it just came as a bit of a shock.'

'What did?'

İkmen thrust a hand out towards the mannequin. 'This,' he said. 'The design and even some of the details are almost

exactly the same as a dress I recently saw on a dead woman
– a victim.'

'Ah, the İpek child . . .'

Not really knowing why he even attempted to keep his
work confidential in this city of twelve million insatiable
gossips, İkmen just shrugged his agreement and then placed
a hand briefly on his daughter's shoulder. Mention of Hatice
had once again made her eyes moist.

'Can you tell me anything about the dress?' İkmen
asked Lazar.

'The design is Ottoman,' the old man said as he moved
up to the mannequin and took one of the delicate sleeves
between his fingers. 'This one is based on a nineteenth-
century wedding gown worn, I should imagine, by a royal
or noble lady of some description. We are making jewellery
in the same style for a wealthy lady who wishes to look like
an Ottoman princess at her wedding.'

'Do you know where she purchased the gown?'

Lazar gave a slow, crafty smile. 'Yes. As I expect you
do also, Çetin Bey, coming as you do from Üsküdar.'

At first İkmen frowned. What had such a magnificent
gown to do with the working-class district where he had
been raised? People there were more likely to require cheap
suits or overalls than magnificent gowns made of expensive
fabric. But then as he continued to look into Lazar's clever,
amused little eyes, it came to him.

'Are we talking about the Heper sisters?' he asked.

Lazar smiled even more broadly. 'The daughters of
General Heper are indeed without equal,' he said. 'Miss
Muazzez's blindness does not seem to affect the quality of
her stitching which still looks as if it has been performed
by a machine. Those women are truly miraculous.'

'And although I know they would never admit it, they are of course products of the old Ottoman ways themselves, aren't they?' İkmen sighed. 'I should have thought of them before.'

'But your head was full of golden coins and little princes and all sorts of other unfinished business.' Lazar placed an arm round İkmen's shoulders and steered him back towards his private room. 'The Heper sisters are old and can therefore go nowhere, Çetin Bey. My exquisite coins, however . . .'

The two young people watched as the men left the workroom. Hulya wiped a hand across her face to remove any stray tears. Then she looked down at the floor.

'I imagine,' Berekiah said as he moved a little bit closer to her, 'that Miss İpek was someone you knew.'

'She was my best friend.'

He reached across and took just the end of her fingers in his hand. 'I'm sorry, Hulya,' he said. 'Really.'

She smiled as the cacophonous sound of numerous police sirens made further conversation impossible.

Metin İskender was not the sort of officer who was easily impressed by celebrity. He had been promoted to inspector at a young age and although still only twenty-nine had dealt with quite a few rich and famous people in his time. Having a wife with a high-profile career in publishing also helped – Belkis İskender was the sort of woman who liked to entertain her clients, and her husband, at extremely smart restaurants. And so when he sat down with Hikmet Sivas and his brother Vedat, İskender behaved rather more 'normally' than the movie star might have expected.

'Apart from yourself, did your wife have any other contacts in Turkey?' he asked, fascinated by the look of horror on Hikmet's face as he surveyed the dismal state of the interview room.

'No.'

'Did anyone apart from your brother know that you were visiting the Republic?'

'Only our sister, Hale, and my son,' Vedat said quickly. 'Hikmet and Kaycee came for a private visit – to the family.'

Hikmet looked at his brother, his face pale with anxiety.

'Yes,' he said. 'A visit to the family. Yes.'

In common with many victims of crime, Hikmet Sivas was currently behaving like one in a dream, answering questions in a stilted manner, looking distractedly around as if he had only just regained the power of sight. The physical symptoms of shock were present too: the way he shivered in the forty-five-degree heat and the bloodlessness of his face.

İskender adjusted his tie so that it sat more stylishly at his neck. A handsome man, he enjoyed exploding the myth that all police officers were by definition unkempt. Together with Mehmet Suleyman and, to a lesser extent, Orhan Tepe, he represented the more modern, professional face of the urban police force.

'I understand from our previous discussion,' he said, addressing Hikmet Sivas, 'that you haven't lived here in your own country for many years.'

'No.'

'My brother is an American now,' Vedat said with rather more pride in his voice than İskender liked.

'I see. However, I do have to ask you whether you have any enemies in this country, Mr Sivas. People who might wish to harm or manipulate you through your wife.'

'No, he doesn't.'

İskender gave Vedat Sivas a stern look. 'I'd rather your brother answered the question,' he said. He turned back to Hikmet. 'Well?'

Hikmet, whose head was now down, his chin resting on the wattled skin of his chest, murmured, 'No.'

'Are you sure?'

'Yes.'

'And in America? Do you or your wife have any enemies there?'

For the first time during the course of the interview, Hikmet Sivas actually looked into the handsome, immobile eyes of Metin İskender. Here was a man, he felt, who approached his professional life with a complete lack of emotion. What he was doing now, opening an investigation into the kidnap of a beautiful young woman adored by her husband, was just an assignment like any other. He'd want to get Kaycee back in order to be seen to be doing his job well, but that was all. There was no empathy in those cold black eyes of his. They reminded Hikmet of some of the eyes he'd seen in the faces of studio starlets he'd worked with years ago – women who screwed well for parts in dire but lucrative movies.

In spite of himself, Hikmet forced a smile as he answered İskender's question.

'I may be old, Inspector,' he said, 'but I am still a Hollywood movie star. Put yourself up on a giant screen in front of millions of people and most of them will like you. But some won't. Some will be envious, some will simply not like you, some will hate you. Some will even like you too much and stalk you.'

'Has that ever happened to you or your wife?'

'What? Being stalked?' He shrugged. 'Years ago there was a man who hung around my house, wanted to talk to me, wore the same clothes, said he loved me . . .' He looked up in order to gauge whether or not this shocked the Turkish policeman. But the cold eyes gave nothing away. 'He was taken to a state mental hospital. He's still there, as far as I know.'

İskender leaned back in his chair and breathed deeply. Beyond the fact that Kaycee Sivas had been abducted in a part of the city where every second person was living beyond the boundaries of what was strictly legal, there was little to go on. Predictably, the young officer who had arrived just after the incident hadn't been able to find any witnesses among the thronging, largely Russian-speaking crowd. Nobody had entered the leather shop that Sivas, who was now not so sure about this himself, had felt his wife had been taken to. And even if İskender did get a very profound feeling that he was not being told everything he needed to know by these men, he couldn't prove it. He surveyed the Sivas brothers with a critical eye. His superior, however, exhibited nothing but star-struck awe when he entered the room. A large man with a high colour that only hinted at the floridness of his temper; he almost fell over his own feet as he nervously presented himself to Hikmet Sivas.

'It is indeed an honour, if a sad, sad duty to serve you, sir,' he said as he took the star's hand in his and pumped it enthusiastically. 'We are ready to receive your commands.'

'Thank you.'

'And please let me assure you that no effort will be spared to locate your wife and return her safely to you,' and then looking across at İskender he said, 'Is that not so, Inspector?'

İskender, now standing to attention, said, 'Yes, sir.'

'I appreciate your concern.' Hikmet Sivas smiled.

'Oh, it is an honour, sir, an honour! The men under my command will not rest until this dreadful stain upon the integrity of our city is put to rights.'

'Thank you.'

'It is nothing.' He turned to İskender and said, 'If you have finished I will take Mr Sivas and his brother up to my office.'

İskender briefly smiled his assent. Up to Ardiç's office for a better class of tea and cigarettes no doubt. How different from the way these things were done with the common man. Fame and money, money and fame . . . As the star and his brother left the room, İskender retrieved his notes from the table and started to make his way out too.

But at the door he met the large bulk of his boss. Quickly, as if checking to see whether anyone was listening, Ardiç looked behind him before whispering to İskender, 'Get on to headquarters in Ankara and tell them. This is international, they have to know. And then find her, Inspector, before Ankara can even think about applying pressure. Tear Beyazıt apart if you have to, but find her.'

By the time İkmen and Hulya got back to their apartment that evening, Bülent had already gone out. Although he was tired and slightly annoyed at himself for spending so much money on what was, admittedly, a very beautiful gold coin, İkmen decided that now was the time to talk to Hulya about Hatice. Armed with, in İkmen's case, a bottle of Efes Pilsen beer and, in Hulya's, a cola, the two of them went and sat together on the darkening balcony.

'So you're sure that Hatice didn't mention anything about

this dancing opportunity to you until the evening before she died?' İkmen asked.

'No, Dad, she didn't.' Hulya looked down into her glass, her face serious.

'And when she did talk about it, she didn't mention Hassan Şeker?'

'No.'

'So as far as you can tell, he didn't have anything to do with this dancing thing.'

'I don't know.' Hulya looked up, her eyes just slightly glassy. 'But I don't think that Hassan Bey would have done anything to hurt her. She really liked him. He wouldn't have raped her.'

'Ah . . .' İkmen looked away.

'What?'

'Well, Hulya, we know Hatice had had sex with Hassan Bey before.'

'You're not saying that because she wasn't a "good" girl before, she couldn't have been raped, are you?'

İkmen took a swig from his bottle before replying. 'No, *I'm* not. But that is what a lot of people will think.'

'What, old men and religious people?' Hulya curled her lip in a sneer. 'I don't care what they think!'

'No, but . . .' İkmen lit a cigarette, exhaling on a sigh. 'Look, Hulya, there's something else too.'

'What?'

'Although this man or men did undoubtedly hurt your friend and had sex with her, we now know that they didn't actually kill her.'

Hulya frowned. 'What do you mean?'

İkmen told his daughter what Arto Sarkissian had explained to him about the nature and probable cause of Hatice İpek's death. As he spoke he watched her expression stiffen, seeming almost to age, as she took in the implications of what he was saying.

At the end of his exposition she said, 'But surely, Dad, even if Hatice did die naturally, you'll still have to find these awful men?'

'Well, of course,' İkmen responded. 'But what I'm saying, Hulya, is that even if I do find them, it would seem that they cannot be tried for murder and to prove that an unmarried girl who was not a virgin was unwilling . . .'

'They hurt her, Dad!'

'Yes, darling, I know.'

'Well then.'

'Hulya, look.' İkmen swallowed nervously. 'I know this is difficult for you to understand, but some people do like pain, it—'

'Men like pain, not women!' Hulya snapped furiously. 'Men beat their wives and force their women to have sex and the law protects them!' She looked down at the floor. 'Not you, I don't mean you.'

'All of those things that you talk about are against the law, Hulya,' İkmen began, 'but—'

'Women have to be "good" women if they really want justice!'

'No,' İkmen cleared his throat, 'but the opinions of those who call themselves moralists do have power. Once all the facts are known, some will feel little sympathy for Hatice. And although I will, as I promised, somehow find these men and bring them to justice, their punishment might not be as severe as I would have liked. If they didn't kill her, if their lawyer convinces the judge that she consented to sex . . .'

They sat in silence for a while, thinking their own thoughts. Eventually Hulya spoke.

'You know, Dad,' she said quietly, 'talking about this makes me wonder whether it is possible for men and women to be equal in this country when some people think that girls have to be good while men can do what they like.'

İkmen smiled sadly. 'I know,' he said, 'but not everyone thinks like that. I don't. As you know, it was part of our Ghazi Mustafa Kemal's mission to set women free to achieve their potential. But some people, even some women, believe that freedom can only be attained through submission to men and to—'

'Allah?' Hulya shook her head. 'You know I think that religion is awful, Dad. Dr Halman once told me that when she was a girl in Ireland, women couldn't have abortions even if they were very sick, because of religion. I don't know how Mum can go along with religion. She's not stupid, is she?'

İkmen laughed. 'No, she isn't,' he said, 'which is why she only pays attention to the bits of Islam that she likes. Turkish women are, on the whole, very sensible, Hulya. Like your mother, many of them pray, stay indoors to care for their families and rule their homes like empresses. If you notice, I challenge your mother only on very big issues concerning our children, and that is all. She rules me and she can vote just like I do too.'

'Yes, but Dad, if the Republic doesn't have a religion, which we're told that it doesn't—'

'Look, Hulya,' İkmen said gravely, 'somehow we're moving into politics here. I didn't want to, but . . . Democracies only strive towards the ideals inherent in that word. Nowhere is, I believe, truly democratic. But one thing that the nominally democratic have to do is they have to listen to and accommodate lots of differing views. Religious people, secular moralists, myself, we all have our view.'

'Yes, but what if I don't like a certain view?'

'Then when the time comes you vote for a party that opposes that view,' İkmen said.

'Yes, but what if—'

'Look, if you don't like something, then you oppose it in whatever way you feel is right. I oppose what some people may think about Hatice and I will fight, within the law, to prove that her attackers are dangerous and deserving of punishment. What I can't do is change what others think or prevent whatever effect that might have on my investigation.'

'But—'

'But if anyone does try to convince me that this case is not worth pursuing, I will fight and if I can't go on, I will pursue Hatice's attackers in my own time.' İkmen put out his cigarette, and took another swig from his bottle. Hulya, who had been watching her father's face harden with the force of his conviction, reached across and took his free hand in hers.

Chapter 8

Something big was happening – something quite separate from the investigation into Hatice İpek's death. Tepe was glad. He hadn't needed Constable Yıldız questioning him first thing in the morning. Especially in view of the fact that the questions involved recent events at the Sultanahmet pastane.

'So you saw Ekrem and Celal Müren and one of their boys at the pastane. So what?'

'They were talking to Şeker's wife,' Yıldız said.

Tepe shrugged. 'So? Did you hear what they were saying to her? Were they threatening her?'

'Well I didn't actually hear . . .'

'Then don't worry about it,' Tepe said.

He had then left Yıldız, who still looked very unsure. Now, however, both he and Yıldız had other things to think about. Ardiç had summoned them all to talk about the fact that the Beyazıt district had been practically disassembled during the night. Or so rumour had it. Why this had happened nobody knew or was prepared to say, except that it was about something 'big'.

When Tepe entered the squad room both the level of activity and noise told him that Ardiç hadn't yet appeared. Neither, as far as he could see, had İkmen. After just a brief nod at Ayşe Farsakoğlu, Tepe picked up a stray newspaper and settled himself down in a corner of the room.

People didn't usually sit in Commissioner Ardiç's office – not unless he invited them to do so. On this occasion, however, he was prepared to make an exception. And so when a pale and drawn-looking Metin İskender entered his office and sat down without being invited, Ardiç made no comment. The man had, after all, been up all night, shouting and threatening his way through the illegal brothels, lower level gangster dens and drug operations of Beyazıt district. He had singularly failed to locate Kaycee Sivas or even acquire any information about a beautiful unnamed American woman. But he and his men had arrested several people wanted for other offences plus they had taken possession of a quantity of cocaine. İskender had, as ever, thrown himself into his work with a will.

Almost immediately after İskender arrived, İkmen appeared. He looked troubled, and Ardiç suspected that before their meeting was over he was going to look even more concerned. As İkmen, following İskender's example, sat down in the commissioner's presence, Ardiç considered how he might avoid a confrontation with his most experienced and successful detective. Basically he couldn't, but he would need to bring İkmen up to speed with events first and so he opted to do this before entering into any uncomfortable specifics.

'As you know, İkmen,' he said, 'I have ordered all available officers to a briefing downstairs.'

'Presumably it's about what happened in Beyazıt last night,' İkmen responded and then turning to İskender he said, 'Quite an event, I understand.'

İskender sniffed and turned his head away. He was only too aware of İkmen's dislike for big, violent operations which, the older man felt, only served to drive the most seasoned criminals further underground.

Ardiç, ignoring the tension between his two officers, continued, 'Last night, İkmen, was all about our attempting to locate a kidnap victim.' He passed a photograph of a young, willowy blonde across the desk. 'Kaycee Sivas was abducted from her brother-in-law's car at approximately four forty-five yesterday afternoon. It happened outside the Antik Leather Boutique on Fetihbey Caddesi.'

'Which is in Beyazıt.'

'Which is in Beyazıt.' Ardiç paused to light a cigar. 'An area not unfamiliar with criminal activity, including kidnap. However, what makes this kidnap a little different is that the woman involved is an American. She is also the wife of the Hollywood movie star, Hikmet Sivas, or Ali Bey as was. Her husband was in the car, together with his brother, when Mrs Sivas was dragged from the vehicle. According to Sivas two, maybe three, men were involved. They dragged Mrs Sivas from the car and disappeared into the crowd.'

İskender turned to face İkmen. 'You won't be surprised to learn that nobody saw or heard anything,' he said.

İkmen grimaced.

Ardiç cleared his throat. 'Now as you can imagine, İkmen, this is big news,' he said. 'It hasn't broken yet, but it will soon and when it does we need to be ready. Beyazıt, as you know, received considerable attention from us during the night but so far we've come up with nothing. I, not to mention our masters in the capital, want this woman found. I want no excuses, no expense spared and I want every available officer working on this.'

'But I'm already working on a case, sir. Hatice İpek—'

'Who Dr Sarkissian tells me died of natural causes,' Ardiç countered. 'Yes, İkmen, I do know. I telephoned him this morning in order to find out whether the girl had been murdered. I needed to discover whether you were free to lead this new investigation alongside Inspector İskender.'

İkmen opened his mouth to speak but was silenced when Ardiç held up one of his large hands.

'The girl died naturally, İkmen, there was no murder. You are therefore free to assist in the hunt for Kaycee Sivas.'

'But sir, murder or no murder, the girl was brutally raped, cut and buggered and her body concealed after her death. A crime has been committed.'

'Yes, but not a murder!' Ardiç shifted his large behind agitatedly in his seat. Why couldn't İkmen just get on and do as he was told without all this argument! Why, come to that, did he himself argue with İkmen?

'Look, İkmen,' he said, 'the İpek girl was not, we know, a nice girl. Young as she was, she was not a virgin. For all we know, she liked it rough.'

'Dr Sarkissian believes there were several men.'

'Some men will pay good money for brutal sex. It went wrong. The desecration of the corpse and its concealment tell us that. Of course I believe that whoever did this needs to be caught and punished, but if the girl was having sex anyway—'

'Sir, I don't believe she consented to it. The place she was found, the clothes she was wearing—'

'You will join Inspector İskender in the search for Kaycee Sivas and that is final!' Ardiç yelled, now finally roused to fury.

İkmen sprang to his feet. 'Oh, I see. And what am I to

tell Mrs İpek? What am I to tell the bereaved family and friends of Hatice? Your girl was a whore and she deserved everything she got?'

'When he returns to duty Inspector Suleyman will be assigned to the İpek case, such as it is.'

İkmen shook his head in disbelief. 'Inspector Suleyman won't be back this week, sir.'

'I am aware of that, İkmen.'

'By which time—'

'Shut your mouth or I'll shut it for you! This case is my priority now! This case involves somebody who might, if we are very fortunate, still be alive!' Up on his feet now, Ardiç pointed his smouldering cigar directly at İkmen's face. 'You will do your duty as I dictate and you will support me when we go downstairs and talk to my men.' And then shifting his gaze from İkmen's furious face to İskender's passive features. 'If you would like to go and tell them that we are on our way, please, Inspector.'

Wearily İskender pulled himself upright. 'Yes, sir.'

When he had left the office and shut the door behind him, Ardiç moved towards İkmen. Taking İkmen's thin shoulders roughly in his meaty hands he held him firmly as he said, 'Of course the truth is that I don't think İskender can do this without you, İkmen.'

Çetin İkmen was not a man easily taken in by flattery and just snorted by way of reply.

'He's very young, he can be impulsive and his manner is not attractive.'

Knowing that he wasn't going to get anywhere with this particular line of argument, Ardiç sat down once again and looked at the floor. It was at this point that he assumed his most casual tone.

'What İskender does know, however, is that Hikmet Sivas is hiding something. He doesn't know what it is—'

'Then how does he know he's hiding something?' İkmen said. 'Does he have a feeling, an intuition?'

'I don't know, İkmen,' Ardiç said as he gathered up everything he needed for the meeting, 'It is a fact that Mr Sivas' brother did try to stop him talking to our officer at the scene. A little strange, I feel. Perhaps if you were to talk to Mr Sivas and his brother yourself . . .'

İkmen knew exactly what his superior was trying to do – piquing his interest – which Ardiç had done. İkmen knew that İskender was not one to give in easily to gut feelings like this, but he had to have them, as all officers did, from time to time. Not that that was relevant; İkmen knew he had to involve himself in this case whether he wanted to or not. It was probably best to pretend he had fallen for Ardiç's clumsy ruse. Then when he was off duty he could do as he pleased, hopefully without questions from Ardiç. In this way it might be possible to continue to investigate Hatice's death and find Kaycee Sivas too. When he would sleep he didn't know, but he'd sort that out some other time. The important thing was to discover who had assaulted Hatice and why. He had made a promise to both Hürrem İpek and his own daughter, and rich American or no rich American, he was going to honour it.

So İkmen smiled at Ardiç and said that he would go and talk to the Sivas family as soon as the briefing was over. He'd had an argument, calmed down and been mollified by a man who thought that he was under his control. And as Ardiç left the room with İkmen respectfully at his heels, the commissioner did indeed feel that he had won. But then this, or rather events like this had happened before – events after which İkmen had gone off and done what he wanted to do anyway. Therefore in order to cover just such an eventuality, Ardiç did take the precaution of turning on İkmen yet again, just before they reached their destination.

Zelfa looked down at the baby sleeping peacefully in her arms and felt nothing except despair. Yes, she could see that he was beautiful and, yes, she was amazed that she could have produced such a perfect late baby. But she didn't feel anything for him. He was there in much the same way as the tube that drained fluid from the site of her operation – something produced by and part of the hospital. When she left she knew that little Yusuf İzzeddin would, unlike the tube, go with her. But she didn't really want him to. Her stomach, which had never in truth been exactly flat, now looked like an enormous deflated bladder, saggy and wrinkled. On the few occasions they had allowed her to get out of bed – they were old-fashioned about bed rest here – she had felt it flop against the tops of her legs, all limp and slimy with sweat.

And he, Yusuf İzzeddin, her baby, had done this. Of course the logical part of her knew that he hadn't. Both as a doctor and as a woman she knew that she and her husband had actually done this to her. But she couldn't blame Mehmet because she loved him, and as for blaming herself, well, that was just faulty thinking, wasn't it? Self blame was pointless, useless – she always told her patients they should have no time for it. It crossed her mind that perhaps this was post-natal depression, but as quickly as the thought came, Zelfa dismissed it. To dignify her feelings with the status of a clinical condition this early on in motherhood was absurd. And yet there was no doubt that she was miserable. Although she managed to keep herself together whenever her husband was with her, as soon as he left she descended into often uncontrollable weeping. Her father was aware of her feelings but, strangely for him, he wasn't much use. But then the aunts were probably to blame for that.

Babur Halman had two sisters, Alev and Zehra, both older and far more outspoken than their brother. Governed by tradition and religious customs that Babur had largely either lost or forgotten during the years he had lived and worked in Ireland, Alev and Zehra had been quick to advise Zelfa about the 'right way' to look after babies. Despite temperatures in excess of forty-five degrees, the child needed to be kept away from draughts and swaddled as tightly as was safe. This, without any reference to Zelfa, the two sisters did while at the same time reminding their niece that when she did finally leave hospital she would have to stay indoors with little Yusuf İzzeddin for at least a month. Babies were susceptible to all sorts of evil forces during the first forty days of life.

And Zelfa's father, a paediatrician, said nothing. Even when that dreadful old bitch of a mother-in-law reminded Zelfa that the announcement of Yusuf İzzeddin's birth in the newspapers should be discreet and tasteful, she knew what the subtext was. Ostentation attracted the 'evil eye' which could bring bad fortune to the child. Nur Suleyman was after all only a peasant in origin, and like Alev and Zehra she believed in these ridiculous practices. Babur Halman, however, was educated, travelled and informed, he had no excuse, and Zelfa was very angry with him.

If things didn't change soon, Zelfa knew that she would probably have to start taking anti-depressants. She didn't want to but even in her distress the professional part of her recognised that this might be essential. In order to allow her feelings for her baby to grow she needed to be relaxed, which was not easy around people and in surroundings that were not her own. Although she had lived and worked in her father's country for the last thirteen years, Zelfa, or Bridget as she had been called back home, was still Irish at heart. And as such she had little time for 'evil eyes' or swaddling or even the enforced bed rest she was currently 'suffering'. But she had to be quite strong when Ireland came into her mind and so she dismissed all thoughts of it. If she didn't, she knew she would just pull the tube out of her stomach and go straight back there now – probably without little Yusuf İzzeddin. Poor little prince. Zelfa started to cry again.

'Sir, I have the utmost confidence in Sergeant Çöktin's abilities as a negotiator,' İkmen said tartly. 'And if it is any comfort to you I can tell you that the methods he uses are similar to those employed by the FBI. I know what value you Americans place on your own institutions.'

He stressed the word 'Americans', but it seemed to be lost on Hikmet Sivas. Clearly devastated by the events of the last twenty-four hours, he paced his now smoke-filled living room, chain-smoking and occasionally exploding into impotent rages.

'But whoever has my wife isn't going to contact me if they know that you're here,' he said, and then more to himself than anyone else he murmured, 'I should have listened to Vedat. I should never have approached that constable.'

'Yes, but you did, didn't you, sir,' İkmen said. 'I agree that whoever has your wife must now know that you have contacted us. But if the plan was to exchange Mrs Sivas for money then I can't see that that can have changed. Kidnappers always think they can outwit us and so I am confident that they will make contact.'

Whilst accepting that İskender had been careful to use other pretexts during the Beyazıt raid, İkmen was not happy – though he would never tell Hikmet Sivas this. Those responsible for the kidnap would know why Beyazıt had been torn apart. İstanbul, as he well knew, could be a very small town at times, particularly within its criminal fraternity. He would not have approached the problem in the way that İskender had done. In spite of this, however, he was still confident that if money were the motive, those holding Kaycee would call. If not, if an element as yet unknown were involved, that could be a problem. According to Çöktin, Hikmet Sivas had not been the most forthcoming crime victim he had ever met and was continuing to exhibit some resistance to the young officer's efforts.

'So, Mr Sivas,' İkmen said as he joined the movie star in his heavy smoking session, 'is there any other reason, apart from money, that you can think of to explain your wife's disappearance?'

'I've told him no!' Sivas exploded, pointing at Çöktin who was sitting beside the telephone extension which was now attached to recording equipment.

'Your brother tried to stop you talking to our officer at the scene.'

'Because he was scared!' the star screamed. 'I've told you people that too!'

İkmen shrugged. Hikmet Sivas was not how he had imagined. Not as tall as he appeared on screen, he looked good for his age but that was all. His hair was quite obviously dyed and the plastic surgery he had no doubt paid dearly for had done little to improve either the wattles on his neck or the slackness around his jaw line. Despite being very upset he was clearly a star, but one who had passed his prime and was fortunate still to be so wealthy. Not all Hollywood's old stars were so lucky – or so İkmen had heard. Unwise investments, drugs, drink, ex-wives and rapacious 'friends' frequently ruined such people. But with his lovely young wife, his homes in Los Angeles, New York, Hawaii and İstanbul, Hikmet Sivas had obviously made the money he had earned in the sixties and seventies work very well for him.

'So,' İkmen continued, 'neither you nor your wife had any enemies.'

'Not that I know of. You know,' he cast a baleful glance at the unfortunate Çöktin once again, 'I really need to telephone my agent.'

İkmen ignored this. 'And there was no trouble between yourself and Mrs Sivas?'

Yet again, Sivas exploded. 'No!' he shouted. 'And before you start speculating about whether my wife might have arranged this herself with some smooth young Turkish lover, just remember that she'd never been to this country before!'

'Sir, I—'

'I don't know why Kaycee has been taken!' he yelled, 'I have no idea . . .'

'It has happened because it is written.'

İkmen turned towards the voice and saw the small figure of a woman carrying a tray laden with tea glasses. She was probably about seventy although her face, albeit stern, was not heavily lined. Swathed in a dark coat, her head covered by a plain brown headscarf, she was obviously, if her words

115

alone were not enough to tell by, a religious woman. Hikmet Sivas went immediately to her side as she placed the tray down on one of the coffee tables.

'Oh, Hale, my soul,' he said, 'I know what you believe but not now, dear sister, please don't say those things now!'

'If you live your life beyond the laws of the Koran, what do you expect? Eh?'

'Hale . . .'

'Running around film sets with naked women! Living like an American! Drink and whores and working for Jews.'

'Hale, I know I am not suitable to pour water to wash your hands.'

The woman snorted, before indicating that the policemen should help themselves to tea. She then left. İkmen had listened with interest to Hikmet Sivas abasing himself so thoroughly and publicly before his sister. Either he was grateful to her for something quite considerable or he was feeling guilty. Perhaps also he wanted something from her. Whichever it was, the interlude İkmen had just witnessed had been both interesting and surprising. In spite of having spent most of his life as an American, Hikmet Sivas had not forgotten the rules of his native land or the formulaic expressions, originating in Ottoman times, that gave shape to how one experienced one's social and moral standing in relation to others. And by not responding to her brother's declaration of inferiority, Hale Sivas had made it plain that she did indeed know that she was exalted above him. Odd, given that he was the rich and famous sibling, the successful child most families would fete, whatever their peccadilloes.

Çöktin and the technician in charge of the recording equipment got up and took tea with İskender who had just returned. İkmen, aware that Hikmet Sivas would need some time to gather his thoughts again, left to go outside. The car Vedat Sivas had been driving when Kaycee was abducted was being investigated by a team from the Forensic Institute. He had left Tepe, who had been rather quiet that morning, in charge.

Outside, İkmen stopped briefly to observe how the midday sunlight hit the glass-like waters of the Bosphorus. This side of town, if not the district, was still home. All through his childhood he had seen İstanbul from this perspective. The imperial mosques were 'across the water', as was Pera, the 'new' city which had all that was European and naughty and tantalising – and important. Asia, where he was now and where he had been born in poor, old, working-class Üsküdar, was different – older almost, he sometimes felt, even though he knew that wasn't so. Perhaps it was a mindset – the Asian mind, hard-working and given to suffering and the reality of death; the whole area was characterised by massive, tree-darkened cemeteries. Even here in smart Kandıllı there was a huge graveyard less than five minutes from where he stood now looking at Tepe watching the activity in and around the car. It was perhaps this fleeting contemplation of death that made him return to the subject of poor little Hatice İpek.

'So,' he said as he offered his inferior a cigarette, 'you don't think that the confectioner Hassan Şeker has anything more to tell us about my daughter's friend?'

Tepe took the cigarette and shrugged. 'Beyond what I told you on the phone yesterday, no, sir. He still maintains their "relationship" was all in the heads of the girl and others.'

'Including my daughter,' İkmen said darkly.

'Yes. But he is willing to give a semen sample for

analysis and he appeared to be confident about that,' Tepe said, attempting to gloss over the reference to İkmen's daughter.

'Mmm.'

'Do you want me to arrange for him to provide the sample?'

'Yes, Tepe, do that,' İkmen said and then he went over to look at the water more closely.

Hulya wasn't lying. Not about this. Hassan Şeker was willing to provide a semen sample probably because he hadn't had sex with Hatice on the night that she died. Tepe had taken statements from employees at the pastane who maintained he had been with them, or at his home, at the time of her death anyway. But then why was Şeker still insisting that he had never had relations with Hatice? True, his wife would hardly be pleased if she found out, but he was a wealthy man and so it was unlikely she would leave him. His continuing refusal to admit to what was an affair with a consenting adult seemed ridiculous – and to İkmen suspicious. For some reason Şeker was trying to distance himself from Hatice İpek.

Ahmet Sılay, like Hulya, also insisted that Şeker and Hatice had been having relations, and Ahmet Sılay had once been a close friend of the man whose wife was now missing, Hikmet Sivas. In order to cover every eventuality, İkmen decided to ask Sivas about his friend, just in passing, to try to ascertain how honest the elderly alcoholic was. He did not want Hulya's statement to become a lone voice of dissent against Hassan Şeker. She was young and susceptible to the sort of fantasies that Şeker claimed both Hatice and Hulya had indulged in about the affair. Perhaps, İkmen expanded, they had even written in Hatice's diary to embellish just such a fantasy. Young girls could and would do such things, he knew. But not in this case. Hulya was, after all, a policeman's daughter. What happened to people who made up stories to the police was well known to her. Hulya had not lied.

İkmen made his way back into the house where he met a worn-out İskender at the entrance to the star's living room. Sivas, seated now, was on the telephone.

'Who's he talking to?' Ikmen asked.

'He kept on berating me about needing to speak to his agent,' İskender responded sourly, 'so I let him.'

Ikmen shrugged and then turned his attention towards Sivas.

'I'm telling you, G,' the star shouted in almost unaccented American, 'my life is over, it's all gone totally wrong . . . It's fucked is what I'm saying! Yes, yes, sure they are, but . . .' He turned his head away from the two officers before he continued. But he was still shouting so they could hear what he said anyway. They and Cöktin, who was also still in the room, shared a disdainful look.

'Have you ever seen Turkish police in action?' Sivas continued. 'Well, imagine a bunch of violent retards and you'll get the picture. No, they won't find her. I need help, proper people. Yeah, I know I gotta go with it, but—'

In the silence during which the agent was no doubt yet again attempting to mollify Sivas, İkmen left. He knew he wasn't a 'violent retard' and he didn't want to listen any more. Sivas was still officially a victim of crime and İkmen didn't want to feel as angry as he was rapidly becoming towards an innocent man.

Chapter 9

When İkmen arrived home that evening he didn't go straight up to his apartment after he had parked his car. He needed yet more cigarettes and so he walked across Divanyolu Caddesi and over to the kiosk. Furnished with forty Maltepe, İkmen crossed back again, passing as he did so the Sultanahmet pastane. Hassan Şeker stood outside smoking a cigarette of his own, but his eyes didn't so much as flicker when İkmen passed even though he must have seen him.

İkmen had heard a few things about Hassan well before all of this business with Hatice began. People said that he was weaker than his formidable father; they said that he allowed some of his employees and his friends to take liberties with his time and his products. Some even said that his cakes and pastries were inferior to those Kemal Bey had prepared. İkmen was doubtful about the latter observation even if he could see what folk meant about Hassan's rather more relaxed attitude towards commercial life. What was fairly clear, however, provided one believed what had been written in Hatice İpek's diary – which İkmen who had now read all of it did – was that he wasn't a beast. Although detailed and specific in her descriptions, Hatice's accounts of her sexual relations with Hassan were neither distasteful nor pornographic. Rather they focused on how his lovemaking made her feel, which seemed to have been very good. And

121

although sometimes he would ask her to do things that she didn't really want to, he would never force her. Hatice, or so it would seem from her diary, achieved satisfaction every time Hassan Şeker licked, caressed and penetrated her body. İkmen wondered how many other women could claim such a record.

He was just turning into the alleyway that cut through to the back of his apartment building when someone grabbed his wrist. Instinctively, İkmen raised his other arm to defend himself. But when he saw who it was, he knew that there couldn't possibly be any threat.

'Oh, it's you,' he said disdainfully as he dropped his arm again and pulled his wrist out of the assailant's greasy grasp.

'Yes, Çetin Bey,' the small, filthy man replied, exposing as he did a set of seriously damaged teeth.

'What do you want, Rat?' İkmen asked although he was rather more concerned with removing all trace of the man's touch from his wrist. Rat, as well as being a somewhat casual informant, was also known to dine out at rubbish bins. Not as destitute as he looked, Rat apparently enjoyed certain aspects of the vagrant lifestyle.

'I want to help you, Çetin Bey,' Rat said, using his accustomed opening gambit.

'Oh, and what do you want to help me with, Rat? Some pickpocketing ring masterminded by an eight-year-old?' İkmen was tired. It had been a long day and Rat's information was rarely worth the price of a visit to a public lavatory. İkmen shook his head and made to move off towards his apartment.

'You know that there are still odalisques in this city, don't you, Çetin Bey?'

İkmen turned. 'Visiting gentlemen from Arab countries

may have more than four wives, girls we would describe as odalisques, yes,' he said. 'What of it?'

'I'm talking about Turkish girls, Çetin Bey. Girls who dress up in beautiful gowns, girls who dance and pretend to men that they are princesses.'

İkmen walked back to Rat and gripped his shoulders with his hands. 'What do you know, Rat?'

'I know that a girl like that died.'

'And do you also know who killed her?'

Rat turned his head down so that he was looking at the ground, his face set and impassive.

'If you do know who killed her, Rat, I can take you down to the station and extract the information from you without any money ever changing hands,' İkmen said with some menace in his voice.

'But I don't know who killed her, Çetin Bey,' Rat replied, completely unfazed. 'All I have heard is that this has not, apparently, happened before.'

İkmen frowned. 'Before? What do you mean?'

'When men have gone with these women before, the women haven't died.'

İkmen pulled Rat deeper into the shadow thrown by the washing the women hung at the back of the apartment building, underneath the place where the antiquated water boiler gurgled and thumped. Then, without offering one to the informant, he lit a cigarette for himself.

'What women are you talking about, Rat?' he said. 'And by men are we talking about customers?'

'It's a great secret, Çetin Bey,' Rat said, his eyes growing larger at the sight of the cigarette. 'I know nothing beyond the fact that young women dress as odalisques and pleasure men. They have been doing it for ever.'

İkmen put his hand back into his pocket and retrieved his cigarettes.

'So these men,' he began, 'are they . . .'

'Oh, I don't know who they are! I know they are important, but . . .' Rat responded, his eyes virtually devouring the cigarette İkmen dangled in front of his face. 'As I said, it is a great secret and has been so for a very long time.'

İkmen handed the cigarette to Rat who lit it with a fluff-covered match.

'I presume the women do this for money,' İkmen said.

'Yes.'

'But someone else organises or controls the trade.'

'Well . . .' Rat looked furtively over his shoulder and only when he was convinced that no one else was around did he continue. 'No one knows who has been doing this, Çetin Bey, no one. But . . .'

'Yes, Rat?'

'But just lately some people involved in "family" business have, well, bought into the operation. I've heard that what was once one thing, unknown to all, is now quite another. Now there is blood.'

'Where did you get all of this from, Rat?' İkmen asked as he tried to control the familiar feeling of coldness that usually came over him at times of revelation.

'Oh, well, it's on the streets, Çetin . . .'

İkmen's hand shot out and he grabbed hold of Rat's skinny neck. He held him firmly up against the wall. The stench and feel of him was appalling, but İkmen knew from experience that there was only one way to deal with the likes of the Sultanahmet Rat.

'Don't fuck me about with "on the streets", Rat,' he spat

through gritted teeth. 'Who told you? Whose window did you listen at?'

'I swear—'

'I can take you down to the station . . .'

'And I will tell you nothing!' the now red-faced little man cried. 'It will do you no good! You can use the bastinado for ten days at a time! I cannot tell you, Çetin Bey. This is a "family" thing, you know. There is nothing the police could do to me that could be worse than what they would do.'

And of course he was right. İkmen loosened his grip on the scraggy neck and then smoked in silence for a while. 'Family' business meant that if Rat was telling the truth, İkmen had all kinds of trouble. The local Mafias, although not as famous as their Sicilian or even their Russian counterparts, were not a force to be taken lightly. For a start, no one was entirely sure where the various families involved in illegal activities were at any one time. They were heavily involved in the drugs trade and tended to move between İstanbul and the eastern provinces and travel abroad – frequently to Germany or England. In fact so mobile were some of these families that it was said informants like Rat, if caught, were never sure who their torturers were. Something else that was frequently said about the families was that the payments they made to certain police officers were considerable. İkmen sighed. With family involvement, the operation Rat had described – prostitution – would take on a much more sinister aspect. One that had possibly cost Hatice İpek her life.

'So if family are involved, why are you taking the risk of talking to me, Rat?' İkmen asked.

'Well, Çetin Bey, as you know I like to help.'

'Oh, please, spare me the usual work of fiction, Rat! You've taken a big risk.'

'I need two hundred million lire to pay my landlord.' Rat's head sank down on his chest. 'I need it today.'

'I don't have that kind of money,' İkmen said. 'And besides, if I'm expected to pay out on the say so of somebody like you—'

'But it's all true!'

'Maybe, but unless you can tell me where this information came from . . .'

'I can't!'

İkmen shrugged. 'Then you're just going to have to get used to sleeping on the street, aren't you? You already eat out of rubbish bins because you're too tight to pay for food. Now you'll have to sleep in them too.' And he started to move off towards his apartment. He was just opening the door to the building when Rat's voice came at him one last time.

'The seamstresses, the Heper ladies of Üsküdar, they know.'

The women who had made the dress he'd seen in the workroom at Lazar's shop. The women who could also have made Hatice's gown. Although quite what two seamstress daughters of an old general had to do with prostitution and 'family' business, İkmen couldn't imagine. But it was the second time that the names of Miss Muazzez and Miss Yümniye Heper had cropped up since Hatice's death and so İkmen took notice, even if he couldn't for the life of him work out how someone like Rat could even know about them.

He took his wallet out of his pocket and dropped notes totalling fifty million lire onto the ground.

'You'll have to sell your arse to a blind man for the rest,'

126

he said and pushed his way into the comparative coolness of the entrance hall.

After he'd made his customary evening telephone call to Fatma, İkmen made himself a glass of tea which he took out onto the balcony. Bülent had left a note to say that he was out for the evening with his friend Sami and with Hulya now back at work at the pastane, the apartment was temporarily free of teenagers. But for now he could be quiet, free to think.

Not that İkmen was exactly happy for his daughter to be working alongside Hassan Şeker once again. But then she had been insistent that she wanted to return to work even though she hated it. Something to do with 'needing' to buy clothes – probably for Berekiah Cohen's benefit. Still İkmen would escort her home later and make sure nothing untoward had happened. It seemed pretty unlikely if Hassan knew he was under suspicion.

It had been a strange day. Hikmet Sivas had not been the easiest victim to inverview and, like İskender before him, İkmen was now pretty sure that his lack of co-operation and at times strange behaviour – around his sister for instance – spelled secrets. Whether or not they were connected to Kaycee's disappearance, he didn't know. Perhaps Sivas wanted his new young wife out of the way for some reason and had set all this up in advance of his homecoming. It was no secret that a lot of Americans considered foreign policemen to be stupid, and Sivas, clearly, was no exception. For an American to commit a murder beyond the reach of the feared LAPD would seem to be a good idea – if one could ignore Sivas's genuine distress at his wife's continued absence, which İkmen couldn't.

Kaycee's disappearance had now reached the ears of the press both foreign and domestic. İkmen had seen some of the headlines over at the kiosk. One of the papers had even printed a rather blurry photograph of Metin İskender. He smiled. Well, it made a change from seeing his own grim visage shouting 'No comment!' followed by a silent 'Fuck off' in his head. İskender by contrast had looked far more relaxed in company with the press. Silent, but polished.

İkmen lit a cigarette and leaned back in his chair. Music, which Bülent had once informed him was called 'rave', thudded rhythmically out of the apartment below, the one just recently let to newlyweds. İkmen didn't like it but he didn't allow it to force him back into the stuffy apartment. Like most Turks he just put up with it and, in his case, thought of something else.

Ahmet Sılay. Now there was an oddity. Like Hulya he had freely stated that Hatice and Hassan Şeker were intimate. He was also, coincidentally, if one believed in such things, an old friend of Hikmet Sivas. In fact it appeared that Sılay made almost a profession out of his long-ago connection with the Hollywood actor. People apparently bought him drinks to encourage him to reminisce at length. What an excellent strategy for an alcoholic. Sivas, for his part, had rather less charitable memories of his old friend.

When İkmen had casually dropped Sılay's name into their conversation at the house in Kandıllı, he had made it clear that the elderly actor was helping the police with another, unconnected, inquiry, which İkmen did not specify. What Sivas had said then, however, had given İkmen pause.

'Oh, I wouldn't place too much emphasis on what Ahmet tells you, Inspector,' Sivas had exclaimed with a snort of a laugh. 'He's a total fantasist, always was.'

He had then proceeded to give İkmen several credible examples of Ahmet Sılay's fantasies and their subsequent exposure. What seemed to be emerging was a picture of a spoilt, wealthy man possessed of both artistic and working-class aspirations. Not overly endowed with talent, Sılay had always been jealous of his more successful friend, who had apparently tried to help him and had even entertained him in America. But Sılay's bitterness and his drinking had put paid to all that some time ago and Sivas had heard not a word from him in five years.

This did rather undermine Sılay's observations with regard to Hatice and Hassan Şeker. Even a mediocre lawyer could argue that evidence given by a known fantasist was at best unreliable. This left only Hulya's observations and Hatice's diary which that same lawyer could argue constituted only girlish yearnings. İkmen strongly disagreed, but that didn't count for anything.

And then only ten minutes ago he had been treated to an audience with Rat. What Rat had said was that someone had been supplying women to act as old-fashioned Ottoman odalisques – a group that could include Hatice İpek. This had been going on for some time but now, for reasons unknown, the business had been taken over by one of the families. Quite why anyone in this day and age would want a heavily robed odalisque when they could have a completely naked Russian woman willing to do anything for virtually nothing, İkmen couldn't imagine. Why he had never heard of this before was also a mystery.

As for the delightful Heper sisters, it was certainly possible that Miss Muazzez and Miss Yümniye had made the gown Hatice had been wearing when she died. But to say that they *knew* something about the use their work was put to had to be ridiculous. Although raised by a man who had been born an Ottoman and who had served in the Sultan's army, the girls, like their father, had been enthusiastic converts to Atatürkism and were consequently both independent and emancipated. Indeed local Üsküdar legend had it that the general's wife, the girls' mother, had been the first woman in all of Turkey to ride a bicycle, unveiled. The Hepers were entirely respectable. İkmen remembered them with affection from his childhood. Miss Yümniye had made his mother's wedding dress – he would have to be careful not to think about this when he presented the ladies with the gown Hatice had been wearing when she died. Because, whatever the truth of it was, he would have to go and see Miss Muazzez and Miss Yümniye and he would also have to persuade Arto Sarkissian to 'lend' him the dead girl's gown – without, of course, alerting Ardiç to this fact. Kaycee Sivas, İkmen knew, was the only young woman he should have on his mind now. Kaycee, who could still be alive somewhere, unlike poor, dead Hatice. But then what Ardiç didn't appreciate was that İkmen had promised his daughter he would find those people who had abused her friend and punish them. And Kaycee Sivas or no Kaycee Sivas, that was what he was going to do.

'Where are we, İskender?' Ardiç didn't even look up from what he was doing.

Metin İskender, as was becoming his custom, sat down before his superior offered this privilege.

'Nobody's talking, sir,' he said as he lit a cigarette with the very stylish silver lighter his wife had bought him. 'Significantly, not even my most desperate informants are coming forward.'

Ardiç looked up from his papers, his large face appearing split by the enormous cigar in his mouth. 'And ransom demands?' he said. 'Anything?'

'Not as yet. Sergeant Çöktin and the technicians have been monitoring all calls to Sivas's house, but there hasn't been anything. Nothing in the post either.'

'And what do you conclude from this?' Ardiç leaned back in his chair. He did this often. It gave his stomach more space and was therefore a much more comfortable position.

Metin İskender frowned. 'I am wary of the silence on the streets, sir. Kaycee Sivas is well known. An informant could get easy money from the press for any snippet about the wife of a movie star. In the normal course of events I would expect some trace of her to have appeared by now.'

'Why do you think that it hasn't?'

'Well, one reason that I can think of, indeed that I have had experience of in the past, is "family" involvement, sir.' He leaned forward to flick the ash from his cigarette into Ardiç's large onyx ashtray. 'There are several clans active in Beyazıt, although we can't rule out those from outside too, I suppose. Edirnekapı, Yediküle . . .'

'But wouldn't the families have asked for money by this time?' Ardiç asked. 'And besides, unless Sivas or his relatives are involved in family business – something we have no knowledge of – how would the mobs have known that he and his wife were even in the city?'

İskender shrugged. 'I don't know, sir. But something is not quite right with all this. Inspector İkmen was out at Sivas's house all day and he found the star's behaviour and attitude as difficult and at times incomprehensible as I did. For instance, Sivas raved for hours about how he had to call his agent back in the States, how he needed to instruct him with regard to press coverage over there. So we allowed him to do this and when he called this man, Gee, I believe his name was . . .'

'Yes? Well?'

İskender shrugged. 'Well, nothing,' he said. 'After all that insistence he told the man nothing beyond the fact that everything had gone wrong in his life and the İstanbul police were stupid.'

'You think Sivas may have set the thing up himself? Possibly with help from the States?'

'I don't know. But if you add together Sivas's assertion that neither he nor his wife had any enemies and the lack of ransom or any other kind of cogent demand then you have to conclude that something isn't genuine. I mean, why take the woman, whoever you are, if you don't intend to do something with her?'

'Do you think he has the ability to organise such a thing himself?'

'He's certainly got enough money to do it, although why he would want rid of such a lovely woman, I can't imagine. He is also genuinely upset.'

'Then perhaps as well as continuing our operations on the street and in Sivas's house we need to find out more about Hikmet Sivas himself. By that I mean the stuff beyond the publicity.' Ardiç re-lit his cigar. 'We all know he is Turkey's only great Hollywood star – the Sultan they used to call him over there in the early days, as I recall.' He smiled. 'But there has to be more to him than just money and fame. He must have friends, ex-wives, this agent . . . In fact, if you think about it, İskender, he has to be quite a person. As I understand it, it is difficult for Americans to break into Hollywood. But for a Turk . . .' He shrugged.

'You're saying that Hollywood bosses don't particularly like us.'

'I mean if you compare the number of Turkish names in Hollywood to the number of other foreigners they have employed, the ratio is not in our favour,' he said. 'I think I might tell İkmen to look into that, he's good with people's pasts. Which reminds me, how are you getting on with Inspector İkmen, İskender?'

'I can't really say, sir. We've been doing rather different things today and have had little time to consult.'

It was a truthful as well as a diplomatic answer and they both knew it. İskender had not, so far, had much to do with İkmen directly, but it was well known that they possessed radically different styles. Whereas İkmen would take time and employ great patience when dealing with both witnesses and suspects, İskender took a more direct and sometimes not altogether pleasant approach. In a world obsessed by results and statistics, İskender was without doubt the more immediately effective of the two. But İkmen still got results, especially in cases like this which could be delicate and protracted. The strange 'feelings' the older man occasionally experienced about cases could be unnervingly accurate. And whatever Ardiç might feel about such occult doings, even he had to admit that they were generally useful. They were, however, only one of the many things that İkmen and İskender were likely to fall out over in the future and so it was a good idea to give them separate tasks for the moment.

'We have a briefing in the morning,' Ardiç said, his eyes returning once again to the papers on his desk. 'I'll decide exactly what I want you to do and tell you then.'

'Yes, sir.'

Without any further comment, Ardiç waved İskender from the room. He worked in silence for a few minutes before he received a phone call from State Police Headquarters in Ankara. After that he was on the line for quite some time, mostly listening to what his superiors had to say. The sunset call to prayer had already finished when at last he put the phone down.

Chapter 10

Hulya İkmen had just shut the door to the family apartment behind her when she caught sight of her dead friend's mother, Hürrem İpek. White-faced, her eyes dark from ceaseless crying, Hürrem was not wearing her customary Zabita uniform and had her head covered by a thick, dark scarf.

'Dr Sarkissian says that I can make arrangements for Hatice's funeral now,' she said as she crossed over to Hulya who, at the woman's approach, felt herself go cold inside. Recalling what her father had told her about Hatice's 'natural' death made Hulya feel awkward in Hürrem's presence. Officially her dad was now working on the Sivas case and even though Hulya knew he was continuing his investigations into Hatice's death, she still felt ill at ease. Not of course that she doubted that her father would do his best. He'd promised her he would and she knew he always kept his word.

'My dad will find out who hurt Hatice,' she said as she placed a hand gently on Hürrem's shoulder.

'Yes.' Hürrem managed just the shadow of a grateful smile. 'They say the case is not a priority, but . . . He's a very good man, your father.'

'Yes.'

'And my daughter was such a bad girl . . .' In spite of

all the dust and rubbish the lazy building kapıcı Aziz had allowed to build up in the hallways, Hürrem İpek suddenly sat down.

'Mrs İpek!'

'She was a whore, Hulya, giving herself to that man – her employer, a married person!' She looked up into Hulya's face, her own features a picture of pain. 'What was she thinking? Did I not teach her enough of the values of her poor, dead father? Am I myself such a bad, bad person?' And with that she took handfuls of the filth around her and, crying now, rubbed it over her face and across her chest as if she were using it for washing.

Hulya, horrified by the depth of agony she was witnessing, tried to stop her, but Hürrem was too strong for her.

'No, I must be punished! I must!'

Cat fur, cigarette butts, dust, sweet wrappers and fragments of newspapers – she threw all of it over her head, until she looked like an old discarded doll, lost and forever alone at the bottom of the dustbin.

'Mrs İpek . . .' Hulya was about to hitch up her long flowery dress so that she could squat down to talk to Hürrem when she heard footsteps on the stairs. 'You've got to get up, Mrs İpek!' She reached down to Hürrem. 'Somebody's coming!'

'No!'

With even more urgency than before, Hürrem İpek scrabbled in the dust, pouring the filthy stuff all over herself, crying and screaming.

'Hulya?'

The girl turned and, when she saw who it was, she blushed.

'Berekiah!'

'Has the lady fallen? Is she ill?' He drew level with Hulya, so close that she could feel the intense heat from the street radiating from his body. She had to swallow hard before replying.

'She's my friend's mother,' she said. 'My friend who has just died. She's upset.'

'As she would be,' Berekiah replied. He squatted down in front of Hürrem and offered his hand to her. As he bent down, Hulya noticed that the crisp, white shirt he was wearing crackled as he stooped.

'Come along, madam,' he said firmly, taking Hürrem's hand. 'Let me help you up and then we can attend to all this mess.'

And as quickly as it had begun, Hürrem's crying ceased. Her mouth opened as if in a silent scream and she toppled forward into his arms, her head tucked into his midriff. They stayed like that for some time, while Hulya looked on and wondered what had brought him to her building in the first place.

The briefing had been shorter than İkmen, at least, had imagined it would be. Basically Ardiç had floated the idea of Turkish 'family' involvement while at the same time emphasising that they should continue to monitor activity in and around the Sivas house. It was, according to Ardiç, rather too early to start actively pursuing families, against which there was, as yet, no evidence. This, from the man who had asked İskender to 'tear Beyazıt apart'! But not antagonising the families did make sense to Çetin İkmen. Nobody wanted a war on the streets.

'Oh, Inspector . . .'

İkmen, who was walking out of the squad room with Tepe,

looked round and saw the small and stylish figure of Metin İskender behind him. Groomed and perfumed to perfection, he was wearing a suit that İkmen had never seen before and which, he uncharitably thought, had to be yet another gift from İskender's very successful wife.

İkmen and Tepe stopped. 'Yes?'

'Did the commissioner talk to you about looking into Hikmet Sivas's background?'

İkmen frowned. 'No. But then having been my superior for many years now, the commissioner knows that I'd do that anyway. The past is usually of some value in situations like this. Why?'

'Oh, just that he mentioned it at a private meeting I had with him last night.' Both the words 'I' and 'private' were heavily emphasised.

'Really?' İkmen looked at Tepe and smiled. 'Well, it's a good thing that I had scheduled in a little research this morning then, isn't it?'

'Yes, Inspector.'

İskender made to go about his own tasks, which involved attendance at the Sivas house, in as businesslike a fashion as possible. But İkmen, who some would say had already bested a man for whom promotion and position were far more important than anything except perhaps wealth, had to push it that little bit further.

'I've actually identified an old friend of Sivas – a man who knew him before he was famous.' He smiled. 'Sergeant Tepe has already spoken to him, haven't you, Tepe?'

'Yes, sir.'

'Oh. Good.' İskender smiled tautly at Tepe. 'Well done.' And then with his back as straight as a broom handle, he marched off down the corridor.

İkmen just shook his head and smiled. Poor İskender. Usually his efforts at self-elevation were successful, but not with him. He was still lead officer in this case and he needed everybody, including İskender, to be mindful of that.

'So will you go and see Ahmet Sılay this morning, sir?' Tepe asked as he followed his superior in the direction of the car park.

'Yes. And I'll ask him a few more questions about Hatice İpek's relationship with Hassan Şeker while I'm there too,' İkmen replied. 'After speaking to Mr Sivas yesterday, I'm not so sure that his evidence is sound.'

'I thought we were supposed to be sidelining that now that we know the girl died of natural causes,' Tepe said.

İkmen took his car keys out of his pocket. 'No,' he said. 'Ardiç might like that to be so, but I intend to carry on pursuing any leads that come my way. And because Mr Sılay is, coincidentally, connected to both cases . . .'

'OK.'

'As I told you earlier, Tepe, I have independent information that the circumstances surrounding Hatice's death are suspicious.'

'Yes.' They'd spoken of it briefly as soon as İkmen had arrived in his office. 'The informant who mentioned family involvement and those Heper ladies you want to see.'

'Yes.' İkmen sighed. 'A person not of entirely good character, my informant, but nevertheless someone it would be stupid to ignore.'

What Rat had told him the previous evening had indeed occupied much of İkmen's thinking time since. Whether or not 'family' members had involved themselves in a prostitution operation of some sort was not entirely germane to how İkmen was approaching the situation. As time had passed the idea of young women dressing up and behaving like odalisques had grown, in his mind, ever more freakish. As far as he could recall, odalisques were renowned for the passivity of their sexual performance. Lying on beds like pieces of wood, offering little more than orifices for their royal masters to gain relief through. Modern men would surely need rather more stimulation than that. In Hatice's case, that had certainly been so. Arto Sarkissian had identified two types of semen in her body and a third in her mouth. No sultan that İkmen knew of ever got his friends round for a gang rape. But he made a mental note to ask Suleyman about palace practices when next he saw him. After all, if a prince didn't know about such things, who would?

Hikmet Sivas couldn't imagine how the box had got into his bedroom. It wasn't small – about three-quarters of a metre in height and quite wide. No one apart from the police and their technicians had entered the house for a day and a half. There had been no post or deliveries. Vedat had been out once, with one of the officers, for cigarettes, but that was all, and besides, if Vedat had placed the box in Hikmet's room he would have told him.

Hikmet knew he should call one of the policemen. The box was large and its contents were unknown. It could be a bomb or even, and this had once happened to a B-list soap star back in the States, a very small admirer. Not that Hikmet believed it was. This was most likely a message of some sort from the kidnappers. And in that respect he'd already made one mistake by involving the police in the first place. So, if this parcel did indeed come from them, he shouldn't really alert Sergeant Çöktin or any of his fellows. He should open the box himself and face whatever consequences might follow. If it was a bomb and he died, well, that was just kismet.

Hikmet walked over to the desk that stood by his bed and picked up the letter opener that lay on top. The box was made of wood, but it was only balsa, by the look of it. It should shift easily under a blunt knife. But it didn't and because it was so very hot, being almost midday, just a couple of abortive attempts to open it wore Hikmet out. Panting, he took some time to sit on his bed, still observing if not touching the box as he did so. It was only then that he noticed the note.

He hadn't looked at the box from this angle before. It hadn't been there when he'd woken so he hadn't seen it from the bed previously. It had turned up sometime between seven am and five minutes ago when he'd returned to his room. And now there was this note . . .

Taped to one of the sides, it was a little pale yellow envelope and it was addressed to him. After first calming himself with a few deep breaths, Hikmet leaned forward and peeled the little missive from the wood. Then he turned it over. The envelope flap was not stuck down but tucked in. He gently lifted it up and looked at what was inside.

The note was folded in half and so in order to read it he had to pull it all the way out of the envelope. When he did read it, however, his face turned from brown to grey and he had to stuff a corner of the embroidered counterpane into his mouth. He didn't want the policemen downstairs to hear his screams.

Now, he thought as he scrambled wildly across his bedroom towards the window, I will have to get out of here and tell G the truth. Now I really don't have anything, of value, left to lose.

'Hikmet was only ever a mediocre actor. He could play one-dimensional heroes but that was about it.'

It was just coming up for 1 p.m. and Ahmet Sılay was already drunk. As he spoke he waved his arms around to emphasise his various points.

'His portrayal of the evil general Bekir Paşa in his last film for Yeşilcam was truly awful,' Sılay continued. 'When he left İstanbul saying that he was going to be a star in Hollywood, nobody believed him. I just laughed.'

'But he did achieve fame, didn't he, Mr Sılay,' İkmen put in. 'While you did not.' Sılay took another swig from his rakı bottle before replying. 'Ah, yes,' he said, 'he did. But it had nothing to do with talent.'

'Then what did it have to do with, Mr Sılay?'

The elderly actor leaned towards İkmen and smiled. His breath, İkmen felt, would have disabled a lesser man than himself.

'He got friendly with some people from Las Vegas,' Sılay said in a heavy stage whisper. 'People who owned Las Vegas at that time, if you know what I mean.'

'This was the early nineteen sixties, wasn't it?'

'When Las Vegas was full of Italians, yes.' His smile was lopsided and bitter. 'When all the stars and their women went to Las Vegas. When a man willing to do anything for such people could do himself many favours.'

Although hardly an aficionado of Hollywood movies, İkmen was aware that the Mafia were known to have had some involvement with the entertainment industry, particularly in Las Vegas, at that time. Rumours had even circulated implicating people as prominent as Frank Sinatra – rumours that, with regard to Frank, Fatma İkmen had always staunchly disbelieved. Nothing was ever proved and neither the name Hikmet Sivas nor the more familiar Ali Bey had been mentioned in connection with such allegations. If they had, İkmen would have known. The Turkish press would have made sure that everyone knew.

But if Sivas had been involved with the Mafia, if he had crossed them in some way, that could explain why his wife had disappeared.

As if reading his thoughts, Sılay said, 'You'll probably find that the Mafia have his wife. He's upset them in some way. Hikmet always upsets people in the end. They're international, these people. They probably waited until he got here to take her because they know Turkish police can't catch a cold without help.'

İkmen turned briefly to look at Tepe who just shrugged.

İkmen looked back into the crimson eyes of Ahmet Sılay. 'Did Mr Sivas tell you he was involved with the Mafia?'

'No.'

'Then . . .'

'Look, he used to write to me, in the nineteen sixties.' He smiled, 'And then ten years ago when I went to see him in Hollywood they were all around his Turkish crescent-shaped pool.'

'Who were?' İkmen asked. 'The Mafia?'

'Italians! Alberto and Martino, Giovanni, Giulia – all around a pool "advertising" this country.' He leaned forward again and the smile returned. 'I tell you, who but someone with powerful connections would tell the world he is a Turk? In America? No. Americans and Europeans hate

143

Turks. Çetin İkmen policeman, you know that, I know it, we are raised to understand that.'

İkmen who had heard and felt such sentiments himself, nevertheless did not encourage Sılay any further down this particular road.

'Mr Sivas says that you make up stories, Mr Sılay,' he said. He lit a cigarette and then provided a light for the ageing actor. 'Would you like to tell me about that?'

Sılay laughed. 'Well, he doesn't want you to know that he works for the Mafia,' he said. 'He knows I'm clever, knows I've worked it out.'

'The subject actually came up when I asked Mr Sivas about your reliability in relation to the Hatice İpek case,' İkmen said. 'If you remember, you said that Hatice was having a relationship with the confectioner Hassan Şeker.'

'Yes, and I stand by it!' Sılay, his eyes now furious, responded. 'Just because I drink—'

'Lawyers regularly rip people like you apart in court, Mr Sılay. People who fuck up their brains every morning before breakfast! I asked Mr Sivas his opinion because I needed to know whether I could even think about going to court if I received further evidence in that case. I suspect it would be difficult.'

'Oh, lawyers, lawyers!' Sılay lifted his bottle up towards the ceiling and laughed raucously. 'Nothing but fucking arse whores for the state! They don't care about the common man, only money, money – just like Hikmet!'

'Money is important, Mr Sılay.'

'No it isn't!'

'To those who've never been without it I suppose it can be peripheral,' İkmen said tartly, mindful of what Tepe had told him about Ahmet Sılay's privileged background.

'Hikmet Sivas sold his body, his soul and his principles for money.'

'Yes, and you may have done the same had you been born into poverty,' İkmen said, his patience stretched to breaking point by this bitter, ruined old rich boy. He would have said more along those lines had his mobile telephone not started ringing at that moment.

He turned away to answer it. Tepe and Sılay both watched the back of his head as he spoke, sometimes urgently, into the small device. The conversation lasted less than a minute. But when İkmen turned back to face the others, his face was the colour of dust. Tepe felt his heart beat faster.

'Sir?'

'We have to go, Tepe,' İkmen said as he rose quickly to his feet. 'Now.'

She'd had all the time that it had taken them to calm Mrs İpek to think about why Berekiah might have come up to the apartment. First she had made tea for her friend's mother, while Berekiah disappeared briefly in order to buy Hürrem a packet of cigarettes. And then they had talked, the three of them. Sometimes about Hatice but usually in more general terms about how cruel life could be and how that cruelty could come about so suddenly. Hulya knew that Berekiah had personal experience of such things himself. There had only been the briefest warning of his older brother, Yusuf's, mental breakdown and there had been no time at all to prepare for the massive 1999 earthquake which had ripped Berekiah's father's legs away.

Hürrem İpek was both charmed and comforted by Berekiah, but all Hulya wanted to know was what had brought him here in the first place.

At last they felt able to leave Hürrem and the two young people walked back into the dusty, litter-strewn hall. 'I actually came to see whether any of your family wanted to go to the hospital to see Mehmet's baby,' Berekiah said. 'Zelfa can't receive people at home in the normal way because she's had an operation. But the family are very happy to see friends at the hospital and I know Çetin Bey has bought a gift for the child.'

'So you came to see my dad then really,' Hulya said as she fought to disguise her disappointment.

'I didn't know who would be at home,' Berekiah replied. 'But today is my day off and I was passing. Do you want to come?'

She did. And so they went together, picking up various items of food, as instructed by Berekiah's mother, along the way.

When they arrived at the hospital, however, Hulya could see instantly that all was not well with the new little family. Dr Halman, as she even now felt obliged to call Mehmet's wife, still looked worn out from her ordeal and barely managed to raise a smile even when little Yusuf İzzeddin was brought in to her. Her father, Dr Babur, made numerous and forced attempts at jolly conversation which worked only patchily. The whole experience was strained in a way that Hulya couldn't understand. When babies came, people were happy. Her mother had always been happy when a new child arrived. She couldn't understand why Dr Halman looked so sad.

But when, a little later, Mehmet Suleyman arrived, Dr Halman's demeanour changed. Now animated, she passed the baby quickly over to her father and then held her husband's hands in hers. Gazing up into his eyes, she laughed wildly at any little comment he made even if it was only remotely amusing. It was almost as if, Hulya felt, Dr Halman and Mehmet were on a first date and she was trying to impress him. Not once did she look at the baby after her husband arrived and when Mehmet himself wanted to spend some time with his son, Dr Halman looked positively jealous. It was all very odd. But Hulya didn't say anything about her observations even after she and Berekiah left.

However, on the way back to Hulya's apartment, to which Berekiah had insisted on returning her, he raised the subject of what they had just seen at the hospital.

'I think that my mother is right when she says that having babies takes a lot of energy out of women,' he said as he took her hand in his to cross the road. 'Zelfa is still, I think, quite ill.'

And although Hulya herself wouldn't have put what she had observed in Dr Halman down to 'illness' as such, she agreed.

'But not all women are ill like that, you know,' she said.

'Oh?' Now that they were back on the pavement he let his fingers gently disengage from hers.

Hulya, feeling the sudden loss of him, forced a smile. 'My mum has always been all right,' she said. 'And I think that I will be too – if I ever have children. Hatice and I always dreamed of starring in the movies . . .'

'Well, you're, er . . .' he looked down briefly and then smiled into her eyes, 'you're very beautiful and so I expect that you could . . .'

Hulya felt her face catch fire and so she looked away from him, fixing her eyes on the side of a passing tram.

'Thank you,' she said.

He pulled her round to face him and put his hand up to her cheek.

It was a touching sight and one that affected Ayşe Farsakoğlu who had noticed one of Inspector İkmen's daughters being romanced by the son of old Cohen the Jew. Ayşe was across the other side of Divan Yolu where, overheated, she'd stopped to buy a drink. Just for a moment she felt jealous. Never again would a young man make her blush, take her hand tenderly in his. Not that she wanted any of that juvenile stuff, of course not. She wanted a man, a home of her own, and not to be pitied by her family any more. If she couldn't have Suleyman, she'd have Orhan instead. As soon as he divorced that wife of his, she could have him and no one would pity her ever again.

But then she tore her mind away from Orhan and looked at the young people once again, this time frowning.

Chapter 11

İkmen looked down at the crumpled figure of Metin İskender as he bent his head over the bucket one more time, retching, but without production.

'How many times has he thrown up?' İkmen asked İsak Çöktin who, together with all the other officers stationed inside the Sivas house, was standing on the landing outside Hikmet Sivas's bedroom.

Çöktin shrugged. 'I don't know, sir,' he said. 'I've not been that concerned with him, to be honest.'

İkmen nodded. He could understand that. Aside from the fact that İskender wasn't well liked, what had taken place in the house in the last two hours overshadowed any other considerations.

At approximately eleven forty-five that morning, Hikmet Sivas had said that he was going up to his bedroom to lie down. He hadn't managed to get much sleep the previous night and he was tired. Çöktin had said this was OK although when, five minutes later, Inspector İskender had arrived he had asked him whether anyone should go with Sivas to his room. İskender had said that wasn't necessary. He would check on the star in a while. Half an hour later he did so. What he found was an absence of Sivas and the presence of an unknown box that he had made the mistake of opening. He had been vomiting ever since.

Çöktin, his hands covered by the familiar thin whiteness of surgical gloves, held a small piece of paper up in front of İkmen's face.

'I found this with it,' he said.

İkmen motioned for him to open the note so that he could read it.

'*Japanese Ivories – to be personally delivered to His Majesty, the Sultan.*' İkmen, strangely, grinned. 'How very apt.'

'Sir?'

'It's to do with history, Çöktin,' İkmen said. 'History concerning perceived betrayal and remarkable cruelty.'

'So what does it mean, sir?' Tepe looked across İkmen's shoulder at the small piece of paper between Çöktin's fingers.

'The words are the same as those alleged to have been written in a note sent to Sultan Abdul Hamid II by the men he charged to execute our great reforming Vizir, Midhat Paşa. Midhat was killed in Arabia, where he had been exiled some years before. So the Sultan in İstanbul didn't actually see his old enemy die. But because he was paranoid, which is why he had Midhat killed in the first place, he couldn't believe it had happened until he saw Midhat's head, which arrived, apparently, some weeks later with a note just like this.'

'Ah.'

'To someone who knows this story, it would make sense. And Mr Sivas obviously did because he didn't open the box.' İkmen sighed and then put his hand up to his head because it was starting to hurt. 'He just ran away from a house full of police officers and is now either in danger or has gone into hiding. How did this happen, Sergeant Çöktin?'

Çöktin, who was well enough acquainted with İkmen to

recognise that his outward calmness was not destined to last, began, 'Well . . .'

'It happened because you all fucked up, didn't it?'

'Er . . .'

'You did not stay with Mr Sivas at all times as you had been instructed and you also failed to sustain effective observation over this property.' He sat down beside İskender on the brocade-covered bench outside Hikmet Sivas's bedroom. 'You all behaved like a bunch of amateurs. You facilitated a catastrophe.'

Metin İskender, who had now just about managed to stop vomiting, looked up.

'Sivas had been up to his room alone before,' he said, 'to go to sleep.'

'Not when I've been in this house!' İkmen roared as the floodgates of his anger finally burst. 'When I've been here there has always been one man at least outside rooms containing Sivas family members! Even when the sister goes to the toilet!'

'Inspector—'

İkmen turned on İskender. 'You and I both felt that Sivas was hiding something. Now that he's gone we have lost the only, admittedly tenuous, connection we might have had with Kaycee's murderers! You have messed up in a big way!'

İskender's already white face turned grey.

'And as lead officer in this investigation,' İkmen said fiercely, 'I am as of now taking personal charge.' He looked around at all the other officers on the landing before he returned his gaze to İskender. 'No more working alongside each other. You do as I say at all times and if you can't do that then you do nothing!'

'But that is for the Commissioner—'

'The commissioner, when he finds out about this, will go berserk!' İkmen shouted into İskender's face. 'You were in charge! You messed up and you will take the consequences like a man!'

He stood up and addressed Orhan Tepe. 'Well, we'd better take a look at what's in there and then I'll have to set about salvaging something from this catastrophe.'

'Yes, sir.'

İkmen walked towards the bedroom door, took a deep breath and entered.

The box was exactly as İskender had left it. The lid was off and the bloodstained newspaper that had padded it out was strewn haphazardly across the floor.

Before his courage failed him, İkmen marched across to the box and looked inside. The face was uppermost, obviously in order to have maximum impact on the person opening the box. And although the eyes were only half open, the look that Kaycee Sivas seemed to be giving him was one filled with accusation. Whoever had severed her head had done it very cleanly just below the chin. They had then pulled her long blonde hair up on top of her head so that it looked like a large pillow at the crown of her skull.

İkmen moved away to allow Tepe to glance just briefly at the head.

'Inspector İskender and I saw a head like this out in Edirnekapı when I worked with him some years ago,' Tepe said, using words to prevent sickness rising in his own throat. 'That's probably why the inspector has been so ill now.'

'I don't really care just at the moment, Tepe.' İkmen sat down on the edge of the bed and lit a cigarette. 'We'll have to inform Dr Sarkissian. See what he can tell us about this thing.'

'Yes, sir.'

İkmen took a deep drag on his cigarette and let the smoke out on a sigh.

'I'll need to interview the brother and sister,' he said. 'Arrange it.'

'Yes, sir. Do you want me to contact Dr Sarkissian too, sir?'

'No. I'll do that.'

Tepe gratefully left the room. İkmen, now alone, took his mobile telephone out of his pocket and keyed in the doctor's number. As he waited for the familiar voice to answer, he looked at the box again for just a second, and then he shut his eyes. Kaycee Sivas had been young and very beautiful and whatever she may or may not have done in her life, she hadn't deserved such an horrific end. She must have been so terrified . . .

But İkmen didn't, couldn't dwell on such matters and when Dr Sarkissian eventually answered the telephone he gave him the information he needed with cold detachment.

The man the whole district knew as Rat was dead. Under torture he had confessed to speaking to İkmen about something he shouldn't. And then they had killed him. Just to be certain they'd also burned his body on some tip up by the wretched Topkapı Bit Pazarı, the 'louse market' where poverty meant clothes that fell apart in your hands and a man's body could be burned like a piece of old rag. Rat, whoever he was, had been, would never be found now.

Hassan Şeker wept as he thought about these things. He wept because he was guilty. If he hadn't let on that he'd seen Rat follow İkmen into Ticarethane Sokak, none of this would have happened. But he had; Rat was a well-known police informant and Hassan had been scared. So scared!

He still was. The fear hadn't receded. As his wife was so fond of saying when one or other of his 'business partners' showed up at the pastane, 'You see these flash, rough boys but you don't really know who they're working for, do you?'

Suzan was wrong in this instance. Hassan did know now, which was why his blood was like ice. Even though he had done everything that he could to please those whose names he couldn't even think of for fear of discovery, he knew that they blamed him for so much that had gone wrong – simply because of his romantic connection to Hatice. If only he possessed his father's strength! Kemal Şeker had always and with passion resisted all advances, offers and threats from such people. No good could ever come of it, he said. And he was right. In spite of all the handouts and favours Hassan had received, what he was experiencing now, the agony of fear, was not worth any of it.

Rat aside, what had happened to little Hatice was beyond endurance. Not that he'd had anything to do with it himself. Indeed if he'd known what had been planned, what had really been planned, as opposed to the half-truths they had fed him he would never have got her involved. The girl, Ekrem said, had been seen and had been greatly desired. And even though Hassan had told them she was in love with him, it had made no difference – not with 'that man' involved. No. But then, if he hadn't given her to them, to that unnameable man, they would have taken her anyway. Nothing would have changed.

But thinking of Hatice's death as an inevitability didn't

make him feel any better. He would miss her, she'd been so sweet. And he'd done himself no good by his actions anyway. Not now that another, more powerful and, to his 'friends', far more useful associate was involved. Apart from the money that he paid them on a monthly basis, Hassan was almost redundant now. Almost, but not quite. Someone to take the blame for their actions was always useful and the policeman İkmen, despite all of Hassan's best efforts, was continuing to pursue him. Soon he would be back, asking questions, moving in. What was Hassan going to say, what could he say without letting something slip?

Hassan Şeker lowered his head into his hands and wept again. This time his wife, hearing noises that sounded like an animal in pain, entered her husband's office without knocking. She stood in the doorway and watched him. Poor weak thing, he'd really made his life a misery getting mixed up with people like Ekrem Müren. Or maybe he was just crying because Hatice was dead. Unlike all the other girls he'd seduced over the years, Hassan had really seemed to care for her. Not that this knowledge made it any easier for Suzan. She loved and hated her husband in equal measure and so instead of going over to comfort him she just pushed the door to his office shut with her foot and went about her business.

'I'm going to need help,' İkmen said as he paced agitatedly backwards and forwards across the room, a cigarette ever present at his lips.

'And you shall have it,' his superior replied. 'Name who and what you want and it shall be given to you.'

Ardiç had been at the Sivas house for just over half an hour. During that time, İkmen and his officers, including İskender, had acquainted him with the facts regarding

155

Hikmet and Kaycee Sivas. At times he had looked thunderous, but he had not gone berserk. In view of what had happened and how it had in effect been allowed to take place, this was startling. Ardiç was famous for his volcanic temper and given the high profile nature of this case, one might expect him to be furious. But he wasn't, which made İkmen feel unnerved and deeply suspicious.

'If Ahmet Sılay is right about Sivas's connections with the Mafia,' İkmen said, 'then I'm going to need to speak to officers in America. In fact I should speak to them now if Sivas is "known".'

'Yes, well in time that will be possible,' Ardiç replied, wiping his heavily sweating face with a handkerchief as he spoke. 'But because that is all rather speculative . . .'

'Well, it's quite enough evidence for me!' İkmen cried. 'Even the suggestion that the Mafia might be amongst us is enough for me. Our own families are bad enough, but these people are experts. They invented organised crime!'

'We have no evidence.'

'I want to know what, if anything, the Americans know.'

'And I'm saying that until we have something more than the bitter memories of a jealous and inebriated rival, possessed of a fertile imagination, I can't just—'

'Yes, you can!' İkmen was close to Ardiç now, close enough to see the agitation in his veined cheeks. 'You are the Commissioner of Police, you have reason to suspect that Hikmet Sivas has connections with the Mafia!' He thrust one arm towards the stairs that led to Sivas's bedroom. 'I've got his wife's head up there! It doesn't get any more serious than this!'

Ardiç, with an act of self control seldom associated with him, lowered his tone. 'As I have told you before,

İkmen,' he said, 'we will observe procedure. You and I will interview Vedat and Hale Sivas. Based upon that and any information our officers glean from people in the surrounding area we will mount a search for Hikmet Sivas.'

'He could be anywhere!' İkmen put what was left of his cigarette out in one of the ashtrays and lit up a fresh one.

'Which is why we need to speak to those closest to him,' Ardiç replied, 'in order to find out where he might have gone.'

İkmen knew that on one level Ardiç was right. Without some sort of notion about where Sivas might have gone, the police would just be moving around to no good effect. Not that either Hale or Vedat Sivas had been particularly forthcoming, as yet. The woman had just spouted religiously inspired laments through her tears while her brother, his face a sweaty shade of grey, had simply sat in silence, like one in a fugue. Undoubtedly shocked, they would, İkmen felt, talk soon. But when they did, what would they say? Their brother Hikmet hadn't lived in the city for forty years; how would they know where he might go? Unless of course they had family connections too. İkmen thought it unlikely that Hikmet had had any part in or knowledge of Kaycee's kidnapping and death. It looked as if he had just read the note pinned to the side of the box, realised exactly what it meant and then in his distress gone to face whatever was in store for him – either that or he had just run away in terror. Written in Turkish, probably so Hikmet could make no mistake about its meaning, the note had been cleverly targeted at a man who was known to be fascinated by his nation's history and whose nickname in his early Hollywood days had been 'the Sultan'.

Ardic, although in no way an intuitive person, was also thinking about the language the note was written in.

'The fact that the note was written in Turkish doesn't suggest the Mafia to me,' he said as he watched the gentle reflection of the Bosphorus waters outside form patterns on the ceiling of the enormous salon. 'I mean, have you ever met an American who can speak Turkish? They have no need for Turkish. And as for Sicilians . . .'

İkmen sighed. He didn't know whether Ardiç was being deliberately obtuse or just plain stupid. 'I hardly think, sir,' he said tightly, 'that Turkish is such an obscure language that sophisticated international crime families don't have access to it.'

'I doubt our own families can even write their own language.'

'Sir, we're not talking about our own families!'

'We were at the briefing this morning.'

'Yes, because Inspector İskender felt that family involvement was possible because of the silence on the streets,' İkmen said. 'But Kaycee's head up there in a box apparently spirited into this house by djinn, together with what I've gleaned from Ahmet Sılay today, suggests a level of sophistication far more advanced than anything one would find in Edirnekapı. According to İskender you yourself wanted me to find out more about Sivas's background. I thought I might start with this agent, Gee.'

'Mmm, we must be careful, İkmen.' Ardiç frowned. 'Sivas is a very respected movie star. He took American citizenship some years ago. He is one of their own now. This country has good relations with the USA. Any suggestion that their crime empires are operating elsewhere could cause offence unless well-founded, and if wrong could be extremely embarrassing for us.'

İkmen, exasperated, threw his arms in the air. 'Oh, please don't let us cause offence or look stupid to the Americans!' He stared into Ardiç's face. 'Has it occurred to you, sir, that their law enforcement agencies might be glad of such information? If we talked to them we could establish where they stand. That's all I want to do.'

'All right! All right!' Ardiç, seemingly defeated, sighed. 'But *I* will speak to them, and to this agent too, if you wish, not you. And from now on we surround this case with silence. The media will report nothing further on the matter – I have already seen to that.'

'Sir—'

'I have taken control.' Briefly Ardiç's eyes blazed. 'I don't want you going off and pursuing your own little theories and suppositions behind my back.' He fixed İkmen with a steady gaze. 'I know you are still meddling in the Hatice İpek investigation, İkmen. I also know that you have deduced, or think you have, some sort of family involvement in that case too.'

'How do you know that?' He knew that he hadn't and wouldn't have discussed any of that with Ardiç.

'Just leave Hassan Şeker alone,' his superior said and, finally tiring of the conversation, he laboriously rose to his feet. 'That is all that I will say, İkmen. You have no evidence against him beyond his romantic involvement with that girl.'

'Did he make a complaint against me?' İkmen felt his face turn red with anger. 'I haven't even spoken to him.'

'Just leave it!'

And so, for the moment, that was what İkmen did. Outwardly cowed, he followed his superior into Sivas's study where Hale and Vedat were waiting, expressionlessly, for them.

Underneath, however, he was boiling. He had seen Hassan Şeker the previous evening when he had arrived home from work, but they hadn't spoken. Had Hassan seen him with Rat? Everyone knew who and what Rat was, but if Hassan had heard information relating to 'family' business, it wasn't clear why he would tell Ardiç. Why Ardiç should only tell İkmen about this now was also a mystery.

Unless, of course, Hassan Şeker hadn't made a complaint against him. Unless the information had come from somewhere closer to home . . .

It was an extreme reaction to a line of questioning that could in no way be called aggressive. It just happened, almost before Vedat Sivas was conscious that it had occurred. He wet himself. The small, thin policeman, İkmen, asked him a question and Vedat, tortured by thoughts about what his brother might be doing now, literally let go.

'I have no idea where my brother Hikmet might have gone,' he said and looked down, horrified, as the wetness from his bladder spread across the red velvet chair cover he was sitting on. 'Hikmet is a big star. I'm just a poor night watchman. I might live in my brother's grand house but I'm still just a night watchman.'

'You chose that,' his sister said as she passed a box of tissues over to him, her face set in an expression of disgust.

'Maybe.' He gave his crotch a cursory dab with one tissue and then, mortified, threw the box to the floor.

They all knew – it was plain to see – what he had done. But none of them mentioned it. Not İkmen nor his corpulent superior, not even Hale.

'Where do you work, Mr Sivas?' İkmen asked. He even smiled as he spoke.

Far down inside, Vedat prayed for death. He needed to be careful, so careful, talking to these policemen. He took a deep breath. With luck he wouldn't be able to take another breath, maybe . . .

But he did and so he had to speak. 'I have several places . . .' His voice trailed off, his throat too dry to continue.

'Oh?' İkmen said with a smile, 'And where are they, sir?'

Hale looked across at her brother and then cast her gaze modestly back to the floor once again.

Vedat cleared his throat. 'I work two nights at the Etap Marmara Hotel, one at Yıldız Palace and one at the Ciragan Kempinski Hotel.'

'But you are on holiday at the moment, aren't you, sir?'

'Yes. To see my brother. I should go back, to the Ciragan, tomorrow night.' He said this with some urgency as if it had only just occurred to him.

İkmen shrugged. 'Well, that may not be possible, sir.' He wrote something down in his notebook and then looked up. 'A murder has been committed here. Nobody can leave. We will need to search this house and its grounds for further evidence, possibly even your sister-in-law's body.'

Hale put her hands over her eyes and said, 'Allah!'

'But what about my work?'

'Did your brother know where you worked and on which days?' İkmen asked.

Vedat felt his bladder slacken once again. 'No.'

'So you don't think he might have gone to one or other of your places of work to wait for you? Both hotels and the palace are considerable complexes. A man could hide out for days.'

'But Hikmet knows I am on holiday.'

'Oh, yes,' İkmen smiled, 'of course.'

'Why we sit here when our brother is spirited away by murderers, I cannot understand,' Hale said, her eyes now glistening with moisture. Although she always gave the outward appearance of being tough, Hale was in fact quite soft-hearted, particularly where Hikmet was concerned. Provided he listened to her religiously motivated speeches once in a while, Hikmet could do as he pleased.

'We are asking you these questions now so that we might have some chance of finding your brother,' the older, fat policeman said.

'But if murderers have him . . .'

'Do you think that my brother may have killed his wife then?' Vedat asked. It was probably stupid to say that. But he had to know, try to discover what was actually in their minds.

The policemen looked at each other and then İkmen, again with a smile, said, 'No, sir, we don't.'

Vedat felt the blood drain from his face. 'Oh.'

Too late he realised that his reaction had been far too muted. İkmen was well into his speech about just how absurd the notion was when Vedat finally managed to look relieved.

Chapter 12

Even now, well into their sixties, Muazzez and Yümniye Heper were 'modern' women. Like Atatürk, General Heper, their father, believed that women could work like men, could make 'men's' decisions and should be valued as highly as sons. The Heper girls had chosen to be seamstresses because they enjoyed sewing and liked fashion, not because they felt that only 'women's' work was open to them. However, even in their sixties, they dressed like neither seamstresses nor *Vogue* models.

A film that had enjoyed some popularity in the 1950s was *Nebahat the Driver*. It told the story of a female cab driver who dressed like a man and joined her fellow, male, drivers in matey banter. Nebahat, though entirely chaste, was one of the boys. And although the Heper sisters were far too posh to behave like that, they both dressed like Nebahat. Miss Muazzez particularly, İkmen recalled, had a great passion for leather jackets and thick, serviceable trousers. He smiled when he thought about it now as he strode along Nuhkuyusu Caddesi towards the sagging façade of the Heper house. There weren't many of these old wooden places in this part of Üsküdar any more, only this one and the slightly smaller one a little bit back towards the cemetery, where İkmen himself had grown up.

Pushing the now heavily splintered garden gate open with

his foot, İkmen took a moment to look at the Heper house. Made entirely of wood, it stood upon a considerable plot of ground, which had its wild unkempt existence between a petrol station and a row of ugly shops which had been built in the 1970s. Like his own father's house, it had always been black, but now the building looked dirty too, paint peeling in long strands from the columns that held the ornate balcony aloft, noticeable gaps in the tiles on the roof. As he mounted the steps which led up to the front door, the boards beneath his feet groaned under his meagre weight. He placed the bag that held the dress Hatice İpek had been wearing when she died down by his feet and rang the doorbell. While he waited for someone to answer, İkmen looked back casually at the street. A short, middle-aged woman with flaming red hair stood by the Hepers' gate, staring intently at him. It was unnerving and İkmen was about to say something to the woman when the Hepers' door opened behind him.

Unsurprisingly it was Yümniye Heper who let him in – she who, as Lazar the gold merchant had told İkmen before, wasn't blind.

'Çetin İkmen!' she said as her elderly and yet still clearly beautiful face broke into a smile. 'Well, this is a surprise!'

She held her hand out to him and İkmen took it in his. Like two men, two European men, they shook hands. Her grip was firm, even though İkmen clearly felt the grind of bone against bone as he squeezed her fingers. Arthritis – that 'gift' of the harsh İstanbul winter. It had plagued his father too.

After dispensing with the traditional inquiries regarding his health and the health of his family, Yümniye Heper led İkmen into a large room at the back of the property, which was graced with numerous comfortable divans and beautiful, if somewhat faded, carpets. When she had settled him on the most comfortable divan and brought him an ashtray, Yümniye went off to get her sister who, she said, was currently labouring in their workroom. During her absence İkmen considered how he might broach the subject of the dress which Arto Sarkissian had so kindly and riskily put at his disposal. The room was not, for him, an unfamiliar space. It hadn't changed a bit, this room the old general used to call his 'salon'. Until the death of his mother when he was ten, İkmen and his brother Halil had been regular visitors to the Heper house. Fittings for little suits, for family weddings, for the occasional party his father gave for members of his faculty and for his sons' circumcision had all taken place here. Occasionally, İkmen recalled, General Heper, still a hostage to his noble upbringing, would put his head round the door and say something in French.

'It has been a very long time since our esteemed inspector sat in this room,' Yümniye Heper said as she re-entered with her sister, an elegant, slightly younger version of herself.

'Indeed.' And Muazzez Heper smiled, her eyes mobile as if they still possessed sight. When she addressed İkmen, however, it was obvious that she couldn't see him. As Yümniye helped her into the only chair which stood over by the French windows, Muazzez spoke to their guest as if he were by the fireplace – until she heard his voice and shifted her leather-clad form to face him.

'So what brings you over to Üsküdar, Inspector?' Muazzez asked when her sister had gone to make tea and collect the requisite number of sweets she imagined their guest might require.

İkmen smiled. Even without sight, Muazzez Heper, who had always been the more direct and 'European' of the

two, could see that this was no social call. After all,
İkmen had only seen the Heper sisters three or four times
since he joined the police in the late 1960s. After that
he and his young bride and infant son Sınan had moved
across the Bosphorus to Sultanahmet. There he had achieved
success, confining Üsküdar and the bitterness that surrounded his mother's death in 1957 to the darkness of
the past.

'I've come to show you a dress actually, Miss Muazzez,'
he said.

'Oh?' She took a packet of cigarettes out of one of her
trouser pockets and lit up. 'Why?'

İkmen bent down to unzip the bag, 'Because I think you
or Miss Yümniye might have made it,' he said. 'Some time
ago, it's old.'

'It's possible.' She shrugged. 'What colour is it? Design?'

'It's similar to one I believe you made recently for a
wealthy bride,' İkmen replied. 'Nineteenth-century Ottoman. I saw the bridal gown at Lazar's in the Kapalı Çarşı.'

Yümniye returned with a tray covered with tea glasses and
saucers containing lokum and chocolates, which she placed
on the table that stood between the divans. She served İkmen
and her sister and only when everyone was settled did she
sit down, next to the policeman.

Muazzez Heper was the first to break the silence. 'Çetin
has a dress to show us, Yümniye,' Muazzez said. 'He thinks
it might be one of ours.'

Yümniye looked at their guest quizzically.

İkmen reached into the bag and pulled the dress out so
that the skirt spread across the floor like a fan.

'Mmm.' Yümniye Heper frowned. 'Yes, I think that you
may be right.'

'It is one of ours?'

'Maybe.' Yümniye took the edge of the skirt between her fingers to examine the stitching on the hem more closely. 'Although it would have to be one that we made a long time ago. It's marbled satin,' she said, looking across at her sister's sightless eyes, 'cream and pink. Faded though, as it does, over time.'

'And the design?'

Yümniye's eyes and hands travelled up the gown to the sleeves. 'Ottoman bridal,' she said. 'Covered with those little fabric roses they used to like so much. You made them out of green netting and—'

'No, not roses.'

Her sister looked up from the dress. Muazzez's face was turned away from her and from İkmen now. Her profile, its strong curves delineated by the light from beyond the French windows, pointed directly towards the old hooded fireplace in the corner of the room.

'Muazzez,' Yümniye began, 'I think that—'

'I made tulips. The tulip is an Ottoman bloom. Roses would have been unsuitable. If roses are involved it can't possibly be one of our gowns.'

'But—'

'No. No it isn't, Yümniye. Roses tell me that it can't be.' She put her cigarette out in her ashtray and lit another immediately. 'You forget these things. I don't. You know?'

Yümniye shrugged and laid the bodice of the gown back down onto the bag and then looked up at İkmen. 'Well, Çetin,' she said, 'I could have sworn it was one of ours, but if Muazzez thinks not . . .'

'My poor sister is afflicted in the same way as the General,' Muazzez said. 'She becomes easily confused.'

İkmen sighed. 'I see.' He looked at Yümniye and added, 'I'm very sorry, Miss Yümniye.'

She just smiled. The story of General Heper and his demise was well known. Some said that his condition had its genesis in the death of his second wife when Muazzez was just twelve, others that what he had witnessed during the First World War and the War of Independence had finally caught up with him. Others still said that his demented state was down to his genes. The fact of the matter was that sometime in the early 1950s General Heper developed a form of dementia which by 1960 resulted in his total removal from social life. He was looked after by his girls until his death in 1973. He received the best medication money could buy and through their talents with needles and sewing machines his daughters succeeded in buying the Heper house from their father's landlord. In this way they secured both their own and his future. Now, though, or so it would seem from what had just been said, things had taken a sad turn. With Muazzez blind and Yümniye apparently in the early stages of dementia, more money than they could possibly raise would be needed. The Hepers, after all, only had each other. İkmen suddenly felt bad for having bothered them. For although her demeanour was now settled, Miss Muazzez had not been pleased when her sister had disagreed with her about the roses on the gown. She had, quite literally, turned away from the subject. That they had, far more recently, made another gown in the Ottoman style that was covered with fabric roses was not a fact that İkmen felt comfortable mentioning.

'So can we know why you have an interest in the gown, Çetin?' Yümniye asked, breaking into İkmen's thoughts.

'It has some bearing on a case I'm working on,' he

replied as he gathered up the gown and replaced it in the bag.

'Oh, so it has some connection with Hikmet Sivas. His wife's disappearance.' Yümniye smiled excitedly. 'I saw you on the television, in the background. Some other officer spoke, but I knew it was you. I think it was some days ago or yesterday. Is that still going on?'

'But that dress can't have anything to do with that, can it?' Muazzez snapped, turning away once again. 'That woman is American. She wouldn't be wearing an Ottoman gown.'

'Ah, yes, but if Çetin knows certain things about it that we do not . . .'

'Actually you are correct, Miss Muazzez,' İkmen said and smiled across at her. 'This dress is not part of that investigation.' He paused for only a second before continuing, a second during which he considered whether he should tell them, or rather Muazzez, the truth. He decided that he would. 'A young girl we think may have become involved in a prostitution racket was wearing it when she died.'

'Really?'

'Yes.'

'How terrible.'

But İkmen couldn't see Muazzez's expression. She had twisted round almost completely in her chair, and her face was now entirely hidden from his gaze. As Yümniye prattled on, irritatingly now, about what an awful place the city had become and how scandalous it was that young women were still so vulnerable to such evil practices, he knew that Muazzez could feel the heat from his eyes on the back of her thick, short hair. When he was a child it had always been Muazzez who had commented on his cleverness; she'd thought it amusing then. İkmen had read from an English poetry book in this very room once when he was only four. Even then his voice had been unusually deep and sonorous and Muazzez had rewarded him with the most delicious chocolate he had ever tasted. It had come, she told him, from Paris. He'd been enormously impressed. Now, however, his presence seemed to be unnerving her. Or rather the subject of his inquiry – the provenance of Hatice İpek's rose-covered gown. He wondered why she had been so vehement about denying her and her sister's involvement in its production. But, amazingly, he felt sure that mention of the dress's latest adventures had shocked her. And in view of the fact that neither of these women shrank from unpleasant words or concepts he could only deduce that something about the connection between the dress and prostitution had caused Muazzez to turn so completely from him. Perhaps as that filthy animal, the Sultanahmet Rat, had told him, the Heper sisters did indeed know something.

'Are you absolutely certain that you didn't make this dress?' İkmen said, addressing his question to both women. 'There is neither shame nor crime in producing gowns for working women.'

'Well, I mean—'

'Yümniye, we have never made anything with roses! Roses are common, they can be made by anyone!' Her face, which was white, was turned back towards them again. Just one small tear stood in the corner of her left eye. 'I've told you that we know nothing about this gown, Çetin, and we don't.'

In the short silence that then occurred, İkmen finished his tea and lit a cigarette. And after that conversation of a polite and general nature ensued until he finally left about half an hour later.

Troubled and also confused, his feet dragged as he made his way back to where he'd left his car in the street behind the property. Surely the Heper sisters couldn't have anything to do with those who had assaulted Hatice? But if they didn't, why had Muazzez been so keen to distance herself and her sister from the gown? Even more confusingly, why had she given him a reason to tell her about Hatice anyway? She could have just let Yümniye prattle on about his involvement with Hikmet Sivas and left it at that, couldn't she?

As he walked down the weed-choked pathway that ran along the side of the Hepers' garden, İkmen looked back up at the house. Yümniye and Muazzez were shouting at each other in front of the closed French windows. And the red-haired woman he'd seen earlier, watching him intently from the Hepers' gate, was still there, her eyes trained unswervingly on his face.

With the setting of the raging summer sun came customers. Although moderately busy during the day, the pastane really came into its own in the evening. Local revellers, tourists and weary business people popping in for a refreshing glass of iced tea or even a sinfully sticky pastry made up the bulk of the business, which was considerable in the summer months. But then if it hadn't been, the Müren family would never have so much as looked at Hassan and his profits. Suzan Şeker glanced anxiously at the door to her husband's office and then turned with a smile towards her customer.

'Good evening, sir. What can I get you?'

'I'll have an iced tea and a glass of water.' The man was good-looking in the way that a professional person, perhaps a lawyer, might be.

Suzan wrote his order down on her pad. 'Very good.'

'Thank you.' He turned his fine head and his attention back to the newspaper he had been reading.

As she replaced her pad in the pocket of her apron, Suzan wondered idly whether this 'lawyer' sulked and sought attention from his wife in the same way that Hassan did from her. He'd been locked in that office for hours now, alone and silent. She'd been in briefly at lunchtime, but she'd heard him turn the key in the lock so she'd kept away. Hassan did such things when he was upset and he was, it had to be admitted, miserable at the moment. But to expect his wife to comfort him for the loss of his mistress was too much. Suzan was happy to keep away from him and willing to do the work of both of them, but she wouldn't show him any sort of affection until this mood was out of his system. If he wanted to stay in his office all night that was all right with her.

Suzan was about to make her way over to the counter to fulfil her various orders when the explosion happened. Or at least that was what she thought it was, though it neither knocked her from her feet nor damaged any of the customers. Their faces, however, were filled with the fear that she also felt at the huge booming sound that had come from Hassan's office.

'Is this your place?' The good-looking lawyer man was on his feet, one hand curled tightly round Suzan's wrist.

'No, it's my husband's, he—'

'Who's in that room?' he hissed. Several of the other customers had also risen to their feet.

'Well, just my husband,' Suzan replied.

'Please stay where you are,' he commanded, his gaze scanning the pastane. 'I am a police officer.'

'But—'

'If you'd all please go to the front of the building.' He waved them away from the partition behind which was the room where the explosion had come from. A strange burnt sort of smell was now emerging from it.

'What's going on?' Suzan asked as she assisted him in ushering the customers forward.

'I don't know,' he said. 'But keep them away. I'm going to take a look.' Then he reached inside his jacket and drew out a pistol.

Suzan, shocked, slapped a hand across her mouth.

'Is your husband alone?' he asked as he made his way up past the partition and towards the office door.

'Yes, um, but the door is . . . it's locked.'

'OK.'

Now standing to one side of the door, he motioned for Suzan to join her customers at the front of the building.

'No!' she said. 'It's my husband . . .'

Inspector Mehmet Suleyman pushed her roughly back behind the flimsy partition and then with a sharp twist of his body he kicked the door in. The wood splintered easily under his foot and the full force of that smell he'd noticed just after the explosion hit him. Smoky and faintly acidic, he knew it had little to do with the overflowing ashtray which stood beside the outflung bloodied arm upon the desk. Somewhere, there had to be a firearm.

'Is he all right?' The woman's voice was tight with anxiety. 'Can—'

'Stay where you are!' Suleyman commanded. 'Keep away!'

Of course she would have to see her husband at some point. Or rather what remained of him. The gun had been fired directly underneath his chin. The result was that part of his skull and most of his brains had hit the wall behind. Suleyman, feeling slightly sick now, looked down at the ground where, sure enough, a shotgun lay beneath the man's desk. It wasn't exactly what he had been expecting when he called in here for a cool drink. Had Çetin İkmen been at home when he called in there he wouldn't even be here now. He took his mobile telephone out of his pocket and punched in a number. As he waited for the thing to start ringing, he noticed a large envelope on the desk in front of the ashtray. It had just one word written on it: 'Police'.

'I'm not saying that Talaat should necessarily come to stay with us,' Fatma said. 'What I am saying is that he should come back to İstanbul. He'll get better treatment at home.'

'Yes. Possibly.' İkmen pushed the telephone receiver hard into the side of his head and then held it in place with his shoulder. He lit a cigarette.

'Well, definitely, or so Talaat's doctor has told him,' the disembodied voice of his wife replied.

İkmen exhaled smoke. He knew exactly where this conversation was going, as did Fatma.

'Yes, but he'll have to stay somewhere when he arrives, won't he?' İkmen said tetchily. 'And forgive me, Fatma, but I just can't see him living with either of your sisters.'

'Well . . .'

'Nilüfer has even more young children than we do and I don't think that Sibel's cleanliness rituals could accommodate a middle-aged man with cancer, do you?'

'My brother does have money, you know!' Fatma said, launching into familiar attack mode. 'He would only need to be with us until he found an apartment of his own.'

'Which I and my sons would have to help him move

into. And which you would visit on a daily basis to see how he was.'

'Talaat is my brother and he's in trouble!'

İkmen slumped down onto the chair beside the telephone table. To be fair, Fatma hadn't called him at the most opportune time. The phone had started ringing as he was opening the door to the apartment, tired and disgruntled after a day of severed heads, Ardiç and the strange and impenetrable doings of the Heper sisters. The last thing he needed right now was the prospect of his brother-in-law coming to stay. The man talked about nothing but beach life, water sports and stupid foreign girlfriends half his age. Though he probably didn't talk about such things now. Ever since February when the pain in his gut had finally been diagnosed as cancer of the colon, Talaat had been much more preoccupied with life-threatening surgery and drugs that made his hair fall out. Poor man. İkmen now felt bad about his lack of generosity and so he did what he always did with Fatma and capitulated gracelessly.

'Well, if the doctor feels it's better for Talaat . . .'

'It'll take us a few days to settle Talaat's business affairs here,' Fatma said in the businesslike fashion she tended to adopt when she'd just won an argument with her husband. 'Haldun has already said that he'll take over the running of the apartments until Talaat is well enough to return.'

'Right.'

Of course it had all been decided before she'd rung.

'So where is he going to sleep?' İkmen asked. 'This place is like a stuffed vine leaf.'

'Talaat can have Bülent's room,' Fatma replied. 'He can move back in with his brothers.'

İkmen's head started to pound. Bülent's shrine to Galatasaray football club was not a room that could be easily disassembled – at least not without a fight. 'Well, you can tell him, Fatma,' he said wearily. 'He waited years to get into that room.'

'Yes, which he'll have to leave soon when he goes into the army.'

'Yes.'

'But if you want me to tell him, then I will. I'm sure that when he hears he's giving it up to poor Uncle Talaat, he'll be only too pleased to do so.'

İkmen, through gritted teeth and cigarette, said, 'Well, let's hope so.'

After that, Fatma wisely moved the conversation on to less contentious territory. They talked about their children, moaned about rising prices and finally spoke briefly about how they missed one another. At this point İkmen called a halt to the conversation. Fatma, for all her forcefulness, sometimes cried at this juncture and he, selfishly he knew, couldn't bear to hear her.

He'd just replaced the telephone receiver when the front door opened and Hulya entered the apartment. İkmen looked at his watch.

'You're early,' he said, frowning. 'I'd have come to get you.'

'Hassan Bey is dead,' she said.

'Dead?' Belatedly İkmen noticed how strained she looked.

'Mehmet has closed the pastane. He was there, having a drink.'

İkmen walked over to Hulya and took one of her hands in his. It was ice cold. He led her though into the living room and then sat her down on one of the divans. Despite the still cloying evening heat, he placed a blanket over her knees and then lowered himself down beside her.

'Mehmet?'

'Suleyman,' she replied. 'He came in for a drink when it happened. I was in the kitchen. There was a shot.'

She told him how Mehmet Suleyman had broken into Hassan Bey's office and found his body, and how Suzan Şeker had, against advice, looked through the office door and screamed like a maniac when she'd seen what was in there.

'Uncle Arto had just arrived as I was leaving,' she said, referring to Dr Sarkissian. 'So I guess if Uncle Arto has been called and Hassan Bey was shot he must have been murdered.'

'I don't know, Hulya,' İkmen said as he pulled her small, cold body in close to his own. In truth, he was beginning to feel slightly chilled himself. Who would want to kill Hassan Şeker? Or had he shot himself? Either way, why?

Rather than go home when he left Hikmet Sivas's Kandıllı mansion, Orhan Tepe went to Ayşe Farsakoğlu's apartment on İnönü Caddesi. He telephoned ahead to tell her he was coming and then waited outside her building in his car. Ayşe's brother Ali, with whom she shared the apartment, was not certain of Tepe's status in his sister's life, but he had in the past made it very clear that he both disliked and disapproved of her 'colleague'. And since Ali was indeed at home at the present time, Tepe's decision not to see him was probably for the best.

When he'd phoned her, Tepe had asked Ayşe to wear something special for their date. Where they were going people only wore good clothes and ate good food. For once, he had enough cash and access to more should he need it later. It was nice to be in control, of his money and entertainment like this, he thought. And as he saw her walk purposefully towards the car, her long dark hair swinging provocatively across her naked shoulders, he hid the rather more troubling thoughts that lay at the back of his good fortune behind a winning smile.

Although her dress was revealing at the top, the red circular skirt covered the length of her fine legs. It was something that she wore often, but he liked it. As she got into the car she had to gather up the full material and pull it inside lest it catch in the door.

'So where are we going?' she asked as she finally shut the car door and turned towards him.

'Well, I thought we'd start with a meal at Rejans,' he said, slipping the car into gear and moving off into the stream of traffic.

'Rejans!'

As well as being expensive, Rejans Restaurant is one of the oldest in İstanbul. Established in the 1920s by White Russian émigrés, it has been favoured by the city's elite for many years. It is and was not the sort of place where an ordinary policeman and his mistress might be found – unless of course that policeman happened to be Mehmet Suleyman. Ayşe Farsakoğlu, only too aware of this, said, 'But what about Suleyman? What if—'

'His wife is still in hospital,' her lover replied, smiling. 'He won't be there. His family might be, but we don't know each other.'

'But it's so expensive!'

'Think of it as an early birthday gift,' he said, turning back up towards Taksim and then on to Galatasaray.

'You said we were going out to Tarabya.'

He shrugged. 'We can still do that. After all, my wife and her family are no more likely to be in Rejans than in Tarabya.'

'But the money! How . . .'

'I just reorganised my finances.' He laughed. 'It was easy enough.' He looked across at her, feeling as he did so that familiar rush of passion to his loins that she so often evoked in him. 'I wanted to please you.'

She smiled. 'Well, you have.'

'Good.' He turned his attention back to the road. After a short silence he said, 'And then afterwards we can go to the apartment. I've told Aysel I'm working tonight. We can fuck until morning. Get in practice for how it will be when we're married,' he said with a smile.

'We will be married, won't we, Orhan?' she said, happy but still touched with anxiety. 'You mean it?'

'Yes, I've told you before. I want a woman, not a child.' He looked across at her again. 'Someone who likes sex as much as I do.' He paused. Still looking at her. 'Did Suleyman like sex as much as I do?'

She turned away, stung by his question. 'Orhan!'

'Well?'

'I, I don't . . .' she stammered, both embarrassed and hurt by his question about a man she still had feelings for.

'Not as big as me, though, is he?' Orhan said. 'Not many men are.' He took one of her hands in his and pushed it down onto his crotch. Just thinking about it had made a large organ even bigger. 'When we're married that will be yours whenever you want it,' he said. 'But tonight we'll eat at Rejans and drink champagne. Then I'll make love to you. You can be my odalisque, if you like.' He laughed again. 'Pleasuring your very grateful Sultan – your husband to be!'

His words and the feel of him under her hand inflamed her. With trembling, eager fingers she unzipped his fly and then took him in her hand.

'Oh, that's good,' he said, as she moved her hand up and down the shaft of his penis.

'You do love me, don't you, Orhan?' she asked as he quickly drove the car into a deserted side street.

'Yes,' he answered thickly. He turned the engine off and reached across to massage her breasts. 'Sorry, Ayşe, I can't wait.'

'And we will be married?'

'Yes, we will,' he gasped. 'I promise. Your mouth, quickly.'

Ayşe lowered her head and Orhan dug his fingers hard into the back of her neck as he climaxed. This hurt Ayşe but she didn't mind. It was just another demonstration of how much he needed her.

And later, at the restaurant, he showed that he loved her in another way, with beautiful gifts and a meal she calculated cost him a week's salary. He counted the banknotes out in front of her so that she could see how much he cared.

They left Rejans at ten and he took her to Pertevpaşa Sokak, which was just a few minutes' walk from the apartment. It was unwise for them to be seen entering the place together and so she agreed to walk from there.

Ayşe Farsakoğlu liked the dress she was wearing. It flattered both her tan and her large, full breasts and she knew it. Ostensibly for Orhan Tepe's benefit, this dress had originally been purchased with the intention of pursuing Mehmet

Suleyman again – she'd even worn it to his wedding. But it had had no effect. The proud Ottoman had married his doctor and now he had a child and there was an end to it, except of course in Ayşe's head. When she had sex with Orhan, even when he talked of marriage as he had done earlier, she usually fantasised about Mehmet. Later, in Orhan's brother's apartment, she'd make him fuck her while she wore the dress. Just thinking about it made her hasten to get to the apartment in Çemberlitaş.

She was just crossing from Pertevpaşa Sokak onto Piyerloti Caddesi when the distinctive sound of an appreciative male hiss reached her ears. Looking as she did, it was not the first time she had provoked such a reaction. And usually she just ignored whatever was hissed or said to her. But on this occasion, possibly because she was feeling so very sexual, after a short tantalising pause she looked round to see who was appreciating her. Unfortunately the men involved were not to her taste. But they were known to her.

Celal Müren, though little more than a child, was an unpleasant individual. He'd spent more time than she suspected he had liked in police custody. On one occasion she had actually arrested him herself – for brawling. And although none of the offences he'd committed were serious in themselves, Ayşe knew that it was only a question of time before he did something really big. After all, with an elder brother like Ekrem, who was standing, smirking, next to him, it was almost a foregone conclusion. Ekrem Müren, like his father, was a gangster. And like his father, Ekrem didn't just confine himself to one kind of illegal trade. During the course of his short life he had been implicated in prostitution and protection rackets, drugs and, it was rumoured, contract killing.

Celal, whose tongue was now literally lolling from his mouth, didn't recognise Ayşe, which was really quite delicious. Everyone knew what the Müren family were even if little could be proved against them – dead people don't give evidence – and so it would be nice to shock Celal and Ekrem just a little. Ayşe Farsakoğlu walked over to them, her long legs now moving casually in lazy, provocative strides. As she came to a halt in front of them, Ekrem ran a hand through his thick waxed hair, licking his lips in appreciation of her.

Smiling, she turned her attention on Ekrem's brother. 'Hello, Celal,' she said. 'I haven't seen you for quite a while. What have you been doing?'

Taken entirely by surprise, Celal just stared.

Ekrem moved forward, in front of his brother. His eyes were level with the top of Ayşe's breasts. He put his hands out towards them, his fingers stopping just short of actually touching.

'And how does a beautiful bird like you know my brother?' he said. 'He's just a boy.'

'Oh, I arrested your brother last year,' Ayşe said, enjoying the sight of the blood running out of Ekrem Müren's face.

'*You* are a policewoman?'

'Yes, that's right, Mr Müren,' a deeper, male voice answered.

Ayşe Farsakoğlu turned and saw Orhan Tepe standing behind her. His face, even through the darkness, looked flushed with fury.

'She's a sergeant,' he continued, his eyes fixed on Ekrem Müren's hands which were now moving quickly away from Ayşe's breasts.

Celal Müren looked at his brother with fearful eyes. 'I

don't remember her,' he said. 'I would have remembered her, Ekrem.'

'Shut up.'

'On your way,' Tepe said coldly and then added, 'boys.'

'We weren't doing anything, *officer* . . .'

'No, but you're scum,' Tepe said and waved the brothers away from the perfumed orbit of his lover.

With one sideways smirk which Ekrem shot at Tepe, the brothers moved off in the direction of the main Okçularbaşı Caddesi. Returning, or so Farsakoğlu at least felt, to their father's apartment in Beyazıt, the family's base.

When they had gone she looked at Tepe, a smile breaking across her face.

'Did you come back to follow me, Orhan?' she said, pleased at the prospect.

'No.' But he looked away from her as he said it.

As a rule they didn't meet in the street. He approached his brother's apartment, or wherever they had agreed to meet, via one route and she via another. It had always been that way. Meetings outdoors could be dangerous – Orhan's wife had many friends and relations – and they, or rather Orhan, always wanted to avoid that eventuality. That they had now come across each other just when she had decided to have a little fun with the Müren brothers was unusual and, Ayşe felt, extremely amusing too. If he had indeed followed her, perhaps he was jealous.

'The Mürens are dangerous,' he said as they began to walk. 'You should keep away from them.'

'I arrested Celal last year,' she said. 'He's a nasty boy, I admit, but—'

'Keep away from them!' He turned quickly and grabbed the tops of her arms.

'Orhan!'

'They're scum and I won't have scum looking at you like that!'

'But Orhan, I was only having a joke with them.'

'Well, it wasn't very funny,' he said through his teeth. 'And you will not do anything like that again, not with any man.' And then, taking one of her hands in his, he pulled her towards him so that his face was level with hers.

'Get in the car. I don't care who sees us tonight. I want you now. I have everything you'll ever need.'

And although she had felt passion for Orhan before, this time it was overwhelming, this time it blanked out Mehmet Suleyman from her mind completely.

Chapter 13

'It was definitely suicide.'

İkmen looked his old friend hard in the eyes, not because he disbelieved him, but because he wanted to make sure that Arto himself harboured absolutely no doubts.

'Not just because of the note that he left,' Arto continued. 'Everything about the scene, not least the fact that the room possesses only one entrance, tells me that suicide has to be the only explanation.'

Mehmet Suleyman sighed. Because he had been the one who had actually found Şeker's body the previous evening, he had joined their early morning conference.

'But if he did, as the note says, kill Hatice İpek,' he said, 'then—'

'Nobody actually killed the girl,' İkmen cut in quickly. 'She died during or just after sex acts were performed on her by several men.'

'One of the chambers of her heart became blocked. Her death was entirely natural,' Arto added.

'Which means that, when Şeker took responsibility for her death in his note, he had to be lying,' İkmen said.

'Or else he just felt responsible because he was one of the men who assaulted her,' Arto offered. 'I mean, was he ever told that her death was natural?'

İkmen shrugged. 'I don't know. I told my daughter and the girl's mother of course, but unless they told him . . .'

'We never did get a semen sample from him when he was alive, did we?' Arto said. 'Perhaps he was afraid of that after all. Time will tell.'

They all passed several minutes in silence, the doctor, the two inspectors and the young constable, Yıldız, who had been first on the scene to assist Suleyman the previous evening. İkmen particularly was troubled. In view of the note Şeker had left admitting to having been responsible for Hatice's death, there was now no hope at all that Ardiç would allow any further work to be carried out on the İpek case. And yet İkmen was still very unsure. Not just because Hassan Şeker, for all his faults, didn't seem to be that kind of man, but also because he had no reason at all to do this. More than one person had seen him go home that night, after Hatice had left.

'Of course there could be another explanation for his death,' said Yıldız, who had been quietly smoking in the corner.

They all turned to look at him.

'And what's that Constable?' İkmen asked, frowning.

'Well, there was some sort of connection with the Müren brothers.'

'Celal and Ekrem Müren?'

'Yes.'

İkmen blanched. 'But they're family, Yıldız! What do you mean, a connection?'

Yıldız shrugged. 'I don't rightly know, sir,' he said innocently. 'All I do know is that when we went to the pastane the second time, the Mürens and some other lad were talking to Mrs Şeker in a rather, well, serious fashion. I mean, Mrs Şeker didn't look happy. She looked across at her husband's office door sort of furtively before she spoke to them, like she wanted them to go away quickly. Sergeant Tepe was in there with Mr Şeker.'

'Why didn't you tell me this before?' İkmen yelled. 'If the Mürens wanted Şeker then money must have been involved.'

'Or drugs or prostitution or contract killing,' Suleyman added, completing the set of likely Müren family crimes.

'Absolutely.' İkmen turned back to Yıldız. 'Well?'

The young man looked down at the floor before speaking, 'Sergeant Tepe told me to forget it, sir, the Müren thing.'

All three of the other men in the room exchanged glances before İkmen looked back at Yıldız and asked, 'Why?'

'Because he said it wasn't important,' Yıldız said.

'Oh, did he?'

'Yes.'

Before anything else could be discussed, the door to İkmen's office opened and Orhan Tepe stepped over the threshold. Although rather tired-looking around the eyes, he was nevertheless smiling. İkmen could see instantly that he hadn't been home to change his clothes. He'd obviously slept elsewhere, hence the smile on his face. It wouldn't take İkmen long to wipe that off.

He waited until the doctor, Suleyman and Yıldız had left before he began.

'Why didn't you tell me that Hassan Şeker was mixed up with the Müren brothers?' İkmen said in the controlled tone he always used prior to exploding.

Tepe smiled. 'Because he's not,' he said calmly. 'Who says—'

'Hikmet Yıldız has just told me what happened when you visited the pastane for the second time, Tepe,' İkmen said.

'About how he saw the Mürens talking to a fearful looking Mrs Şeker.'

'Well, I didn't.'

'I don't care whether you saw it or not!' İkmen roared. 'When Yıldız told you what he had seen, it should have set off sirens in your head!'

'I—'

'What possessed you to tell the boy that seeing the Mürens at the scene was unimportant? Family are always important! If you paid as much attention to your work as you do to your sex life . . .'

'Sir!'

'Oh, don't get offended with me!' İkmen growled. 'Don't—'

He was interrupted by his telephone. İkmen pointed Tepe towards his own desk. 'Don't go anywhere,' he said. 'I haven't finished with you.'

He picked up the receiver. 'İkmen.'

'It's İskender.' The voice at the other end of the line sounded uncharacteristically nervous.

İkmen's eyes were still disapprovingly on Tepe. 'Yes?' he said into the phone.

'Vedat Sivas has gone missing.'

İkmen sat down, his face white. 'Tell me this is a joke, İskender,' he said softly.

'It isn't. I wish it were. Men disappearing without trace, gruesome boxes appearing from nowhere – am I going fucking mad or—'

'Look, try and hold yourself together until I get there,' İkmen said, interpreting İskender's uncharacteristic use of swear words as well as the obvious nervousness in his voice as signals to get over to the Sivas house very quickly. 'Does Ardiç know?'

'No.' İskender sighed. 'He stayed here until after midnight last night. I don't suppose he's in yet, is he?'

'Not yet,' İkmen said as he cast a nervous eye towards the door lest his superior be lurking somewhere outside. 'I presume you have Miss Hale Sivas with you.'

'Yes. Yes, I haven't managed to lose her yet,' İskender replied wearily.

'Well, just keep hold of her until I get there.' İkmen grabbed his jacket from the back of his chair and started to put it on. 'She doesn't even get to go to the toilet on her own, do you understand?'

'Yes.'

'I'm on my way,' İkmen said and then without another word he replaced the receiver and threw a set of car keys across to Tepe. After all the shocks he'd had in the last twelve hours, he felt driving was far too stressful for his nerves. 'You drive,' he said. 'To the Sivas place.'

Tepe stood, 'But sir . . .'

'Oh, don't worry that I've finished berating you, Orhan.' İkmen checked his pockets for smoking requisites. 'I'll carry on when we get in the car.'

'Sir . . .'

'You drive, I'll shout, but when we get to the Sivas place we act like professionals. Apparently Vedat has gone missing too, Allah alone knows where.'

'Vedat Sivas? The brother?'

'Yes, Tepe.' İkmen shook his head in disbelief. 'First Hikmet, now Vedat . . . All this on top of Hassan Şeker.'

Tepe frowned. 'Hassan Şeker? What do you mean?'

There hadn't been time to tell Tepe why Suleyman, Yıldız and the doctor had been in his office that morning. İkmen had intended to tell him when he was interrupted by İskender's call. After all Şeker's death was entirely germane to the argument he had put forward to Tepe regarding the Müren brothers. Had he known of their involvement he could have got them off the street and away from Şeker, which might have prevented their leaning on him for money or whatever else had caused Şeker to end his life. It occurred to İkmen that Hassan Şeker may have killed himself and left that incriminating note in order to remove all suspicion of family involvement in Hatice's death, because of threats against his wife and children. Nasty and violent as they were, Ekrem and Celal Müren were hardly godfathers; that honour belonged to their father, Ali. But they could certainly frighten someone like Hassan Şeker, and bugger little Hatice İpek. Once he'd dealt with İskender's latest incompetence, İkmen intended to go looking for them.

'Hassan Şeker is dead,' he told Tepe baldly. 'He committed suicide yesterday evening. And before we leave here I'm going to ask Inspector Suleyman to speak to the widow about the Müren brothers.'

Tepe's face drained of all colour and İkmen noticed that his hands had started to shake.

Although large, Hikmet Sivas's Kandıllı mansion didn't possess any exits that couldn't be easily observed. The front door had been under guard ever since the police had gone to the house with the movie star in the wake of Kaycee's abduction. Men had been stationed in both the house and the garden day and night. And although the back of the property faced directly onto the Bosphorus, neither the boathouse beneath the yalı or indeed the craft within it had been roused from their dust-encrusted torpor for some long time. Unless Hikmet and Vedat had swum away . . .

'A person would have to know this bit of Bosphorus very well,' İsak Çöktin observed when İkmen put this possibility to him. 'As I understand it, it's easy to get pulled all over the place even in a boat. The currents are complex and very dangerous. If one or both of the men swam out, even close to the shore, they're probably dead by now.'

'You observed nothing untoward during the night?' İkmen asked as he sat down in one of the richly upholstered chairs that commanded stunning views of the Bosphorus. The water lapped and gurgled underneath the open window before him.

'No. Even the commissioner was here until one o'clock.'

'Mmm.' İkmen looked across at the face of the elderly woman sitting next to him and sighed. 'Well, Miss Sivas,' he said, 'it would seem that your brothers have disappeared via magical means.'

Hale Sivas leaned her weary head back and then closed her eyes. 'Such things are possible,' she said. 'As I know you know.'

İkmen frowned. 'What do you mean?'

'I was born in Haydarpaşa district,' Hale said, opening her eyes which she trained upon İkmen with great intensity. 'Close enough to Üsküdar for me to have knowledge of the witch Ayşe İkmen.'

'Yes.' İkmen nodded. 'Sad, isn't it, that even with such a famous woman for a mother I am still a poor man. But with all due respect to my mother, I don't believe your brothers just melted through the walls of this yalı, Miss Sivas.'

'No?'

'No. I think that they left via a method we don't as yet understand. I think also,' he paused briefly in order to light a cigarette, 'that you know more about their motives for doing so than you are telling us.'

'What do you mean?'

İkmen looked up at Çöktin, indicating that he wanted him to leave them alone. When the Kurd had gone, İkmen said, 'Your brother's wife was not abducted and murdered for no reason. The appearance of her head in this house tells me that someone was sending a message to your brother Hikmet, a threat or a warning.'

'An American,' Hale said firmly, her lips pursed in disgust around the word.

'Possibly.'

'I know nothing of Hikmet's life in America.'

'Oh? When I was here before you appeared to know quite a lot about how he runs around with women and works for Jews.' She turned her eyes away from him and so İkmen moved on to another tack. 'You know about your brother Vedat's life, though, don't you?'

She shrugged. 'Vedat works at hotels, palaces. We live here together.'

'And very comfortably too,' İkmen said as he looked around the large, tasteful salon approvingly.

'We are family. I have never married. Hikmet loves us.'

'I'm sure he does,' İkmen replied with a smile. 'Which is why it strikes me as somewhat odd that Vedat still lives the life of a poor man.'

'He doesn't,' she snapped.

'What I mean is, he's widowed but has not remarried, and he works in humble employment.'

'He chooses to.'

İkmen flicked the ash from his cigarette into an ashtray made of solid gold. 'Yes. Although of course none of this explains why Vedat, according to the young officer who was at the scene when your sister-in-law was taken, was so very anxious for Hikmet not to involve us in the crime. Why was that?'

Hale Sivas' face didn't show any sort of emotion as she shrugged once again. 'Vedat, like everyone, doesn't trust the police.'

'Is that so?' İkmen smiled and rose to his feet. 'You know, criminals are always saying that to me. Isn't it odd?' He straightened up and moved towards the centre of the room. 'But maybe you're wrong about Vedat. After all, he isn't a criminal, is he? Nevertheless, neither Inspector İskender nor myself got the impression that either of your brothers was telling the whole truth when we spoke to them.'

And then without another word he left the salon and made his way into the large, airy entrance hall. Metin İskender, his eyes red from lack of sleep, was leaning against a kilim which hung on one of the rose-coloured walls.

'I just needed a moment,' he said as İkmen approached. 'Can't seem to sleep when I'm here at night.'

The sound of many people exploring many rooms floated to them from every part of the building.

'Nothing unusual as yet?' İkmen asked after he had stubbed his cigarette out in the golden ashtray he had carried with him from the salon.

'No. But we're working on it. Some in a rather more fanciful way than others.'

'What do you mean?' İkmen asked.

'Hikmet Yıldız is convinced there's a secret passage somewhere in the house. He keeps tapping the walls.'

'He may well have a point,' İkmen said with a shrug. 'It could explain how a large box materialised in an upstairs bedroom and how two grown men disappeared without trace.'

'Well, yes, but we're not exploring the interior of a Rhineland castle here.' İskender wiped the sweat that had gathered on his forehead with the back of his hand. 'You've spoken to Miss Hale?'

İkmen lit up another cigarette. 'For all the good it did me. By the way, why haven't we got a female officer on site? We should have.'

'Farsakoğlu was due to relieve Gün at eight,' İskender replied, 'but she's sick.'

'Oh?' Tepe, or so it had appeared to İkmen, had been somewhere he shouldn't last night. Could it be the lady was 'recovering'?

İskender shrugged. 'That's all I know,' he said. 'I hear that confectioner you persisted in pursuing killed himself yesterday.'

Angered both by the implication that he bore some responsibility for Hassan Şeker's death and by İskender's casual attitude towards it, İkmen said, 'Yes, he did, Metin. But I don't think it had anything to do with me. I would tell you what my suspicions are with regard to that situation but since I'm not yet ready to have Commissioner Ardiç privy to my thoughts, I'll keep them to myself for the moment.'

'Çetin . . .'

'Well, somebody told Ardiç I was still making inquiries about Hatice İpek's death!'

'And you think I did?' İskender shook his head in disbelief and lit one of his own cigarettes before answering. 'Now look, Çetin, whilst acknowledging that you and I are very different men, I think that we concur in the professional respect we have for each other. I don't like you as a person, I could never be your friend, but I have to respect the decisions you make in a case that I am not involved with and have no knowledge of. We've all been in the position you are in at one time or another.'

İkmen frowned.

'You wanted to continue your investigation,' İskender said and then lowering his voice he went on, 'Ardiç who is so very far from the ground and, let us face it, knows so little takes you away. Of course I guessed what you were doing. But on my honour and with my hand metaphorically on the Koran, I swear to you that Ardiç did not learn what you were doing from my lips!'

In spite of İskender's rather pompous statement about how they were supposed to have professional respect for each other, İkmen believed him. He was ambitious, inclined to be headstrong and lacked charm, but Metin İskender was not known to be dishonest. His manner made him difficult to warm to, but that was all. İkmen had looked at him closely as he gave his little speech and he was sure that Metin was not dissembling. And so for once İkmen actually apologised, albeit very quickly and without waiting around for any sort of acknowledgement.

'I'm very sorry, Metin,' he said, 'I misjudged you,' and he walked towards the open front door of the yalı.

He went out into Hikmet Sivas's lush, green garden and stared at the large fountain which stood in the middle of the driveway. Adorned with poorly executed plaster swans, it was a very bad copy of the magnificent fountain which stands before the entrance to the Dolmabahçe Palace. Perhaps Hikmet Sivas possessed regal pretensions. İkmen smiled briefly at the thought. Art imitating life or, in view of Sivas's fantastic riches, life imitating art?

İkmen glanced up at the house and spotted movement near a window. It was Tepe busying himself in one of the bedrooms. İkmen could just see the greyness of his face, studded with those sealed-in eyes of his. In the normal course of events İkmen would have sent Tepe to question Mrs Şeker, but given his earlier omission with regard to the Mürens, İkmen didn't want him anywhere near the İpek case again. Mehmet Suleyman, although still officially on leave, had readily agreed to go and see the confectioner's wife. He must have spoken to her by now.

Ayşe knew that soon she was going to have to do something about her situation. The weather was hot and so lying naked on top of her bed, face down, very still, was quite a good idea. The fact that she had no choice but to do this was another matter.

How she'd got home from Orhan's brother's apartment was still a mystery. Oh, she knew Orhan had brought her, in his car. He'd helped her up the stairs to her apartment and had even, amazingly, managed to deliver her to her bedroom without waking Ali. What she couldn't remember was how she'd dealt with the pain.

It had all begun so well. As soon as they'd got to his brother's apartment he'd started kissing her passionately, telling her how much he loved her, caressing her body as he did so. She'd been so aroused that when he'd suggested they play a game, it had simply excited her further.

'Imagine we're in the cells,' he'd said, 'and you are my prisoner.'

He'd made her strip. He'd enjoyed watching her. Then he'd taken his handcuffs out of his pocket. She should have stopped it then, but she hadn't. She had let him put them on her wrists; it was exciting, kneeling between his legs, pleasuring him, cuffed. And when he'd come, he'd called her filthy names which, because they were playing a game, was perfectly permissible and, again, exciting.

But at some point things changed. It was all a blur now. He ordered her to tell him how good he was, which she did, and then, somehow, she was cuffed to the bed. She thought he was just simply going to enter her from behind, he'd done it before . . . But she should have known something different was about to happen.

'I'm going where Prince Mehmet has never been,' he'd said breathlessly. The pain as he'd pushed himself into her anus was excruciating. She'd begged him to stop, but he'd just carried on, hitting her on the head as he did so, gasping words into her ears. 'Tell me I'm better than him! Tell me I'm bigger!'

And she had. In pain and terrified, she had still done what he asked.

'Filthy whore!' he'd said when he'd finished. 'Tell me again!'

'You're fabulous,' she'd lied, 'the best lover in the world!'

'Better than Suleyman?'

'Yes!'

Then for a while there had been silence. Too frightened now to look round to see what he was doing, Ayşe just lay on the bed, panting with fear. Her real ordeal was yet to come.

'I do wish I could believe you,' he'd said and then his belt came down across her back. She'd screamed as the leather and the thick metal buckle bit into her flesh.

'Flaunting your body in front of that Müren scum!'

'No! Orhan, no!'

Eventually she had passed out for a few moments. And when she came round he had mercifully stopped hitting her. But her respite was short-lived. She could hear his breathing, rough and laboured, somewhere behind her. Slowly she turned her head to see what he was doing. Naked now, one knee on either side of her buttocks, Orhan Tepe was masturbating onto her bloodied back, his eyes intent upon and fascinated by her wounds. As soon as he had obtained relief, he toppled forward onto her and kissed her face and hair with passion and tenderness.

'I do love you, you know,' he'd said afterwards as he'd helped her gently back into her dress. 'I love you so much, I need to be inside your flesh. I need to fuck every part of you.'

There had to be something wrong with Orhan to make him say and do such things. What he'd put her through hadn't been a game. It was sadism. He'd always been a very hard and masculine lover who enjoyed taking and giving pleasure roughly, but she'd never, until now, considered him a beast. But that was what he was, and he was consumed with jealousy of Mehmet Suleyman. The two men could not be more different. Mehmet was in a different class altogether. Sophisticated, considerate and skilled as a lover, he knew that you didn't batter a woman to give her pleasure. That was why she thought about him all the time, yearned for just a smile or the occasional touch of his body as he brushed past her on the street or in one of the station corridors.

Hot and dehydrated, Ayşe reached over to the cupboard beside her bed for her bottle of water. As she did so her hand caught against something hard and sharp. Oh yes, the jewellery. Earrings and a matching bracelet, gold and diamonds. Orhan had given them to her at Rejans. Where he'd got the money from to buy them, she couldn't imagine. She picked up the bracelet and looked at it. She would have to give it back. She couldn't possibly keep anything of his, not after what he'd done. But that would mean having to see him alone again. Just the thought of it made her flesh tremble with fear.

More immediately, however, she would have to try to encourage her body to heal as quickly as possible. Tomorrow she would have to resume her duty. To do anything else would excite comment and may arouse suspicion. İkmen, if no one else, knew that she and Orhan had some sort of 'arrangement' and the last thing Ayşe wanted was for the inspector to turn up on her doorstep. How she would explain the blood to him she didn't know. As it was, she would have to wash her sheets and the clothes from the previous evening before Ali returned.

But that would have to happen later. For now all she could do was lie on her bed under her open window and pray that the tiny breeze from the Bosphorus soothed her bleeding wounds.

By the time the pastane re-opened for the evening, Hassan Şeker, who had blasted his own life away only the night before, was in his grave. His widow, despite the disapproval of her father-in-law, had gone straight from the graveside back to the pastane.

'I need the money,' she'd told Kemal Bey when he had tearfully croaked his displeasure at what he perceived as her lack of respect for his son. 'My husband spent so much of what we had keeping gangsters happy.'

Well, she had told Inspector Suleyman about the Mürens,

why not Kemal Bey? It wasn't as if he hadn't suspected. Hassan had tried to be one of the 'lads' with the thugs who terrified him, welcoming them in and gaily socialising with them. Suzan had already decided that things were going to proceed much more straightforwardly now that she was in charge of the business – much more, in truth, like the way Kemal Bey had run things. That was why she'd told Inspector Suleyman about the Mürens. Let them come and threaten a widow woman, she'd told him defiantly; I'll have nothing to do with them. Now, however, Suzan wasn't so sure she'd done the right thing.

Inspector Suleyman had been impressed. He had also been worried. The Müren family was controlled by a powerful crime sultan. They had, it was believed, connections to very frightening people in narcotics and racketeering. They would make trouble for Suzan and her children if they knew she had spoken to the police. And so he had told her that if either Ekrem or Celal came to see her, she was to be as pleasant as she could and say she would get some money to them soon. If they even let her speak and didn't just beat her. The boys, so Inspector Suleyman had said, were due a visit to his cells. Apparently Hulya's father Inspector İkmen had some business with them. He had been investigating that little slut Hatice İpek's death . . .

'Mrs Şeker?'

And here suddenly was Hulya İkmen, friend and cohort of the whore who had obsessed her husband. The girl looked very cool and pretty in her long blue cotton dress. All of Suzan's pent up anger spilled over.

'What do you want?' Suzan said, eyeing Hulya and the tall young man with her distrustfully across the confectionery display case.

'I didn't think that you'd be opening the pastane today,' Hulya began.

'Yes, well, you were wrong.' Suzan reached into the cabinet to get a chocolate éclair for the man sitting on his own at the front window.

Although Hulya was unnerved by both the lack of customers in the usually bustling pastane and by the widow Şeker's hostility, she went on, 'But you can't work alone, not—'

'I can do what I like!' Suzan's face was bright red now and the tendons in her neck pressed tightly against her flesh. Berekiah Cohen, alarmed by this fierce visage, placed a protective arm round Hulya's shoulders. Unfortunately this one small gesture of affection inflamed Suzan Şeker to breaking point.

'Get out of my pastane, Hulya İkmen!' she screamed. 'And take your latest conquest with you!'

'But Mrs Şeker—'

'You didn't waste any time taking up with another pair of trousers as soon as my Hassan had gone, did you!'

The man who was patiently waiting for his éclair over by the window cleared his throat in a very obvious manner. But Suzan only gave him the briefest of glances before she continued her tirade.

'You think I'm stupid?' she shouted into Hulya's shocked face. 'You think I believe that Hassan completely bypassed you when he gladly fucked every other young girl who ever worked in this place!'

'No, It's . . . that's not true!' Tears, more of anger than of misery, sprang into Hulya's eyes.

Suzan moved quickly round the counter and approached her, the éclair and the plate upon which it sat trembling in her hands. The man over by the window quickly folded up the newspaper he had been reading and left.

Before she had time to resist, Berekiah Cohen moved Hulya behind him and put his hand up to Suzan.

'Now, madam—'

The pastry caught him right between the eyes, chocolate and whipped cream dripped down his nose and onto the front of his shirt. Suzan Şeker, as if suddenly coming to her senses, put her hand over her mouth and burst into tears.

Hulya, not really knowing whether to go to her or help Berekiah clean himself up, moved forward with one hand outstretched. Suzan, however, refused this gesture.

'No!' Suzan cried and then ran weeping towards the back of the building. 'I'm so sorry!' She disappeared into the room where her husband had taken his life and closed the door.

Berekiah had by this time removed the éclair from his face and was cleaning his nose. He looked at Hulya. 'It has to be grief,' he said quietly. 'Mum said a few crazy things too when Yusuf became ill.'

'I didn't ever sleep with Mr Şeker, you know,' Hulya said as she passed him a stack of paper napkins from the top of the counter. 'You must believe me.'

Berekiah took the napkins from her and smiled through chocolate and cream. 'But of course I do,' he said, and then as if truly he lent Suzan's outburst absolutely no credence, he added, 'We'd better get this place cleaned up or she'll lose even more business.'

After glancing around to make sure no one new had entered the empty pastane, Hulya reached up and kissed him on the cheek.

Chapter 14

Although not entirely fruitless, the day had proved frustrating for those involved in trying to solve the riddle of how Hikmet and Vedat Sivas had left the yalı without being seen. Every room, every wardrobe, every outhouse and abandoned old 'oriental' lavatory had been pulled apart, investigated and in some cases turned upside down. But to no avail.

'There's nothing even a little odd about this house or any of the things in it,' İskender said as he wearily joined İkmen at one of the windows overlooking the now dark Bosphorus. From another part of the property the sound of anxious feet on stairs and floorboards was vaguely registered by the two exhausted men.

'Çöktin just called in from the palace,' İkmen said as he offered İskender one of his cigarettes. 'Vedat hasn't appeared.'

İskender took the cigarette with a nod of thanks. 'Did you expect him to?'

'No. But Çöktin and Avcı are going to stay and look around. Yıldız Palace is a big, dark and mysterious site. They are, apparently, getting the guided tour.'

'He was definitely supposed to be working at the palace tonight?' İskender asked.

'Yes, the hotel manager was adamant that Vedat Sivas

203

was not due to work at Cirağan again until next Tuesday. They were expecting him at Yıldız.'

'You don't think that Vedat himself, in his distress about recent events, just got confused?'

'It's possible,' İkmen said. 'Yıldız Palace Museum, Cirağan Palace Hotel – I can see where confusion could arise. But there's a chance that Vedat was lying in order to steer me away from Yıldız Palace because that is where he and possibly his brother had planned to be for some reason. A very clumsy deception, if that's what it was.'

A Bosphorus ferry, alive with lights, if not people, passed in front of the yalı, heading for the Kandıllı boarding point. Very few people would get on now that darkness had fallen. In all probability the ferry would just continue its journey up to the very brink of the Black Sea at Rumeli Kavaği, eerily free of human cargo.

İskender wiped away the sweat that clung to his face like a sickly mask in the humid night. 'I can't really see them meeting representatives from the Cosa Nostra in the grounds of Yıldız,' he said.

'Stranger things have happened,' İkmen replied and then as if the sound of running feet he'd been vaguely aware of for some time had suddenly increased in volume, he said, 'What is that noise?'

'It's Constable Yıldız,' İskender said wryly, 'still convinced this yalı hides secret passages, no doubt concealing a lot of Greek gold. He runs from room to room. The mystery is driving him insane, like the rest of us.'

'One brother we could lose through incompetence, but two?' İkmen shook his head. 'Even the stupidest constable surely couldn't be that useless, let alone someone as sharp as Çöktin.'

'I'm just grateful that Ardiç was called away to Ankara,' İskender responded darkly. 'Of course we'll have to face him eventually.'

'Yes.' İkmen stubbed out his cigarette and lit another. 'After I've faced the children I've been neglecting.' He smiled weakly as he looked at İskender. 'My wife is away looking after her sick brother and so I've been left with our two teenagers.'

İskender nodded. 'Ah.'

'I tremble to think what they might have done to the apartment,' İkmen said and turned to walk away from the window. 'Come on, let's go and tell Yıldız to give up for tonight. The thought of him running about like that is exhausting.'

They'd told her she could go home tomorrow. But it wasn't good enough. Mehmet had only been to see her once today and then only for five minutes. He'd been called back to duty – or so he said.

Zelfa knew that wasn't true. He had another woman – he had to. He was a good-looking and charming man. She, on the other hand, was fat, old and exhausted. Sometimes the detached psychiatrist in her would make a brief appearance through the many veils of depression that stifled her mind. But not for long. For most of the time now she was just like a stone, hardly noticing her baby, roused only to resentment, when Mehmet cuddled and soothed the infant.

It was the child that he wanted, that was obvious. And now that he had the child – a male, so beloved of these Turks – she was entirely redundant. He would throw her away in just the same way that her mother had thrown her father away all those many times when she ran off with boys half her age. The embarrassment as well as the hurt had damaged poor Babur. It had made him passive and under-confident. Zelfa didn't want to be like that.

She felt tears start in her eyes but she choked them back. No time for crying now, too much to do. She already had her coat on, over her nightdress. Apart from the slippers she looked quite normal. She wouldn't have to walk very far anyway. Just down the corridor and round to the front entrance. There were bound to be taxis on the street and at this time of night it wouldn't take that long to get home. And as soon as she was, she would confront Mehmet. She might even find him with another woman – in *her* house. People did such things, she knew.

Zelfa swung her legs down onto the floor and picked up her handbag. It still hurt to move. It was bound to so soon after surgery, but she suspected that she might have an infection too. It had been so very hot lately and besides, she didn't trust the antiseptic agents they used here. She didn't trust 'them' at all – apart from her father. She opened the door of her room and shuffled out into the corridor, a conspicuous foreigner wearing a huge winter coat. Looking first left and then right, she moved as quickly as she could down towards the entrance. She imagined that she looked rather like one of those staunch Allied prisoners of war in old British Second World War films. Big coat, head down, trying to get past the guards without being seen. Zelfa laughed, if silently, at the image. Well, at least she could speak the language!

Back in her room little Yusuf İzzeddin slept on, oblivious to the fact that his mother had deserted him.

* * *

'The thing is, sir,' Hikmet Yıldız said as he hunkered down beside the small glass structure, 'there's a well or a gap of some sort underneath this . . .' He struggled to find the right word and failed.

'It looks like a frame people sometimes grow plants under,' İkmen said with a frown. 'Not that I'm any expert.'

'Cellars sometimes have skylights like this,' İskender added.

Yıldız instantly became excited. 'Exactly!' he said. 'Exactly!'

Being outside in Hikmet Sivas's moonlit garden had not been İkmen's original plan. He had intended to tell Yıldız to go home and then take turns with İskender in getting some sleep themselves. But the boy had been so animated.

This frame or window he had discovered was on the eastern side of the yalı, attached to the building, just above ground level. And although it wasn't possible to see what was underneath the structure, it was obvious that there was some sort of void. What was also obvious, however, was that this hole was not going to be big enough to allow even the thinnest person, such as İkmen, access.

'So what is inside the building at this point?' İkmen asked slowly.

'Nothing.' Yıldız sighed. 'I've looked and looked. There's just a blank wall. Miss Sivas says there isn't a cellar. She doesn't know what this . . . thing is for.'

'And is this wall solid?' İkmen asked, knowing that anyone looking for secret passages was bound to have checked it out.

'No, but then there are lots of hollow walls in this yalı,' Yıldız replied. 'Back in the old days some paşa had those big panels put in, to make the place look more like a French castle or something so Miss Sivas said.'

'Miss Sivas seems to know quite a lot,' İkmen commented. 'So what is on the first floor?' He looked up at a darkened window nestling beneath the overhanging roof.

'That's Hikmet Sivas's bedroom,' Yıldız said.

'It's panelled, isn't it?'

'Yes, but there's a recess into the window. You have to open a set of doors to get to it,' Yıldız replied. 'It's a bit weird.'

'Let's go and have a look at it,' İkmen said.

Yıldız rose to his feet. 'But sir, it's upstairs.'

'I know that, Yıldız.'

İkmen, followed by İskender, was already on his way back inside. Yıldız ran to catch up with them.

'Back in Ottoman times servants used to sleep in cupboards like this,' İkmen said as he surveyed the small wooden cubicle, its plain glass window affording a wide view of the garden. 'The window would have been screened then, as opposed to curtained,' he smiled, 'Ottoman gentlemen being most particular about their privacy.'

İskender walked into the cupboard and looked around at the ornate doors and thick, green curtains, which were open.

'Doesn't appear to be used for anything now,' he said.

'No.'

'So why would they have taken the screens down then, sir?' Yıldız asked. 'Some of the other windows still have them.'

'Who knows? Maybe this set rotted away.' İkmen rubbed a hand against the side of one of the doors. 'They do sometimes. Or maybe they were removed for another, unknown, reason.'

They all stood in silence for a few moments. İkmen looked around intently, frowning.

'Although young Yıldız here is a little over-keen on the idea of secret passages,' he said after a pause, 'I do believe that he is only responding to something that resides in his blood and that we all share.'

İskender walked out of the cupboard and stood in front of the older man, looking confused. 'Inspector?'

'I don't know whether it's to do with this city or whether it's to do with being a Turk,' İkmen said. 'But when you, Inspector İskender, said that looking for secret passages was something rather more appropriate to Europe than here you were not entirely correct.'

'What do you mean?'

'This city is littered with underground passages,' he said. 'The Greeks before us tunnelled under the city to construct their cisterns.' His face momentarily darkened. 'Places where modern men hide young girls' bodies, in my all too recent experience. There are also cellars and tunnels of Turkish construction across the whole of the old city district. We were the first country ever to have an underground railway with our Tünel in Beyoğlu. As a friend of mine who comes from an old Ottoman family himself always says, the Ottomans liked their private lives to be walled. They were secretive, dark. Their sultans scuttled around the city in disguise at dead of night, picking up cheap women.' He smiled. 'And we are their descendants, Turks who still partly adhere to the secretive strictures of our ancestors and, of course, to the modesty required of our women by Islam.'

İskender, who had heard how İkmen could 'go off' when

either formulating a theory or tackling a problem, cleared his throat.

İkmen smiled. 'I expect you think I'm losing my mind.' He walked into the cupboard and looked first around the walls and then up at the ceiling. 'But the more I think about this . . . There is no reason to suppose that people living outside the old city didn't build tunnels too. There are underground constructions in Beyoğlu.'

'In Beyoğlu, yes,' İskender responded, 'and maybe even here too. But Inspector İkmen, we are on the first floor of a wooden building. Constable Yıldız has explained that there are cavities in the walls.'

'Yes. But what he hasn't explained or maybe even noticed is this.' İkmen showed his colleague the end of what looked like a curtain rope pull.

'It's for the curtains,' Yıldız began, 'it—'

'No, it isn't.' İkmen pointed up towards where the other end of what he was holding disappeared into a hole in the cupboard ceiling. 'Stand clear.'

'What are you doing?' İskender asked as he watched İkmen unravel the rope from its cleat on the wall.

'I'm going down into whatever lies beneath that skylight, I think,' İkmen said.

And sure enough, as soon as he had unravelled all of the rope, the bottom of the cupboard started to move slowly downwards.

'You see, this is a lift,' İkmen said as his head drew level with İskender's waist. 'It's primitive but it moves easily so it must have been oiled recently. I suspect the Sivas brothers may have done that.'

'You mean Hikmet and Vedat Sivas had this thing constructed?'

'I doubt it,' a muffled voice from a now invisible İkmen replied. 'It looks far too old for that. No, I think they probably found it . . . It's very dark . . .'

'Do you have a torch, sir?' Yıldız asked anxiously.

'Yes.'

İskender and Yıldız looked down into the hole where the cupboard floor had been. By the time the roof of the lift came to a halt, all they could really see was the rope disappearing down into a deep and almost tactile darkness.

'Inspector İkmen . . .'

For a few moments there was nothing. The two officers looked from one to the other, their eyes suddenly anxious. İskender was beginning to think that he should never have allowed İkmen to enter an unknown place on his own. OK, the older man was known to be impetuous, but that didn't necessarily absolve İskender from any blame should anything untoward occur. He could have got into the lift with him. Allah alone knew what might be down there.

'There's a passageway.' İkmen had to shout to make himself heard.

İskender breathed a sigh of relief. 'Come up,' he said. 'We'll go down with you.'

'All right.'

Something from the depths of the hole started moving upwards once again.

İskender looked across at Yıldız who blurted, 'I told you it had to be a secret passageway – sir.'

İskender, unusually in the face of even mild insubordination, laughed.

Hale Sivas wasn't aware of the existence of the tunnel that led, via that strange and archaic lift, from her brother's bedroom to the row of small Ottoman houses that stood outside the garden walls. Built on a dirt track which ran along the eastern side of the garden, these tumbledown structures were completely deserted – or at least they were when İkmen and his colleagues climbed out of the tunnel and into the kitchen of the middle house. Not that they had told Miss Sivas any of this – yet.

'The little houses belong to the yalı,' she said as she sat herself down in one of the chairs that faced the now jet black Bosphorus. She couldn't understand why Ayşe the witch's son had roused her from her sleep to talk about the property when Vedat and Hikmet were still possibly in some sort of danger. Pulling the edge of her headscarf as far round as she could without completely obscuring her face, she added, 'Hikmet has never done anything with them. I would have objected anyway had he wanted to. They are in a terrible state.'

'What were they used for?' İkmen asked, lighting his own and İskender's cigarettes. 'They look nineteenth century to me.'

'Yes, they are,' she replied, her face now tauter than it had been before, as if it were closing in on something difficult or unpleasant. 'It is said that they were built by Mahmud Effendi.'

There was a silence during which she averted her eyes.

'Mahmud Effendi?'

'The paşa who owned this yalı at the time,' she said. 'An unpleasant and immoral man. I told Hikmet he shouldn't buy this place, that no good could come of it. And I have been proved right.'

'Meaning?' İskender asked.

'Meaning that some places are haunted by misfortune,'

she said, looking all the time at İkmen. 'You know what I mean. They say that Mahmud Effendi was one of those who supplied the Sultan Abdul Hamid with information about people – untruths. Those people would then be tortured. Many died.' She shook her head sadly. 'Other stories tell of his unnatural vices. The houses you were asking about are where he kept his real harem – of boys. I have even heard tell that he had a passage built underground from this yalı to the houses, so that he could visit the boys whenever he wanted without being seen. But that may be just a myth. People's lives were walled in those days.'

'You've never found such a passage?' İkmen asked.

'No.'

İkmen, İskender and Yıldız exchanged glances.

İkmen cleared his throat. 'You said that, in your opinion, no good could come of owning this yalı.'

'It has an ill-omened history.' She hesitated. 'Not just Mahmud Effendi . . . I wouldn't tell you this if Hikmet and Vedat were here but,' she looked at each of the policemen in turn before she continued, 'my brother bought this house with dirty money.'

'What do you mean, Miss Sivas?' İkmen asked.

She paused for a moment before replying. 'I only went to visit Hikmet once when he moved to America. Vedat goes every year. But when I went, Hikmet had only just finished his second Hollywood movie. He took me to Las Vegas. I saw Frank Sinatra sing with Dean Martin. Then Hikmet introduced me to them.' She smiled. 'They were very charming to a young Turkish girl with no English.' Her face darkened. 'But then later when we met some of his, shall I say, closer friends, things were not so good. I have no English and so I don't know what was actually said, but . . . I am not stupid. I have eyes to see when money changes hands, I have ears to hear the sounds of unnatural acts in big hotel bedrooms. Hikmet often looked strained . . .'

'Strained?'

'I don't know what Hikmet is or was involved with, or Vedat. I only say that Allah will punish them in the end and Hikmet, I know, is torn to pieces inside.'

'Why didn't you tell us any of this before?' İkmen asked.

Hale Sivas shrugged. 'Tell you what? That my brother mixes with bad people?'

'Who may be responsible for what happened to your sister-in-law,' İkmen countered, 'yes.'

'But how can that help?' The old woman shook her head. 'I don't know who any of them are. They are foreigners, I don't speak their language.'

'So you never asked either Hikmet or Vedat about them?'

'I tell my brothers only to behave like proper Muslims and reject the infidel. They both know what I think. The world loves Hikmet Sivas, but he is a disappointment to me.' Tears began to well up in her eyes now and her voice cracked with emotion. 'I tell him not to go to America, to make films here, but he goes there without a care for me! I tell him not to marry infidel women who will give him only Christian children, but he ignores me. I tell him not to buy this yalı and he does so. Oh, he's always very, very sorry afterwards, begging forgiveness of me all the time, promising that Vedat will always be here to take care of me . . .'

'Why do you live here if you disapprove of this yalı and its associations?'

Hale Sivas turned to look hard at İskender. 'Because I must live with my brother Vedat, there is no one else to care for me. I live where he lives, and with my prayers and the purity of my life I work to keep the evil ghosts of Mahmud Effendi and his crimes at bay. Maybe Allah in his wisdom will see my suffering and will forgive my brothers for their womanising and their badness.'

Yıldız, for whom talk of ghosts was a more unusual experience than it was for İkmen, coughed in spite of himself.

Hale Sivas gazed at his face.

'You don't believe in ghosts?' she asked gruffly. 'You don't think that the damned walk abroad? Too sophisticated, are you?'

'No.' But the young man bowed his head.

'I don't think that Constable Yıldız, Inspector İskender or myself are in a position to refute the possibility of such things after what we have just experienced,' İkmen said.

She turned to look at him. 'Oh?'

İkmen smiled. 'You see, Miss Sivas, Mahmud Effendi's secret passageway does exist. Behind some of his stylish French panels, via a lift. We've just been down there. The passage leads from your brother Hikmet's bedroom underneath the garden to the houses. It's very dark and very eerie, but it has been used recently. We think your brothers may have used it to disappear.'

Hale Sivas looked genuinely shocked.

'The only thing we don't know is why,' İkmen said. 'If neither of your brothers killed your sister-in-law then they had no reason to leave – unless they knew who had killed Kaycee.'

'But wouldn't they have told you?'

215

'Not if they were involved in some sort of illegal activity with these people themselves,' İkmen replied. 'As I told you before, right at the beginning of this investigation. Vedat tried to prevent Hikmet from involving us. There must have been a reason for this beyond your own explanation which, if I recall correctly, was distrust of the police. I personally believe that your sister-in-law's murder had rather more to do with Hikmet's associations than hers. I think, as I've also told you before, it was some sort of warning.' He leaned in closely to her and said, 'What do you think?'

Hale Sivas, unable to sustain İkmen's gaze for long, averted her eyes.

'I don't know,' she said sadly. 'Sometimes Vedat begins to talk about his anxieties but I always turn my head away and block up my ears. I don't want to know about evil. It can taint a soul . . .'

'Well, that's a great pity,' İkmen said as he rose angrily to his feet in one quick movement. 'Had you taken a risk with your soul we might now have some idea where your brothers are and with whom. Las Vegas, where you once met Frank Sinatra and Dean Martin, was owned by the Mafia in the early nineteen sixties, and if Hikmet and Vedat are, or were, connected to them, then they're probably well beyond your prayers now.'

And with that he left the room. İskender and Yıldız followed soon afterwards, leaving as quietly as they could while the old woman wept into the thick folds of her headscarf.

Chapter 15

Muazzez Heper allowed her sister to escort her to the pavement and even to hail a taxi for her, but nothing else.

'It's me he's asked to see,' she said, clinging to Yümniye's arm as they moved towards the pavement. 'I've always said that you know nothing.'

Yümniye, unbeknown to her sightless sister, frowned. 'We should have told Çetin.'

'You nearly did,' Muazzez replied acidly.

'Yes.'

'This is far bigger than you know, Yümniye.'

'Yes, but we had nothing whatever to do with that girl's death!'

'That is irrelevant!' Muazzez turned her blank eyes in her sister's direction and scowled. 'Now get me a taxi, please. I've no time to waste.'

With a reluctant sigh Yümniye released her arm from Muazzez's grasp and approached the road. One of the many things of which İstanbul has an abundance is taxis. Bright yellow and sporting their registration numbers on the side, they are driven by a group of people committed to the twin macho ideals of speed and positional supremacy on the road. One skidded to a halt in front of the two women almost immediately.

Yümniye opened the back door nearest the pavement

and helped her sister into the vehicle. It was unwise to sit alongside the driver, especially in the older cabs, like this one, which could have old and inefficient brakes.

'My sister wants to go to Sultanahmet, İshak Paşa Caddesi,' she said, 'just before the railway underpass.'

The driver shrugged and then put his foot down.

'Be careful, Muazzez,' Yümniye said as her sister sped away towards the Bosphorus Bridge. Away to meet 'him', the one Yümniye had never met but had always wanted, in spite of anything, to do so. He had, after all, made their lives possible. He had saved the General from ignominy.

İkmen saw Ardiç speak briefly to İskender outside in the garden. İskender had been on his way home. He had probably had even less sleep than İkmen. Hikmet Sivas's furniture, though beautiful, was hardly comfortable and all night long both men had shuffled around trying to get settled while at the same time listening for strange sounds in the house and the telephone. It had been awful and probably the last thing İskender needed now was Ardiç, who, it seemed, hadn't exactly lingered in Ankara.

İkmen took the small glass of tea offered to him by one of the younger policemen and sat down. Çöktin, who had now also returned to his home, had discovered nothing useful at Yıldız Palace the previous night. Staff there knew Vedat Sivas, they also knew who his brother was. Vedat had worked every day at the palace when he started there forty years before; now he worked there once a week. He kept his own counsel and did not get too close to colleagues. Maybe having a famous brother was the reason for this. İkmen doubted that any of Vedat's colleagues lived in anything like the splendour he enjoyed.

A bustlingly impatient sound behind him alerted İkmen to the fact that Commissioner Ardıç had entered the building. He turned and saw that Tepe, looking pale and anxious, was standing in Ardıç's considerable shadow.

'You look like a vagrant,' Ardıç said disapprovingly as he came and sat down next to İkmen.

'I didn't get a lot of sleep last night, sir,' İkmen replied.

Ardıç turned to Tepe. 'Well, go about your business then,' he said and waved a dismissive hand towards the sergeant.

'Yes, sir.' Tepe walked smartly out of the room.

'What's he doing?' İkmen asked, tipping his head in the retreating man's direction.

'I want him to make sure there are no pressmen waiting outside,' Ardıç said.

'I thought you had negotiated a blackout.'

'I did but you know what they're like. We can't afford any slip-ups. No one must know what's going on in this house. As far as the world is concerned, Sivas is here.'

'And if anyone sees him on the street?' İkmen inquired.

'Well, nobody will, will they, İkmen!' Ardıç lit up one of his fat Cuban cigars and then leaned back into the over-stuffed chair. 'He's gone.'

'They might,' İkmen mumbled as he lit a cigarette that had been far too long loose in his pocket. 'It's possible.'

Ardıç coughed. 'Well, whether it is or it isn't, it doesn't concern you, İkmen,' he said. 'Not any more.'

İkmen, his eyes narrowed against the rancid smoke from his ancient cigarette, leaned forward and furrowed his brow.

'Sir?'

'I want you to go home and take a few days' leave.' Ardıç shuffled in his seat, rearranging himself to make his large stomach more comfortable. 'For the moment I'll work with İskender.'

'But I don't want to—'

'That's an order, İkmen,' Ardiç said in the low, menacing voice he used only when he was being deadly serious. 'Go home, see your children, eat something. You're looking even more skeletal than usual.'

'I don't eat when I'm busy, I can't.' İkmen lowered his head and then asked, 'Why?'

'Because I tell you to,' Ardiç responded mildly. 'Because it must be.'

İkmen looked up. This wasn't Ardiç's idea. This was something he'd been told to do. 'Who told you to get rid of me? You've just come back from Ankara . . .'

'I'll need a report on this case,' Ardiç said, changing the subject without a flicker.

İkmen, incensed, sat up smartly. 'Very well,' he said, 'although Metin and I have become rather more accustomed to each other of late and I think he is fully up to date.'

'Write it down anyway, İkmen. Go back to the station, write your report and then go home. You have so much leave owing it's almost incalculable.' He looked at İkmen steadily. 'Take a week.'

'A week!'

'A week, İkmen,' Ardiç growled. 'With your children. It will be very nice.'

Tears of frustration and anger rose behind İkmen's eyes. He'd worked hard to get where he was with this case. Now someone in authority over Ardiç was discarding him. Why? But there was no point arguing, that was evident from the look on Ardiç's heavyset face. 'Yes, sir,' he said miserably.

And then Ardiç, uncharacteristically, smiled. 'Forget about all this,' he said as he waved his cigar expansively in the air. 'Get your strength back. People will always be greedy, violent and unreasonable, there will still be plenty to do when you return.'

'Yes.' İkmen's face, which was heavily lined and rumpled at the best of times, looked crushed now and, as if moving underneath the weight of an enormous burden, he rose slowly and wearily from his seat.

He had in fact, to Ardiç's obvious relief, turned to go when he swung back again suddenly. He couldn't let this just go!

'Was it the same people who told you to get me off the İpek case?' he said, his voice husky with bitterness. 'Did they tell you to get me away from here too?'

'The İpek case, as you put it, barely exists,' Ardiç, his eyes now dangerous, said. 'The girl died naturally. Suleyman will take any necessary action against any attackers.'

'Just as soon as he returns to work and the trail has gone cold, yes,' İkmen said, 'I know.'

'It's a non-case, İkmen!' Ardiç's normally ruddy complexion had turned an alarming shade of grey. If İkmen hadn't been so very angry himself he would have paused to consider what effect his words might be having on his superior's state of health. But he was beyond that now.

'I am making progress here!' he yelled. 'I've discovered how the Sivas brothers melted out of this building, I've discovered yet more evidence of a connection between Hikmet and the Mafia.'

'Put it in your report and I will read it!' Ardiç tried to spring furiously to his feet but only succeeded in lumbering slowly upwards.

'All right, sir! All right.' İkmen leaned forward so that his nose was almost touching Ardiç's face. 'But I'm telling you, if you don't immediately contact the American authorities as I suggested originally—'

'I will do whatever is necessary!'

İkmen backed off. He stood for a moment regarding his boss with deep disdain. 'Even if those who are, for whatever reason, pulling your strings at the moment don't want you to?'

Every one of Ardiç's chins shook with indignation. 'Don't be so fucking insolent! Now get out before I do something you'll regret!'

İkmen turned about smartly and started walking towards the door.

'Tell Metin I wish him good fortune,' he said as he opened the door and then turned back to look at Ardiç once again. 'I hope that whatever game is going on here doesn't end up tainting him too.'

Ardiç sat back down again and re-lit his cigar. İkmen shut the door quietly behind him.

The southern end of İshak Paşa Caddesi disappears underneath the railway just before Cankurturan station. For those with sight, the station is visible as one descends into the underpass. Now just a suburban railway, this line used to carry the famous Orient Express to and from glamorous Paris. Muazzez Heper remembered it well. Not its plush and luxurious heyday of course, but its slow decline in the 1950s and 1960s when it was mostly used by peasants going to or returning from their Gastarbeiter jobs in Germany. Nevertheless she had still dreamed of riding its shabby carriages one fine day.

As soon as the General's mind started to deteriorate, however, all such dreams had disappeared from her young life. It was as much as she and Yümniye could do to pay for his treatment and try to keep on top of the rent without thinking about foreign travel. Sometimes, however, Muazzez, unable to stand her father's ravings any more, would have to cut loose and take a glimpse at life beyond the house in Üsküdar. Sometimes she would just go for a walk, but occasionally she would scrape together whatever money she could and go to the Alkazar cinema in Beyoğlu. There she would gaze upon large-breasted heroines trembling before bristling moustachioed villains in the latest Yeşilcam epic, or clap gleefully as the latest offering from Hollywood – films of unbelievable sumptuousness – featuring real stars like Cary Grant, Frank Sinatra and Marilyn Monroe. It was at the cinema that she had met the man who had changed her life forever – in ways both good and bad, but mostly good. After that meeting the rent hadn't been a worry any more and with the occasional big commission from the same source to augment their other work, the Heper sisters had done really very well. Muazzez had never managed to ride the Orient Express or get across to Europe by any other means, but one could not have everything. The general had lived and died with dignity and that was worth everything. That was why she had done it in the first place and why, in spite of what would be said about it by friends, neighbours and even relatives should they ever get to know, it had been the right thing to do. Muazzez regretted nothing.

Wearied by the heat, which wasn't tempered by even the lightest breeze from the Sea of Marmara, Muazzez leaned back against the wall of the underpass. She was too old to stand around for long periods in strange places. Where was he? Heavy vibrations in the concrete wall of the underpass told her that a train had just arrived at Cankurturan station. Outside of commuter times not many people opted to travel to the city by train and so there was no great flurry of activity around the train's arrival. Just more heat and a quietness punctuated by the distant voices of children at play in the shabby streets of Cankurturan district. Muazzez smiled. At night this place had a reputation as a haunt for robbers, prostitutes and drunks. But by day it was all right, or at least she thought it was.

The train started to pull out of the station and rolled across the underpass. The car which had been stationary two hundred metres up on İshak Paşa Caddesi came to life and moved forward. Gathering momentum in line with the departing train, the white Volvo estate was travelling at quite a speed as it rounded the bend into the underpass.

Muazzez, who was concentrating on the sound of the train above her head, didn't hear the car until it was too late. Even when its heavy metal bonnet smashed into her legs, she didn't for a second imagine that what had happened was anything other than an accident. But when the car reversed and then, still under cover of the noise from the train up above, came at her one last fatal time, she knew she was meant to die. And as the reality of impending death engulfed her she was saddened that after all these years he had felt he had to do this in order to silence her. He should have known there was no need.

As the car disappeared down Kennedy Caddesi at high speed, Muazzez Heper died on the ground, alone.

Sometimes, even with the greatest of one's friends, certain things are hidden. You know it from the way the friend behaves, from the atmosphere inside the room, house or apartment. Like an intrusive odour, it lingers, weighing down the most ordinary conversation with its spaces full of silent questions.

İkmen knew that there was something odd happening in Suleyman's house as soon as he crossed the threshold. Not only did Mehmet look uncharacteristically unkempt, he had a very unpleasant scratch on his face as well. İkmen did not mention this even though he noticed old Dr Halman, who entered the salon carrying the baby Yusuf İzzeddin, look at the wound with undisguised concern. And then there was their visitor. İkmen couldn't recall his name but when the young man descended from the bedrooms upstairs, İkmen recognised him as one of Zelfa's psychiatrist colleagues. Babur Halman went to meet him. And even though Mehmet closed the door after his father-in-law had left the room, İkmen could hear the sound of their voices talking quietly for a long time afterwards.

But then Mehmet was an Ottoman and kept his home life private. It was his prerogative and his choice and so İkmen ignored the strangeness around him and launched into the background to his recent dismissal from active duty.

'Ardiç has been *told* to remove me from the Sivas case. I know it!' he said, leaning back into Babur's faded wing chair and lighting a cigarette. 'He went to Ankara to see his superiors. Things must have been said.'

'Sivas is a Hollywood star, Çetin,' Mehmet said gently. 'You and I both know how things are with Americans.'

'You mean that the world bows down to them.'

'Because most of the world owes them either money or gratitude, yes.' Suleyman smiled. 'They probably want someone stupidly youthful who doesn't smoke.'

'Metin İskender smokes!' İkmen retorted.

'Yes, which means that they may make him work under somebody else,' Suleyman said. 'A man from Ankara maybe.'

'A Turk who doesn't smoke?' İkmen shook his head in disbelief. 'Apart from you when you were young, I've never met such a creature. It's ridiculous!'

Suleyman shrugged. 'Whatever the rights and wrongs of it, that is how it is, Çetin.'

'I mean, if I'd just been allowed to speak to the Americans . . .'

'Yes, but Ardiç didn't let you, did he?' Suleyman rubbed his forehead with a very tired hand, 'And anyway, if Sivas does have Mafia connections, that's for the Americans to deal with, isn't it? We have enough trouble with our own families without importing murderers from New York and Chicago or wherever.'

İkmen, temporarily drained of all energy, closed his eyes. He knew he should be back at the station now writing that report on the Sivas case for Ardiç. After all, what he had discovered had to be valuable to Ardiç and/or whoever came after him. Secret tunnels, whispers of Mafiosi, the strange and rapid rise to stardom of a young boy from İstanbul, in a country where seemingly nobody likes Turks . . .

'So Suzan Şeker told you that her husband was paying the Müren brothers,' İkmen said, abruptly changing the subject to his other previous case. His mind did, after all, have to do something if it couldn't busy itself with Hikmet and Vedat Sivas.

'She isn't prepared to go on record though,' Suleyman replied darkly. 'She was, very brave and determined at first but she changed her mind. She phoned me. I said that you had an interest in talking to the Mürens but she wasn't impressed. I think that Mrs Şeker will carry on where her husband left off. The reality is that she has little choice.'

İkmen sighed. 'You know, unless we're prepared to take on organised crime in this city we're going to lose control.'

'Oh, and we do that by starting a war with the Müren family, do we?' Suleyman stood up and walked agitatedly up and down for a few moments. 'Çetin, we don't know that the Müren family were involved in what happened to Hatice İpek.'

'Rat told me that family were behind a prostitution racket.'

'Rat!' Suleyman took a packet of cigarettes out of his pocket and lit up. 'He's insane!'

'He also told me that two seamstresses from my old district, the Heper sisters, knew all about this high-class prostitution thing.'

'And did they?'

İkmen shrugged. 'What they didn't or wouldn't say suggested to me that they probably did.'

Suleyman sat down again. Although far from convinced that the notoriously unreliable informant known as the Sultanahmet Rat did indeed know anything of value about the İpek case, he didn't doubt what İkmen had experienced with the Heper sisters. Employed over many years and in numerous cases, İkmen's instincts were only ever questioned by Ardiç, who generally lived to regret his scepticism.

'How do you think these sisters might be involved?' Suleyman asked.

'They definitely made that dress I told you about,' İkmen said. 'The one Hatice was dressed in when she died.'

'But they didn't or wouldn't say that they had made this dress?'

'No. Which suggests to me that they know more about or have greater involvement in this,' he shrugged, 'I don't know what to call it. This trade in prettily dressed girls which has recently been taken over by families, according to Rat.'

'According to Rat. Mmm.' Suleyman looked at İkmen with a jaded eye. 'That for me, I must say, Çetin, has to be the flaw in all of this.'

'Rat?'

'Yes. He's both unreliable and stupid.'

'Well, I can't argue with you about that,' İkmen said. 'Usually Rat is a waste of time. But he was scared on this occasion.' He frowned at the memory of it. 'OK, he wanted money as usual, but that doesn't detract from the risk that he took, in my opinion.'

'So this prostitution . . .'

'My understanding of it is,' İkmen said, 'that someone has for a long time provided odalisques for men with a taste for the old days. Rat said it had been operating for years. But now one of the families has taken it over and people, maybe not just Hatice, are getting hurt.'

'Well I suppose that having a woman totally subservient to one's every whim or, in some cases perversion, can be compelling,' Suleyman observed. 'Traditionally, odalisques were female servants who attended to the Sultan's needs both in bed and as domestics and entertainers. An odalisque, as well as learning sexual submission, would be trained to dress beautifully, sing, play an instrument and wash clothes. She also had to be perfect.' He smiled. 'Allah's Shadow on Earth could not be subjected to the sight of physical defect.'

'So perhaps the families are now cashing in on the fantasies of deviants,' İkmen said. 'Although if the Heper sisters made the gowns for these modern sex slaves, the service can't have come cheaply. Rich weirdos—'

'Now possibly paying one of the families?'

'Ah, but which family?' İkmen raised his hands as if inviting an answer which Suleyman couldn't supply. 'The only family connection to any of this is the Mürens' connection with Hassan Şeker who was having an affair with Hatice İpek and who in his suicide note claimed to have taken her life. I still don't believe that. The Mürens could have had sex with her, yes. But to take over something as, well, classy, sophisticated, well-researched as this seems unlikely. Ali Müren is as scummy as his sons, he's basically just a thug. No. They're too stupid to get involved in what sounds like a labour-intensive operation. If we were talking about the Galikos or the Edips, I would say yes, but not the Mürens.'

'Then perhaps another family lies behind the Mürens,' Suleyman said. 'The Galikos maybe. Perhaps even the Bulgarian.'

'I thought he was dead.'

'Apparently not.' Suleyman let his tired head droop down towards the floor. 'He's alive and kicking, so I've heard.' He looked up and waved his cigarette in İkmen's direction. 'Now he is dangerous,' he said. 'Metin İskender tried to get him a few years ago. He and his team, which I believe included Tepe, worked hard for nearly six months on Zhivkov and his gang. Then when they raided his place they found it empty save for the impaled head of the Bulgarian's wife, Nina – İskender's informant.'

'Metin still has problems with that. He reacted very

badly to what we found in Hikmet Sivas's bedroom. But is Zhivkov associated with the Müren brothers?'

Suleyman shrugged. 'I don't know, but it's possible. Like all of these people, the Mürens are difficult to find when you want them but you could try having them followed. Or you could just ask them of course.'

İkmen shook his head in disbelief and lit up another cigarette. 'This is no time for levity, Mehmet.'

'No, I'm serious,' Suleyman, who was generally serious, responded. 'If you can get them in, or rather if you can use the right incentive to get them in, then I think they might be persuaded.' Seeing the confused look on İkmen's face, Suleyman amplified. 'I'm talking about Alev Müren, Çetin. The little sister from hell?'

'Oh.'

Suleyman smiled at İkmen's expression. 'Bring Alev in and the boys will follow. It won't be difficult, she's incapable of shopping without stealing at least half of her purchases.'

'So I just have to lurk around in shopping malls, do I?'

'Get one of the younger men to follow her to Galeria or Akmerkez,' Suleyman said, naming two of the city's new and popular American-style shopping malls. 'Alev Müren is a fashion diva, she shops from dawn till dusk. Daddy gives her money to shop every day. But when that runs out she steals. She's stolen from shops all over the city. You can bring her in on her reputation alone.'

'And then?' İkmen asked.

'As soon as the boys know she's in custody, they'll come,' Suleyman said. 'They'll try and buy every officer they bump into on the way. But when they get to you, make it clear that you're going to keep hold of Alev this time. You might even intimate that you like her.'

'What a distasteful thought that is,' İkmen said, recalling the plump, self-satisfied features of Alev Müren.

'If they think that Alev's honour might be in danger, they may talk,' Suleyman said. 'Old Ali Müren would certainly kill both of them if he thought they had allowed his little girl to be violated. Then you can ask them about other families.'

'You think that they would inform on the Bulgarian?' İkmen asked doubtfully.

Suleyman shrugged. 'I don't think it's impossible. If anything is their collective Achilles heel, it is that dreadful girl. Anyway, Çetin, what else have we got?'

There wasn't much. There was, in truth, little beyond rumours, suggestions and feelings. The only concrete fact was that a girl had been horribly violated and her body dumped in a minor cistern, and now her mother and her sister cried ceaselessly in her memory. İkmen felt his eyes start to sting again.

'The problem is, I'm supposed to be on holiday now,' he said as he looked questioningly into Suleyman's face.

'Oh, I'm having to take a little more leave myself, Çetin,' the younger man replied as he held his hands aloft to signify his detachment, 'Zelfa still needs, er, she isn't, uh . . .'

İkmen smiled. So Zelfa was having a few problems. Some women did. İnşallah whatever the problem was would pass quickly. 'That's OK,' he said. 'You take care of your family.'

'Çetin, I'm sorry . . .' Suleyman looked away.

'Well, don't be.' İkmen leaned across and placed a small dry hand on Suleyman's shoulder. 'Take care of the living, your wife and your son.' He put his other hand into his jacket pocket and retrieved a small, shiny box. 'Give this to him,' he said and rose to leave. 'I'll deal with the dead people.' Then he left.

Suleyman, who was in reality exhausted from Zelfa's accusations and delusions, simply sat and felt inadequate. Later he opened the little box and found inside a moderately sized gold coin dating from the reign of Sultan Abdul Mecit whose blood ran in his veins and those of his son. How İkmen could possibly afford such a thing he didn't know but he smiled anyway.

Chapter 16

The sun had set by the time İkmen got back to the police station. He'd been vaguely aware of the sunset call to prayer as he berated his teenage children for the appalling state of the apartment. But then he'd gone out, leaving the place as messy as he'd found it – to do Ardiç's bidding and try to think about what he might do now about his 'holiday' and how he could further his investigations into the 'dead' İpek case. He could hardly carry on alone but he didn't want Tepe with him. The man, at best, had exhibited sloppy thinking with regard to the Mürens and their involvement with Hassan Şeker. At worst, well . . . Perhaps it was best not to ponder upon how many and who amongst the officers that he had known over the years had had some financial link to members of the underworld. Besides, Tepe seemed to be working directly for Ardiç now. Maybe the commissioner wanted to keep him close in order to watch him. Ardiç was, after all, nobody's fool even if he was currently having his mouth moved for him by faceless creatures in Ankara – or maybe Washington.

'Would you like some tea, Inspector?'

İkmen looked up and saw the pale face of Ayşe Farsakoğlu gaze quizzically over at him from outside his office.

'Yes, please. Large,' he said and then turned back to the computer screen which was currently showing him that he had a very long way to go with his report. İkmen sighed. He'd made a lot of discoveries during his short time in and around Hikmet Sivas's home, but of the man himself he'd learned little.

His mobile telephone started to ring. İkmen picked it up and grunted into the mouthpiece.

'It's Cohen,' a smoke-scarred voice said. 'I thought I'd better ring because I know you knew the lady . . .'

'What lady? What are you talking about, Cohen?' He was really too tired to listen to Cohen's gossip right now. İkmen sympathised with the ex-constable's situation; if he had been crippled by the earthquake he'd probably live his life through gossip too, but now was not a good time.

'The seamstress,' Cohen said. 'Muazzez Heper. Knocked down and killed by a car in the underpass at Cankurtaran railway station.'

İkmen felt the hairs rise on the back of his head. 'Are you sure?'

'Avcı told me,' Cohen said, referring to one of his old colleagues in uniform. 'Happened at about midday. Whoever did it just drove away. She was alone, Miss Muazzez. A man who was leaving the station at the time caught sight of a white car, but he couldn't tell what it was. Muazzez and Yümniye Heper made my Esther's wedding dress.'

'You're sure it was Muazzez and not Yümniye?' İkmen asked. What would a blind woman be doing alone in a district so far from her home?

'Oh, yes,' Cohen said, 'definitely. Tragic.'

Yes, and chilling, İkmen thought. The last time he'd seen Muazzez Heper she'd been mouthing furiously at her sister after he'd shown them both that awful, beautiful dress. Just before he saw that odd woman with the red hair again, staring at him from outside the gate.

'But life goes on,' Cohen said with a sigh, 'especially for my son and your daughter.'

İkmen, whose mind hadn't caught up with this rapid change of subject, just grunted.

'Yes,' Cohen continued breezily, 'they've been seeing quite a lot of each other lately. You and I will have to watch the situation closely.'

'What do you mean?' It sounded very much, to İkmen, as if someone had intended to kill Muazzez Heper. But who and why? Surely not just because of that dress?

'Well, in case they want to be together,' Cohen said.

İkmen, who had now managed to catch up with the conversation, frowned. He knew that Hulya liked Berekiah, but what of it?

'I can't see anything wrong with that,' he said. 'Berekiah is a very nice boy.'

'A very nice Jewish boy, yes,' Cohen replied somewhat tartly. 'Your Hulya is a Muslim.'

'Oh, Cohen, don't tell me you've suddenly become religious! I can't think of one of your mistresses who was Jewish.'

'Yes, but my wife is! Estelle is! And she's the mother of my children. Five hundred years my family have been here and not once have we married out! It's important to me, Inspector, to Estelle, to my brothers!'

Ayşe Farsakoğlu entered İkmen's office bearing a steaming glass of tea which she placed in front of him on his desk. He looked up and smiled wearily at her.

'Well, Cohen,' he said, 'let's see what develops, shall we? At the moment they just like each other.'

'Yes, but what if my boy comes to you, asks you for Hulya?'

'Well, Cohen . . .' İkmen began.

Ayşe Farsakoğlu turned to go while İkmen still, vaguely, watched her.

'It's important that we talk about this, Inspector,' Cohen said.

'I've got to go, Cohen,' İkmen said, smacking the end button as quickly as he could with his finger. 'Sergeant Farsakoğlu!'

She turned. 'Yes, sir?'

İkmen stood up and walked round the side of his desk towards her. 'You've got blood on the back of your shirt,' he said. 'Have you been involved in something?'

She turned her head and her back away from him. 'No.'

'Well then, have you had an accident?'

The uneasy look that had settled onto her face gave İkmen a very bad feeling. 'Ayşe?'

'I fell at home,' she said, 'against the stove. In the kitchen.'

İkmen moved to look at the large bloodstain but she shifted away again.

'When did this happen?' he asked.

'Oh, last night . . .' It was obvious she had just picked this out of the air.

'Quite a sharp-edged stove you must have,' he said. 'Have you seen a doctor?'

She lowered her eyes. 'No.'

'Well, I think you should.' Gently but firmly he took hold of her elbow and attempted to move her around so that he could look at the stain once again.

'Sir!'

But he was stronger than her and managed to move her so that he could see the stain easily. Not only was it very large but the blood was obviously fresh. İkmen frowned. 'Has anyone else commented on this?'

'No, sir.' And then gently she began to cry. 'People don't get involved . . .'

'Get involved with what?' İkmen asked. 'Somebody hurting you?'

'No!'

'Ayşe, is somebody, a man—'

'Mind your own business!' she screamed. 'This has nothing to do with you!'

But İkmen had seen enough of domestic violence and its results during the course of his career to know the signs. He briefly loosened his grip on her elbow and moved forward to shut his office door. Then he stood behind her and took a deep breath. The stain was actually darker in some places than others, a horizontal pattern ran across it, presumably in line with the wounds.

'Well, if you won't go to a doctor, you'd better let me see. Take your shirt off,' he said.

Her tear-stained face whipped round in shock. 'No!'

'That's an order!' İkmen barked. 'Lose your job or take your shirt off, it's up to you. I won't move round to look at your chest, I just want to see your back.'

'No!'

'Do it!' He placed a warning hand on her collar and applied just a little light pressure. 'Please.'

Her sobs came even harder. With every button she undid, her distress and humiliation grew. And by the time she had slipped the shirt off her shoulders, she was bent almost double, shielding her chest with her hands.

İkmen looked at the stripes and gouges on her back and felt sick. He'd come across men who liked to do this sort of thing before, men he had wanted to beat senseless. But that would make him just like them and so he had always stayed his hand – he was famous for it. Now, however, the urge was very strong. He clasped his hands tightly behind his back.

'Did Orhan Tepe do this to you?' he asked quietly.

She turned and looked at him, saying nothing, but he knew.

'Oh, Ayşe,' he said sadly. 'You silly girl.'

Orhan Tepe, like İkmen's half-written report, wasn't going anywhere. Both he and it would wait. And besides, İkmen thought, he could hardly confront Tepe in front of his wife. Maybe he whipped her too? Who was to know? Old Ottoman mores died hard, İkmen knew that. So many lives were 'walled'. Smart-suited government ministers could fulminate all they wanted about the evils of wife-beating and how it had no place in a modern society, but some men would always do it; men in even the most 'advanced' cultures did it. He just hoped that Ayşe Farsakoğlu would do as she had said and keep away from Tepe in the future. Give him back all the expensive baubles he had somehow acquired for her, forgo the meals in smart restaurants and go back to what she was before, a sad young woman in love with Suleyman who only had eyes for his newborn son. A real Ottoman patriarch at last, to Zelfa Halman Suleyman's dismay and incomprehension, or so it seemed.

What a mess.

* * *

İkmen looked up from the tip of his glowing cigarette and into the liquid eyes of Yümniye Heper.

'Tell me everything,' he said. 'I'm helpless without the truth.'

The elderly woman seemed crushed. What a terrible day this had been for her. Not only had she lost the only relative she still possessed, she had also lost her soulmate, the reason for her existence. Yümniye and Muazzez – the names were as one, they were always spoken in the same breath, like a never changing phrase or formulaic spell. Neither worked on its own. Even this wakefulness in the darkness of the hot miserable night was an abomination – because she was alone.

Yümniye Heper dabbed her eyes with her handkerchief and leaned back into the large brown chair that had once been her father the General's favourite seat.

'By nineteen sixty Father's illness had taken a terrible toll on our finances,' she said sadly. 'The landlord was threatening to evict us. I was paralysed with fear. But Muazzez was made of sterner stuff than myself and she continued to pursue her life as she always had.' She sighed. 'It seemed like a miracle when she came home after being away all of that strange night, clutching enough money to buy this house.'

'How did she get this money?' İkmen asked. 'What happened?'

Yümniye smiled sadly. 'Sex is what happened, Çetin,' she said. 'She met a man at the cinema. To this day I still don't know who he was – is. But he paid Muazzez that money to have sex with another man, a foreigner.'

'Did she know the foreigner?'

'No. But then she said very little about it. I mean I know

239

that you know the General raised us to be independent,
liberal-minded women, but Muazzez was ashamed. To be
used by men like that . . . They wanted her to dress like an
Ottoman princess. In that gown, the very one you brought
to show us. The one that girl died in. I knew I'd seen it
before. I know I'm vague now, but . . . Muazzez made
it. At first, after the meeting at the cinema, she believed
that the commission was just for the dress, but then the
man said that he wanted Muazzez to wear it and . . . do
things. Afterwards there was no sex ever again. Muazzez
was only asked to make dresses for other girls. And so
we made several gowns every year from then on, for other
girls to wear while they pleasured men. Given the amount
of money my sister was paid, the men had to be wealthy,
and again foreign, I think. Muazzez always arranged for
their delivery. We were very well paid for them.' She
paused briefly to sip her tea. 'Muazzez was chosen to go
with that man because Father was an Ottoman general. The
man knew of us, the high-born Heper sisters who liked to
dress like boys.'

'Everybody knew you,' İkmen said with a smile. 'You
were always the finest seamstresses in İstanbul.'

'Yes.' She looked over at the portrait of a stern-looking
military man wearing a fez, which hung over the empty
fireplace. 'They wanted real Ottoman girls for their harem
– that's the term this man and his customers used. Muazzez
was perfect. Later, any girl would do, provided she wore the
right clothes. Things changed recently, don't know how, but
Muazzez became frightened. She went to meet her man this
morning, he'd called her.'

'Did you speak to him?'

'No. Never.' She looked from the portrait back to İkmen.

'Muazzez made sure I was always kept away from this business. She loved me . . .'

'Yes.' İkmen leaned forward, frowning. 'So this harem, Miss Yümniye—'

'I don't know where this activity took place, Çetin,' she said as she wiped the tears once again from her eyes. 'I asked Muazzez once, at the beginning, but she said only that she was taken to the place blindfolded. She had no idea herself. The only detail she ever offered was that it was reached through a wood or park of some sort. She did this thing only once, in a room full of silk, crystal and gold.'

'Like a palace.'

'Well, yes, where else would one take an Ottoman princess?'

İkmen looked down at the floor and shook his head. 'And yet it could be anywhere, couldn't it, Miss Yümniye? It could be a secret room in the vastness of Topkapı or it could be a mock-up at the back of some ghastly gecekondu.'

'Given the money she was paid, I would think the former more likely,' Yümniye said. 'It was a great deal of money, Çetin.'

'For a Turk, yes, but not necessarily for a foreigner. This place was very cheap to Europeans in those days.'

'I don't know if he was European,' Yümniye replied. 'Muazzez only alluded to his foreignness.'

'But this harem persists to this day.'

'Yes. With new girls and new dresses. Although as I said before, Muazzez wasn't as comfortable with it as she had been. And when you told us that that poor girl had died wearing one of our dresses . . . I wanted to tell you, but Muazzez was adamant. It was far too dangerous, she said. This harem thing was big.'

'Big?' İkmen put his cigarette out in the ashtray and lit another. 'What do you mean?'

Yümniye shrugged. 'I don't know, Çetin. I'm using Muazzez's words. All I do know is that although both of us were aware that what we were doing, making the dresses, was wrong, Muazzez only became scared this year. She was, as you know, always very brave and anyway she and I were both grateful to that man she met outside the Alkazar cinema all those years ago. He gave us this house, a decent living and he almost single-handedly enabled the General to have some dignity in his final years. I always wanted to meet him.'

'You don't think he killed your sister then?' İkmen asked.

Miss Yümniye looked shocked. 'Oh, no,' she said, 'I don't think so. I mean, why would he after all this time?'

'Maybe he or one of his people saw me come to this house. I'm a well-known officer, Miss Yümniye.'

'Yes, you are,' she said. 'You've done very well, Çetin. But how would Muazzez's man know you came here to ask about the harem? You had that dress in a bag and anyway he knew Muazzez would never have told you anything. Even after we knew the girl had died in that dress, Muazzez was still adamant. We argued about it. She said that it was utterly impossible for her man and his customers to have killed that girl. I asked her how she knew but she said that she just did and not to ask. Others, she said, must have done it.'

'But she didn't say who?'

'No.'

İkmen leaned back into the slack softness of the sofa and sighed. So Rat had been right all along about the odalisques. They had been 'sold' in modern İstanbul for many years. A Turkish 'delight' of sorts for curious, rich and probably sated foreigners. Silly old Europeans who, for the price of a whole Turkish house, could play at being sultan for an hour with a 'genuine' Ottoman princess. But then perhaps not. Perhaps those involved hadn't been so silly, perhaps they'd been better than that, more important. After all, it had been a great and well-kept secret. And if, as Rat had said, families were now involved, they must feel the harem's customers were wealthy and powerful enough to justify their time.

'Miss Yümniye,' he said slowly, 'have you ever heard of a family by the name of Müren?'

Yümniye looked blank. 'No. Why?'

'Oh, no reason.' İkmen shrugged. 'Just a thought.'

They both sat quietly for a few moments until Yümniye, frowning as if she were making an effort to remember something, said, 'You could speak to Sofia, I suppose. If you want to know more about the harem.'

'Sofia?'

'Yes, Sofia Vanezis. You know, about your age. Very pretty girl she was, a little slow.'

'Was that the girl who came to live at Panos the shoe-mender's?' İkmen inquired.

Yümniye smiled. 'Yes. She and her mother moved here from Fener when Sofia's father died. Panos was, I think, his brother.'

'Yes.' İkmen nodded. 'They were very poor. But her mother was a proud woman, always well-dressed.'

'Maria Vanezis was a Phanariote, old Byzantine aristocracy,' Yümniye said. 'One of the last. But, as you say, living in very reduced circumstances when she came here. Like all of us.' She sighed, her face sad again at yet another mournful memory. And then for a few moments she just sat, lost in some small corner of the past. But then İkmen cleared his throat and the sound brought her back to him.

'Well, anyway,' Yümniye continued, 'the point is that when Maria was dying, Sofia needed money. She was quite young and she was afraid. She couldn't work because she was slow and Panos wanted her out. Muazzez felt sorry for her and so she arranged for her to, er, work at the harem. Muazzez always liked to believe that I didn't know, but I heard them talking. Sofia still comes – came – to see Muazzez from time to time. She's grateful, you see. Through Muazzez she got treatment for her mother and bought that little boarding house she lives in now.'

'So Sofia had sex for money.'

'Yes. The poor thing had been letting men touch her for several years because she knew no better. Muazzez must have felt that this was the only way she'd ever have any money and she was probably right.'

İkmen lit up another cigarette. 'The attraction, I presume, was Sofia's Phanariote background.'

'I suppose so.'

'But you think she might talk to me about the harem, do you, Miss Yümniye?'

'I don't know,' Yümniye replied. 'If she did talk to you, she could probably tell you quite a lot. She has a remarkable and very precise memory. It's the way she is. I can talk to her, try to persuade her. But she never actually utters a word to me. She just stands gawping with all that mad red hair of hers.'

So that was the woman who had stared at him when he'd visited the Hepers with Hatice's dress. Weird Sofia. It all came back now – İkmen's guilty secret. The first female breast he'd ever seen in the flesh had belonged to weird

Sofia. She'd been very pretty then and he'd had fantasies about her. He was twelve at the time. She'd aged frighteningly badly. He wondered whether she'd recognised him.

Upbringing can be a wonderful indicator with regard to what a person can tolerate. The Yıldız family were a case in point. Mustafa and Arın Yıldız, although village born and bred, had lived in the livelier quarters of the city for nearly thirty years. First in a gecekondu shack in Gaziosmanpaşa where their three sons, İsmet, Hikmet and Suleyman, had been born and then later in the three-roomed apartment they lived in now. Almost as small and noisy as the gecekondu, the Yıldız high-rise apartment overlooked the Londra Asfaltı highway and was situated, together with numerous similar blocks, about four kilometres from Atatürk Airport. Packed with noisy adults, screamingly loud adolescents and hordes of children, the blocks resounded day and night to the sound of television, Arabesk music and frayed tempers. Not that any of this had any effect upon Constable Hikmet Yıldız and his brothers as they slept soundly upon the hard divans that had always been their beds. Even when the telephone rang just after midnight, none of the boys stirred. It was up to Arın to get Hikmet up to answer it.

'It's somebody from the police,' she said nervously as her son staggered, sleep-sodden, into the tiny grey-painted hall. Even with a son in the police force, Arın still felt cold every time they contacted the Yıldız home. Back in the village all those years ago, the police had been both feared and appeased in equal measure. They had never been liked.

Hikmet took the receiver from his mother's hand. 'Hello?'

The voice on the other end sounded urgent, fevered even. 'Hikmet, it's Inspector İkmen.'

'Oh, hello, sir.'

'What time do you come off duty tomorrow, Hikmet?'

'Um,' he had to think for a moment, 'er, three.'

'Look, Hikmet,' İkmen said, 'do you trust me? My judgement?'

Hikmet frowned. What was this? 'Yes,' he said, 'of course.'

'And so if I ask you to do something you might find strange or irregular, offering absolutely no explanation for it, you would do it for me?'

'Well, yes, I suppose . . .'

'Good,' İkmen replied, 'I'll call you tomorrow.'

'Sir, is it—'

'Don't ask, Hikmet, I won't tell you. The less you know, the better. Now you're sure you're OK with this?'

He wasn't entirely but he said yes anyway, and İkmen cut the connection.

Hikmet replaced the receiver to the sound of his father's snoring and a blast of garage music from the apartment across the corridor. Neither the noise nor the troubling nature of İkmen's request would keep him awake, however. He needed his sleep. Only he and İsmet had employment at the moment and the young policeman knew that if he was late or didn't do as he was told the consequences could be dire.

He flopped back down onto his divan just as İsmet murmured a woman's name and groaned.

Chapter 17

Orhan Tepe rubbed his bloodshot eyes with the heel of his hand and then sipped his coffee. Sitting on the small balcony at the back of his apartment he could observe the comings and goings at the büfe opposite. The sun had only been up for just over half an hour and most of those purchasing börek and tea from the büfe were poorly dressed peasant workers – taxi drivers, simitcis, security men. One uniformed cop was amongst their number, a younger man whose clothes fitted badly. Orhan wrinkled his nose into a sneer. Allah, but this country needed something! Not that he knew what that was. He supposed it had to be an attitude more akin to that which he had witnessed when he'd taken Ayşe out amongst the smart folk at Rejans. A cleanliness, a confidence – a whole package that only money could buy. One day, he smiled, one day soon. But the thought did not make him feel better; actually it made him feel worse and the smile faded from his lips. Perhaps when he got off duty later on he would buy one of those CD players he had been hankering after for so long – perhaps that would make him feel better. Maybe he'd get one for Ayşe too . . .

The door from the living room opened, interrupting his thoughts. Orhan looked round and saw his wife, Aysel, smiling at him.

'Çetin Bey has come to see you, Orhan,' she said and

moved aside to allow the small crumpled figure to walk out onto the balcony. 'Would you like some coffee, Çetin Bey? It's French and very good.'

İkmen smiled. 'Thank you very much, Mrs Tepe,' he said, 'that would be nice.'

Aysel left. The two men heard her wittering happily to her child Cemal as she went to the kitchen.

'So how goes your search for Hikmet Sivas and his brother?' İkmen said as he eased his tired, cigarette-reeking form into the chair opposite Tepe.

'I thought you were on holiday,' his junior replied with a bluntness that İkmen would have challenged had he had any sleep the night before.

'Yes, I am, Orhan.' He took what was left of a soft packet of cigarettes from his pocket and lit up something that looked like an old piece of string. 'But even though Ardiç denies me access to the house in Kandıllı, I can still show an interest. That he cannot prevent.'

'No.'

'And so?'

Tepe shrugged. 'We're interviewing known associates. Had a look at the old paşa's tunnel. Commissioner Ardiç is basing himself at the house. In case someone calls.'

'Has he contacted the authorities in America?' İkmen asked.

'I don't think so.'

'Poor Metin İskender must feel as if this case is going to be the one to bury his career,' İkmen responded tartly.

'Why?'

'Because I can't see that any of you are doing very much,' İkmen said. 'Both the sister and Ahmet Sılay have intimated that Hikmet Sivas has Mafia connections.'

248

'Commissioner Ardiç says that's only hearsay.'

'Yes, but he should still check it out. I would! Stupid—'

Aysel returned with the coffee at this point, cutting off İkmen's rant against his superior. As she placed the cup in front of him, he looked up at her and smiled. 'That smells very good, Mrs Tepe,' he said.

'We've got crystal sugar too,' Aysel replied, placing the bowl of sparkling sugar down beside his cup.

'How lovely!' İkmen bowed his head in appreciation. 'French coffee and crystal sugar. Win the lottery at last, did you, Orhan?'

Only İkmen and Aysel laughed, and then she left to return to her domestic duties. İkmen stirred his coffee thoughtfully for a few moments before speaking again.

'But I haven't come to talk to you about Sivas or even about this very expensive coffee.'

'I have a credit card,' Tepe responded tightly.

'Oh, do you? Well, don't get into difficulty with it, will you?' İkmen said. 'Coffee, meals out at Rejans and diamond earrings can rack up, you know, Orhan.'

Tepe looked down and sipped his own coffee, frowning.

'Yes, I've come to talk to you about Ayşe Farsakoğlu,' İkmen said. 'I've come to tell you that it would be unwise to buy her such extravagant presents again.'

'It's my money.'

'No it isn't. It's a credit card, or so you say.' İkmen paused. 'But money and baubles are not the issue here.' He leaned forward. 'Not when they're given to women in exchange for perverted sexual favours.'

The colour in Tepe's face flared. 'What do you mean? What's she been saying?'

'It's not often, fortunately, that I get an opportunity

to see someone's back when it's been whipped,' İkmen said through his teeth, keeping his voice low so as not to attract Aysel Tepe's innocent attention. 'You touch her again, Orhan, and I'll finish you!'

'I didn't do anything to her!' Tepe, his face now contorted with anger, hissed. 'She's lying! She's a whore who will give herself to anyone! You've seen how she dresses.'

'I don't care how she dresses!' İkmen retorted. 'I know that you've been seeing her. I know you've promised to leave your wife for her. I know how used and cheated she feels.'

'Lying, greedy bitch, I never said I would marry her! She's a cheap slut, only out for what she can get!'

'I don't know about that. But even if she is, she doesn't deserve the disfiguring beating you gave her! She doesn't deserve to be lied to!'

'If she's accusing a serving officer of sexual violence then she insults our security forces and our nation,' Tepe said. 'She could go to prison.'

'Oh, yes,' İkmen said, smiling now, if unpleasantly, 'that law. Which I will not comment upon except to say that Sergeant Farsakoğlu is a serving officer too. So any legal action could go either way. I personally would support Ayşe.'

'You've always hated me!' Tepe spat as he searched furiously and in vain for his cigarettes. 'Like that bitch, you too resent the fact that Mehmet Suleyman left you.'

'At my recommendation, Orhan,' İkmen corrected. 'I wanted Suleyman to progress because he is a good officer. I took you on because you were a good officer. Ayşe, I will admit, has not been good for you. She thought she had a chance with our resident prince but she didn't and so she turned to your very willing, if second best, arms instead.

I don't know when your obsession with Ayşe and your jealousy of Suleyman turned you into a sadist, but it has to stop.'

'Or else?'

İkmen sipped his coffee for a few moments, put his cigarette out and lit another. He didn't offer his packet to Tepe.

'Or else I will ruin you,' the older man said simply. 'I can do it, Orhan, and I will. Leave her alone and also give some thought to your career. I can't have someone on my staff who beats other officers and who also talks about my activities to our superiors behind my back.' He wanted to address this particular suspicion. After all, if İskender hadn't spoken to Ardiç about Hassan Şeker . . .

Tepe's face whitened, which seemed to confirm that it was indeed he who had spoken to the commissioner about İkmen's continued involvement in the İpek case.

'Any request you make for reassignment will be fully supported by me,' İkmen said as he finished his coffee. He rose to his feet. 'Think about it. Soon.'

At the door he paused.

'Oh, and the coffee was excellent, best I've had all year.' He smiled. 'My compliments to your credit card.' Then he left.

Tepe put his head in his hands and closed his eyes against tears of rage. He hadn't dreamed that this could happen. Lots of other things could and had gone wrong, but Ayşe he had absolutely counted on. He'd done all this for her – people had died, indirectly of course, he was no killer after all, so that she could have what she wanted. All he'd ever wanted in return was some acknowledgement of him as a man, some validation of his needs, of his superiority over

'Prince' Mehmet. What he was going to do now he didn't know. He needed to be on duty in Kandıllı in less than an hour, but how could he concentrate with all this on his mind? If İkmen was going to send him off into some sort of service wilderness he'd have to try and get his hands on money. More money. He'd have to sell something, just like he'd done the last time. There had never been any possibility of going back anyway. Hassan Şeker had made that quite plain when he'd interviewed him for the second time, alone, at his place of business. Hassan Şeker who had blown his own brains away with a shotgun . . .

'Well, give me the money then!' the girl said and snapped her pudgy fingers at the elderly man sitting in front of her.

'Only if you go with Abdullah,' Ali Müren replied sternly.

'Oh!' His daughter stamped her wedge-heeled foot hard against the floor.

'I'm sick of having to pay off clothes shops you have stolen from when you've spent all my cash, Alev,' her father retorted. 'When it's gone Abdullah can bring you home.'

'But he's such a freak! I can't take Abdullah to Akmerkez or Galeria!'

'Then go somewhere else!' Ali Müren stood up. He wasn't a tall man but he was considerably larger than his daughter. He looked down at her with a mixture of frustration, fury and adoration in his eyes. 'Go to İstiklal Caddesi.'

'That's old and boring!' Alev pouted.

'Go there anyway.' He handed her two enormous rolls of banknotes. 'One is for yourself, take the other to Türbedar Sokak.'

'Oh, I don't have to see Grandma, do I?'

Ali sighed with exasperation. 'Yes you do, we owe her,' he said and then turned to the middle-aged man who sat silently in the corner of the room. 'Take my daughter to Türbedar Sokak and then on to İstiklal Caddesi, Abdullah, and make sure she doesn't steal anything.'

'Yes, Ali Bey,' Abdullah gummed through broken, nicotine-stained teeth.

Alev tossed her coiffured head and made her way petulantly towards the door. As she moved, the rolls of fat on her back wobbled with each heavy footstep. Abdullah rose from his chair and followed her.

When they had gone, Ali Müren opened the door out onto his considerable balcony and smiled at the tall blond man who was standing looking down into the teeming street below.

'My daughter. My youngest,' he said, joining the other man at the rail. 'She's expensive, but . . .'

'You love her,' the other responded in his deep heavily accented voice. 'You'll be able to give her everything she wants soon.' He smiled.

'İnşallah!'

They both watched as Alev and the tried and trusted Abdullah got into a large Japanese car and drove off just ahead of a very sorry-looking Mercedes. Both cars and a horse cart made slow progress through the heavy multinational Beyazıt crowds.

'Come on,' Ali said as soon as he was sure that his daughter was well on her way. 'Let's eat lunch and talk business.'

The other man's pale blue eyes sparkled appreciatively.

* * *

Zelfa was full of tears now. Whatever arcane psychiatric narcotic Sadrı had given her to calm her down had now worn off and she was full of remorse. How could she have been so cold towards their son, the most precious child in the whole world? How could she have attacked Mehmet with such ferocity? He had just been sleeping, alone, in their bed, after all. What on earth had possessed her?

'Post-natal depression can be a terrible thing,' her father said as he rocked her gently back and forth to comfort her. 'You know that.'

'Yes, I have patients . . .'

'Ah, but it's not the same as experiencing it yourself, is it?' Babur Halman said gently.

'No.' She looked up into his eyes, her face pale with tension. 'Mehmet will forgive me, won't he, Dad?'

'As long as you don't slap him again, yes,' he said with a smile.

'I lost touch with reality, didn't I?'

'For a while. It happens. And you're not going to get over this in five minutes, Zelfa. Sadrı will still have to monitor your condition for a time. But hopefully the worst has passed now. Babur moved from behind his daughter and stood up. 'You had to have surgery, it was very traumatic, the experience temporarily heightened your insecurities.'

'Yes, but I should have known!'

'Because you're a psychiatrist?' Babur smiled. 'Zelfa dear, do you remember that story I once read to you from the *Irish Times* about Dr McConnell?'

She looked at him blankly.

'He bricked himself into his own office so that he could have a little peace and quiet,' Babur said. 'He was an eminent Belfast psychiatrist.' He smiled again. 'Now try and get a little more sleep. I'll send Mehmet up later once his father has gone.'

Zelfa lay back down against her pillows and closed her eyes. 'Thanks, Dad.'

'You're welcome, darling girl,' he replied in slightly Irish-accented English.

Babur closed the door behind him and went downstairs to where Suleyman and his father were sitting silently in the living room. Strangely, Muhammed Suleyman had come to visit them without his forceful wife. Babur knew that Mehmet had told his parents nothing about Zelfa's troubles, and had discouraged them from visiting her whenever he could, which must have seemed odd to them. Turkish grandparents, generally, have absolutely free rein with their children and their infants. Perhaps Muhammed had just dropped by to try and work out what was happening for himself – and of course for his wife.

As he entered the room, Babur gave Mehmet, who had been staring at the front of his father's upheld newspaper, an encouraging look.

'She's fine,' he said quietly. 'But sleeping. See her later.'

Mehmet, whose face had become rather thinner and more strained since the birth of his son, smiled.

'You know I've looked all through this paper and I cannot find any information about the kidnapping of Hikmet Sivas's wife,' a deep, cultured voice from behind the newspaper, *Cumhuriyet*, boomed. 'It's almost as if the entire event has disappeared.'

So what İkmen had told him about a press embargo was true. Mehmet Suleyman raised a wry eyebrow.

'I expect more important stories have superseded it, Father,' he said. 'These things happen.'

Muhammed Suleyman let the paper drop down onto his lap. Although elderly and quite grey, he was still, like his son, a very handsome man.

'You weren't working on the case, were you?' he asked.

'No, Father. I've been rather busy with other things.'

Babur Halman left to go and make tea. Mehmet and his father had an odd, frosty relationship that he didn't really understand and so leaving was probably rather a good idea at this point.

'Mmm.' Muhammed Suleyman fitted a cigarette into the end of his silver holder and placed it in his mouth. Mehmet, as he knew he must, walked over to light it for him. 'I saw Hikmet Sivas, the Sultan, once. Must have been in the late fifties.'

'Did you, Father? Where?'

'My uncle, Selim, had been allowed home after many years in exile. Malta, I believe.' He smiled. 'He'd been raised in Yıldız Palace. He showed me around. Extraordinary place if you saw all of it as I did – not that you can these days. Like a template or plan of the mind of his uncle, the Sultan who designed the thing. He was a very disturbed man, the Sultan Abdul Hamid – your wife would have found it fascinating.' He raised his newspaper again.

'Yes, Father. And Hikmet Sivas?'

'Oh, yes.' He put the paper down again. 'They were filming there, some historical epic. A Yeşilcam film. Sivas wasn't of course famous then, but I recognised him later from a Hollywood movie. Oddly, he was dressed as a Janissary which was absurd given that Mahmud II destroyed the Janissaries before Abdul Hamid was even born. He, Sivas, was standing in front of the Sale Pavilion, the one that looks like a Swiss chalet. It was an incongruous moment which is why I suppose it has stayed with me.'

Mehmet smiled. 'Indeed.'

'Yes.' And Muhammed disappeared behind his newspaper once again.

In common with so many of his aristocratic forebears, Mehmet's father was becoming more eccentric by the year. But unlike some of his more famous and powerful ancestors, many of them sultans, Muhammed's peccadilloes were neither lethal nor deranged. Weak, profligate and uneasy with strong emotion, he had come to Mehmet's home not only at the behest of his nagging wife but also because he was worried about Zelfa. Unlike Nur, he liked the little Irish woman and he loved his grandson, Yusuf İzzeddin. Not that he, a man, would have asked to see the baby himself. But when Mehmet did eventually suggest that they have a quick look at the sleeping child, Muhammed Suleyman leapt from his chair with alacrity.

İkmen looked more like a wraith than a person as he pulled a terrified Hikmet Yıldız into Saka Selim Sokak opposite the Church of St Anthony of Padua.

'What are you doing on İstiklal Caddesi?' the older man asked, his voice low and sibilant as if he were trying not to be overheard. 'Why aren't you in Kandıllı?'

'I was told to report back to the station.'

'That doesn't explain why you're here.'

'I came on the bus, sir,' he said. 'Commissioner Ardiç told lots of us to go – Inspector İskender, Sergeant Çöktin, the technical man. All the cars were full and so I had to come on the bus. I got off at Taksim. I'm going to walk down through Karaköy and across the Galata Bridge.'

İkmen, his face grey and drawn with exhaustion, grimaced. 'I don't believe this,' he said. 'I don't understand. What is going on?'

Yıldız shrugged. 'I don't know.'

'Oh, Allah!' İkmen coughed. 'Well, now that you are here, you can help me,' he said. 'In fact your being here now could be fortuitous.'

'Oh. Right. So you want me to do that thing we talked about last night. Ask no questions and—'

'There is a ladies' clothes shop less than a hundred metres down İstiklal on the right,' İkmen said. 'It's called the XOOX Boutique.'

Yıldız, who came from an almost exclusively male household, didn't like the sound of this. He frowned.

'I want you to go in there,' İkmen continued. 'Pick a small item off one of the shelves, drift around looking for a while and then arrest the very fat girl dressed in pink and black as she leaves the premises.'

Yıldız, shocked, said, 'What for? Why would I arrest her?'

'For theft, Yıldız! Theft of the small item you will drop into one of the many carrier bags she's walking around with!'

'You want me to set up a young girl?'

'Yes.'

'But—'

'I know you have experience of the Müren family, Hikmet,' İkmen said, rummaging for cigarettes he knew he did not have.

Yıldız looked up at the clear blue sky and narrowed his eyes in thought. 'Drugs, prostitution, some protection . . .'

'Yes, plus a relationship of sorts with the late Hassan

Şeker.' İkmen put one arm round Yıldız's shoulders and moved him forward onto the main thoroughfare. He pointed at a trendily monochrome shop to the right. 'Well, Alev Müren, old man Ali's dearest daughter, is the said fat girl in that shop.'

'Oh.'

'Right. So you go and buy something for your sister.'

'I don't have a—'

'Then pretend!' İkmen said through gritted teeth. 'And when you bring her out I will be waiting. I've been following that spoilt child around for more time than I care to think about. I know what she's been up to,' he added cryptically. 'And I know what that could mean for her brothers.'

Chapter 18

İkmen flicked his head in the direction of the nearest interview room.

'Put him in there,' he said to the thickset officer who was holding Ekrem Müren's arm halfway up his back.

'If any harm comes to my sister . . .' Müren spluttered, his face red with fury.

'Yes, yes,' İkmen said in a bored tone as he followed the struggling officer and his prisoner into the room. 'You'll pull my arms and legs off and feed them to the wolves.' He sat down and lit a cigarette.

While the other officer, Roditi, struggled to seat Ekrem Müren, Hikmet Yıldız entered the room and sat down at the table beside İkmen.

'You've no reason at all to hold Alev.'

'Ah, but we have,' İkmen said with a smile. 'It was a scarf Miss Müren attempted to liberate from the XOOX, wasn't it, Constable Yıldız?'

'Yes, sir, blue.'

'How very attractive,' and then with a lightning change of mood and tone, İkmen hissed, 'Sit down and shut up, Müren!'

'If any of those animals down there touch my sister,' Ekrem said, referring to the small contingent of very large officers İkmen had introduced him to when they visited Alev in the cells. 'If they—'

'So it's very important that we get her out of there soon then, isn't it?' İkmen said, 'and your sitting still so that Constable Roditi here can have a little rest is a first step.'

Still struggling, Ekrem sneered, 'Bastard.'

'Is that really the best you can do?' İkmen said. He sighed with weariness. 'Look, Ekrem, I want to do a deal so just stop struggling and let's all get down to business.'

Ekrem Müren eyed İkmen suspiciously. He'd felt Suleyman and İskender's hands upon his neck before – he'd had other more pleasant dealings with lesser policemen – but he'd never had personal experience of İkmen. As he slowly allowed his body to relax as much as it could, he thought about this man's reputation as a person of total incorruptibility and how oddly that sat beside the notion of a deal. But then not all of those around İkmen were straight, as Ekrem knew from personal experience, and so perhaps the stories about honest İkmen were just, well, lies.

He looked behind to where Roditi was still standing, though not touching him any more, then swung his head round to stare at İkmen.

'How much do you want?' he said. 'I can have any amount here in an hour.'

'Oh, that's good,' İkmen said and then, turning to Yıldız, he added, 'That's very quick, don't you think?'

'Yes, sir.'

'So how much do you want then? While we talk my sister's down there with them!' Anger made him rise to his feet, and immediately the hard hand of Constable Roditi made him sit down again. Hot and stuffy, Interview Room

2 only served to heighten the heat that had filled his mind as soon as he'd heard about Alev.

İkmen pretended to study his fingernails for a few moments until Ekrem appeared to be settled. Then he looked up and smiled. 'I don't want your money,' he said simply. 'It's of no use to me.'

For a moment, Ekrem looked flummoxed, eyes darting in all directions. He was truly confused. 'Well, what—'

'If you want Alev to come home at some point tonight with her face and her honour intact then I need to know who it is you work for,' İkmen said, stubbing his cigarette out on the floor. He lit up another.

'I work for my father.'

'Yes, I know that!' İkmen waved a dismissive hand in front of Ekrem's face. 'But who does he have connections with, Ekrem? He's good, your father – in the traditional way – prostitution, drugs, extortion . . .' He leaned forward across the table so that his face was almost touching Ekrem's. 'But he isn't very imaginative, is he? I mean, it's all tired old whores giving blow jobs, that's his level, isn't it? He doesn't work with elegant young women wearing the dresses of princesses, does he? Or at least he didn't.'

'I don't know what you're talking about!'

'Hassan Şeker didn't kill himself because of the protection money he had to give to you,' İkmen said. 'He could afford it. He didn't finish himself because he'd killed Hatice İpek either, because he hadn't. He left her when he finished his work and went home. But he knew who did kill her and so, I think, do you.'

Ekrem turned sideways in his chair and looked at the wall. 'That girl has nothing to do with me.'

'Hassan Şeker died and implicated himself because he wanted to protect his family from someone who must have really frightened him.'

Ekrem shook his head, not realising how white his face had suddenly become.

'We know that you and your brother collected money from Hassan Şeker,' İkmen said.

'That's a lie!'

'I also discovered, from your sister actually,' İkmen continued, 'that your father's mother lives next door to the property of a Mrs Oncü, the lady who owns the entrance to the cistern where we found Hatice İpek's body. Care to explain?'

A moment of silence passed, time during which Ekrem Müren appeared to think.

'You're in a bit of a corner here, aren't you, Ekrem?' İkmen said.

'But none of that proves anything!' Ekrem blurted. 'We didn't kill that girl!'

'So you and your brother won't mind providing me with some samples for forensic analysis.'

Ekrem nodded. 'We can do that.'

'Good. And the friends you were working for?'

'You've got nothing on us, İkmen,' the gangster sneered, 'nor will you get it.'

İkmen's tired face suddenly reddened. 'I haven't got time for this,' he said and then quickly turned towards Yıldız. 'Give me your gun.'

'Sir?'

'Give it to me! A child lies dead. I've promised her mother I'll find who did it and I'm fucking exhausted!'

With some reluctance, Hikmet Yıldız put his hand into the

holster at his side and withdrew his pistol. İkmen snatched if from him and pointed it at Müren.

'Hold him in that chair, Roditi,' İkmen said to the other, now rattled officer.

'Inspector . . .'

'That is an order, Roditi!'

The officer pinned Ekrem Müren's arms behind his back. Ekrem's eyes widened in alarm as İkmen took the safety catch off and moved forward.

'If you don't tell me who you're working for and what involvement those people had with the death of Hatice İpek, I'm going to kill you,' İkmen said quietly and shoved the weapon up against Ekrem's temple.

'I've told you, there's nothing to tell.'

'Wrong! Try again!'

Yıldız and Roditi exchanged alarmed glances. Much as they liked and respected İkmen, this had gone too far. The inspector, obviously sorely in need of sleep and nourishment, wasn't himself. İkmen didn't hurt people, he didn't even carry a gun of his own.

'How are you going to explain it if you kill me?' Ekrem, who had now lost his earlier cocky demeanour, trembled.

İkmen moved his face close in to his prey. 'I don't know and I don't care,' he said. 'My wife is hundreds of kilometres away, there's nothing to eat at my apartment, my superiors tell me they don't like me any more and I see no reason why I shouldn't take all of that out on you. Now tell me who's behind your recent interest in fancy-dress prostitution!'

'I can't!'

'Why not?'

'Because . . .' Ekrem slid his eyes over towards the barrel of the gun. 'Because they and my father . . . No . . .'

'You have two choices, Müren,' İkmen said, his voice thick with tension. 'Either you keep quiet and die at my hands or you tell me and I give you the protection that you need.'

In spite of the seriousness of his situation, Ekrem laughed. 'Oh, you stupid fucking—'

'İkmen!'

Ardiç's voice ripped across the room as the door flew open.

'I'd like you to come out in the corridor now please, Inspector,' he said as his furious eyes took in what appeared to be a scene of old style, now supposedly outlawed, intimidation.

'But sir—'

'*Now!*' Ardiç turned on his heel and left.

İkmen, the gun still in his hand, his head lowered, followed him.

'What the fuck do you think you're doing?' Ardiç hissed, thrusting his large face at İkmen's.

'He was just about to tell me—'

'Is that weapon disabled?' Having just noticed that the gun was still in İkmen's hand, Ardiç's face whitened in alarm.

'Of course it is,' İkmen said wearily. 'What do you think I am?'

'I think,' his boss said with some acidity, 'that you're a fucking mess! When did you last sleep, İkmen? Or eat? Or wash?'

'I finished that report for you. I've been busy.'

'Busy? You're not even supposed to be on duty!' Ardiç looked at him with distaste. 'You look like a drunk! You're a fucking disgrace!'

İkmen straightened his back. 'Müren was just about to tell me who he's working for, the person I believe was responsible for Hatice İpek's—'

'Not that again!' Ardiç took hold of the front of İkmen's shirt and pulled him forward. 'I've told you to leave that alone! It's a non-case. And before you start telling me that you promised the girl's mother you would find her attackers, may I remind you that the girl, who was anyway less than perfect, died of natural causes!'

'Yes, I know,' İkmen said, his mouth now just centimetres from Ardiç's hot, sweating face, 'but she was raped and cut. And besides, sir, I've discovered what I think might be a conspiracy, an organisation around girls like Hatice, girls supplied to act like odalisques for rich, select people. I think Müren might recently have become involved.'

Ardiç, his face now more concerned than angry, loosened his grip on İkmen's shirt. 'Where did you come by this information?' he asked.

'From several sources.'

'What sources?' Ardiç looked at İkmen severely. Officers were frequently reluctant to name their informants, even to their superiors. İkmen had always been one of the worst culprits. 'Well?'

'One of my informants,' İkmen said, 'was a man known as Rat.'

Ardiç rolled his eyes.

'Also two very well-bred and respectable elderly ladies, one of whom is now dead. Muazzez Heper, she died yesterday under the wheels of a hit and run driver.'

'Which you believe, I assume, is connected to this . . .' he paused to find the right words, 'bizarre Arabian Nights fantasy these misfits have fed you?'

'Sir, this organisation, the Harem, they call it, is—'

'Oh, spare me! The Harem?' Ardiç threw his arms in the air and laughed. 'This is nonsense, İkmen! Discrete items of information that you have decided to slot into some weird conspiracy theory.'

'Rat told me that families are now involved with this organisation. The Mürens were connected to Hassan Şeker who could have been instrumental in getting Hatice involved in it. In his suicide note he said that he killed her but we know that he didn't, he was definitely at home. He must have been protecting his family from someone, maybe the Müren boys. Or maybe someone they have dealings with, someone more powerful and sophisticated than Ali and his brood. Sir, Muazzez Heper made the dress Hatice was wearing when she died. She made it in the early sixties when she herself was involved with the Harem.'

'But you say she is now dead? Is that right?'

İkmen lowered his head, much of his energy spent. 'Yes, sir.'

'And does the sister who remains know the Müren family?'

'She says not, sir, but she is in contact with another woman who—'

'And Rat?'

'I haven't seen Rat for a while. He moves around.'

'I see.' Ardiç sighed and then held his hand out towards İkmen. 'Give me the gun, İkmen.'

He handed it over automatically and without a word.

'Now go home,' the commissioner said quietly, 'and stay there, as I orginally instructed you, for a week.'

İkmen looked up, his eyes shiny with tears of exhaustion. 'You don't believe me, do you?'

'No,' Ardiç replied as he weighed the pistol agitatedly in his hand. 'I believe that you believe it, but I don't. You've been fed a fantasy, a silly film script.'

'Have I?'

'Yes. Now go home, İkmen. Come back to us when you're feeling better.'

Ardiç moved as if to go back into the interview room where Müren and the two junior officers were still sitting, no doubt in the kind of silence that allows people to hear what is going on beyond closed doors.

Before he got there, however, İkmen spoke. 'What are you going to do with Ekrem Müren now, sir?'

'He is my concern, not yours.' Ardiç pointed an accusatory finger at İkmen. 'Go home!'

'You're going to let him go, aren't you?'

'Go home!'

İkmen turned and made his way falteringly down the corridor towards the stairs. It hurt that Ardiç didn't believe him but then it had hurt when the commissioner had taken him off the Sivas case. This, he believed, was informed by 'others', Ankara people, who had ordered Ardiç to remove him: a sort of high-level conspiracy . . . Allah, but weren't they just appearing everywhere all of a sudden! The Harem, the intimation of Mafia involvement in Hikmet Sivas's past, and maybe his present too, Ardiç's rapid flight to the capital . . .

Perhaps, İkmen thought, I really am going insane. Maybe exposure to so much of an 'exotic' nature in such rapid succession coupled with a lifestyle just waiting to catch up with me has finally taken its toll!

He felt the blood drain from his face as his body responded to this fear. But then he straightened up and walked on with more purpose. The fact was that these things he'd spoken to Ardiç about had happened. Hatice had died in the costume of an Ottoman odalisque, Hassan Şeker had killed himself and Muazzez Heper had been run down at what, if Yümniye and Rat were correct, seemed a very convenient time. Somebody didn't want this affair to come to light. Maybe even Ardiç himself . . . It had, after all, been Ardiç who had effectively closed the case on Hatice İpek. Maybe Ardiç had himself visited this Harem. İkmen shuddered as he tried to turn his mind away from the image.

Although the assumption that Belkis İskender was exclusively wedded to her career was not far shy of the truth, she did give some of her time to her husband who had always excited both her passion and her sympathy. After all, although considerably shorter than her and not nearly so astute, Metin was a good-looking man who enjoyed literature and cultivated company. She could talk to him about her work which he appeared to understand. The same could not be said for her attitude to his employment which Belkis didn't want to know about or understand. Authority and artistry didn't gel and so most of the time Belkis chose to ignore the fact that her husband was a policeman.

This evening, however, was different. Metin had come off duty much earlier than Belkis was accustomed to and in a bad mood. No, not a bad mood, upset. This was why they were now in the Malta Kiosk in Yıldız Park, as opposed to some stylish city centre restaurant which was Belkis's usual preference.

'I could have solved it, you know,' he said as he pushed his aubergine salad disinterestedly around his plate with his fork. 'Given time. İkmen and I were making progress. But first they get rid of him and then I go.' He waved his arms in the air in agitation. 'I was on television, at the beginning. Fame for a moment. Now this.'

'I think you should consider doing something else, darling,' his wife replied, draining the last of the champagne into her glass. 'You know I would support any project you decided to undertake.'

He smiled weakly. 'I know.'

'I always hoped that after that terrible business in Edirnekapı you'd give it up,' she said, alluding to the difficult time her husband had had after his abortive and bloody altercation with an eastern European drug dealer.

'But you know I can't,' he replied. 'I've got to do this and succeed, Belkis.'

She reached across the table and touched his arm. 'Why?'

'Because much as you might like to dress me up in designer suits and thrill to my enjoyment of books, I am still that kid from Umraniye,' he said. 'I joined the police to get out of there, which I did. I educated myself, married a beautiful, successful woman, but I still need to prove myself in their eyes,' he said, alluding to the impoverished family he still visited weekly.

'But you could do that in another career. You know all the people I work with.'

'But policing is a man's job!' he said as he broke free from her grasp and then turned to look down the wooded hill towards the distant Bosphorus. 'My father and brothers would never understand book publishing. If I joined your company they would view me as even more of a lap dog than they do now!'

'Metin, darling, you must let go of the past.' Belkis rested her head in her hands and sighed. 'You're a sensitive person.

You could exorcise so much if you had time and space and could just sit down and write. You don't have to join my company. I know you have a book in you, I would support—'

'Oh, Belkis, leave it, please!' he said. They'd been here before – so many times.

Belkis put her hands in her lap and cast her eyes down sadly. As far as she was concerned the only thing to be done with Metin's desperate childhood in Umraniye was to write about it and then forget it. He was a success already. In spite of growing up without the benefit of running water in a district where rubbish dumps smouldered constantly and exploded occasionally, he had educated himself, climbed the ladder of success very quickly and looked good enough to eat. Why he still wanted to prove himself to people who were illiterate, filthy and frequently criminal, she couldn't think. But then she couldn't even imagine what went on inside her husband's head.

Metin let his eyes rest on the path that ran along the top of the wooded hill to the restaurant. Couples and a few families were approaching, puffing and sweating their way to their evening meals in the graceful setting of the Malta Kiosk. Well-dressed, clean people who knew, as he did, that the gorgeously Italianate building he was sitting in front of had once been used to imprison poor Murad V, the Sultan who had drunk much and reigned little. Nobody in Umraniye would know that. Nobody in Umraniye had nice clothes, unless they had stolen them. He still remembered sorting through the smoking rubbish piles for winter shoes. He would never forget. Because you didn't. Things came back, all the time, just like the man whose thick blond hair shone so brightly in the setting sun as he materialised onto the path in front of Metin İskender. Allah, no! And for a moment the world became silent and fixed – a spell only broken by Belkis as she thrust her face into his and shouted, 'Metin! Metin, what is it? Darling!'

Chapter 19

Mehmet Suleyman should have known better. One never just turned up at Çetin İkmen's apartment and expected to leave after half an hour. What had begun as a mid-morning social call, to thank İkmen for the gift he had given to baby Yusuf İzzeddin, became a lengthy conversation.

'What I don't understand,' Suleyman said as he finished his second glass of tea and then lit a cigarette, 'is how, given that this Harem exists, we've never heard about it before.'

'If they used only quality girls, as apparently they did,' İkmen replied, 'they wouldn't talk. Women like the Heper sisters would rather die than have it known they've had sex for money.'

'But that doesn't explain Hatice İpek, does it?'

'No.' İkmen lit yet another Maltepe cigarette. 'But if both Miss Yümniye and Rat are correct about a recent change of ownership of this operation then Hatice İpek would fit. I mean, if one or more families are involved then I can't see even the brightest of them having any understanding of what a lady may have to offer as opposed to some pretty kid or cheap gecekondu girl. And anyway, how many girls are there now who possess connections with the old order?'

'Mmm.' Suleyman frowned. 'Except that surely the nature of the Harem would demand ladies. As I understand it, the originators were selling an Ottoman fantasy. Genuine paşa's daughters sold at high cost to foreigners and maybe even Turks. Although I suppose that if we consider Hatice's death, it could be that the clientele has changed.'

İkmen shook his head dismissively. 'I don't think so,' he said. 'If the families wanted to start an operation like this of their own, there is nothing to stop them. According to Miss Yümniye and Rat, the original clients were rich and important, and I think the families took over this operation because they wanted to gain access to these important clients.'

Suleyman leaned forward in his chair and put his chin thoughtfully in his hands. 'But why? Why would these men accept ordinary working girls if they've had the real thing before? Shop girls and the like wouldn't know how to behave appropriately. But then some of these original clients must be quite old now, mustn't they?'

'Old, rich and important,' İkmen said with a thin smile. 'In the early hours of this morning I thought about the possibility of blackmail.'

The sound of the front door buzzer sounded from the hall outside, making both men look towards the living room door.

'Hulya will get it,' İkmen said and then just to make sure that she did, he shouted her name.

Suleyman, his mind still on their talk, sighed. 'What I also don't understand is how, given that it was supposed to have been such a great secret, the families got to know about the Harem.'

İkmen who, in spite of having got at least some sleep the night before, was still extremely tired, just shrugged.

The living room door opened and Hulya came in.

'Dad, Inspector İskender has come to see you.' She

turned to beckon the young officer into her father's presence.

Both İkmen and Suleyman made to stand up, but İskender motioned for them to stay where they were.

'Sit down, Metin,' İkmen said. 'Can I offer you tea?'

'Yes. Thank you.'

He looked nervous, his hands fidgeted in his lap, like a man at an important interview.

İkmen turned towards his daughter. 'Can you do that please, Hulya?'

'Yes, Dad.'

It really was quite amazing how much more pliant and even pleasant she had become since she had been seeing Berekiah Cohen. Balthazar could say what he liked about the children's religious differences, but if this was the result, İkmen was glad – not that he had been bothered in the first place.

After checking to see whether her father or Suleyman also wanted tea, Hulya left.

'So to what do we owe the pleasure of your company, Metin?' İkmen asked and then added, 'I can tell something is wrong.'

'I've seen Zhivkov,' İskender replied.

'Well, I'd heard he was alive,' Suleyman said, 'but I didn't know he was actually in town.'

'Oh, he's in town.' İskender reached into his pocket and took out his cigarettes.

'You're sure it's Zhivkov?' İkmen asked.

İskender lit up. 'I watched him for nearly six months,' he said. 'There are hundreds of photographs of him in all sorts of situations on his file. Sometimes even now I get them out. It's as if I keep having to remind myself about the true appearance of evil. It was him.' İskender looked down at his cigarette. İkmen and Suleyman exchanged concerned glances.

'Where did you see him, Metin?'

Hulya entered briefly at this juncture to give the three men their tea. Only when she had gone did İskender reply.

'Well, that was the really frightening thing,' he said. 'He just appeared.'

'He would do,' Suleyman said. 'You weren't expecting to see him and there he was.'

'No, Mehmet.' İskender put his hands over his face. When he had composed himself, he said, 'Look, I know it sounds crazy, but Belkis and I were having dinner at the Malta Kiosk in Yıldız Park last night. We sat outside. I was watching the path that runs to the kiosk across the top of the hill. I saw families and couples puffing after the climb – and then there was Zhivkov, suddenly on the path, as if he'd jumped out of a trap door in the ground.'

'Maybe he was behind the families and couples,' İkmen said.

'I don't think so.'

'They could have obscured your view of him.'

'Yes, but they didn't!' İskender shook his hands out in front of himself in order to emphasise his point. 'That's just it! One moment the people were there with no one behind them and then suddenly there was the Bulgarian.' He looked at the sceptical faces around him with something approaching panic. 'Belkis will tell you. She thought I was having a heart attack!'

'I don't doubt that it looked like that, Metin,' Suleyman said.

'I tell you, Mehmet,' İskender insisted vehemently, 'it

was just like that show Belkis and I once saw in Paris. David Copperfield, the American illusionist. One minute he wasn't there, the next . . .' He clicked his fingers.

'Yes, but—'

'No, no.' İkmen, who had been quietly deliberating for the last few moments, held up his hand to silence Suleyman. 'Whatever you or I may think, Metin has had a genuine experience, I can tell that from his voice, and besides, I know him to be an honest man.'

'Thank you.'

'If all life, as some believe, is an illusion anyway, then who are we to say what is and isn't so?' İkmen smiled. 'And what was it Sherlock Holmes used to say? When you've ruled out all other logical explanations, whatever remains, however improbable, has to be the solution, or in this case the reality.'

'So are you saying,' Suleyman said, 'that we should seriously believe that Zhivkov materialised out of thin air?'

'Or appeared to do so, yes.' İkmen looked at the two troubled faces in front of him. 'Any ideas?'

He'd been frightened twice in as many days. First by İkmen's threats and then by the news that the informant known as Rat was dead. The latter, if not the former piece of news, had been designed to frighten him. The caller, someone whose voice he didn't recognise, had gone into lurid detail. The lopping off of ears and other, more delicate parts . . . Saying, of course, that 'this is what we do to those who betray us'. As if he needed reminding. As if, now, it had anything to do with him! The man he'd been well paid to protect, Hassan Şeker, was dead. It should have ended there. But it hadn't and as Orhan Tepe knew only too well, it had everything to do with him because, and only because, of his insatiable desire for money. Of course, once one was involved in this sort of thing, one was in forever. If only he hadn't needed to impress Ayşe so much! If only he, as İkmen had so acutely observed, hadn't been so eaten up with jealousy of Suleyman.

Hassan Şeker had been fucking Hatice İpek for over a year. He liked the girl and Tepe had believed him when he'd said that he hadn't killed her. He knew who had, although he never revealed who it was. The only certainty was that it was neither Ekrem nor Celal Müren. They were, as Tepe was beginning to appreciate, only messenger boys – for whom he didn't know. Soon, however, he was going to find out.

A favour was, apparently, needed. Ekrem said that Tepe's presence would be required at some time during the course of the weekend. Tepe looked across at the elderly woman sitting opposite him, apparently asleep, and silently cursed his bad fortune. He was supposed to be on duty here in Kandıllı until Sunday morning. What was he going to do if he was wanted before then?

'I would suggest that you attend to your Koran,' Hale Sivas said, opening her eyes. 'I can read in your face that your mind is troubled. But every answer to every question lies within the pages of the Holy Koran.'

Tepe attempted a smile and said, 'Yes, thank you, Miss Sivas, I'll bear that in mind.'

The old woman straightened in her chair and then scrutinised Tepe even more closely. She shook her head sadly.

'No you won't,' she said. 'My brothers always agreed far too readily to my suggestions, just like you. Neither of them has so much as opened the Holy Book for decades.'

'Well, when we find your brothers you can ask them, can't you?'

'No.' She gripped the arms of the chair tightly and then pushed herself up to a standing position. 'My brothers are dead. Being with bad people rots the soul, you know, at first. Then later it takes the vile body with it. My brothers are dead and I don't have enough piety even in my good soul to save them from hell.'

She moved slowly towards the door, her headscarf pulled down tightly across her hair. Tepe briefly wished her dead. Ungrateful old bitch! Oh yes, she could afford a blameless soul living in a fantastic place like this, leeching off the successful brother she both loved and despised. If Hikmet Sivas had indeed come by much of his wealth by less than legal means then he'd done it in part for Hale. He loved her, according to İkmen; he deferred to her, wanting always to please her.

He'd been like that himself with Ayşe. He'd so wanted to please her, he'd got into this mess in order to please her. But she, just like this old Sivas woman, hadn't appreciated it. The one time he'd done something to fulfil his own needs and fantasies she'd first behaved like some stupid cock tease and then she'd gone crying to İkmen who had taken her side. Bastard! How he could call himself a man when he obviously didn't understand a man's needs was beyond Tepe. The fact remained, however, that İkmen would make trouble for him now. He'd have to get himself reassigned, and quickly. He shouldn't think about that particular event with Ayşe now. No. The thought of how she'd looked, naked, afraid and bleeding, would only make him hard and there was no outlet for that here. With Ardiç in the building he couldn't even find an empty bedroom in which to relieve himself – that would be too risky.

Ardiç was watching him. He was convinced of it. He'd got rid of İkmen first and then İskender and had taken personal charge. But he'd kept him. Other junior officers, that old fool Yalçin, and him. What was Ardiç doing? All any of them did was wait, but for what? The only sensible thing that Hale Sivas had said during the course of her last little homily was that her brothers were probably dead. The people who had killed Kaycee hadn't been messing around. And so if Hikmet or Vedat or both were mixed up with these people they were certainly in a lot of trouble. If the Mafia, which was the name being mooted in some quarters as the culprit in Kaycee's murder, were involved, Tepe hardly dared think what might be happening to the Sivas brothers.

'The fact is,' İkmen said as he rose to pace his living room, which was something he did when he wanted to explore ideas, 'that İsak Çöktin and a group of junior officers spent almost a whole day exploring Yıldız and its environs after Vedat Sivas went missing. Bar the cellars, everything they looked into was well and truly above ground.'

'Well, it would be,' Suleyman responded. 'There is nothing else, apart from a stupid old story about secret tunnels.'

İkmen, frowning now, stopped pacing. 'I know the legend you mean. It would explain—'

'Oh, come on, Çetin!' Suleyman shook his head in disbelief. 'I know Abdul Hamid was paranoid, but the old stories about his moving from place to place in tunnels because he was frightened of assassins were just journalistic sensationalism. If the tunnels existed, the staff at the palace would have taken Çöktin and his boys down there when they were looking round the place.'

'If they knew they were there,' İkmen said.

'Well, of course they'd know!'

'If the tunnels were blocked up many years ago—'

'Only to be miraculously discovered by Zhivkov?' Suleyman flung his hands petulantly in the air. 'Oh, please!'

İkmen turned away from Suleyman towards İskender. 'Yıldız Park has undoubtedly featured in our lives of late. We searched the place because Vedat Sivas has worked there for many years.'

'And Hikmet himself worked there too.'

İkmen and İskender both looked at Suleyman.

'My father saw him there in costume, making a Yeşilcam film,' he said. 'He was supposed to be a Janissary.'

'When was this?' İkmen asked.

'Before he went to Hollywood,' Suleyman replied. 'My great-uncle Selim, who was born in Yıldız, was showing my father around at the time.'

'Ah,' İkmen said.

'My father didn't mention tunnels, Çetin,' Suleyman said with a smile.

'Did you ask him?'

'No. He'd think I was crazy.'

İkmen took his mobile telephone out of his trouser pocket and handed it to Suleyman. 'Perhaps you ought to put that assumption to the test, Mehmet.'

With a disgruntled shake of his head, Suleyman took the phone from İkmen's hand and stood up.

'I'll do it,' he said, 'but if one of my wife's colleagues comes for me with a straitjacket, I'll hold you responsible.'

He walked out onto the balcony for privacy – not from

İkmen so much as from İskender. İkmen was familiar with the strained conversations that took place between members of the Suleyman family; Metin İskender was not.

When he had gone, İskender turned to İkmen. 'We still want Zhivkov for the murder of his wife,' he said, 'amongst other offences.'

'Yes.' İkmen, frowning, lit another cigarette. 'Has he been seen anywhere else in the city lately?'

'Not that I know of.'

'So, given the strangeness of his appearance by the Malta Kiosk, he could be hiding out at the palace.'

'I guess so.'

'Mmm.' İkmen sank back into the depths of his old, battered armchair. 'Do you remember,' he said, 'when you and I were first working on the Sivas case, you felt that family might be involved somewhere along the line?'

'Yes.'

'And then we talked about Hikmet Sivas's possible connection to the Sicilian Mafia.'

'Which Ardiç saw no virtue in pursuing,' İskender said regretfully.

'Are you suspicious, Metin?' İkmen asked. 'Of Ardiç.'

The younger man lowered his eyes, saying nothing but speaking volumes through his movements.

'I thought so.' İkmen shook his head sadly. 'I am too. Nobody remains from the original team except Ardiç, old Yalçin, still strangely eluding death, and Orhan Tepe. I don't like it. We've got Vedat Sivas, brother of movie star Hikmet who, it seems, has significant Italian connections, works at Yıldız, has done so for forty years. Zhivkov, Bulgarian gangster and man who decapitates women, seen emerging from the ether in Yıldız. Kaycee Sivas, decapitated—'

'But by a different method,' İskender said. 'Kaycee was killed cleanly with one blow. Poor Nina Zhivkov had her head sawn off with a bread knife. Dr Sarkissian said it could have taken her up to an hour to die.'

'What bothers me,' İkmen said, 'is that our families and theirs – the Americans, Sicilians, whatever – may have for some reason come into conflict in this city via Hikmet Sivas.' He put his head on one side, frowning. 'And police officers are in there somewhere too, senior police officers . . .'

İskender nodded. 'You mean Ardiç, I take it.'

'No,' İkmen said, 'I don't actually.' He looked at İskender with a serious expression on his face. 'Men from Ankara. If you remember, Metin, it was after Ardiç went to Ankara that I was taken off the case and everything constructive about the investigation ceased.'

They sat in silence for a few moments as the implications of this deduction sank in.

Suleyman, returning from the balcony, placed İkmen's phone down by his ashtray and resumed his seat.

İkmen, watching him with red, tired eyes, asked, 'Well?'

Suleyman shrugged. 'You were right and, astonishingly, I was wrong. There are tunnels, or rather subterranean passages, constructed by the Sultan to allow him safe transport from one part of the palace to another. My father went down into one underneath the main palace complex with his uncle. He thinks some of the other passages had been blocked off.'

'And the Malta Kiosk?'

'He doesn't know. And that's the point really.'

'What is?' İskender asked.

'Nobody knows,' Suleyman replied. 'Abdul Hamid used

separate architects and artisans for every different part of his palace. The men worked in shifts and were forbidden to associate. Only the Sultan knew the whole picture. The only clue we have is that the Malta Kiosk was at one time used to imprison the Sultan's alcoholic brother Murad. According to my father, Abdul Hamid used to like to go and gloat over his elder sibling's misfortune from time to time, so there could be a passage from the main complex out to the kiosk. And if that is the case it may pass underneath or near the path you observed Zhivkov on, Metin.'

'And both Hikmet Sivas and whoever murdered his wife knew of the legends of Yıldız,' İkmen said.

'Did they?' Suleyman asked. 'How do you know?'

'Well,' İkmen replied, 'whoever sent Kaycee's head to her husband had pinned a very pertinent note to the side of the box. It alluded directly to one of those legends.'

'Yes,' İskender said excitedly, 'that's right! You said at the time that Sivas probably knew what was in the box just from the words in the note!'

'It would seem like it, wouldn't it?' İkmen said softly. He leaned his head back still further and closed his eyes. 'Yıldız is connected to Vedat and Hikmet Sivas. Zhivkov appeared there yesterday. The question is, what is the connection, if any, between Zhivkov and the Sivas brothers?'

Chapter 20

When Suleyman and İskender left, Hulya broached the subject of Berekiah Cohen with her father, but the front door buzzer cut her short.

The visitor, who was a short, middle-aged woman, had the reddest hair Hulya had ever seen. She wanted, she said, to see Çetin İkmen. Hulya led her through into the living room.

İkmen's face showed true surprise when he saw her. 'Sofia Vanezis!'

'You touched my breast in nineteen fifty-nine,' Sofia replied as a shocked Hulya left the room and shut the door behind her.

'I—'

'Miss Yümniye Heper told me I had to see you.' Sofia sat down heavily in the chair nearest the door. 'Miss Muazzez Heper is dead.'

'Yes, I know,' İkmen, who was unaccustomed to embarrassment of this order, rubbed one of his hands nervously across his chin. 'Would you like some tea?'

'Miss Muazzez always said I should never say anything and I never have,' Sofia continued. 'But now Miss Yümniye has told me that I must. So I will, but not all. Miss Muazzez said I must never tell all. I remember everything.'

'Do you?' İkmen sat down on the sofa opposite his guest

and lit a cigarette. Sofia, with her swollen legs and stomach like a football, in no way resembled the girl whose breast he'd briefly squeezed in 1959. Only that red hair and that monotonous speech of hers, devoid of all emotion, were familiar.

'Nineteen sixty-five. There was a room with no windows,' she said, 'gold cloth on all the walls, silk kilims on the floor, a very big bed, shiny sheets.'

'This is the Harem.'

'It is a place for sex. There was a man.'

'And do you remember—'

'I can't tell you who he was. Miss Muazzez said no, under no circumstances. Miss Muazzez arranged everything so I could have some money from this man. He told me I had to forget what happened in that room with gold cloth walls, which I did. He gave me some money. I left. I was there thirty-one minutes. Exactly thirty-one minutes.'

Sofia Vanezis had always been odd. Some people, like Yümniye Heper, said she was 'slow'. But that was a very long way from the truth, as İkmen could now appreciate. Sofia Vanezis was sharp, observant and almost certainly, he felt, autistic. And, if he was right about this, as long as he didn't ask her for her opinion about anything or ask directly for this person's name, he might yet find out who he was. Autistic people couldn't, İkmen had heard somewhere, lie. They were, in effect, slaves to facts, devoid of the ability to fabricate.

'This man . . .'

'He had black hair, brown eyes. He wore a blue shirt and black trousers. I know his name, but I won't tell you that. I saw him in a film once, before nineteen sixty-five. Mama

288

took me to see it in nineteen fifty-nine. I don't know what it was called, I can't read. Nineteen fifty-nine. When you touched my breast. September. I told you to. I let you. It was Thursday.'

She rose, with some difficulty, as if to leave.

İkmen, impulsively, leapt from his seat and blocked her exit with his body. The man, the Harem customer Sofia had serviced, had been a film actor.

'Sofia,' he said hurriedly, lest she interrupt him again, 'this man you saw in the film in nineteen fifty-nine, who was he in the film? Not his name, but the character he played. Do you remember?'

She looked at him without emotion.

'I remember everything,' she said. 'He was Bekir, a very bad general.'

Ahmet Sılay had used the word 'evil' as opposed to 'bad' when he'd talked about that particular film. Hikmet Sivas's performance in the part had been, Sılay had said, truly awful.

'Dad?'

Hulya had come into the room and seated herself opposite İkmen without his even noticing.

He looked up wearily and then smiled. 'Hulya.'

'Who was that woman?'

İkmen sighed. 'I don't really want to talk about it right now, Hulya.'

'Yes, but she said—'

'I know what she said,' he replied evenly. 'And for the record I was twelve and she was about, I suppose, sixteen when the incident she mentioned happened. Boys touch girls and girls touch boys. It happens. Human beings, particularly young human beings, develop fancies for each other from time to time.'

'Yes, I know.' She looked down at her hands which were clasped nervously in her lap. 'Dad, Berekiah Cohen has escorted me to work a couple of times and we went to visit Dr Halman together at the hospital.'

'Yes, Hulya, I know. What of it?'

The girl looked shocked. 'You know?'

'Yes.' Why did teenagers always think that their parents were completely ignorant about their lives? 'You're friends,' he said. 'What of it?'

'Well, Mr Cohen, Berekiah's father, wants us to stop seeing each other!'

'But you're only friends, aren't you?' İkmen watched her closely to gauge her reaction.

Hulya duly lowered her eyes. 'Yes.'

'So there isn't a problem then, is there?'

'No.' She looked up sharply now, with a challenge in her eyes. 'But if Berekiah and I developed fancies for each other . . .'

'Then that would be another matter,' İkmen said. 'You're very young and as your father I would want some sort of assurance from Berekiah that he would treat you with respect. I am sure that he would.'

'So you wouldn't object to him because he's a Jew?'

'No.' İkmen leaned forward and looked his daughter straight in the eyes. 'But if Mr Cohen is worried because he fears you two might become involved then we have to respect his point of view, Hulya.'

Tears suddenly sprang into her eyes. 'What do you mean?'

'I mean that the Jews of İstanbul have a very longstanding

and honourable tradition in this city. Berekiah's family fled here from Spain five hundred years ago and although they have always taken part in the life of our country, they have never married outside their religion.'

'How do they know that?' Hulya asked disdainfully as she roughly wiped a tear from her eye. 'How can they know that?'

'I don't know,' İkmen replied with a shrug, 'but that is what they say. And it is important to them, so we have to respect that point of view.'

'Yes, but Dad, what I want to know is whether you agree with it,' Hulya said urgently. 'I mean, if I wanted to marry Berekiah, say, what would you do?'

'Beyond placating your mother and wondering where I might get some money to buy you a bed and a kitchen, you mean?'

'So you would . . .'

'I wouldn't stop you, Hulya. But Mr Cohen and your mother might and I would be lying if I said that I'd actively fight them for you.' He sighed. 'However, I do hope that all of this is some way down the line,' he said gravely. 'I trust the two of you are still just friends. To marry someone so different requires sober thought. One has to consider language – the Cohens speak Ladino amongst themselves, you don't – and children and, like it or not, the opinions of others.'

'You always used to say that you didn't care what other people thought,' his daughter countered with some petulance.

'I don't,' İkmen replied. 'But I have skin like a crocodile's.'

Hulya, in spite of herself, smiled.

'I just don't want you to get hurt,' her father said earnestly. 'Maybe you should stop meeting casually. It makes parents deeply suspicious. Ask Berekiah to come to dinner with us when your mother returns. Mr and Mrs Cohen will, I know, reciprocate. They might not like it, but they will do it.'

'Mmm.' Hulya looked down at her hands again and sighed.

'I'm saying that I think you should take things slowly,' İkmen said. 'Marriage, even without all the cultural differences we've been talking about, is a very big step. You have to be certain it's what you want and that the man you wish to marry is someone you can spend the rest of your life with. Sometimes that takes time. As you have unfortunately discovered today, I had feelings for at least one other girl before I met your mother. But since I've been married to her, there hasn't been anyone else. But you're still very young.'

'A lot of girls get married at my age.'

'Yes, I know, but not usually ambitious, educated girls like you.'

She looked gravely up into her father's face. 'I don't think I want to be an actress any more,' she said, 'not after what happened to Hatice.'

İkmen got up from his chair and went and sat down beside his daughter. He put his arms round her shoulders. It was good that she was no longer considering entry into the uncertain world of entertainment, but now that her attention had moved towards Berekiah Cohen, life was no less problematic. What was it with this girl? She'd never been easy – Fatma said she'd been born with an 'attitude'.

The sound of a door slamming across the corridor made İkmen jump. Bülent was up and about. Obviously still furious about having to surrender his bedroom, the İkmens' other teenager was showing some attitude of his own. İkmen closed his eyes and hoped that his son didn't decide to come in and have yet another argument about his room. He needed quiet in order to think about what Sofia Vanezis had just told him, and where he might need to go with that information.

The tip of the knife was so very close to the main artery in her neck that Suzan Şeker hardly dared breathe for fear of bleeding to death.

'I know that you told the police about our arrangement with your late husband,' Ekrem Müren said as he moved the blade just fractionally away from her so that she could talk. 'Who else would've done that? It had to be you.'

'No!'

'They arrested Ekrem!' Celal, his brother, put in from where he was leaning against the kitchen door. 'They let him go, but they did arrest him. They said we collected money from Hassan.'

'Shut up wittering, Celal!' Ekrem leaned into Suzan's face, blasting her features with beer fumes. 'I don't actually care anyway,' he said, 'because our association with you is about to end.'

Suzan, her lips quivering with fear, closed her eyes. So this was it. This was where she joined Hassan in whatever darkness and pain awaited the unclean soul in the afterlife. Her children would be orphans! Her eyes flew open at the horror of this image and she swallowed hard. How could she have been so stupid? One never spoke to the police about arrangements! Not even off the record. There was no such thing. Suleyman had used the information against her wishes. What had possessed her? The grief following her husband's death? A desire to impress her father-in-law Kemal Bey with courage that his son had never possessed? She didn't know. The only thing she was sure of was that she wasn't going to beg these brutes for her life. It's what they would want, but it was the one thing, given that no one was going to come to her aid from beyond the locked doors of the pastane, she had the power not to give them.

'Do what you will,' she said, looking fiercely into Ekrem's eyes. 'Just leave my children alone.'

'Oh, we have no problem with your children,' the gangster replied. 'We have no further interest in this business.'

'We won't need to do shitty little collections like this any more,' his brother boasted. 'We're going to be so rich, my dad says—'

'Celal!'

The younger man bowed his head and murmured, 'Sorry.'

'So you're going to kill me.'

'Oh, no,' Ekrem said. 'No, no, no!' Once again he pushed the blade upwards so that it just dented the skin on her throat. 'No, you will have to pay us what you owe, but we've sold this business on.'

'Who to?' Suzan asked carefully so as not to jog the knife in her tormenter's hand.

'To a less, shall we say, experienced group of young men,' Ekrem replied. 'Far more unreasonable than us.'

'Azerbaijanis.'

'Celal!'

'Well, she has to know.'

'Shut up!' Ekrem laughed into Suzan's white face. 'They'll like you,' he murmured softly. 'I like you. Maybe they'll let you pay them without money.'

'I—'

'Look upon your new masters as punishment from me,' he said. 'And remember that if you ever cross them they will cut your children up in front of your eyes.'

Tears burst out of Suzan's eyes like the overflow from a swollen river.

Ekrem smirked. 'But now you must pay your debt to me,' and he pushed down hard against her shoulder with his free hand.

'But I've put all the money in the bank,' Suzan stammered as she sank to her knees in front of him.

'That's all right,' Ekrem said. 'I'll take payment in services.'

He unzipped his trousers and pulled her head roughly towards him.

It was far too hot to be out and about. Even with the shade thrown by the trees it was close, humid and uncomfortable. If he had any sense he'd be at home, drifting in and out of consciousness in front of some rubbish on one of the satellite channels. With both balcony doors wide open, the apartment he shared with Belkis could be very airy and there was a huge jug of iced tea in the refrigerator . . .

Metin İskender looked across at the Malta Kiosk. He'd have to go up there soon and buy a cold drink, some of the diners outside were beginning to give him strange looks. He'd walked this path, just the section one could see from the kiosk, for some time. Up and down, his eyes trained on the ground and amongst the thick foliage beside the path. So far he'd found nothing. He wasn't sure what he had been expecting to see. A wooden trap door that sprang outwards when activated by some sort of device under the ground, a suspicious-looking drain cover, some odd and unexplained clearing in the foliage . . .

But, he knew, it wouldn't be any of those things, this mechanism that raised a man from the 'subterranean passages', as Mehmet Suleyman had described them. No, if attending that David Copperfield show in Paris had taught him anything it was that the best illusions were simple and involved the manipulation of perception. Somehow the eye was diverted from what was really happening to something far more interesting or active within the immediate environment. İskender sat down on one of the low stone walls beside the path and lit a cigarette. The main distraction in this environment was the Malta Kiosk itself. Always busy, especially at weekends and on warm summer evenings. Nobody who dined there was poor; indeed, when Zhivkov had appeared on the path in his pale grey summer suit with the fine Italian shoes, he had looked just like any other prosperous man out for a little al fresco dining. Not that Zhivkov had dined. He'd walked round the restaurant, following the path across the vine-covered loggia and then, presumably, down the hill towards the entrance on Cirağan Caddesi. İskender, though attended by a most concerned Belkis at the time, had nevertheless followed the gangster's every move.

He put his hand up to his forehead to wipe away some of the sweat that had collected there and then ground his cigarette out on the path. Now he just had to get a drink. He crossed to the veranda in front of the kiosk and ordered some water and a can of cherry juice. Sitting at the table just to the left of the one he'd shared with Belkis, he let his eyes roam down and along the path, picking out any salient features on the way. He was only just awake now. He hadn't had very much sleep the previous night, tormented as he was by pictures of Nina Zhivkov's severed head. Then at İkmen's apartment, the three of them had feverishly tried to make sense of the many seemingly discrete and confusing events. As his eyelids drooped under the weight of what felt like iron bars, he was conscious of something niggling away at the back of his brain, but he didn't know or even now care what that might be. He needed sleep whether or not he was in a public place.

His chin had dropped down to his chest when the sound of a familiar voice made him open his eyes. Amazed, as people always are, at just how immediate the reaction to anything familiar is, he shook his head to clear it so that he could address his colleague who seemed to be just behind him.

'You said eight,' he heard the voice say as it passed beside him and began to move off the veranda.

'Yes,' the man who was with him replied. 'Here at eight.'

İskender, who had already seen his colleague's companion in profile, quickly put on his sunglasses. Even underneath the large hat and the unaccustomed moustache, the nose and the fine eyes, just like his brother's, were unmistakable.

İskender watched fascinated as Vedat Sivas took Orhan Tepe's arm in his and together they walked towards the loggia, using the exact same route that Zhivkov had taken the previous day.

İkmen leaned forward onto his elbows and rubbed his hot face with the cologne Suleyman handed him.

'We, or rather you, Metin,' he said, addressing a travel-weary İskender who sat on the other side of the table, 'should tell Ardiç.'

'Yes, I know.'

The kitchen descended into silence for a few moments as all three men attempted to deal with both the heat and the disturbing nature of what İskender had seen. Assembled for the second time that day, these officers were, they all felt, quite alone with the information that had come their way.

'But can we trust Ardiç?' Suleyman offered his cigarettes to his colleagues and then took one for himself.

'I don't know whether we can trust anyone,' İkmen responded gloomily.

'If Ardiç is taking instruction from Ankara,' İskender offered, 'then it's possible that Tepe is part of that. He could be setting Vedat up in some way.'

'True. Although Orhan, it would seem, has obtained rather a lot of money very quickly. He told me he has a credit card. But according to Ayşe Farsakoğlu he paid with cash for their meal at Rejans, which included French champagne. I can't see Ankara paying Tepe extra to do what would seem to be police work and is therefore his duty anyway.'

'That's true,' Suleyman said, 'but still we might be interfering in an operation deemed to be way above our heads.'

'Then perhaps we shouldn't interfere but merely observe,' İkmen replied.

İskender frowned. 'But how would we know, without more information, what we were observing?'

'I don't know,' İkmen said, 'but I do feel that we should be there. Something is happening in that park tonight at eight and I want to know what it is. Vedat Sivas is alive and apparently in good health. He is doing something with Tepe. There may or may not be a connection to Zhivkov but one thing is for certain: after forty years Vedat knows Yıldız very well.'

'He must know you two quite well too,' Suleyman said, looking both of his colleagues up and down.

'Well, if anyone, you'll have to track him, Mehmet,' İkmen said. 'Metin can give you a description – if, of course, you want to come in on this with us?'

'Why shouldn't I?'

'You're a new father,' İkmen said. 'You might not want to take such a risk with your career.'

'Or your life,' İskender added. 'Whatever else we may think we know about this business, one fact that is irrefutable is that Kaycee Sivas was brutally murdered. And whoever the killer is, he's dangerous and ruthless.'

'Think about it, Mehmet,' İkmen said gravely.

Suleyman smiled. 'Without me it's going to be difficult for you to follow Vedat.'

'Difficult, but not impossible. We can stay out of sight and keep in contact by mobile.'

'Yes, but I can follow him overtly, right up until he meets Tepe. I want to do this, Çetin,' Suleyman went on. 'I always remember you telling me the story of that London murderer Jack the Ripper. You said no one will ever now know who he was and how frustrating that was. I know this isn't the same, but it is a mystery, and no one else seems keen to unravel it. More to the point, our superiors could be involved, and if they are, I want to help get to the bottom of it.'

'Well, if you're sure.'

'I am.'

They agreed to meet at a büfe they all knew in Beşiktaş at six. From there it would take them about ten minutes to get to the palace gates and, although they were as yet unsure about what they might then do beyond observing what may or may not unfold, İkmen for one felt that it was important their activities were not heavily proscribed. They had to be both mobile and reactive since they had no idea what they might find at the palace. In a sense they didn't want to think about that too deeply.

İskender left first. Like the others he wanted to get changed.

When he'd gone, İkmen turned to Suleyman. 'I think,' he said, 'Hikmet Sivas may have been one of the Harem's customers.'

Suleyman's face assumed a grave expression. 'Why do you think that?'

'I have a rather unusual source.'

'Someone very odd and unreliable,' Suleyman said, only too familiar with the sort of informants his former boss seemed to attract.

İkmen smiled. 'You could say that.' Then his expression sobered. Although the decision to get into whatever it was they were about to embark upon had been jointly reached, he still felt responsible. Against orders he was taking two young men into something that could either ruin or kill them all.

Chapter 21

Tonight was the night when all things became possible. The moment he had thought about, planned for, done the most awful things to facilitate was about to come to pass. Sometimes he had thought that it would never happen, that Hikmet's 'friends' would simply overwhelm them all. And indeed without the intervention of the Bulgarian they would have done. It was why Vedat had sought him out in the first place. Alone, even with all the knowledge that he had, he could never even have considered it. Zhivkov's money had bought so much: silence, fear, loyalty, death. Even the police.

In spite of the steepness of the climb, Vedat smiled. That young sergeant was going to be struck dumb when he saw who he was going to be sharing a dinner table with tonight. In years to come people would talk about this night with awe. But only some people. Most would never know that a 'new order', as Zhivkov had put it, had been imposed. As long as they had TVs and mobile telephones, people cared little about who actually pulled the strings.

Strange to think that what was about to happen had been born out of weakness. Hale had always said that only damnation and death could come from licentiousness and greed and she had been right. Vedat himself had never been troubled by too many sexual feelings, and as for being greedy, well, he was only getting what he deserved, wasn't he? He'd spent years and years in those brainless security jobs, taken just to help Hikmet and his 'friends', watching as his son went to university courtesy of his film star uncle and all the time knowing what was going on, why and by whom. Hikmet had to be cursing himself now for sharing it all so willingly with his poor, dull brother.

There had been moments of fear. When Hikmet simply ran out after discovering Kaycee's head, Vedat had been afraid. Bent upon revenge as he had been, there was always the possibility that Hikmet might kill Zhivkov. In addition, he couldn't be sure that the police wouldn't find the old paşa's tunnel and cut off his own escape route. But by the time that happened he had gone, out through the ruined houses at the edge of the estate, Mahmud Paşa's boyish harem. Vedat would have smiled if this had been the only association those tatty buildings had for him, but there was something else. Kaycee, too, had in a sense been in those houses . . .

For that alone Vedat Sivas knew he would certainly burn in hell. But not yet. Death was still, he hoped, a long way off; he had time to enjoy the largesse of the high and mighty before the flames detached the flesh from the bones of his soul, like a virgin removing her nightgown. Forcing a smile, he looked around the private room that the maître d' at the Malta Kiosk had prepared for them. Buying all this had been costly for Zhivkov – not so much the food as the silence of the maître d' and a few significant others, the men and women the police had interviewed without learning a thing. Not that they really knew anything beyond the fact that Vedat had never really been missing. Billions would be on offer here tonight, but they would never know that, only a very few would ever know that.

After briefly inspecting the cutlery and glass that adorned the long mahogany dining table, Vedat walked back outside again. Although it wasn't yet evening there was a vague sense that the temperature might be about to drop a little. That would be a relief. Walking around in disguise took it out of a person, especially that huge, stifling hat. The only consolation was that he was better off than his brother. Everyone had to be better off than Hikmet. Vedat looked down at the honeycombed earth of Yıldız Palace beneath his feet and smiled.

'I thought we were going to spend the evening together,' Zelfa said as she watched her husband put on a clean, blue shirt. He'd finished showering some time ago and, as was his custom, had taken care to style his hair and inspect his clothes before dressing.

'Yes, I'm sorry,' he replied, 'but I've got to go out.'

Zelfa scowled. 'Where?'

'As I told you, it's work,' he responded calmly.

'But you're not back on duty until—'

'I'm helping Çetin with something, Zelfa.' He took his trousers off the end of the bed and put them on. He purposefully avoided her eyes as he did so.

'So what is it?' she asked. 'This thing you're helping Çetin İkmen with?'

Mehmet zipped his trousers and then looked down at his wife who lay on top of the covers on their bed.

'It's not anything I can talk about, Zelfa,' he said. 'I'm sorry.'

303

'Something dangerous then,' she said petulantly.

'No.'

'Something mad then, knowing İkmen.' Rapidly changing language into her native English, she added, 'Boys out chasing the bad guys just for the craik.'

'What?'

'Oh, you're like fucking kids, all of you!' Zelfa exploded. 'Guns and football, strutting about.'

'Oh, so now I'm some sort of football thug, am I?' Mehmet responded, as he wrestled with the fury he could feel welling up inside him. 'First I was out chasing other women and now—'

'I apologised to you for that!' she shouted. 'I said I was wrong!'

'Yes.' He snatched his keys and cigarettes off the table beside the bed. 'You did. And I accepted your apology. I was very insulted that you would even entertain the idea that I could have an affair while you were having our son, but I did forgive you.'

'Oh, do you have to make it sound like you're doing me some great favour.'

'Just leave it!' He was shouting now. 'Go no further, Zelfa! I'm going out.'

'Mehmet!'

Following precisely the pattern of behaviour she had exhibited when she'd discharged herself from hospital to come home and accuse Suleyman of infidelity, Zelfa suddenly came back to herself and started crying. This time, however, her husband didn't go over to comfort her. He fastened his watch on his wrist and then placed various items in the pockets of his jacket.

'Mehmet, I'm—'

'Yes, I know you're sorry, Zelfa,' he said, in a tone that was more controlled than affectionate.

'Well, I am, really!' she sobbed. 'It's just that—'

'I don't know when I'll be back,' Mehmet said as he moved towards the bedroom door, still avoiding her eyes. 'So don't wait up.'

'Mehmet!'

'Goodbye.'

He opened the door, stepped outside and then slammed it shut behind him.

Zelfa's cries became bitter, waking the tiny baby who had been sleeping in the small nursery next door.

She wasn't wealthy enough for gestures. Film stars, pouting Arabesks and pampered odalisques could throw away the jewellery their faithless lovers had given them, fling it out into the street like shit from an old-fashioned chamber pot. Some princess or other had even ground a great diamond her husband had given her to dust which she had then flung into his eyes, along with her sharp fingernails – or so it was said. Anyway, far from being faithless, her own lover had been too attentive, far too keen to know her, to see the woman beneath the skin – literally.

Ayşe moved the jewellery away from her open bedroom window and replaced the items in their boxes. Just because she wanted nothing to do with Orhan Tepe ever again didn't mean that she had to beggar herself. The pieces were lovely, valuable, she liked wearing them. Why shouldn't she have them? After all, if money became tight, she could always sell the stuff.

The mobile telephone in her pocket trilled and vibrated against her thigh. Painfully, for her back was far from healed and still quite raw in places, she reached down to retrieve it from the pocket of her trousers.

'Hello?'

'Hello, Ayşe.'

'I don't want to talk to you, Orhan,' she responded sharply.

'Because you told our bedroom secrets to İkmen? I can understand that.'

'No!'

'But I forgive you for that and so you don't have to worry, you know,' he said.

'Just leave me alone.' She could hear the tremble in her voice, feel it as it shimmied its way down her arms and into her hands.

'Oh, Ayşe.'

Why was she so frightened? It wasn't as if he was in the room with her, she had nothing to fear. There was just his voice at the end of the telephone, a voice that was so cool and normal, though she knew how strong he was, strong enough to beat and rip . . .

'Get out of my life!' she yelled and pushed the off button, then turned the whole thing off. As the liquid crystal display on the face of the phone dimmed to nothing, Ayşe threw it roughly onto her bed and looked away from it.

But try as she might, she couldn't stop her eyes being drawn back to it. Orhan had said that he would leave his wife for her. Perhaps he still meant to do what he had promised and make her a proper married woman.

Stupid girl, she thought as she looked out of the window at one of her prim, headscarved neighbours hanging her washing out on her balcony. You'll never be fat and contented like her. Orhan would always want you to be lithe and provocative, ever ready for sex. His own particular brand of sex . . .

Quietly, lest Ali, who was still ignorant of her recent experiences, should hear her, Ayşe began to cry. She was on her own again now and that hurt far more than her physical wounds. Orhan, for all his beastliness, represented what might have been her last chance at marriage. She was so sick of being the spinster in her family. Her mother and father were uneducated peasants who believed that marriage was the most important and sacred thing in a woman's life. She knew they suspected she had lost her virginity and believed that this was what was keeping her single. She couldn't explain, because she feared their outrage, that she'd only let her first lover take her virginity because he'd promised to marry her if she did. She'd given him what he'd wanted in the same way she'd give in to Orhan. Orhan had wanted her in order to assert his superiority over Suleyman, at least in part. But unlike her first lover, Orhan, hadn't dumped her when he'd achieved his objective. He called. He loved. But he'd almost beaten her senseless. She couldn't tolerate that, not again!

Weeping even harder now, Ayşe opened the small boxes containing the jewellery he had given her. She was going to be thirty very soon. Alone and thirty! It was horrible. Better women than her took beatings from their husbands all the time, Turkish peasant woman often suffered in return for a secure home. And Ayşe, for all her loose morals and pretensions to sophistication, was just a girl from a peasant family. She snatched up the mobile phone and switched it on again. She knew his number by heart and she punched it in as soon as the instrument was active. But he wasn't answering, so she left a message.

*   *   *

She didn't want to burden him with her concerns. She'd been told many times that the case was as good as closed. Her daughter, a whore, had died a natural death whilst pleasuring several men. The confectioner hadn't been enough for her, the dirty pig! But as quickly as Hürrem's anger rose, it subsided again. Watching İkmen come out of his apartment, a small hug for Hulya on the threshold, she knew he wouldn't be angry if she did just mention it . . .

'Inspector?'

He turned. 'Mrs İpek.'

Hürrem moved towards him, her head slightly bowed. 'Inspector, I know it is a trouble, but . . . but Hatice . . .'

'I know.' His thin face eased slowly into a sad smile. 'Her death is never far from my thoughts and I will, as I promised you, Mrs İpek, find out who defiled your daughter.' He looked down at the litter-strewn floor and sighed. 'But with so little assistance from my superiors, it will take time.'

'I know! I know!' Hürrem wrung her hands nervously in front of her chest.

Impulsively İkmen reached out and lightly touched her elbow. 'Look,' he said, 'you're in the service, you know I can't tell you anything until I'm certain about the information that I've gathered.'

'I know.' She moved her arm until it was no longer in contact with his hand. A decent widow lady.

'But I promise you that I haven't been idle.'

'Oh, Inspector, I never—'

'I've given you my word I will bring Hatice's tormentors to justice and I will do that.'

And then he left.

Alone again in the hot, dark hallway, Hürrem İpek fought

against the images that kept torturing her mind. Pictures of Hatice running in from school, her face flushed with the innocent joy of being home with her beloved mother and sister once again. Where was that little girl now?

Chapter 22

It was an ideal evening for eating al fresco. Warm and still, the awful heat of the day had given way to the kind of evening that was perfect for a meal with one's lover. He would be dressed in the lightest of summer suits, she wrapped in delicate white muslin; they would enjoy a meze with champagne which would be French because only the best would be appropriate.

Silly thoughts! Suleyman smiled. His idle musing was beginning to remind him so much of his father it was frightening. But this place did tend to nudge one's thoughts towards the hopelessly romantic. The Malta Kiosk, Yıldız Park, with its panoramic views of the distant Bosphorus, the elegant restaurant, echoing with Ottoman grandeur . . . Suleyman looked around at the numerous other diners on the restaurant veranda and wondered how they would react if they knew this was, in a sense, his home they were eating at. He also wondered how Vedat Sivas, that shadowy figure, just inside the entrance to the building, could be so calm in such a public place. He was, after all, in hiding from the police at the very least. But then he had other activities and people on his mind. People like Orhan Tepe who, observed by Suleyman from behind sunglasses and an open newspaper, had been ushered by Vedat into the depths of the building some time ago, together with a very smart, possibly foreign man, and Ali Müren. İkmen and İskender were somewhere in the thick foliage that smothered the hillside. İkmen had been surprised when Suleyman had used his mobile to tell him of Müren's presence. Ali Müren was nothing, a cheap gangster in charge of a second-rate family – a thug. But still, he had connections. Through his sons he could be linked to the Hatice İpek case, which in turn had a tenuous connection to Vedat Sivas, via his brother, Hikmet. İkmen now believed Hikmet had been one of the Harem's high-class customers. And so if Ali Müren was here with Vedat and a group of obviously wealthy men, it might mean this meeting had something to do with the Harem. It was all rather Byzantine though.

Suleyman sipped his very expensive coffee and lit a cigarette. A young woman with straight black hair cut to look like an ancient Egyptian headdress smiled at him from the table opposite. The policeman returned the greeting and then he lowered his eyes behind his sunglasses. Zhivkov hadn't made an appearance yet. Various men had arrived after Tepe and his new friends but Suleyman hadn't recognised any of them. One had looked obviously foreign. He had spoken as he'd entered the kiosk, and Suleyman had caught the American-accented English. He and the foreigner who had entered with Tepe had both looked uncomfortable and tense. Neither of them had taken Vedat Sivas's outstretched hand as he greeted them. Not like the Turks, assuming the dark-haired, Turkish-speaking men he had seen were in fact Turks. Eastern Europeans, as well as Georgians and Azerbaijanis, adapted quickly and soon learned to speak Turkish.

Suleyman flicked his ash into the ashtray and then leaned back in his chair. Two men were coming along the path and onto the veranda. The one leading, tall and elegant, had his head turned in order to talk to the man behind, who was young and whey-faced, with hooded Mongolian eyes. He looked nervous. Turks, probably. But then they weren't necessarily going to whatever event Vedat Sivas was holding in the kiosk. Suleyman watched them anyway. As the taller and older man turned away from his friend and looked up at the kiosk, his face was clearly visible. Since his eyes were hidden behind his glasses, Suleyman could afford to stare. He wasn't alone, others looked too as the senior and well-known army officer and his aide walked past Suleyman and into the kiosk. Only Suleyman, however, was curious enough to peer in after them. He saw General Pamuk give Vedat Sivas his coat and then disappear in the same direction as that taken by the foreigners, Ali Müren and Orhan Tepe.

Shortly afterwards Vedat disappeared down the same corridor that all of his guests had taken and someone unknown shut the door to this portion of the kiosk behind him.

'In some countries generals are almost invisible to the public,' İkmen said to a still incredulous İskender. 'But here, because we have this long military tradition, they are pampered, famous and revered.'

'Which only makes the fact that General Pamuk is apparently consorting with wanted men, gangsters and who knows what else all the more incredible,' İskender replied.

'Yes.' İkmen pulled a few leaves from a nearby bush and dropped them by his feet. 'And in plain sight.'

'Exactly. What is he doing?'

İkmen shrugged. 'Things are happening, have been happening for some time that we don't understand,' he said, 'things way above our heads.' He looked up into the now darkening canopy of leaves and murmured, 'Everything has taken place in broad daylight. Kaycee Sivas's abduction, the delivery of her head, Tepe's meeting with Vedat. Whatever hand is guiding events belongs to someone very confident and secure.'

'No sign of Zhivkov, though,' İskender said.

'No. Unless he's already in the kiosk.'

'Or unless he's got nothing to do with this after all.'

'You know,' İkmen said after a pause, 'Miss Yümniye Heper thought that this Harem her sister became involved with could have been situated in one of the palaces.'

İskender clicked his tongue tetchily. 'That's a separate matter,' he said. 'This has to be about Hikmet Sivas and Kaycee.'

'About enemies, their enemies, families,' İkmen said, 'people involved in murder and extortion, prostitution. Something that was hidden and now isn't, just like Rat said.' He went on to tell İskender what Sofia Vanezis had told him about her long-ago experiences.

'So,' the younger man said when İkmen had finished, 'this here tonight, this could be the Harem?'

'It's possible,' İkmen said thoughtfully. 'It's possible.'

He looked around at the trees and bushes, the grass and the occasional flower, and at the path.

'Metin, I think we should return to where you saw Zhivkov.'

'But I've been there,' İskender said on a tired sigh. 'You know the path. There's nothing there.'

'Well, humour me anyway.' İkmen lit a cigarette and started walking towards the path.

*   *   *

As soon as he saw that inner door close, Suleyman paid for his coffee and then casually walked round the entire building. But wherever the men had gone was not obvious from the outside. In spite of the heat, none of the windows was open and there was no noise other than that coming from the veranda. And so in line with İkmen's instructions to remain at the scene, he returned to his previous table, intending to order a snack.

'We're closing,' the waiter said.

Suleyman looked at his watch. 'But it's only eight forty-five,' he said. 'I understood you were open until ten.'

'We're closing.' And with that the waiter walked off to clear a recently vacated table.

Suleyman leaned back in his chair and sighed. So what now? He couldn't just sit where he was. It was obvious that something out of the ordinary was happening and that the staff knew it. Soon they would ask him to leave. He looked across at the path and saw İkmen and İskender emerge from the undergrowth. Should he go and join them?

The 'Egyptian' girl at the table opposite was just finishing a large plateful of baklava. She smiled at him again as she placed the last spoonful into her mouth. This time Suleyman returned her smile properly and then lit a cigarette.

There was nothing.

'I told you,' İskender said as he watched İkmen walk up and down the path, looking intently at the ground.

'Show me again exactly where you saw him.'

'There.' İskender pointed to a slight curve in the walled path in front of a very large tree.

'Mmm.' İkmen scowled. 'Just walk back towards the kiosk, will you, Metin.'

İskender looked over his shoulder and briefly caught Suleyman's eye. 'I thought we were supposed to be keeping a low profile,' he said.

'Vedat and his friends are inside now,' İkmen replied, 'and anyway quite a few ordinary diners seem to be leaving. Just walk over there, will you?'

İskender walked up the path for a few metres and then turned. İkmen was nowhere to be seen. A young couple and a child, on their way back down from the kiosk, passed İskender, the child skipping happily as she went.

İkmen reappeared on the path. Frowning, İskender went to join him.

'How did you do that?' he said. 'That's exactly the way it was with Zhivkov!'

İkmen smiled. 'I just stepped out from behind that tree,' he said, pointing to the large yew on his left. 'I put my foot onto the wall and then jumped onto the path.'

'Yes, but—'

'There's no mystery,' İkmen continued. 'When you saw Zhivkov, just as a moment ago, your eyes were distracted by other figures.'

'But they weren't. I was staring down the path and he just materialised.'

'Behind other people,' İkmen said. 'Very rarely do we look at just one item in a scene, especially if we're not trying to focus on it, which you were not. You didn't expect to see Zhivkov, his appearance came as a shock. I think your eyes were focused somewhere other than on the tree when Zhivkov appeared. It looked as if he'd materialised because one doesn't expect to see people come out of the undergrowth and because of factors peculiar to you.'

'What do you mean?'

'I mean that you've got a history with him. Zhivkov is a gangster of mythic proportions. His crimes are violent and bloody and he has escaped us and his rivals many times, over many years. You've seen his work first hand, and I'm not saying this to denigrate you, Metin, but I think he frightens you. Personally I think that's a most sane reaction.'

İskender nodded his head slowly. 'So it was an illusion, sort of, as I first thought. I could have saved my energy earlier, instead of combing the place for tunnels like an idiot.'

'I'm glad you did,' said İkmen. 'If you hadn't, you wouldn't have overheard Orhan Tepe arrange to come here and we wouldn't know that a man I want to question about the death of his sister-in-law is currently in that kiosk with, amongst others, a very important Turkish general and the aforementioned Tepe.'

'So I'm not a complete fool then?'

İkmen smiled. 'No more than the rest of us.'

He lit a cigarette and the two men stood in silence for a moment. Up at the kiosk Suleyman was almost entirely alone now.

'So what now?' İskender asked.

'I think we all need to get back together,' İkmen said and reached for his mobile.

Officially the gates to the park closed at ten. But with the Malta Kiosk closing early, it was possible the park would follow suit. If it did, security officers would soon be prowling the highways and byways, looking for those who were lingering: the lonely romantics, the sex-starved couples, the occasional slavering peeper. İkmen was confident they wouldn't be found if they kept their heads down.

He wanted to stay to see the eventual break-up of the party inside the kiosk. Quite what good that would do them, he didn't know, but if it meant they could follow Vedat Sivas and find out where he was staying, that had to be something. Ardiç surely couldn't afford to ignore such significant information. Unless of course the commissioner, too, was in on whatever the hell was going on inside the kiosk.

'That's the last of them,' Suleyman whispered as he nodded towards the figure of the restaurant's maître d'.

The man was standing in just enough light for the officers to see that he was probably in his forties. He closed the main door behind him and left. He didn't lock the door or check that it was properly closed.

'Since he didn't lock that door, we could get in,' İkmen said.

'And do what?'

'Find out where the men went and what they're doing.'

'But we have no idea what we might be getting ourselves into,' İskender replied. 'I'm sure Ardiç got rid of us two and kept Orhan Tepe for a reason. He must have.'

'As I've said before, I believe it's enough that one of my officers is consorting with a man wanted in connection with a murder,' İkmen said. 'And then there is the tantalising possibility of the Harem.'

'But even if we were to find that something illegal was taking place, what could we do?' Suleyman asked. 'There's a general in there.'

'Who is just as subject to the rule of law as any of us,' İkmen said. 'I also want to know what Ali Müren is doing in there. When I dragged Ekrem into the station he gave me the impression that the Mürens were not acting alone these days. There are foreigners in there who could be Mafia.' İkmen stared at the darkening façade of the kiosk.

'You're not trying to tell me that a man like General Pamuk, who has acquitted himself with such honour, would sully his hands with the Mafia, are you?' İskender protested.

'I hate to smash your illusions,' İkmen said tartly, 'but contrary to popular belief, anyone can be corrupted. I know that we're encouraged to think that all of our soldiers are perfect—'

'A notion not extended to ourselves,' Suleyman put in.

'No. And over the many, many years I have been doing this job,' İkmen said, 'I have always tried to seek out the best in even the most highly placed individual. I have, as a result, been disappointed many times which means that I now trust very few and take no man at face value.' He smiled. 'It's a scepticism I suggest you cultivate, Metin.'

İskender looked miserably at this feet. Like a lot of young men, he had always revered the army. When he was a child his greatest wish had been to try and gain entrance to military school. And although boys from poor families did gain places, boys from Umraniye were another matter. Even if his father had sobered up enough to take him along to apply for a place, he wouldn't have had anything to wear that didn't smell of the refuse tip and dead animals. He'd had to fight his corner to get into the police, battling mainly against his parents whose attitude towards the law consisted of breaking it in order to survive.

'You don't have to come, you know,' İkmen said, breaking across İskender's thoughts. 'I know how important your career is to you. And this is, well, it's not exactly sanctioned or necessarily even the right thing to do.'

'I do know that I come across as a stiff, ambitious bore,' İskender responded bitterly.

'With integrity,' Suleyman put in. Although he had never actively liked Metin İskender, he did respect him and he was disturbed by this sudden descent into verbal self-flagellation. He himself was not wholly certain that he wanted to do what İkmen had proposed but what he did know was that now was not the time for self-defeating thoughts. 'You've worked very hard to get where you are now, Metin,' he added, 'and I respect you for it.'

İkmen, who was rapidly losing patience with the very Turkish niceties that were currently taking place, cleared his throat.

'Look, are either of you going to come in there with me or not?' he said, pointing an unlit cigarette at the kiosk.

Suleyman sighed. It would be so easy to just get up and go home now. İkmen wouldn't reproach him for it. But he trusted İkmen and his hunches. They rarely proved unfounded. And if something corrupt was occurring, he wanted to know what it was, not that the knowledge would necessarily mean they could do anything about it.

'Well, I'm in,' he said before he could think any more and change his mind.

'And so, I suppose, am I,' İskender said glumly. 'I have to take some risks.'

'And you want to know the truth just as much as I do,' İkmen said with a smile. 'Are you armed?'

'Of course.'

'I take it you aren't, Çetin?' Suleyman said, knowing already what the answer would be.

'No.' İkmen looked at the incredulous expression on İskender's face and smiled again. 'You didn't know? I never am. If I can't talk my way out of a situation then I don't deserve to do this job. But I know that you two both carry, and that's up to you. All I ask is that if anything does happen, you don't just react without thought. We don't know what we might be getting into here. Our aim is just to observe without intervention, if possible.' He looked at them sternly, each in turn. 'Agreed?'

İskender and Suleyman both nodded their assent.

'OK, let's try and find out what all this is about then,' İkmen said. 'We'll split up, check out the area and then, if it's clear, meet at the front entrance.'

'You think they might have people outside?' Suleyman asked.

'I have no idea,' İkmen replied, 'but if General Pamuk had anything to do with the organisation of this meeting, or whatever it is, then I think it's very possible. Keep quiet, keep low and use the undergrowth for cover.'

Suleyman agreed to take the back of the building while the other two approached it from opposite sides. There was some moonlight, just enough to give the front of the building a faint silvery glow. Ghostly. This place, with its unknown tunnels and its even darker history . . . Suleyman, at least, recalled the story, recounted in tones of sad regret by his grandfather, of how this palace had been captured by Young Turk troops back in 1908. Moving stealthily through the woods, every nerve straining against the noises made by the Sultan's menagerie of exotic animals, these young men had known exactly where the monarch was, due to the strange and disordered sound of his piano playing. Not that they went in to confront him. No, the madman of Yıldız had to wait until morning to find out what he must already have known, that he was deposed, that the people had finally and unalterably spoken. Now, in a direct reversal of that situation, the old Sultan's descendant moved to retake the palace, though he wasn't sure who exactly his adversaries were and with no music to guide him he didn't know where in the building they were either.

Chapter 23

Keeping low wasn't difficult for Metin İskender. Keeping quiet was another matter. In all this foliage, every step seemed to bring with it a burst of cracking twig or crunching leaf. His ears cringed with every sound and his heart thudded heavily against his ribs. There might be nobody out here in the heavy greenery around him, and if he had to he supposed he could try to do what İkmen apparently always did and talk his way out of trouble. With any luck, park security might just think him a straggler. After all, it wasn't even the official closing time for the park yet. He could be anyone, some poor sad pervert who'd spent the day in the bushes, wanking as the pretty girls passed by. He didn't think that he looked like a wanker, but . . .

If they were discovered and General Pamuk and his associates weren't doing anything untoward, he could finish someone like İskender. General Pamuk could finish him even if he were doing something untoward. And İkmen and Suleyman. However, the fact remained that İkmen had been right. He, İskender, needed to know. Ardiç had just dismissed him from the Sivas investigation, thrown him away like a bag of rubbish. This image made İskender smile. Rubbish. That's what he'd come from, and he wasn't going back to it for anyone. His visits to his family made him want to heave. The smell of it all, the rot and the filth. But they didn't have to live there, not now. It was their, or rather his father's, choice. Both he and his sister Meral had good jobs and would have gladly helped the senior İskenders, provided his father didn't spend the money on drink. But he would. Haldun İskender was an alcoholic. Metin's mother could make all the excuses for her husband that she wanted, but that was the truth.

İskender could see the shimmer of the marble staircase leading up to the kiosk now. There wasn't, as yet, any sign of either İkmen or Suleyman. And until he had some sort of idea of their whereabouts he didn't want to go up there alone. He could not see, hear or in any way sense the presence of anyone in the vicinity. He began to question why they were in the park at all. Some rather mismatched men were meeting, maybe even having a meal in the Malta Kiosk. Nothing wrong with that – except of course the presence of Vedat Sivas and the nasty feeling at the bottom of his stomach, the one that had been there ever since Zhivkov had 'appeared' to him. Stupid! The tree solution had been obvious, he had even sat on that wall and considered the possibility of a simple optical illusion of some sort. So why hadn't he worked it out for himself? He had been utterly convinced that he had seen Zhivkov spring out of thin air.

Perhaps it was his peasant background. Peasants were always only too willing to believe the miraculous. Every year his mother would take his father out to that Armenian church, the one where a miracle cure was supposed to take place at one or other of their festivals. Nothing ever happened, but his mother still went, a headscarved Muslim woman, dragging a rakı-soaked lush in her wake. Mystery and magic. Like the way Zhivkov, pure evil in his eyes, consistently escaped death. Some sort of demon, he had to be! Peasant thinking again. Suleyman thought rationally about tunnels built by his fabulous, aristocratic ancestors; he conjured up devils and djinn and things that reach out and grab you in the night.

His heart missed a beat, he felt it distinctly. Not even a second's warning. Something large and black wrapped itself round his throat and lifted him clean off his feet.

'I'm a police officer!' Suleyman held his ID aloft to the eye slits in their balaclava helmets.

The one who had his foot on Suleyman's chest glanced at it briefly before shrugging at his colleague in what might have been a meaningful fashion. Who were they, these huge, black-clad men bristling with guns?

'Who are you?' As soon as he'd asked the question he knew it was pointless. Their only answer was to roll him over on his stomach and cuff him. Next came a rough piece of cloth which covered his eyes. Clearly his police ID did not impress them. Did they even recognise it for what it was? Were they going to kill him?

He felt one of them squat down beside him, heard something unzip beside his ear.

'Sleep,' a voice said, just before something painful speared his bicep. Sleep, one word, short, staccato, in *English*. Suleyman's mind flew down a deep black hole with sickening rapidity.

He'd been right, the door was unlocked. In an effort to contain his nervousness İkmen put a fist up to his mouth and bit down hard on his knuckles. Briefly he looked around. There was nothing to see beyond the trees and bushes sweeping away down to the blackening mass of the Bosphorus at the bottom of the hill. No Suleyman or İskender, yet. They would come but in the meantime he felt exposed. There was no evidence to support the idea that there was anyone about but themselves but just in case security should pass and glance up at the building, he ought to get inside.

The door moved easily and without squeaking. İkmen entered the dark hall, his eyes quickly scanning for the door Suleyman had described, the one all the men had walked through. There it was. He put his head back round the main door and looked for his colleagues again. They were both taking their time. That was unlike Suleyman at least. İkmen frowned. If anything had happened to either of them he would never forgive himself. He looked at the inner door again. There didn't appear to be any kind of light behind it, suggesting that wherever the men had gone was some distance from it. He hoped it, too, was unlocked. If it wasn't he could probably get it unlocked. It would be nice to know for certain, however. He looked outside once again. Nothing. This was getting worrying, he was older and far more unfit than the others.

He returned his gaze to the door inside. It couldn't do any harm just to check it out while he was waiting. And so he did, unable to believe his good fortune when the thing sprung soundlessly open under his hand. Whatever else they may have done, the old sultans always made sure that their palaces worked. Best builders, best carpenters, plumbers who really understood water tables. Pity the criminals who'd built all those abominations that had folded in on themselves during the earthquake hadn't looked to history for a little guidance.

Where were Suleyman and İskender? He looked over his

shoulder at the open main door and felt his heart begin to pound. Nothing. This wasn't good. Something must have happened. Either that or they'd just gone. Neither of them had been happy about this. Oh, but that was preposterous. İskender might possibly have left but İkmen couldn't believe that Suleyman would desert him.

If they hadn't deserted him but had come to some sort of harm, shouldn't he try and find out? Where to start looking? Beyond the doorway in front of him lay a long corridor flanked by other doors and culminating in a very large portal, under which he could see a sliver of light. If he really strained his ears he could hear voices.

To listen outside the door was going to be too dangerous. No, he'd have to try and glean what he could from whatever lay behind one of the adjoining doors. But what about Suleyman and İskender?

There was no sound or movement from outside and standing where he was he was totally exposed. He'd have to assume they weren't coming. If he stood here wondering why, he'd never achieve anything. He took a few steps forward onto the carpet and paused. The floor beneath was marble and so it wouldn't creak. Briefly he reminded himself just who was behind that door at the end and moved rapidly towards the door beside it.

Sweating heavily now, he checked all round the door for chinks of light. There were none. A raucous laugh from the lit room beside him caused him to react without thought and the next thing he knew he was in an entirely black room. He wasn't alone, however.

'They won't buy it, you know. They'll kill you all in the end.'

The voice was American, the words English, tinged with a Turkish accent.

Although his hands really didn't want to move at all, İkmen took his pencil torch out of his jacket pocket and switched it on. At first he had thought he recognised the voice but he couldn't equate it with the figure tied up against one of the huge old imperial radiators. Spattered with blood, half of its hair pulled out by the roots, it looked more like an incomprehensible work of modern art than a person. Only the extraordinary and mesmeric eyes confirmed that İkmen had indeed recognised the voice.

'Mr Sivas?'

'And what is your particular method of torture?' Hikmet Sivas said acidly.

'Mr Sivas, it's me,' İkmen said in Turkish. 'Inspector İkmen.' He stepped over to the prone figure and squatted down beside him. 'What has happened to you?'

He started to work at the ropes with his fingers. The great dark eyes looked up into his. 'Is this a trick?'

'No! Mr Sivas, what are you doing here?'

'I came to kill the man who murdered my wife. But now,' he smiled crookedly, 'he's going to kill me.'

'There are some men meeting in the room next door to this. Some of them are very bad men. One of my officers is with them.' İkmen looked through the blood-stained lashes and into the bruised eyes. 'I want to know why.'

Hikmet Sivas started to laugh. İkmen slammed a hand over a mouth now ruined by broken teeth. 'Be quiet!' he hissed.

When Hikmet Sivas eventually managed to regain his composure, İkmen took his hand away and resumed his work on the ropes.

'Well?'

'They're all here because of me,' Sivas said, 'because I always wanted to be the centre of attention.'

İkmen frowned as he worked one of Sivas's hands free.

'I wanted to be a movie star.'

'Which you are.'

'Which is an honour that I bought,' Sivas corrected. 'I sold the cream of Turkish girlhood, not to mention my own sense of who I was, to a group of very highly placed Sicilian American gentlemen who, in return, made me a star. I know you've seen one of the gowns we dressed the girls in, Muazzez Heper told me. Muazzez and Yümniye dressed all of my girls, you know.'

İkmen stopped what he was doing and sat back. 'The Harem. *You* ran it?'

'Yes, I started it. It was my idea. Some cheap little Neapolitan, the only Hollywood executive who would even let me through the door when I first arrived there, told me that the only thing about Turks that people were interested in was their harems. He'd read that the odalisques would do anything for their master without a word. He said to me that as a Turkish national I was of no use to him, Valentino and all that Middle Eastern vogue was over. If, however, I knew of a harem . . .'

'Well, you can't have done. Nobody could in the nineteen sixties, there weren't any.' İkmen shook his head at such ignorance.

'No, of course not, which is why I had to create one. In the early days they were genuine Ottoman ladies. Desperate, poverty-stricken aristocrats,' Sivas said as İkmen freed his other wrist. 'I thought I'd only have to do it once. I came home. I set it up. I invited the Neapolitan to come visit our exotic homeland. I even, because Vedat worked here, said he could fuck them in a genuine palace.' His eyes glazed over at the memory of it. 'I got Muazzez and three others, separately you understand. He did everything it's possible for one human to do to another and they, poor desperate things, didn't even squeak. He, the Italian, really got off on it. He liked the silence, the compliance – it was like playing with fat, dusky dolls, he said.'

'And so this Neapolitan rewarded you.'

'He told his friends.' Sivas scowled. 'It was so different. They'd done everything else, his friends. Starlets, kids, boys, Marilyn. Now Turks, silent, subhuman, fat princesses. And so in return for giving the Cosa Nostra and their friends a genuinely Ottoman experience I became a star. In the sixties everyone came here,' he continued bitterly. 'Some of them on state visits. They even paid me. They still do.'

'You entertained them all here?'

'In the rooms the madman built underneath the palace. The Republican government had bricked them up but the people who worked here knew where they were. Everyone searches for treasure under the pavements of this city, Inspector. İstanbulis are always on the lookout for a quick fix. So once a year I would come home and once a year Vedat would dress the rooms most beautifully.' He smiled unpleasantly. 'We entertained only the very best: godfathers, politicians, movie stars, world leaders. No one in their right mind would ever have thought that such a thing could happen in a backwater like Turkey. My customers were thrilled. I was thrilled. A peasant boy from Haydarpaşa who was not only a movie star but also the originator of the most exclusive club in the world.'

'Which you also used yourself,' İkmen said, recalling the story told to him by Sofia Venezis.

Hikmet Sivas frowned. 'No, why would I? I was young and attractive. What makes you think—'

'Sofia Venezis, a Greek woman,' İkmen said, 'does the name mean—'

The wounded star interrupted him with a soft laugh. 'If you mean the idiot girl that Muazzez made me meet,' he said, 'then I know who you're referring to but I can assure you that I never had sex with her. I couldn't use her either for my customer or myself. She was like a running commentary of inconsequence. For Muazzez's sake I listened, told her not to say anything about our meetings to anyone then gave her the money she could have earned. I was rich by that time.'

Suddenly the door to the room adjoining banged open. Laughter followed. İkmen, his hand over Hikmet Sivas's mouth once again, switched off his torch.

'I trust your journey will be a comfortable one,' a deep voice said in heavily accented Turkish.

A smooth, native voice replied, 'It's been a pleasure.'

'Your involvement will be invaluable, General.'

'As will the money we will make.'

And both men laughed.

'Goodnight.'

Only when he was absolutely certain that no one was outside did İkmen switch his torch back on again.

'Do you know what's going on?' he asked Sivas as he held the torch close up to his once handsome face.

'Well, of course I do,' the star replied haughtily. 'Everyone in there wants my photographs.'

'What?'

'Even when I was young I believed in the value of

331

insurance,' Sivas said, rubbing his freed wrists with his bloodied hands. 'I photographed everyone who used the Harem, *in flagrante*, you understand. Not for blackmail but, as I said, for insurance should any of the studio bosses I worked with decide to curtail my contract before I wanted them to or in case somebody even more important should decide to reject my application for American citizenship. I keep them all in sealed envelopes . . . somewhere.' He smiled. 'Nobody, apart from Vedat my brother, knew about the photographs until last year.'

'And so what changed?' İkmen asked.

'Vedat changed, Inspector,' Sivas replied. 'I thought at first that this Bulgarian person, Zhivkov, was simply emulating my idea. OK, I couldn't understand how he'd managed to find out, how he'd been able to force Vedat to give him the girls' costumes and introduce him to our clients, but Vedat was here, I was in the States. I've always loved my brother. I closed my mind. But then some of our clients told me Zhivkov was trying to blackmail them.' He sighed. 'Even then I continued to ignore it. And then, one day, after a very severe beating, or so he claimed, Vedat called to say that Zhivkov knew about the photographs and wanted them. I told him to go to hell.'

'So who else knew what was going on?' İkmen asked.

'No one. Oh, my Italian friends and people a little higher up, shall we say – knew about the blackmail and got really wired. But they didn't know about the photographs. I couldn't tell them. They'd have killed me. But then when Vedat called to say they'd killed a girl in one of our dresses . . .'

'Hatice İpek.'

'I don't know what the kid's name was. Anyway, Vedat hadn't been honest with me. There'd been no beating. Vedat wanted the photographs just as much as Zhivkov. I have pictures, Inspector, of people so important that they would silence even the most prominent members of the Cosa Nostra – some of whom are in that room now.'

'So what you're saying,' İkmen said slowly, 'is that Zhivkov wants to get hold of these pictures so he can have power over the Mafia.'

'Amongst others. People don't like to see pictures of desperate young girls going down on their leaders. They tend to vote such people out. They don't like to see their role models jacking off as they watch top Mafia godfathers fuck little princesses up against walls.'

'You have photographs of such things?'

'Almost every prominent man connected with the Cosa Nostra for the last forty years. Men who either belong to the organisation or men the mob put where they are today. You'd be amazed at the number of faces you'd recognise – not all of them American.' He smiled. 'If I'd wanted to I could've brought down governments with what I've recorded. Not bad for a stupid Turk.'

No, it was very clever. In fact for a poor boy from Haydarpaşa whose only experience of the world at that time had been through his involvement with the Egyptian film industry, it was remarkable. There had always been rumours that certain criminal organisations controlled politicians in certain countries; they were also rumoured to run Hollywood, some union organisations, etc., etc. Now here, suddenly, or so it would seem, was the proof. Gleaned, almost innocently, by a man who just wanted to cover his back.

'And your wife?' İkmen asked. 'You said you left your house in order to avenge her.'

Sivas' eyes filled up immediately. 'They killed Kaycee

in order to show me they meant business about the photographs,' he said, his voice catching. 'I came to İstanbul to try and sort things out – about the dead kid and of course I needed to lay it on the line to Zhivkov about the photographs. But he pre-empted me. I couldn't believe how I underestimated him. He took Kaycee. Without thinking I involved the police and Zhivkov killed her. There was no blackmail involved. He'd always intended to kill Kaycee. He felt it would be an object lesson for me – like "You're next unless you do as I say." Stupid bastard didn't know how much I loved her. I'll never give him his photographs now. And anyway those who really hold the power, I don't mean those godfathers in there, know now. I made some calls before Zhivkov caught up with me.'

'Then why are the Mafia bosses in there with Zhivkov now?' İkmen asked.

'Zhivkov's told them he already has the photographs. He's impatient. Vedat can describe them; he's seen them, after all,' Sivas replied. 'Of course he needs them in actuality at some point, which is why I understand they're coming back later to try and persuade me all over again.'

'Sssh!' İkmen switched off his torch and held his breath. He was certain he could hear movement outside the door. As his eyes adjusted to the lack of illumination in the room he noticed that the radiator he was leaning against was next to a window, in front of which hung a pair of full-length, heavy curtains. What made him pull the curtains round himself he didn't know; it was just a feeling, 'that thing you do, like your mother' as his father used to say.

The younger son of the witch Ayşe İkmen concealed himself behind the curtains just before the door to the room flew open and the light came on.

Chapter 24

Ali Müren's hand hadn't even managed to get inside his jacket, much less reach for his gun, before they eliminated him. The silenced shot hit him in the heart, killing him instantly.

There had been fourteen men sitting round the table; now there were thirteen.

Zhivkov, who was at the head of the table beside Vedat Sivas, made as if to stand up.

'Sit down!' The black-clad figure spoke in English. Others, also all in black, spread out around the room.

Orhan Tepe turned to the man sitting next to him, one of Zhivkov's bodyguards and said, 'What is this? What—'

'Shut up!' The butt of a hand weapon hit him on the back of the neck, silencing him.

The room was full now. Two men in black for every man at the table. In response to some sort of signal, one of each pair placed his handgun up to the head of the man sitting in front of him.

Some of them whimpered, one of the Americans crossed himself. Tepe just kept thinking that he was going to die and it was all his own fault. There was no reason for him to be here, apart from his greed, apart from the fact that he'd had to have Ayşe. Even now on the point of death she was in his mind, the image of her blood dripping sensuously down his fingers. He felt himself stiffen and it almost made him smile.

The next act involved certain men being pulled from their seats: Zhivkov and two of his minders; Vedat Sivas; Zhivkov's brother-in-law, the Georgian, Lavrenti; two heavies who had belonged to Müren; and Tepe. As they started to move out of the room, it occurred to Tepe that only the Americans were staying behind. But there was, he knew, no point in questioning this. Whatever the reason for this, he would have to wait until the answer became apparent rather than question any of these faceless ones – whoever they were.

As Tepe and the others left the room, the shivering and bloodied figure of Hikmet Sivas passed from the room that had been his temporary prison and into the room they had just come from. He was being escorted by what seemed to be a most solicitous black-clad person. Perhaps they were Special Forces, maybe even the FBI, here to try to get hold of the photographs. Was that why this was happening? If only General Pamuk hadn't insisted they all eat before Zhivkov gave Hikmet that drug to make him talk! The foreigners wouldn't have known any different, they understood nothing beyond what Zhivkov had told them, namely that he already had the photographs which were going to cost them dearly. But General Pamuk had talked endlessly about how this knowledge was going to give them all so much power in the future. He had monopolised Zhivkov's attention for the entire evening. And then he had left.

Tepe felt his whole body start to shiver. Suddenly unmindful of the gun at his head, he turned sharply to look at Zhivkov.

'Pamuk set us up!'

'Shut up!' Both of them pistol-whipped him from behind. By the time they reached the stairs that led down to the place that Zhivkov and Vedat knew so well, Tepe was vomiting blood.

Five men remained at the table, six including Hikmet Sivas.

The oldest and certainly the fattest of the group turned his heavy Roman head round to face his captors and said, 'So you killing us or what?'

Two of the figures who had been conversing quietly in the far corner of the room turned around.

'Well?' The big man, whose name was Bassano, shrugged. 'Do I need a priest or what?'

'Get up!'

Bassano was pulled out of his seat with tremendous force. The other Americans, and Hikmet Sivas, received similar treatment.

'Don't ask any more questions!' one of the figures said as the men were moved forward by guns.

Sivas glanced at the room where İkmen was still hidden behind the curtain but didn't say anything. If they were, as Bassano, and indeed Sivas himself, felt, about to die, why take another innocent soul with them? They were trash to a man – Bassano, di Marco, di Marco Junior, Martin, Kaufman and himself. İkmen was something else, İkmen was what Hikmet had once been. Just a guy. And anyway these creatures, professional killers, would probably find him in the end.

The six men were herded outside into a night filled with small animal noises and the gentle rustle of cooling plants, across the veranda and out onto the path. On the path, its back doors open, stood a dark transit van. The cab was blocked off from the rest of the vehicle. The men were pushed onto rough bench seats in the back. As he climbed in, urged on by the ubiquitous gun in his back, Hikmet fought to beat away thoughts of what these men, G's men, they had to be, would do to him in order to get at those photographs.

When they were all seated, the black-clad guards closed and locked the doors on them. After that there was nothing – no sound, no light, no feeling save the pounding of their hearts.

Nobody had entered the room since the men, he assumed they were men, dressed in black had come for Hikmet Sivas. It seemed reasonable to assume they were Special Forces. They looked right, conformed to the mental picture one had of such people. But they could just as easily be gangsters or even some sort of foreign force. They had, after all, spoken to Sivas in English; the accent could have been American or English or Australian. Not that speculation of this sort really helped İkmen in any way.

The fact was that whoever they were, they were heavily armed and they were fulfilling some sort of brief within this palace with this motley collection of lowlifes and Orhan Tepe. But if what Hikmet Sivas had told him about his photographic collection was the truth, any one of the powerful men depicted could have decided to deal with the situation in this way. Even in the twenty-first century, even in the most liberal parts of the West, photographs of this nature could bring governments crashing down. Men on state visits stopping off at their Turkish 'club' for a blow job given by a beautifully dressed, desperate,

sad-eyed little princess and being photographed – where
the hell was their security? People like that lived behind
steel doors, slept in fucking nuclear bunkers! But then if
they trusted Hikmet – no, more likely they dismissed him
as an amusing 'primitive'; perhaps the idea that one day he
might use his knowledge of their activities to harm them
had never occurred to them. It can't have done.

As far as İkmen could tell, the men in the room next door
had been moved out to somewhere else now. And although
sound was still coming from that area he suspected that it
was probably the black-clad soldiers or whatever they were.
He wondered how long they would be in there, how long he
would have to stay behind this curtain, in a brightly illumi-
nated room with the door ajar, unable to have a cigarette.

Damn. He hadn't even thought of cigarettes until that
moment. But now that he had, he couldn't think of anything
else. Perhaps if he just took one out of his pocket and placed
it, unlit, between his lips . . .

The room Tepe and his fellow captives were taken to was
stunning. Windowless walls draped in shimmering gold
fabric, high-class, almost iridescent kilims on the floor. The
furniture was minimal, just a bed and a table covered with
the accoutrements of wealth and of passion: Spanish fly,
French champagne, a disposable syringe, a metal, probably
gold, dildo. For the old ones who just couldn't get it up
any more. This was the room where princesses sucked on
presidents, where a thousand and one delusional Arabian
Nights were fulfilled.

Apparently Hikmet Sivas had been imprisoned here since
Zhivkov captured him. In this fantastic room, almost certainly he would have told Zhivkov of the photographs –

the fabulous photographs. Drugs could, Tepe knew, loosen the tongues of men who may have been tortured for weeks without success.

He wondered whether Hatice İpek had been brought here. Hassan Şeker, the confectioner, had had no idea what he was getting into when he supplied his little mistress to Zhivkov via the Mürens. And then with the girl dead, with his fingerprints, metaphorically, all over her body, he'd been scared, and only too willing to part with some cash for a little police protection. Şeker hadn't realised that the Mürens and through them Zhivkov would be so interested in his new friend from the police force. Neither, come to that, had Tepe, not until yesterday when he'd gone to meet Ekrem Müren and found Vedat Sivas instead, and all of İkmen's ravings about some nonsense called the Harem became a reality.

Tepe looked at Vedat now, standing to one side of the door, unmoving, his eyes cold and glazed, while Zhivkov in contrast moved across the room towards the bed, apparently at ease in familiar surroundings. The other men, the now terrified underlings and henchmen, stood in a group, looking uneasily at their captors.

'Get down, on your stomachs!' one of them shouted in Turkish, which was obviously not his own language.

Nobody moved.

'Now!' He raised his short-nosed submachine gun and pointed it at them.

As Tepe slowly lowered himself towards the gorgeous pattern on the pure silk kilim, he considered the two most likely outcomes from such a scenario as this. They could be about to search them or, given that people shot in this position made less mess than those shot on their backs or standing up—

'Fuck you!'

As Tepe turned his head to look at Zhivkov, a shot rang out. The force of it threw Zhivkov back onto the richly covered bed where he lay, his mouth open, looking like an unfit if sated sultan.

'Get down!' the man repeated. 'Heads to the floor. Don't look at me! Look down!'

Look down! Look down! There was no choice, and anyway, what good would looking up do? OK, there was something noble about looking one's enemy in the eyes, but that was for heroes and Tepe knew he wasn't a hero. He wasn't even a policeman, not really, not now. Now he was one of them; like Müren and Vedat, a man corrupted by wanting what he shouldn't. And then he smiled, wondering suddenly what his lovely Ayşe was doing now.

The burst of gunfire lasted less than twenty seconds. Anyone still alive after that they finished off with handguns.

Chapter 25

Commissioner Ardiç was rarely sick. In fact he prided himself on the strength of his stomach. But not tonight. Not with eight men dead in that blood-spattered room smelling of metal and cordite. Eight men slaughtered.

When he'd cleaned himself up and had a drink of water, he went outside. A tall figure wearing a thin summer suit greeted him on the veranda. He offered Ardiç a seat, one that was usually used by diners, and then sat down himself, smiling.

'Your assistance has been invaluable, Commissioner,' he said in a voice which though obviously not Turkish in origin spoke the language perfectly. 'Without yourself and Pamuk things would have been so much more difficult.'

'You shot one of my officers.'

Ardiç was offered a cigarette. Unusually he accepted the offer.

'Yes,' the man replied smoothly, lighting both his own and Ardiç's cigarette.

'You told me that Tepe would be given back to us.'

The man shrugged. 'I lied.'

'Yes, you did, you—'

'I lied, you chose to believe me, end of story.'

Ardiç, angry now, roared, 'I didn't choose to believe you, I did believe you!'

'Well, that was foolish of you, wasn't it?' The man narrowed his eyes at Ardiç. 'When you came to Ankara it was agreed that every loose end in this situation should be tied up. Your officer knew far too much.'

'Oh, and Zhivkov's other heavies don't?' Ardiç retorted.

'Not now,' the man replied with a thin smile. 'My goodness but the İstanbul police have been busy cleaning up this town tonight!'

Ardiç, speechless, stared at the man with horrified eyes.

'You won't have to bother about that small quarter of Edirnekapı for some time.' The man continued and then looking into the commissioner's grey tinged face he said, 'Don't worry, Commissioner, we were very careful, very neat.'

'I have no doubt that you were,' Ardiç said thickly.

'Thank you.'

Quietly and with calm efficiency, black-clad figures began coming out of the kiosk carrying body bags. A closed army truck down on the path was their destination. Ardiç glanced at this grisly scene then turned back to the pale features of the man sitting in front of him.

'And the sons of Ali Müren?' he asked. 'What of them?'

'Oh you'll need some live bodies in order to tie all of this into an ordinary gangster scenario of kidnap, murder and prostitution.'

'Which it was,' Ardiç interjected.

The man laughed. 'On your side of things, yes, Commissioner.'

'And on yours?'

The man's face assumed an impenetrable expression. 'You know what it was from our side, Commissioner,' he said, 'so don't fuck with me. The Müren brothers at the very least disposed of the girl's body once she so very inconveniently died while Zhivkov and his horrors were 'interviewing' the poor bitch. She was very pretty, that girl. We know that the Mürens were also involved in killing some local character, a vagrant who had spoken to your man İkmen. Zhivkov's guys killed the old woman, the seamstress. Through the Mürens, Zhivkov got to hear that she might say something unwise to İkmen. Although he didn't know precisely what the connection might be at that time, your young officer passed the information on like the good little doggy he was.'

'How do you know that?'

'Because we had their meeting room wired for sound.'

'Nothing I can use, I suppose,' Ardiç replied bitterly.

'No.' He ground his cigarette out on the marble floor. 'And by the way, I've had your two officers, İskender and Suleyman, taken to the American Admiral Bristol Hospital.'

Ardiç peered at the man, horrified. 'What are you saying?'

'Three of your officers decided to see what was going on up here tonight. Very remiss of you not to know about that, Commissioner, but I'll let it pass. The two younger ones may be rather disorientated for a while. You'll have to explain to them that they really shouldn't get involved in special operations against the mobs in future. Next time the gangsters could kill them. As for İkmen—'

'İkmen!' Ardiç felt his heart jump in his chest. If İkmen wasn't with İskender and Suleyman . . .

'Don't worry, he's alive,' the man said pleasantly. 'He's still hiding in the room where they kept old Hikmet. I expect he spoke to him. Perhaps you'd like to find out what they talked about for us. We'd be grateful.'

'What, so that you can—'

'We agreed no loose ends, Commissioner.'

'So why didn't you just shoot him like you did Tepe!'

The man looked down and sighed. 'Well, in truth, we were rather slow getting to him, and if he really doesn't know anything . . . He's something of a character, shall we say, in the force. I don't think his death would be very good for police morale. It was never our intention to damage you.' He smiled. 'We contained the situation and neutralised the threat.'

'The situation as you call it got rather out of hand, in my opinion,' Ardiç snapped. The man's hand whipped across the table and gripped Ardiç's throat.

'I don't care!' he hissed. 'You are nothing. The images on Hikmet Sivas's photographs are everything.' He let go of Ardiç's throat as quickly as he had taken hold. 'I'm paid to maintain the status quo.'

Despite being red-faced and obviously frightened, Ardiç said, 'So you protect the Mafia.'

'The one we understand, yes,' the man responded. 'Some people have so much knowledge, Commissioner, that they become untouchable. Hikmet Sivas is strictly an amateur, taking photographs for insurance purposes. The "foreign" gentlemen here tonight have something on almost everyone of great power a man can name. We know how they operate, we know they will only use their knowledge under certain circumstances and that those circumstances can be dealt with without altering the status quo. He smiled unpleasantly, 'Hikmet was a wild card, didn't understand the rules.'

'What do you mean?'

'He's a loose cannon, he took those photographs to protect himself, they could end up anywhere. He'll give them to us, of course he will, but he would've given them to Zhivkov, in the end. And Zhivkov,' a shadow crossed his features, 'would have used them.'

'Yes, but the Mafia, your Mafia . . .'

'Those we understand, we can control,' the man said. 'Those we don't, those who may wish to buy plutonium, for instance, with just one of these images . . .'

'He could have blackmailed your government?'

'Govern*ments*.' The man emphasised the last syllable. 'I don't work for a government, Commissioner. I work for democracy; it's a very big club.'

'Yes.' Ardiç threw down the long ago dead cigarette butt. 'And if İkmen does know something?'

'I will know,' the man replied gravely.

'And what will you do?'

The man rose from his chair and pushed it neatly back under the table. 'I will neutralise the threat,' he said and then with yet another smile he turned and made his way back towards the marble stairs.

It was only when he had gone that Ardiç realised that so had everyone else. No black-clad figures from Allah alone knew what part of the world, no bodies, no blood – nothing. Just himself, the welcome sight of his car in the car park, and İkmen, somewhere inside the kiosk.

For a while Ardiç toyed with the idea that he might go and seek him out. But then he decided against it. Knowing İkmen, he would have pieced together quite a lot of information. The pale man, however, was a shadowy figure about whom Ardiç knew little. He could not judge the degree or extent of his power, or what access he had to what information. Listening devices could have been planted on both himself and İkmen, for all Ardiç knew. There was no way of knowing with such people, that much had been apparent in Ankara. No, best leave İkmen. He would find his way out, get home; İkmen was good at that sort of thing. Ardiç stood up and looked down at his car. He would see İkmen tomorrow. Yes. Give him the chance to lie about his knowledge. İkmen was sensible – sometimes; he'd know what to do for the best.

The truck took the men out onto the tarmac, right up to the plane which was already fuelled, cleared and ready to go. As far as Hikmet Sivas could see, nothing else was moving, only them.

As the anonymous figures that had brought them to the airport ushered them up the steps and into the plane, Hikmet said, 'Where are we going?'

One of the men, a particularly tall example, shouted, 'Have a good flight, sir,' through air thick with heat and fuel fumes.

Hikmet continued to climb the steps, questions juggling for supremacy inside his head. Where was Vedat? Curse his soul to hell! Whatever he had done, he was still his brother and Hikmet needed to know where he was. Where were G's men taking him? What would happen to Hale? He would have returned to his sister after he'd dealt with that Zhivkov scum. She must be worried. And Kaycee. Poor, darling Kaycee. Where was she, her body? Had it been given a Christian burial?

As he entered the aircraft, Hikmet felt himself start to cry. What a nightmare! What a mess! In attempting to please people he couldn't understand, he'd succeeded in killing or corrupting so many. When he'd first found Zhivkov, he'd nearly been murdered himself. Why had he done such insane things? Because he wanted to be famous? Because he wanted to get one over on Hollywood? But then he was Hollywood, wasn't he? He was American, now. He'd managed to get rid of the Turk inside him – except that he hadn't. Hikmet Sivas had a harem, Hikmet Sivas got work because he had a harem. Ali Bey, the Sultan – laughable. A naive Turk in American clothing, taking pictures he'd never had to use. A man with a harem needs nothing beyond the jaded lust of others to ensure his continued survival. Why hadn't he realised that? Why did he have to go just that little bit further? He'd tried to put it right. That's why he'd called G, to get help. It was G who had organised this bloody operation, who had 'fixed' it all so decisively. But was G going to 'fix' him too now? There had to be some kind of punishment. He'd known that as soon as he'd contacted G.

'We're taking you back to the States.'

The man was tall, fair and possessed an indeterminate accent.

'Why?' Hikmet asked, knowing what a stupid question that was.

'Because it's where you belong,' the man replied. 'You always wanted to belong there, didn't you, Hikmet?' He smiled, a cold thing. 'Money, Hollywood, the dream. The Turk is dead isn't he, Mr Sivas? Just like you wanted.'

The man took Hikmet's elbow and led him, past Bassano and the others, towards the back of the plane.

He went willingly, as if in a daze. That was it. What this man had said, that was it. Killing the Turk. Doing what they wanted, always, in order to kill that thing that always held him back. Kill the Turk and replace him with a cardboard sultan. Do it because it sells. Sells like the comfortable, compliant Ottoman fantasy girls, like the vision of something that had disappeared, like a bad, bad movie. And all the time he had been invading their privacy, snapping something men would kill for, just to keep that dream alive, just to make sure that the Turk remained where he was, in his unloved grave.

As Hikmet and the man sat down, side by side, the man's smile widened.

'When we get to LA,' he said as he buckled himself into his seatbelt, 'you will take me to those photographs.'

'And if I won't?'

'You'll do it or I'll kill you, Hikmet,' the man responded simply.

Hikmet looked into eyes that were indeterminate in colour. It was a nondescript face, pale, smiling, completely unreadable.

'What exactly is your interest in the photographs?'

'It's nothing personal.' He settled himself comfortably into his seat and closed his eyes. 'That mutual friend you called when you were in trouble, the one who organised tonight's little party, wants me to burn them,' he said. 'Or rather one in particular. I'm sure I don't have to spell it out to you, Hikmet.'

Hikmet Sivas looked down at the floor with haunted eyes.

'That way,' the man continued cheerily, 'we can all go on just as before, which will be very nice, I'm sure you'll agree.'

At first Zelfa thought that the ringing sound was part of her dream. One of her teachers from school, Sister Immaculata, was, for reasons that were totally incomprehensible, getting married to Burt Reynolds. Church bells were ringing to celebrate this momentous occasion which, amazingly, seemed to please Burt greatly. Burt and the nun, in full habit and without a scrap of make-up, were just about to kiss when Zelfa realised that the ringing came not from bells but from the telephone beside her bed.

With some difficulty she opened her eyes just enough to allow her to locate the phone, which in the hot and heavy darkness of her bedroom looked not unlike a strangely animated bone. Her hands, which were clumsy with sleep, dragged the handset from its cradle and then held the thing shakily to her ear.

Someone said something odd in a foreign language.

'What?' she croaked thickly in English. 'Speak fucking sense, will you!'

'Zelfa, it is Ali, Ali Ozakin.' The man spoke in heavily accented English.

Zelfa frowned. The name was familiar.

'We have worked together some few times,' he said. 'I practise neurology.'

'Oh, yes, Ali,' it was all coming back now, 'at the Admiral Bristol. The woman with aphasia . . .'

'Damage to Broca's area, yes,' he said. 'You referred her for therapeutic intervention. She is making some progress.'

'Good . . .' Although why he would telephone her about this unfortunate woman at what she saw from her clock was nearly one o'clock in the morning, Zelfa couldn't imagine. 'Ali . . .'

'Zelfa, I'm calling because your husband has been admitted to the Admiral Bristol.'

'Mehmet!' Suddenly and shatteringly she was awake.

'There is no cause for alarm.'

Stupid, stupid, stupid job! Hadn't she told him it would be like this one day? Hadn't she always feared that one night would bring fear and gut-grinding bloody torture! No cause for alarm, indeed!

'Inspector Suleyman has sustained a wound to the head,' Dr Ozakin continued calmly. 'Not of a serious nature.'

Which meant? 'What do you mean? Is his skull cracked? Is he conscious? What?' Her heart was hammering so fast now she could barely breathe. Mehmet! She'd been such a prize bitch to him the last time they'd been together! Oh Jesus, Mary and Joseph!

Ozakin cleared his throat. 'His skull is not damaged,' he said. 'But he is not conscious at the moment. He will regain consciousness.'

'Oh, yes? And how do you know that?'

'Well,' he cleared his throat noisily once again, 'I have a lot of confidence—'

'I want to see him for myself,' Zelfa said determinedly. 'Now.'

'Zelfa, that is not going to be possible.'

'I'm his wife!'

'Ah, yes, but . . .'

Even in her distress Zelfa was certain that something, possibly a hand, went over the mouthpiece at Ozakin's end. She even thought she heard the sound of muffled voices somewhere beyond the obstruction. Muffled, angry voices. Cutting a patient out of a conversation was of course something that doctors did sometimes, or perhaps the neurologist was communicating with one of his colleagues. But if he was, he should allow her, Zelfa, as a fellow professional, some input, even if the patient was her husband.

'Ali,' she said sharply. 'What's going on?'

A few more moments of muffled sounds passed before Ozakin spoke again.

'Come and see him in the morning,' he said. 'He will be able to talk to you then.'

'No, I want to come now!'

'You will not be permitted to see him,' the neurologist replied tightly. 'I am in charge of his care and that is my decision.'

It was, Zelfa knew, useless to argue with a clinical decision like this. She had done the same with relatives of her patients on many occasions. But it still rankled, and it hurt too. Mehmet was injured and she wanted to be with him, whatever his state of consciousness.

'Was he alone when he was brought in?'

'I cannot comment upon his admission,' Ozakin said, Zelfa felt, a little snottily. 'But he is safe and he is stable and you will be able to see him in the morning.'

Zelfa sighed. 'OK.'

'Now I must return to my work. Goodnight, Dr Halman.' And before she could reply he cut the connection.

Mehmet injured. How? Well, in any number of ways, Zelfa knew that. Christ, the man was a policeman in one of the most populous and edgy cities in the world. The place was rife with all sorts of tensions – ethnic, drug-fuelled; just living in the damn place created tension, what with the overflowing buses, the choking traffic and the ever present threat of earthquakes. And then there was İkmen. Mehmet had gone out with him, working, to somewhere unspecified to do something unspoken. Not that there was anything unusual in that. But the older man did have a propensity for getting himself and others into awkward situations. İkmen, much as she liked him, made Zelfa angry – anyone who took Mehmet's attention away from her made her angry. Her eyes grew wet with the beginning of tears; automatically she looked through the darkness towards the door of the little room where Yusuf İzzeddin lay sleeping.

'I do hope this isn't what I think it is,' İkmen said as he cast a stern eye over the figures of two young people on the sofa.

Hulya, her eyes large and bright like those of a small animal caught in a car's headlights, sat up.

'Dad!'

'The very same,' her father replied. He flung himself down into a chair and rubbed his forehead with one weary hand.

'You look terrible,' Hulya said, moving herself as quickly and as far away from Berekiah Cohen as she could.

'Yes,' İkmen responded curtly.

'What—'

'I have no desire to get into the where and with whom of my evening,' he said. 'Yours and Mr Cohen's, however, I could find fascinating.' He caught Berekiah's doe-like eyes in his hard gaze.

'Çetin Bey—'

'Dad, I asked Berekiah to come over when you didn't come home,' Hulya put in forcefully. 'I tried ringing your mobile, but it was off. I rang Berekiah because I was scared for you and I didn't want to be in this place on my own. I've never been on my own before and I don't like it.'

İkmen sighed. Allah, but he was tired, tired and confused and, it had to be admitted, scared too. Even though whoever they had been at the palace had cleared up after themselves, he knew the odour of blood when he smelt it and the air had been thick with it. All those men, gangsters, police-men, Vedat Sivas, gone, replaced by the metallic tang of blood . . .

'So I take it that your brother, Bülent, is out?' İkmen asked, returning to what was becoming his second nightmare of the evening. Hulya and Berekiah alone in the dark, on the sofa, the unmistakable sound of kissing reaching his ears as he had turned the light on.

'He went to Sami's,' Hulya said, 'hours ago. Thought you'd be back, I expect. Not that you've been around that much lately.'

'If you,' İkmen said, turning his attention now exclusively to Berekiah, 'have taken advantage of my daughter—'

'That is not the case! I swear to you, Çetin Bey!'

'Well, I hope so, Berekiah, because both your father and I would be deeply disappointed if we thought you had lied.'

'We didn't have sex!' Hulya spat, her face a picture of dis-gust. 'But only because Berekiah said that we shouldn't!'

'Hulya!'

'No, I'm going to tell him!' she said imperiously to Berekiah and then turning to her father she continued, 'I would have liked to but he said that it was wrong, that we should wait. Wait for what, I don't know, because nobody wants us to be together.'

'Hulya . . .'

'And anyway, Dad, I was really frightened. You still haven't caught Hatice's killer and I was here, a girl on my own!'

'Yes, yes, yes.' İkmen put his head in his hands and closed his eyes. These two were more serious than he'd thought, his Hulya and the Jew, Berekiah Cohen. Son of a friend, nice, nice boy. One of many. He'd searched high and low for Suleyman and İskender among the undergrowth of Yıldız Park, but he hadn't managed to find them. Where were they? Why wasn't he down at the station trying to find out? Because they, like Berekiah, were somewhere they shouldn't be. He had been where he shouldn't have been – talking to a movie legend about something that sounded like a cross between a spy story and a snippet from the *Arabian Nights*.

'Çetin Bey, if I could only court Hulya in the usual way . . .'

İkmen raised his head. The boy looked so worried, so earnest.

'I do love her.'

And he did. Even through his tiredness and the sounds and smells that kept returning to assault his mind since his experiences in Yıldız, İkmen could see that Berekiah was completely genuine. He loved the girl and despite the difficulties İkmen knew lay in wait for this couple, mainly in the shape of her mother and his father, he knew that he at least should give them a chance. He had, after all, always said that he would never stand in the way of any of his children if true love were involved. In fact not long ago, admittedly during the course of a row, he had told Fatma that the children could all marry gibbons so long as the apes in question were kind, employed and didn't smell too bad. But whoever the suitor was, now was not the time to be discussing such matters. He had to sort out his thoughts about what had just happened first. At present he couldn't even remember how he'd managed to get out of the park, much less try to work out what it had all been about.

'We'll have to talk about this another time,' he said gently.

'Oh, so that you can side with Mum and Mr Cohen.'

'No!' İkmen made a conscious decision to lower his voice. 'No. So that I can be quiet and get a little rest, Hulya.'

'Have you been having some problems tonight, Çetin Bey?' Berekiah asked in that serious, understated way of his.

'Yes.' İkmen finally smiled. 'Yes, you could say that, Berekiah.'

Identifying exactly what those problems were was another matter. The Harem went far beyond just the servicing of a few bored businessmen. It seemed that those who ran the world went to Hikmet Sivas to have their secret and shameful appetites satisfied. And Sivas, clever man, had recorded everything, photographing the great and the good abusing little girls. Pictures that could change the world. İkmen tried to get to grips with what he'd rather clumsily stumbled into.

'I think it best if I go.' Berekiah rose to his feet.

Hulya began to protest but was halted by her father's stern upheld hand.

'Yes, I think that's a very good idea, Berekiah,' he said. 'We're all too tired and, for our own reasons, upset to talk about any of this now.'

'I'm sorry, Çetin Bey, to have—'

'Just go home and get some sleep, Berekiah,' İkmen interrupted. 'See your guest out please, Hulya.'

As soon as the young people had gone, İkmen put his head in his hands once again. What a mess! Not knowing where Suleyman and İskender might be, not knowing where Tepe was, for that matter, or even how he could find out was driving his over-strained mind to the edge of craziness. This could be how I really fuck up, he thought, where I place everyone in danger because I always have to know what I shouldn't. Why do I do that? What compels me to want to dig and dig like some ghastly psychological excavator?

'I really think that we should talk now, Dad.' Hulya was standing in the doorway, her hands stroppily braced against her hips.

İkmen sighed. 'I disagree,' he said wearily. 'You—'

The ringing of the apartment telephone cut off any further conversation. İkmen picked up the receiver while Hulya, still standing, fumed silently.

'Hello?' İkmen said into the receiver. Frowning, he added, 'Zelfa? What?'

During the course of the conversation that followed İkmen's face drained of any colour it may have had previously. And Hulya, despite her earlier petulance, soon became alarmed. As he continued with his conversation she came and sat down on the floor in front of him, hooking her hands across his thin knees. He stroked her hair as if comforting himself with its softness.

Chapter 26

'I've told you that the patient is unconscious and cannot receive visitors,' Dr Ozakin reiterated to the small, raving figure in front of him.

'Yes, and as I've told you, Doctor,' İkmen answered through tightly gritted teeth, 'I've seen him. You yourself opened the door just now, and he's awake!'

'It's three o'clock in the morning.'

'Not the perfect time for a social call, I'll grant you,' İkmen said, 'but I don't really care.'

'I have asked you to leave . . .'

İkmen slid a hand inside his jacket and produced his gun, which was as usual unloaded. 'You either let me see Inspector Suleyman or I shoot you.'

The small nurse, a woman in her early fifties who until that time had stood beside 'her' doctor, edged herself away.

'This is a hospital!' Ozakin cried, his voice trembling with fear.

'I know,' İkmen said and pushed the door to Suleyman's room open and placed a foot across the threshold, 'Well observed.'

'I'm going to call your superiors!'

'Good.'

İkmen let the door swing shut behind him and then turned,

his gun still in his hand, to look at the pale but conscious figure lying on the bed.

'Doctor?'

İkmen made his way over to the bed and sat in the chair beside it.

'No, it's Çetin.'

'Çetin?'

'Yes.'

Suleyman, though conscious, looked appalling. His face, which was white to the point of green, was covered with a lot of small, surface bruises which made him look uncharacteristically dirty. But it was his eyes that were the most disturbing feature of his countenance; eyes that rolled around in his head, sometimes disappearing completely.

'Look, I haven't got long,' İkmen said breathlessly. 'What happened?'

'What . . .'

'Mehmet, you've got to tell me!'

'I . . .' The eyes rolled.

'Look at me!'

But he couldn't. There could be no doubt that he was trying, but something was preventing him.

'Mehmet!'

Ozakin would have called for assistance now and it wouldn't be long before it arrived. İkmen had had to negotiate his way past two half-asleep uniforms in the reception area and he knew he wouldn't get away with it again.

'Mehmet! Please!'

But the eyes continued to roll, and occasionally Suleyman's tongue lolled, thick and dry, out of the corner of his mouth. İkmen felt himself begin to descend into despair. What had happened to Suleyman? The official line was that he had been beaten, which was possible, but İkmen could see no sign of any wounds serious enough to cause disconnection like this. And why had the doctor lied? His insistence that he could not see his friend seemed rather more zealous than the usual doctor/patient relationship warranted. Suleyman sighed and then moved one of his arms out from underneath the bedcovers. The top of the arm was bandaged. Suleyman moved his head in uncoordinated jerks towards it.

İkmen watched, puzzled.

Suleyman then repeated the process, moving his head towards the arm and then looking, unfocused, back in İkmen's direction. İkmen stood up and looked closely at the bandage – not that there was anything to see. It was clean, the arm wasn't or didn't appear to be swollen at all. He must have injured it during the course of the fight or whatever it was he had been involved in . . .

'Does it hurt?' İkmen asked. 'Do you want me to get the doctor?'

'Drug . . .' The unfocused eyes lurched wildly to the side as Suleyman began to struggle in order to breathe.

'You want some more painkiller?'

'Drug!' Suleyman did that head movement towards his arm again and suddenly İkmen understood. He sat down and took his friend's hand in his.

'Somebody drugged you, didn't they?'

The struggle for breath, the panic, subsided and Suleyman raised his head slightly from the pillow and made a sound somewhere deep inside his throat.

'Nobody hit you, you were drugged.' Shaking now, İkmen ran his fingers through his hair and then reached into his pocket for his cigarettes.

Drugged. If he had been frightened before, it was only

a pale reflection of what he was feeling now. Even in the palace he hadn't felt the way he did now. Back there, there had been nothing to see, just the smell of blood and cordite and the sound of men moving other men around, violently. But here he was looking at a man, a friend, drugged almost to paralysis, to idiocy. He had no way of knowing whether Suleyman would recover without talking to that doctor who insisted he had sustained a head wound. Lies! All the way along there'd been nothing but fucking cover-up, deception.

'İkmen!'

The door had opened without him noticing. And if the voice that called his name hadn't been familiar he probably wouldn't have reacted at all. As it was, he turned only slowly, the gun still hanging from his hand, infuriating Ardiç almost beyond reason.

'Give that thing to me,' the commissioner hissed as he stomped angrily towards İkmen, his hand outstretched to receive the weapon.

İkmen tossed it unceremoniously into Ardiç's hand and then turned back to look at Suleyman once again. His superior turned away briefly to check the weapon, grunting as he did so. İkmen pressed his head close to Suleyman's ear as if in a final, affectionate embrace. 'Don't say anything about the drugs to anyone,' he whispered. 'No one.'

Suleyman's eyes rolled wildly before closing.

İkmen heard Ardiç say 'Bring him!' just before two pairs of hands grabbed his shoulders and pulled him to his feet. He found himself looking directly into his superior's furious eyes.

'You're coming with me now, İkmen,' Ardiç said tightly. 'And you will do everything that I ask of you.'

*　　*　　*

Cemal had improved. Aysel, despite the bags under her eyes and her constant yawning, had to remind herself of that. Less than a year ago the baby had been waking at least five times every night whereas now he stayed asleep, although he rarely settled before ten and he always woke between five and six. She slept – sometimes. Sometimes she didn't, most often due to influences outside of Cemal. Orhan mainly.

Aysel cradled Cemal in the crook of her arm and placed the milk bottle between his lips. Although he now ate solid food with relish he still liked his bottle first thing in the morning, cuddling up to her, his eyes all dizzy with pleasure. If only Orhan could see this, she thought sadly, even he would have to be touched by it. But Orhan wasn't in, which wasn't an unusual state of affairs. The Sultan of his own home, he only told her where he was going if it suited him. But she knew. If it wasn't work then it was Ayşe Farsakoğlu. Aysel had known almost from the start; she had, after all, had some warning. He had wanted to do those sick things, while she had not. His attitude alone had told her that he would go looking elsewhere for satisfaction. Then at Inspector Suleyman's wedding she'd seen just where he was looking – at a tall policewoman in dramatically revealing clothes. One didn't have to be a witch to know these things. But one did need to be made of stone not to be affected by it.

She glanced up at the clock on the wall when the doorbell rang. It was five fifteen. Very early for anyone to be calling. Perhaps Orhan had misplaced his key – perhaps he'd left it in his mistress's bed. Aysel put the now sleeping Cemal down on the sofa and walked out into the hall. In line with what her husband had told her about security, she opened the door just a crack at first. But then almost immediately she opened it all the way. It was only İkmen.

'Good morning, Çetin Bey,' she said and tucked a few stray hairs back behind her headscarf.

'Aysel.' His voice was very cracked this morning, very smoke-dried. 'May I come in? I need to speak—'

'Orhan isn't here, Çetin Bey.' She smiled, noticing that he didn't. He did usually, he was very nice.

'It's you I need to speak to, Aysel.'

'Oh.' Lightly she stepped aside to allow him to enter. Even then she was aware that the casualness of her manner wasn't natural.

But she carried on anyway. She offered to make Çetin Bey a drink – the good hostess, entertaining her husband's superior. He declined, both that and a seat, but he made her sit.

'Aysel, I'm afraid there has been an incident,' he said looking down at her with very tired, very serious eyes.

'Oh? What sort of incident?' Still light, still smiling happily.

'Some of our officers were involved in an operation up at Yıldız Palace last night.' İkmen found and then lit a cigarette. 'They were attempting to smash one of the gangs. Some officers got hurt.'

'Ah.' She looked down at her hands which were fidgeting in her lap.

'I'm afraid Orhan—'

'Is he dead?' It sounded so matter-of-fact, almost heartless.

İkmen took a deep breath. 'Yes,' he said, 'I'm afraid he is. I'm so terribly sorry.'

'How did it happen? Was he shot?'

'Yes, he was.' İkmen sat down in the chair opposite her. 'He died trying to make İstanbul a safer place. I know that's no consolation right now, but I believe that it will be one day.'

Aysel looked up with eyes that were perfectly dry, only the hollowness of their expression hinting at the slow caving in of the soul that was happening out of sight. 'It was good of you to come and tell me,' she said. 'Thank you.'

'It's not a part of my job that I grow accustomed to,' İkmen replied sadly. 'Orhan was a good officer and I will miss him.'

'Yes.'

They sat in silence for a while as Aysel stared glassily in front of her, completely impassive – outwardly, at any rate. Not a murmur from Cemal; he must still be asleep. Good.

After a deep, rather shaky sigh, İkmen spoke again. 'Is there anyone I can contact for you?' he asked. 'Your family, someone in Orhan's family?'

'My parents . . . They live in Aksaray. I'll do it.'

'Are you sure?'

'Yes.' She looked down at her hands once again. 'Will you tell Sergeant Farsakoğlu?'

When he didn't say anything, she prompted him. 'Will you?'

'All the officers your husband worked with will have to be told.'

Aysel looked up sharply. 'I do know, you know,' she said. 'About Orhan and the sergeant.'

'Aysel . . .'

'It's all right though.' She made her face move into the template of a smile. 'I never had a problem with it.' Then she stood up and walked to the stove. 'Are you sure I can't get you some coffee?' she said. 'It's French and very good. We have crystal sugar too . . .' Then very suddenly she began to cry. And as her self-control collapsed Aysel gave herself over to one long, awful scream.

It was six thirty by the time they reached the Yerebatan Saray, the most comprehensively explored and exploited of all the city's cisterns. At first İkmen thought that for reasons his fogged and battered brain could no longer fathom, they were going to his apartment which was round the corner from the cistern. But a grimly determined Ardiç, who uncharacteristically had driven the two of them there, had other ideas.

As they came to a halt outside the unprepossessing little building that serves as entrance to the cistern, he turned to İkmen and said, 'My brother will open up for us. He is the custodian.'

İkmen, who hadn't ever given a thought to Ardiç's family beyond his wife and horribly overweight twin sons, was mildly surprised. Ardiç seemed so well-heeled, with his house on Büyükada and his little chats with the mayor and other dignitaries. It was odd to think that his brother gave out tickets to tourists and cleaned up the water that constantly dripped from the roof of the cistern onto the walkways below. Maybe if he was lucky they let him put on the music that accompanies the coloured lights which play up and down the rows of ghostly ancient columns. But this inequality between brothers was not such an odd phenomenon. His own brother was a very well-connected and wealthy accountant, while he – well, he did as he had always done and coped, with the job, with the endless children, with the lack of money.

'Come on,' Ardiç said and opened the door on İkmen's side of the car. İkmen slid rather than stepped out onto the pavement, a small corpse-like figure with eyes so tired they had all but disappeared. A thin version of his superior ushered them down into the cistern where, rather kindly İkmen thought, the other Ardiç had switched on all the coloured lights plus some Western classical music that he didn't recognise. It was pleasant and not too loud. It also provided some cover for the potentially irritating sound of dripping water. Supported by 336 eight-metre-high columns, this vast space had been built specifically to supply water to the Great Palace of the Byzantines. A vast imperial and administrative complex, the Great Palace stood beside the Hippodrome and covered that patch of land that is now called Cankurtaran. Little remains there now of old Byzantium, beyond the meagre fragment of wall that is the Bukoleon Palace, a haunt of drunks and drop-outs, just minutes away from the house of Ahmet Sılay, the self-styled film star. As İkmen descended the stairs into the cistern he thought how odd it was that Ahmet Sılay and indeed the memory of that quite different cistern where they had discovered poor little Hatice's body all seemed so very distant now. At some point, the nature of what he was doing and why he was doing it had changed. A new dimension had been introduced, much of which he didn't understand.

Ardiç sat himself down at one of the small tables in the café area and indicated that İkmen should join him.

'Osman is making us some coffee and then he will go,' Ardiç said as İkmen dropped heavily into the chair opposite. 'He'll have to come back at eight to open up properly, which will give us nearly an hour and a half.'

İkmen looked up with a doleful expression on his face. 'What for?' he said. 'What now?'

If he hadn't been so exhausted he would have dressed his speech up a little more for his superior's benefit. But he hadn't slept, he'd just told Aysel Tepe that her husband was dead and he was confused. Something dreadful had happened and, although he had some ideas about why, he felt that he really didn't *know* anything.

Ardiç cleared his throat. 'When Osman has gone we will talk,' he said. 'Just you and me. No notes, no records, just a conversation that will never have happened and will never be spoken of again.'

'More mystery.' İkmen lit a cigarette and looked glumly down at the damp floor. Well, at least it was cool in the cistern, that much could be said for it.

Osman Ardiç came over with two cups, a pot of coffee, milk and sugar. He didn't speak, just smiled at his brother and then left.

As soon as he'd gone, Ardiç poured coffee for both of them and then lit a cigar. He eased his large body back into the chair until he was comfortable and looked across at İkmen.

'I need to know everything that you know, İkmen,' he said.

'What do you mean?'

'I know that you, Suleyman and İskender were in Yıldız Park last night when certain incidents took place.'

'You mean when something terminal happened to my sergeant?' İkmen thought about adding to that the fact that Suleyman and possibly İskender had been drugged, but he thought better of it.

'Orhan Tepe was on the Mürens' payroll.'

'Presumably he got in via Hassan Şeker.' İkmen sighed. 'I assume it was Tepe who told you I was still pursuing the confectioner. Tepe was paid to make sure that we didn't pursue Şeker with regard to Hatice İpek.'

'He was very willing and wanted to do as much as possible for the organisation,' Ardiç said. 'Tepe had lots of expenses and so he would do almost anything for money. I trust Mrs Tepe was content with your version of events, İkmen?'

'Yes,' he responded dully. What he'd told Aysel Tepe had been both kind and necessary, but he hadn't enjoyed it.

'The media have been told that our men were involved in a gun battle with various crime families up at the palace last night,' Ardiç continued matter-of-factly. 'A major criminal of Bulgarian origin died. We sustained one casualty but apart from that the operation was a success.'

'Until Zhivkov's thugs start picking off our men in the street.'

'That won't happen.' Ardiç paused to drink some more coffee.

'Why? All dead, are they?' İkmen smirked at the absurdity of the notion.

Ardiç fixed him with very grave eyes, 'Yes,' he said, 'they are.'

İkmen paused just briefly before he replied 'And we . . .' He stopped as if the words had caught in his throat.

'Yes, we did that too,' Ardiç flicked his eyes away as people do when they lie.

'Well, haven't *we* been busy, then?' İkmen said acidly. 'Makes you wonder, what with us being so very good, why we left it so long? We could have flushed Zhivkov and his friends out a long time ago, couldn't we? My—'

'Yes, all right, İkmen, I think I get the point!'

369

İkmen tasted his coffee and, finding it rather bitter, loaded three large spoonfuls of sugar into his cup. He finished his cigarette and then lit another.

'So I'm prepared to accept that we dealt with Zhivkov's men,' he said, 'and that we both know, you by some means I don't yet fully understand, that I was at Yıldız last night, that just leaves one question: who were the men in the Special Forces-style clothes?'

'I don't know.'

'Oh, come on!'

'No, really, my hand on the Holy Koran.'

'They were totally invisible until the last minute, they were armed with just about everything a person can be armed with, they spoke to each other in English—'

'I don't know who they were!'

'You must do!'

Ardiç, infuriated, leaned across the table at İkmen. 'I don't know,' he said tightly, 'because I never asked! I don't want to know and neither do you!' As quickly as it had arisen, Ardiç's anger subsided. 'Now I have to know whether Hikmet Sivas spoke to you.'

Immediately İkmen's guard came up. 'Talked to me when?'

'When you were hidden in that room with him last night.'

'Oh, so you even know where in the building I was.'

'The only reason you are still alive is because I know, İkmen.'

The two men looked at each other for a moment as the import of what had just been said sank into İkmen's mind.

'He told me about some photographs he'd taken of

prominent people involved in this Harem thing.' He looked directly into Ardiç's eyes. 'I assume you know about it.'

'An exclusive, sexual venue for the rich and powerful, yes,' Ardiç replied, a look of extreme distaste on his face. 'Started by Hikmet Sivas to further his career.'

'He told me that his brother, Vedat, effectively sold it on to Zhivkov. Is that right?'

'Yes.'

'And what he also sold was the promise of these photographs which, I understand, Hikmet had taken as a sort of insurance against these men should they try to get rid of him.'

Ardiç nodded. 'Hikmet Sivas got involved with some very dangerous people in order to further his career. He had to have insurance.'

'He only got involved with them because he was Turkish,' İkmen responded bitterly.

'What do you mean?'

'Sivas told me that when he first arrived in Hollywood, no one would see him. No one. He was good-looking, young, could speak English, would do anything, but no one would see him.' İkmen picked up his cup and drained what was left of his coffee. 'And even when one of them did, all he was interested in was our harems, or rather his conception of them. Hikmet Sivas created the Harem in order to get started. The prejudice he encountered is sickening!'

'I agree,' Ardiç replied. 'But that doesn't mean that he's blameless. He shouldn't have done what he did. Two women have died because of him, not to mention Tepe and . . . some others.'

'Zhivkov.'

'And Ali Müren and other assorted scum, yes.'

İkmen poured himself more coffee which he again loaded with sugar. 'And Muazzez Heper,' he added bitterly.

Ardiç sighed. 'Yes.'

Slowly and wearily, İkmen shook his head. 'You know, I don't think Hikmet told me everything about Hatice's death.'

'And you want me to tell you?' Ardiç asked.

'Well, do you know?'

'I suppose so,' he said. 'It was Zhivkov and his men. Unlike the Sivas brothers, Zhivkov took an active role in recruiting girls to the Harem. Ekrem Müren and his brother were directed by their father to look for suitable girls. They weren't told why. As I understand it, Ekrem saw Hatice at the pastane when he was collecting from Şeker. It would seem that Şeker handed her over even though he was using her himself. But then one didn't say no to Zhivkov, did one? I didn't know this until we had actually started working on Sivas's disappearance.'

'When you went to Ankara?'

'You were taken off the Sivas case precisely because of what you are doing now, İkmen.'

'What?'

'Asking questions.' Ardiç re-lit his cigar and smiled. 'I'll tell you what I can and then maybe you'll stop, for your own sake as well as mine. Agreed?'

'Possibly,' İkmen said, keeping his options open.

Ardiç sighed. 'Zhivkov came on the scene about a year ago. He started to run the Harem with Vedat according to his own rules, which included blackmail. Hikmet's American friends didn't like Zhivkov's methods, but it wasn't until Hatice İpek died that Hikmet was forced to come to İstanbul to try and regain control of the Harem and reassure his

American associates. There was another reason too Vedat had told Zhivkov about the photographs some time before. Here was a man who was powerful enough to get them and use them in a way that Vedat wanted – to gain power. Hikmet hadn't told his Mafia and other friends in the US about the photographs – they'd have killed him if they'd known – but after Kaycee was killed and he escaped from you, he again called the man he said was his agent – Gee – and told him about the pictures. Shortly afterwards, Zhivkov captured Hikmet and, confident that he could obtain the photographs from him, got Vedat to invite some of the higher order mob bosses to what was in effect an auction at Yıldız. G, meanwhile, with the help of one of those bosses and a lot of, shall we say, influence, was planning a more permanent solution to the problem. Some armed individuals arrived from an unknown source, the Malta Kiosk staff were instructed by myself to leave the building unlocked and everything was set.'

'But who are these people? Who is G?'

'There you go again, asking questions.' Ardiç topped up his coffee from the pot and offered more to İkmen, who declined. 'I don't know, İkmen. People. I don't ask questions. I was put in charge of this operation, from our side, because I don't ask questions.'

'Sivas and all his associates are American, so—'

'My orders came via many intermediaries, from people so exalted you cannot imagine who they might be,' Ardiç said, 'which is why you and I are having this conversation in a damp tourist attraction and not at the station or at my house or your apartment.'

İkmen suddenly felt several, noticeable degrees colder. His hand shook slightly as he raised his cigarette to his lips.

'The "businessmen" these people routinely associate with are bad,' Ardiç continued, 'but we, the world, understand them and they understand us. They may run drugs, extort money, put their puppets into positions of power. But that is how it has always been. They may decide from time to time to blackmail people in the public eye, but they do it according to certain rules that are very well understood. Zhivkov, on the other hand, didn't know the rules, acted in haste and was extremely greedy—'

'Is my apartment bugged?' İkmen interrupted.

'Blackmail was obviously one attraction but the fear was he might not be above trying to sell those photographs to governments who are, shall we say, outside the loop, or using them to obtain weapons I don't even want to think about. Zhivkov was an ambitious, unscrupulous psychopath.'

'You haven't answered my question,' İkmen said. 'Is my apartment—'

'I don't know!' Ardiç exploded. 'But I wasn't prepared to take that risk! If they knew that you knew any of this they would kill us both!'

'So why are you telling me?'

'Because I know what you're like! I know you'll carry on digging until somebody somewhere blows your brains out!' He raised a hand to his sweating brow and flicked the moisture onto the floor. 'They knew you could be in the palace grounds and they had taken your presence into account. Everything went according to plan.'

'What? Even Tepe? You let Tepe—'

'Tepe wasn't meant to die. I asked to have him handed over after the operation,' Ardiç shook his head regretfully, 'but they shot him.'

'And General Pamuk?'

'I think it is best to gloss over what the general's connection might have been to Zhivkov and company. But let's just say that Zhivkov wanted something from him and that was a request he couldn't refuse. Unknown to Zhivkov, however, G had also, via sources this end, made contact with Pamuk. The general readily agreed to pass on details about the layout of the room, who was carrying weapons and so on to the forces who eventually took the kiosk.'

'But you said that one of the foreigners knew what was going to happen?'

'Yes. But obviously he wasn't in the same position as Pamuk who, once he'd given Zhivkov whatever it was he wanted, could leave. All the foreigners flew safely out of the country some hours ago.'

'So,' İkmen began. 'This thing Zhivkov wanted from General Pamuk?'

'I wouldn't think about that if I were you, İkmen,' Ardiç put in tersely.

The two men lapsed into an uncomfortable silence.

İkmen looked around at the ancient, wet columns and wondered, not for the first time, at the vast history of secrecy that had grown up in this city. Whether the Greeks, who had been famous across the world for their Byzantine spies, had started this tradition, he didn't know. But it had certainly gone from strength to strength since. Perhaps people took their cues from structures – labyrinthine palaces, vast and impenetrable underground cisterns, places where, literally, bodies could be hidden by gangsters and, İkmen couldn't help thinking, by generals too.

'The Mürens put Hatice's body in that cistern on Türbedar Sokak because they knew about it from their grandmother's neighbour,' İkmen said, switching back to the matter of his neighbour's dead child. 'Whoever did it laid her out quite carefully. I'd like to talk to Ekrem and Celal.'

'I won't stop you – this time,' Ardiç said. 'Last time you were just a little bit too close. We couldn't afford to alarm anybody at that stage. But the Müren boys didn't harm the girl. It was Zhivkov, that much we do know.'

'He killed Kaycee Sivas,' İkmen said.

'As soon as he'd taken her off the street apparently,' Ardiç replied. 'Poor woman. Zhivkov liked taking heads. If we hadn't arrived, Hikmet Sivas would have been presented with it as soon as he got to his yalı. As it was, Zhivkov had to be rather more devious about its delivery and used the old passageway you found in order to get it to him. I'm not sure whether Vedat Sivas knew that was the plan or not. But both men left through the passageway so he obviously knew it was there. He must have told Zhivkov about it.'

'And where is Hikmet now?'

'On his way back to the USA,' Ardiç replied, 'where he will no doubt be relieved by someone of the burden of those photographs.'

'And the world will once again be safe from megalomaniacs,' İkmen said in a voice heavy with irony. 'And all due to those ever unfashionable Turks.'

Ardiç shrugged. 'Look at our neighbours and ask yourself whether we could afford to have someone like Zhivkov running loose with, well, let me see anthrax, smallpox . . .'

'Do you honestly think that those photographs are worth that much?' İkmen said, frowning. 'I mean if President Clinton can admit, on television, to having oral sex with some girl in the Oval Office and survive, surely those photographs aren't going to topple governments.'

'But we didn't get to see Clinton doing it, did we?' Ardiç replied with a small smile. 'In the photographs we would be able to see princes and presidents, lots of them.'

'I'm still not entirely convinced,' İkmen said. 'At first I was, but thinking about it seriously I feel that there must be more, to explain all that trouble and effort. There's still something hidden.'

'I don't know,' Ardiç said, 'but don't go looking for anything. After today we must draw a line under this thing.'

'So that the civilised world can live on in its usual deluded state. So that the people who control us can carry on controlling us.'

'Yes.'

İkmen crossed his arms and leaned back in his chair so that he was looking at the herringbone domes up above. 'You know, sir,' he said, 'one day somebody isn't going to care about what people like us or these other nameless people you speak of might think or do about their activities. One day someone is going to try and change all this and they're going to do it in such a way that we won't be able to do a thing about it. These people who choose to kill a young, if misguided, policeman because of fears for their own security just shouldn't be where they are now.'

'Are you saying that people like Zhivkov should?'

'No.' He looked down. 'I'm saying that there's no real right and wrong when it comes to power. I'm saying that I wish my country, and every other country, could be truly independent, so we can't all be moved around by so-called businessmen and their henchmen and flunkeys.' He laughed, suddenly and with a lot of phlegm. 'I sound like one of those mad conspiracy theorists, don't I?' But then just as suddenly his face became grave. 'But if what we've been talking about is true . . .'

'I think we'd better get back to the station now,' Ardiç said. 'We may need to answer some questions about last night's successful operation against the Zhivkov/Müren organisation. I've issued instructions for Mrs İskender and Dr Halman to be briefed upon their arrival at the Admiral Bristol.'

İkmen looked deeply sceptical. 'And what about Inspectors Suleyman and İskender? They know—'

'They will know only what I have instructed them to know,' Ardiç said coldly. 'They will repeat word for word what I told them while you were with Mrs Tepe.'

'But Suleyman was almost in a coma!'

'Yes, from which he was roused.' Ardiç began the long and laborious process of standing up. 'There are certain drugs, you know . . .'

'Yes, I do,' İkmen said as he rose and went over to help his superior regain a vertical position. The two men shared a brief look and then broke away from each other.

'Don't speak of these things with Suleyman.'

'No, sir. I'd really rather he stayed alive.'

'Good.' Ardiç smiled and began to move towards the stairs. 'You must give some thought to who you want to replace Tepe,' he said. 'I know you might feel it's a little early . . .'

'I'd like to have someone I can trust,' İkmen said as he drew level with the commissioner. 'I think a woman would be a good idea.'

'I hope you're not going to suggest the adulteress Farsakoğlu,' Ardiç responded tartly.

'She's a good officer.'

The large man stopped in his tracks and looked down at his inferior with very hard eyes. 'I do hope, İkmen,' he said, 'that this is no more than another example of your peculiar sense of humour.' He turned and started moving again.

İkmen, following, said, 'I don't think it's any more amusing than the notion that my apartment might be bugged.'

Ardiç kept on going, his broad back heaving forward in front of İkmen. 'Ah, but you only talk about family matters there, don't you, İkmen? Just like I do.'

İkmen raised his hands up to his tired head and rubbed his brow. 'Yes, sir,' he said.

But as he left the cistern İkmen felt as if he'd been violated. Lied to, bugged, his men attacked, one of them killed and for what? He still didn't really know. Powerful people, somewhere, had been in danger and the resolution of that danger had cost him what felt very much like his innocence. No, they wouldn't speak of it again. He would arrest the Müren brothers, he would feel awkward around Suleyman and İskender for a while and then life would continue as normal, the illusion restored. But there was one thing more he had to say before they left the dubious protection of the cistern – something he had to get out while he still could.

'I want you to know, sir, that I consider and will always consider Tepe's death an execution,' he said.

Ardiç stopped but he didn't answer.

İkmen stared at his superior's back. 'I thought you should know,' he said through gritted teeth. 'Just in case you get a chance to pass that on to someone powerful you know nothing about.'

Chapter 27

Fatma, her hands on her hips, looked up at the girl with fury in her eyes.

'You didn't tell your father. You forgot,' she said tightly.

Hulya bit her bottom lip and looked down at the floor. 'Yes.'

'So where is he?'

'I don't know,' Hulya responded quietly. 'Dr Halman called and he had to go out.'

Fatma turned to face the tall, rather sallow middle-aged man behind her and said, 'What did I tell you? Always elsewhere!'

'If he'd known that you were coming . . .' Hulya began.

'Oh, I admit there might have been some chance of his being somewhere in the vicinity,' Fatma said, 'but when your father is off out saving the world, who knows?'

'Well, we're here now, aren't we?' the man said as he sat down in one of the living room chairs and closed his eyes. 'There's no problem really, Fatma.'

The sound of children's voices and feet drifted in on the hot air from distant areas of the apartment building.

Fatma, deflated now, sat down beside the man and took one of his hands in hers. 'I'm sorry, Talaat.'

'There's no need.' He opened his eyes again and smiled. 'We got a taxi from the bus station, it was OK.'

Talaat Ertuğrul was five years younger than his sister Fatma. Not that this was immediately apparent. Thin and exhibiting the first pale signs of jaundice, Talaat had aged considerably in the three months since his condition had been diagnosed. No longer the waterskiing, parascending lothario of old, the lines that had, almost overnight, appeared on his face were tangible proof that here was a man who had not only accepted the idea of his own mortality but had smashed up against it a few times too. And much as she had disapproved of his previous life of rampant bachelorhood, Fatma hated seeing him like this, hated thinking about where all this pain would lead.

Hulya, who had been too nervous to approach her mother, now sat down beside her. 'Mum? I'm sorry.'

Fatma turned towards her, her anger gone. She reached across and touched her daughter's face tenderly.

'I'm sorry too, Hulya,' she said. 'I know how difficult it is first to find your father and then get him to listen.'

'Bülent has cleared most of his things from his bedroom,' Hulya said, 'although there are still Galatasaray posters all over the walls.'

'Well, as a lifetime supporter of Beşiktaş,' Talaat put in gravely, 'I really should get him to take them down.'

'Oh.'

'But I won't.' He laughed gently. 'After all, it's only football.'

'Don't let Bülent hear you say that,' Fatma responded sharply. 'To that boy it's like religion. To so many men it's like religion.'

'Oh, I don't know,' Hulya said, smiling now that she was

no longer the object of her mother's wrath. 'Dad has never had any time for it and Sınan hates it. Berekiah says that it's just like a modern version of what used to take place in the Hippodrome – gladiators and violent mobs and things. I agree with that totally.'

Fatma, who had not been a young girl herself for very many years, nevertheless felt the skin on the back of her neck prickle. Mention of a young man's name combined with respect for his opinion and blushing was significant.

'Berekiah Cohen?' she said calmly.

'Yes,' Hulya said and turned slightly away from her mother.

Fatma and Talaat raised their respective eyebrows in unison.

'Berekiah sometimes brings me home from work,' the girl continued. 'Dad's been so busy.'

'Mmm, well, it's very noble of Berekiah to come all the way across from Karaköy just to escort you a few metres.'

'There have been some terrible crimes around here, you know!' Hulya exclaimed.

'Yes, your father told me, and you and I spoke of poor Hatice.'

'So then you know—'

'I know that my daughter is besotted with a young Jewish boy.'

Hulya's cheeks flared. 'Mum!'

'We won't talk of this now, Hulya,' Fatma said firmly. 'I think you should really go and make some tea for your uncle.'

'But—'

'That would be very nice,' Talaat said with a smile.

For a moment, Hulya did consider pushing her argument

further but then she thought better of it. Her mother hadn't, as yet, gone berserk, as she'd imagined she would, and so Hulya decided to accede to her request as gracefully as she could.

'Of course,' she said and rose to her feet.

'Thank you,' Talaat said with a smile.

When Hulya had gone, Fatma's face assumed a strained expression. But she didn't discuss what had just passed between herself and her daughter with Talaat. He, poor soul, had enough to deal with. After all, unknown to Hulya, Çetin or any family members beyond Talaat and herself, her brother hadn't come back to İstanbul for any further treatment. He'd had everything he could have and none of it had worked. Talaat Ertuğrul had come home to die.

İkmen had only been in his office for five minutes when he was told that he had a visitor. At first he was loath to receive anyone, much less a weeping young woman (another of Orhan Tepe's conquests perhaps?). But when he found out the person's name, all of that changed.

'Please do come in and take a seat, Mrs Şeker,' he said as he held the door open to allow the tear-stained young woman to enter. 'Can I get you tea or—'

'Inspector İkmen, I know I let Inspector Suleyman down, but I need your help,' Suzan Şeker said as she sat down opposite the vast amount of paper and cigarette ash that covered the top of İkmen's desk. 'I've thought about it a lot and I heard what happened up at Yıldız Palace last night on the news.'

'Yes?' İkmen, frowning, sat down opposite her.

'Inspector, the Mürens have sold their interest in my business to an Azerbaijani family.'

'How do you know this, Mrs Şeker?'

She looked down at her hands and, although she was no longer actually weeping, her eyes were wet.

'Ekrem and Celal came to see me,' she said. 'They told me they didn't need my business any more and that they'd sold it on.'

'I see. And have this new family contacted you?'

'No. But . . .'

'When they do you want us to be waiting for them.'

She looked up, and her face was contorted with fury. 'I'll never be free unless you do! They drove Hassan to kill himself! Ekrem Müren made me do a disgusting thing! How do I know these other people won't do that too?'

İkmen sighed. 'You don't.'

'You completely smashed that family who were using the palace. You killed Ali Müren! To be honest I've never really had any confidence in the police, but your actions last night made me think differently.'

İkmen smiled. He didn't want to discuss the previous night's operation but at the same time he didn't want to dissuade this woman from pursuing a course of action that could improve both her life and her bank account. Suzan Şeker, poor woman, had suffered enough. 'This disgusting thing you speak of—'

'I don't want to talk about it!' She turned her face away from him, towards the window.

'You will have to if the case comes to court, Mrs Şeker.'

'Ekrem Müren made me suck him!' She looked at İkmen's face defiantly, her lips tight with indignation. 'There!'

İkmen wearily rubbed his forehead with his hands. 'I'm so sorry, Mrs Şeker. But I had to ask.'

'Yes, I know.' She paused to wipe her eyes and regain her composure. 'And so?'

'And so, provided you are willing to give evidence against them, I will order the arrest of Ekrem and Celal Müren. I will interrogate them and I will find out the name of the family Ekrem has sold your business to. But you must be willing to follow this through and you must be prepared for the attention, not always pleasant, that this will bring to you and your family.' He looked at her steadily. 'Think carefully.'

'I've done that already,' Suzan replied hotly, 'and I want to do it. Hassan let these people move him around like a Karagöz puppet and then when he couldn't stand it any more he killed himself! I don't want to be like that, Inspector. I don't want to pass a business that isn't really mine on to my children.'

'No. No, of course you don't.' İkmen looked down at his hands. He felt dizzy with tiredness. This woman had courage. By doing what she proposed she was laying herself open to intimidation from the Azerbaijani family and to the shame that her admission would bring. And she wanted to do it based upon what was in reality a lie. Those who had killed Ali Müren and the others had nothing to do with him or his men, he didn't even know who they were, only that they had succeeded in protecting those who did what had been done to Suzan Şeker at a much higher level. Good gangsters against bad gangsters, but they were all one and the same at the end of the day. He had to somehow stop thinking about it now. Thinking could lead to unguarded words, unwise actions. The Müren boys knew nothing about the Harem, but they would be very rattled in the wake of the deaths of their father and Zhivkov.

Now was an excellent time to get them for extortion and sexual assault.

İkmen lifted his telephone receiver from its cradle and dialled a number. 'Let's set this in motion,' he said as he took a cigarette from his packet and lit up.

Suzan Şeker smiled.

To say that there are many attorney's offices in Los Angeles is rather like saying that İstanbul has some mosques. The stars, for all their money, power and influence, still need representation by persons qualified in the law should their charmed lives take unexpected and messy turns. The man had made it his business to know all the most prestigious names; he knew where they all worked, lived and jogged. He'd even spoken to some of them during the time he had worked on this Sivas thing. None of them had known anything about Hikmet Sivas or his photographs.

The Turk, it would seem, placed little trust in lawyers. The photographs were where they had always been apparently: at the bottom of an old writing paper box in Hikmet Sivas's bedside cabinet.

'You kept them here?' he said as he shuffled through the large stack of mainly black and white photographs.

'Yes.'

Although it was his bedroom and the man was sitting on his bed, Hikmet was loath to sit down beside him. Instead he placed himself in a wicker chair opposite; he could just see the tops of his palm trees through the window behind the man's head.

'I told no one where they were,' Hikmet continued. 'Not even Vedat. I felt it was safer that way.' He laughed, but without humour.

The man shuffled and riffled, his eyes fixed on the images, showing acts sometimes odd, sometimes sensual, often distasteful and sadistic. The only thing they had in common besides sex was that the male participants were all well-known. More official images of them had appeared in newspapers all over the world or in files held by criminal investigation organisations. As he shuffled, the man tried to work out what a collection like this might be worth to its owner and decided that it was totally incalculable.

'It amazes me that you never tried to use any of this, Hikmet,' he said. 'You could have been a billionaire.'

'I have enough for my needs,' Hikmet replied tightly. 'As I've said before, I only took them to protect my life here. It was the only way I could make sure that a young man from Turkey would be listened to, respected.'

'But you never had to use them, right?'

'Right. But I never knew whether I would have to. I had to protect myself.'

The man looked up and smiled unpleasantly. 'Shame about your brother then.'

'I should never have revealed what I was doing to him.' He shook his head. 'I should never have allowed him to run the Harem without me.'

'Did Vedat take pictures too?'

'In recent times, yes. He was fine until he met Zhivkov.'

'How'd they meet? D'you know?'

Hikmet sighed. 'In a little street of bars we call Çiçek Pasaj,' he said wearily. 'Vedat has always gone there. But in recent years a lot of mainly foreign gangsters go there too.'

The man looked down and started sorting through once again, his brow furrowed in concentration.

'So it was like an accident, a coincidence?'

'Yes.'

'No, Hikmet.'

'What?'

'There are no coincidences,' the man said harshly. 'This could still rear up and bite us on the ass unless we tie up every loose end.' He paused, raising a single photograph up in front of his face. 'Oh, well, look here.'

'That's the one that you want?'

'It's the only one that could change the face of the world map, yes.' The man regarded the image from several angles before continuing. 'Some ambition you must have, Hikmet, to allow someone like him to do something like that to them.'

Hikmet Sivas looked down at the floor. 'His appetites . . . He demanded . . .'

'Yeah, right.'

Hikmet's anger flared. 'Well, would you have said no? To him?'

'No,' the man replied simply. 'But then people like me are paid very well by people like him to say yes all the time. It's also an idealistic thing, if you know what I mean. I take care of the world as we know it, I keep it that way.'

'So are you going to destroy that one?'

'I'm going to destroy them all, Hikmet.' He spread the whole stack out on the highly polished wooden floor and then looked at them each in turn once again. 'You developed them here.'

'Yes,' Hikmet said, 'as I've told you.' Then suddenly he smiled. 'My friend Ahmet and I learned how to develop pictures when we worked in Egypt. One of the cameramen taught us. The first one I ever did was a picture of Ahmet. I was so pleased.'

'And the negatives?' The man hadn't been listening, just looking at the pictures, thinking.

'All of them are in my darkroom downstairs.'

The man stood up, pulling on the waistband of his trousers as he did so.

'Good job it's all going then, isn't it, Hikmet.' He smiled. 'And, sadly, that means you're going to have to go too.'

'What?'

The two men who had accompanied the man into Hikmet's house emerged from the shadows, one with a can of petrol, the other with a knife.

Hikmet was terrified. 'But if you kill me someone will investigate, someone will know!'

'Oh, I don't think there's any chance of that happening,' the man said calmly. Then the taller of his two associates cut Hikmet Sivas's throat as if he were a common hillside goat. 'Bye Hikmet.'

When the house was well and truly soaked with petrol, the man threw a match into it and left. Separately and silently, he'd shot his two associates just before he torched the house. They'd been kindly supplied by di Marco, trash he'd been wanting to offload anyway.

The man left the house, the state and then the country. There were other things to be done elsewhere.

Despite the best efforts of the Los Angeles fire department, only the great crescent-shaped pool at the back of the house remained intact; everything else burned to the ground.

Hürrem İpek stared fixedly out of her kitchen window, her eyes focused on nothing. The sky was darkening now and the man who sat with her, on the other side of her table, looked more like a shadow than a person.

'So this Zhivkov, this monster, is dead.'

'Yes,' İkmen replied. 'We killed him last night. In the operation up at Yıldız.'

'Who?' She turned away from the window, her eyes seeking his. 'Who killed him?'

'We . . .'

'Which officer? What is his name?'

İkmen, blinking hard just to stay awake, glanced away, edging to the corner of the lie.

'I don't know,' he said. 'It was all very violent, very confusing.'

'I'd like to kiss him,' Hürrem said hollowly. 'I'd like to take him in my arms and kiss him. You know?'

'Yes.'

'He avenged my daughter. I owe him everything I have.' She put her head down and silently started to cry.

'He also did his duty,' İkmen said softly, not enjoying the deception but nevertheless feeling that he had to elaborate it for her sake. 'His reward and yours is that Hatice can now rest in peace.'

She was crying too hard to answer him. Her head was in her hands, her whole body heaving with grief, tears running through her fingers and down her arms. And for İkmen, too, there was pain here in this small, darkening kitchen. This poor woman deserved the whole unexpurgated story, she should be aware that many years before, forces over and above the terrible Zhivkov had in fact set up the apparatus that had led to Hatice's death. But to tell her would be to put her at risk and he couldn't do that. Bad enough that somebody, somewhere, might come and ask him about what and who he knew in this affair. Somebody with power he couldn't even imagine.

'And you,' Hürrem said, raising her head, 'you promised me you would do this for me, Inspector. You did it. I throw myself at your feet!'

Which is exactly what she did. Falling from her chair she prostrated herself before him, her sodden face pressed down into the cheap linoleum on the floor.

İkmen, shocked and embarrassed, leapt to his feet. 'Mrs İpek!'

'I am not fit to pour out water for you to wash your hands!'

That expression again. Almost word for word the same as Hikmet Sivas had said to his sister Hale when he attempted to atone, just a little, for the shortcomings of his lifestyle. The formulaic creation of a mismatch between one person and another, that old remnant of the rigid Ottoman system of lofty exaltation and cringing servility. Even if Hürrem's total abasement at his feet had been deserved, İkmen would have felt uncomfortable; under the current circumstances it made him feel fraudulent and tainted. Beyond discovering much that he shouldn't know up at Yıldız, he'd done nothing. He hadn't made Zhivkov pay for anything, no one had. The Bulgarian had lived a violent, no doubt exciting and rich life, exploiting and killing wherever he went, activities he enjoyed. Even in death he'd been fortunate. Cleanly shot dead, no pain at all. No time for retribution, no payment exacted for crimes committed, at least not here on earth.

No. Zhivkov was free, whereas this grieving mother? İkmen began to feel tears of misery, weariness and frustration well up in his eyes and so without another word to the woman still cringing at his feet he left that apartment and went out onto the landing. There, in front of his own apartment door, he slid down onto his haunches and wept. Beyond the door, the entrance to what he had always considered his own private and secure space, he listened to the sound of his younger children's games. As he wept he wondered who else might be listening and for just a moment the rage within him was so strong that it frightened him. How dare they! Whoever they were and whatever their motives, how dare they do this to him, to his family, to the few certainties of his way of life.

Chapter 28

Celal and Ekrem Müren were eventually tracked down in the early hours of the following morning. Holed up in their dead father's apartment, they were both angry and distraught with grief. Despite this they didn't allow the police to come in without a fight. And so the man leading the small group of arresting officers, İsak Çöktin, gave the order to break into the apartment. Leading as ever from the front, Çöktin only narrowly escaped a bullet from Ekrem's gun. One of the other men took a shot in the leg.

It took the police longer than they had hoped to bring the situation under control. The brothers fought with a reckless ferocity that eventually resulted in Ekrem sustaining a chest wound and Celal's death. It wasn't the outcome they had been hoping for and so Çöktin, rather than call İkmen who he knew was exhausted, informed Ardiç directly. After all, Ekrem would have to be treated in hospital before he could be questioned by İkmen and Celal's body would need to be removed to the mortuary. As the officers were leaving, Alev Müren, the little sister from hell, arrived with her grandmother from the old woman's home on Türbedar Sokak, having been alerted by sympathetic neighbours. Both women screamed at the police, calling them 'Bloody murderers!' while the neighbours peeped silently at the scene from behind their curtains and blinds. And Çöktin, ever obliging, duly rewarded this strange, silent vigil by arresting both women when Alev attacked Constable Yıldız. Even by Beyazıt standards it was a very dramatic event.

İkmen, in contrast, began the morning at a very slow pace. Last night he had, with no more than three words to his family, fallen into bed and a mercifully dreamless sleep. When he did finally wake it was to the unusual sight of a high sun outside the window and Fatma watching him intently from where she stood at the end of their bed.

'Çetin, I'm sorry,' she said as she polished the old brass bars that made up the bed's footboard, 'but you have a visitor.'

'Ardiç . . .'

'No. No, if it had been work I'd have sent whoever it was away,' Fatma responded tartly. 'No, this is a friend, Çetin.'

'Oh.' His voice was husky and cracked and he coughed violently as he swung his legs over the side of the bed and retrieved his clothes from the floor. 'Who is it?'

'It's Arto,' she said, removing more dust than she was accustomed to from her furniture, 'and Miss Yümniye Heper.'

İkmen looked up, his eyes bleary with weariness and surprise.

'Poor Miss Muazzez,' Fatma continued. 'I didn't know she had died. Such a terrible thing!'

İkmen walked over to her. 'I'm so glad that you're back,' he said.

She smiled and then he kissed her, a long, lingering kiss that spoke more effectively than words ever could about how much he had missed her.

The doctor and Yümniye were sitting at the kitchen table

when İkmen entered. Yümniye, away from her normal surroundings, looked somehow older and smaller than usual. The two men embraced and then İkmen seated himself opposite his guests, while Fatma, who had followed him in from the bedroom, gave them all coffee. She then left to attack the rest of the apartment which was, by Fatma's standards, filthy.

'I'm going to release Miss Muazzez's body for burial today,' Arto Sarkissian said as he stirred an enormous amount of sugar into his drink.

'I was so pleased when I heard Arto's voice this morning,' Yümniye said, smiling at both of the men. 'It was so nice to know that her poor body had found its way into friendly hands. I can still remember you two playing with your brothers in our garden when you were little boys. You were all such good boys.'

İkmen and his friend shared a small, secretive smile. Yes, they'd all really liked General Heper's garden, it was true. Plenty of fruit to steal from the trees.

'I brought Miss Yümniye to see you,' the Armenian continued, 'because she'd very much like both of us to attend Miss Muazzez's funeral.'

'I have only distant family now that Muazzez has gone,' the old woman said sadly, 'and you both remember her when she was young and vital. You've both tried very hard to do your best.'

'We're still looking for the car that ran Miss Muazzez down,' İkmen said as he lit his first cigarette of the day. 'I have hopes . . .'

'That you will find those responsible for the Harem?' Yümniye shook her head. 'Ah, but you won't, will you, Çetin? No.' She looked up into the confused face of Arto

Sarkissian and shrugged. 'People don't keep things like that a secret for forty years only to lose it all over an old woman. I never did know anywhere near as much as Muazzez, but I do know that. I don't suppose that idiot Sofia—'

'Did I miss something?' Arto interrupted. 'Harem?'

İkmen, mindful that not too much of this type of talk could be risked in his apartment, especially if the names of others involved were going to be used, changed the subject.

'So what will you do now, Miss Yümniye?' he asked.

The old woman sighed. 'Oh, I will go on as before, I suppose,' she said. 'It is important for me to keep my father's house, until I become too confused.'

'I will visit you,' İkmen said determinedly. 'I would like that.'

'Would you? In addition to all these children you have, all this work you have to do?' She turned to Arto Sarkissian. 'I don't think he looks well enough to take on any more responsibilities. So thin now! What do you think, Krikor dear?'

'Arto.'

'Pardon?'

'It's Arto, Miss Yümniye, Krikor is my brother,' Arto explained gently.

'Oh, I'm so sorry,' she said, looking down at the floor, embarrassed and flustered. 'My silly head.'

'I think that if Çetin says he will visit you there is little you can do to stop him,' Arto said with a smile.

'And we will of course both attend the funeral,' İkmen added. 'Now you will need some help with the arrangements, won't you?'

She said that she would appreciate that. And so that was what was discussed until the old woman and Arto Sarkissian left some time later. And despite the fact that İkmen, though tired, retained a reasonably cheerful countenance during the course of their visit, he quickly descended into dark thoughts afterwards. Sacrifice was a word that kept crossing and then re-crossing his mind. So many lives sacrificed and for what? So that those one didn't even dare think about might sleep a little easier in their beds? So that the present sick, ruined and corrupt state of the world could be perpetuated for eternity? He and everyone he knew were just used. Shut up, speak out, sit down, do your duty, die. Where was the value or the latitude in that? Nine children he'd brought into the world, nine people to be moved around and manipulated like mannequins. He thought that he might cry again but he didn't. There wasn't anything left inside him to cry with and so instead he took Tepe's mobile telephone out of his pocket and looked at it.

The phone had been amongst the effects İkmen had been given to return to Aysel Tepe. Before he did so he thought that he might just check the instrument for messages, and sure enough there was one, which he played.

'I'm sorry, Orhan,' Ayşe Farsakoğlu's rather muffled, miserable voice said. 'I'm so alone. I miss you. Please call.'

Desperation. A need for closeness whatever the price. A universal and, İkmen felt, a beautiful need. Because that was the point, wasn't it? Men and women may be pushed around by those they cannot know, but if they can find closeness, that hedge against the darkness that is always lurking . . .

He started the erase sequence on the phone just as Fatma came in and kissed him on the top of his head. With sudden energy he jumped to his feet and took her passionately into his arms.

*   *   *

Three days later İkmen made arrangements to meet his colleagues early, for breakfast. That way they would avoid the heat of the day and the hordes of people who tended to gather in and around the Eminönü docks later on in the morning – commuters and tourists. However, none of them was so early that they risked missing the fishing boats. The catch was in and the fishermen, dressed as ever in their ornate just-for-tourists Ottoman waistcoats, were cooking it up for the excellent sandwich breakfasts they served. Indeed Metin İskender was already buying his. İkmen was sitting on a bench back towards the road, almost hidden behind a copy of *Cumhuriyet*. İskender turned briefly to ask him whether he would like some food too, but he declined.

Mehmet Suleyman smiled. İkmen probably wouldn't ever now get to grips with eating. Perhaps, like himself, it was because the older man had never truly been hungry. Although far from wealthy, the İkmens had never been dirt poor, not like Metin İskender, who had the largest fish sandwich possible wedged in his hungry mouth. Fish was still a feast for him, notwithstanding his wealthy wife. But then in the slum where he'd been raised, the people lived on whatever they could get and it was possible that Metin hadn't eaten fresh fish at all until he was an adult. Other people's discarded food, yes, but not all his own, paid for with his own money.

As he watched the fishermen, Suleyman thought contentedly that so far it had been a very pleasant morning. Zelfa was a lot happier now that she had a definite date when she could return to work. Just the knowledge of it seemed to settle her and, for the past two days at least, she had appeared to be much more at ease with their son, Yusuf. She had even, strangely for her, admitted to some feelings of regret about having to return to her practice. She was, she said, starting to enjoy the baby and would miss him when Estelle Cohen took over the baby-care role in four weeks' time. Life was good, or rather it would have been if there wasn't still this terrible blackness that surrounded the events up at Yıldız Palace.

As İskender joined them on the bench, İkmen, still hidden by his newspaper, spoke. 'Hikmet Sivas is dead,' he said flatly. 'Had his throat cut. Apparently the perpetrators then proceeded to burn his house down. They must have been the most incompetent arsonists one can imagine. Stupidly, they failed to get out themselves.'

'Who were they?' İskender asked through a mouthful of bread and fish.

'No one seems to know.' İkmen folded his paper and placed it on his lap. 'But Miss Hale is insisting that his body be returned here. She believes he won't rest unless he's interred next to their mother and Vedat. I must say I don't know about the latter.'

Suleyman lit a cigarette and sighed. 'I wish I knew how and when he returned to America,' he said. 'I wish I knew something of the truth.'

'You know that Vedat Sivas was involved with Zhivkov,' İkmen said as he, too, lit a cigarette. 'You also know that Zhivkov killed Kaycee Sivas.'

'I don't know why,' Suleyman snapped.

'No.'

The three men, each of them avoiding the others' eyes, sat in silence save for the sound of İskender's voracious chewing.

'Zhivkov was involved in so many things,' İkmen said

at length. 'It's a pity we weren't allowed to know what those higher up had planned for him. We stumbled into something.'

'The man who,' Suleyman stopped himself alluding to what had actually happened to him, 'assaulted me was European.'

İskender looked briefly into Suleyman's eyes and then away again. The two men hadn't spoken of their experiences since they'd been discharged from the Admiral Bristol. First Ardiç and then a very smart man wearing a genuine Rolex watch had, separately, advised them against it.

'Zhivkov was involved in both the Sivas and the Hatice İpek case,' İkmen said, omitting all details. 'He had a prostitution thing going, based on some old legend, Vedat became involved and—'

'You were convinced that the Harem thing was a fact,' Suleyman said sharply. 'You said that Hikmet Sivas had used the Harem.'

'The Müren boys disposed of poor Hatice's body. Apparently Celal rather liked her which was why she was laid out so sympathetically.'

'I don't really see where the Sivas people come into it,' İskender said, watching, big-eyed, as yet more fish were thrown onto charcoal grills on board the gently bobbing boats. 'I mean, why kill the sister-in-law of the man you're working with?'

'Zhivkov wanted Hikmet to bankroll his activities. Vedat had fallen under the Bulgarian's spell,' İkmen replied simply. 'Unfulfilled younger brother – you know how it is.'

'I don't know why a great big, effectively foreign movie star who, you always said, had Mafia connections, could allow himself to be attacked by Zhivkov, Vedat notwith-standing,' Suleyman said angrily. 'None of it makes any sense to me! And we've been as good as gagged.'

'And you would do anything to know the truth, would you, Mehmet?'

Suleyman looked at him. 'You know, don't you?' he said coldly 'You got into the palace – with Vedat and the foreigners and General Pamuk.'

'General Pamuk helped us, er, our forces, get to Zhivkov, Müren and the others,' İskender put in nervously. 'It's quite—'

'I was drugged, you know that!' Suleyman said in a low, angry voice to İkmen. 'You came to see me in the hospital. I remember!'

'I'm going to have to go,' İskender said suddenly, dis-carding what was left of his sandwich and rising to his feet. 'I can't be here.' He looked at Suleyman who returned his gaze with pitiless eyes. 'I'm sorry, Mehmet.' And then he walked, very quickly, in the direction of the Galata Bridge.

As soon as he was out of earshot, Suleyman turned to İkmen once again. 'Something very big happened, didn't it, Çetin? Something foul.'

İkmen looked down at the ground, the smoke from his cigarette causing him to squint. 'It was Zhivkov.'

'Not only Zhivkov!'

İkmen looked up, straight into Suleyman's eyes. 'You have to do what Metin has done, Mehmet,' he said softly.

'So you asked us here to enjoy a fish sandwich, put aside any questions and then just walk away from this thing?'

'I have to be certain that you will walk away,' İkmen said. 'Absolutely certain.'

'It's that big then, is it, Çetin?' Suleyman asked, still with a lot of anger in his voice. 'It goes right to the top, does it, just like we said before that bloodbath? I thought that you, of all people, opposed that sort of thing.'

İkmen's hand was at his friend's throat before Suleyman could take a breath.

'This goes beyond anything any of us understands!' he hissed. 'Beyond our city, beyond our country!'

'Çetin!'

'You mustn't even dream about what you think happened that night, Mehmet! Don't think about it, don't speak about it – to anyone. That way you might stay alive!' Aware that some of the few people around them were looking, İkmen let go of Suleyman's throat and placed his hands back on his newspaper again.

Suleyman breathed in deeply to steady his nerves.

'We smashed a major crime family,' İkmen said. 'The bad men have gone. We did well.'

'Yes.'

'You've a brand new son and life is good.'

'Yes.' But when Suleyman looked at İkmen, his eyes were full of tears. 'I've always looked to you for the truth, Çetin.'

İkmen turned his head away. 'Then perhaps in future you would be better served by looking to yourself,' he said.

'Maybe you're right.'

He had invited that response but it nevertheless hurt İkmen deeply. He glared at Suleyman.

'You of all people,' he said bitterly, 'should understand that rulers keep their own secrets, rulers employ lots of people to help them do that.'

'Oh, so now you throw my ancestry at me as a way of salving your conscience!'

'You built the palaces, threw up the walls, dug the secret rooms deep into the earth!'

Suleyman, enraged, sprang to his feet.

'Every man who sets himself above others is a flawed man,' İkmen said, looking up into the burning eyes of his colleague, 'They move people about like pieces on a chessboard. They make us do things, seal up our mouths, rip away even the deepest things inside us! Rob us of our honour!' Despite himself, tears came to his eyes. 'I cannot and will not tell you anything!'

'After everything we have been through together, I don't understand how you can trust me so little!'

'And I don't understand,' İkmen said wearily, 'how you can fail to appreciate that I'm doing this not because I don't trust you but because I care too deeply about you to share something that will endanger and dishonour you.' Roughly he wiped away his tears. 'Isn't it bad enough that I stink of it?'

Suleyman sighed and then, somewhat deflated, sat down beside İkmen once again. He offered him a cigarette and then lit one up himself.

'So where does all of this leave Jack the Ripper then?' he said gently. 'The agony of not knowing the truth?'

A small flock of seagulls landed on top of what was left of Metin İskender's fish sandwich and fought amongst themselves for the most succulent parts.

İkmen smiled. 'There's something uncannily pertinent to this case about Jack the Ripper,' he said thoughtfully.

'Oh?'

'Yes. One of the theories about that mystery concerns

the possible involvement of the British establishment at the time. The story goes that one of the British princes made a prostitute pregnant and that Jack was a government agent charged with clearing up his mess.'

'But didn't the killer murder several women?'

'Yes. Only one of whom was the royal prostitute, or so it is said,' İkmen explained. 'The others were killed in order to build the legend of Jack the Ripper, to distort the truth and manipulate the common people like chess pieces, as I said before.' He looked at Suleyman. 'And we will never know the truth,' he said, 'because it is further postulated that everyone who knew about it who shouldn't met a similar fate to those prostitutes.'

'So this thing with Zhivkov . . .'

'All you may safely know is that the world remains the same,' İkmen said, staring not out at the brightening waterway in front of him but at the dull pavement beneath his feet. 'As a prince you would know everything. But you're not a prince any more, Mehmet, and so the secret chambers beneath the streets are forbidden to you. I've looked, as you know, into the face of something that I shouldn't have and I wish that I hadn't. For me the world has changed.'

They both sat in silence for a while then. As the morning began to bustle around them, people getting on and off the hooting ferries, simitcis and vendors of all sorts of useful and useless things shouting their wares to the scurrying public, they seemed for a while to be a small pool of silence, a stopping place, an absence. It wasn't that people avoided them, they didn't seem to know that they were there.

To İkmen this separation made some sense and in a way crystallised the difference he now felt between himself and others. But to Suleyman the experience was unnerving and so, with a brief touch of his colleague's hand, he left. Without another word.

İkmen, alone now, knew that they would never speak of what had happened up at Yıldız on that awful evening again. What they would talk of and how they would talk when next they met, he didn't know. Nothing, no secret thing, had ever come between them before. Would it ever go away? İkmen wondered.

A waft of foul-smelling air from somewhere deep within the ancient sewers beneath the city hit İkmen's nose and made him get up and move. For a while it seemed to follow him, but then when he lit up one of his pungent cigarettes it began to abate. Turning his face away from where he felt the source of the smell to be, İkmen dragged heavily on his Maltepe and walked with purpose back to the station and the company of those who knew nothing but kept him close.